About

Rachael Stewart adore[...] heartwarmingly romanti[...] writing since she could p[...] scrawled-on pages in her loft will attest to. A Welsh lass at heart, she now lives in Yorkshire with her very own hero and three awesome kids, and if she's not tapping out a story, she's wrapped up in them or enjoying the great outdoors. Reach her on Facebook, Twitter (@rach_b52) or rachaelstewartauthor.com

Brenda Jackson is a *New York Times* bestselling author of more than one hundred romance titles. Brenda lives in Jacksonville, Florida, and divides her time between family, writing and travelling. Email Brenda at authorbrendajackson@gmail.com or visit her on her website at brendajackson.net

Reese Ryan writes sexy, contemporary romance featuring a diverse cast of complex characters. She presents her characters with family and career drama, challenging love interests and life-changing secrets while treating readers to emotional love stories with unexpected twists. Past president of her local RWA chapter and a panellist at the 2017 *Los Angeles Times* Festival of Books, Reese is an advocate of the romance genre and diversity in fiction. Visit her online at ReeseRyan.com

Secrets and Seduction

Secrets and Seduction:
One Night to...

RACHAEL STEWART

BRENDA JACKSON

REESE RYAN

MILLS & BOON

First Published in Great Britain 2022
By Mills & Boon, an imprint of HarperCollins*Publishers,* Ltd
1 London Bridge Street, London, SE1 9GF

www.harpercollins.co.uk

HarperCollins*Publishers*
1st Floor, Watermarque Building,
Ringsend Road, Dublin 4, Ireland

SECRETS AND SEDUCTION: ONE NIGHT TO... © 2022
Harlequin Enterprises ULC.

Getting Dirty © 2020 Rachael Stewart
An Honorable Seduction © 2018 Brenda Streater Jackson
Seduced by Second Chances © 2019 Harlequin Enterprises ULC.

Special thanks and acknowledgement are given to Reese Ryan for her contribution to the *Dynasties: Secrets of the A-List* series.

ISBN: 978-0-263-30469-5

GETTING DIRTY

RACHAEL STEWART

For my sister Louise and her fabulous husband, Mark, for inspiring the inclusion of the Highlands with their awesome road trips!

And to my talented editor, Sareeta, for loving this story line when it was just an idea! I hope I've done it justice. ;-) Thank you for being so great at what you do!

Happy reading DAREdevils!

Rxx

CHAPTER ONE

I LOVE MY line of work. People bitch and moan about their careers but not me.

Clients task me with a job and I get it done. I don't run an empire. I don't employ anyone full-time. I only have myself to watch out for and that's the way I like it.

This job earned my family back a shred of their respect a decade ago and I've been dishing the dirt on corrupt arseholes, playboys and spoilt little rich girls ever since.

I didn't set out to be a private investigator. It's a job that chose me when my family needed it most and it turns out I'm a natural. If there's dirt, I'll find it.

And right now, that dirt is sitting across the softly lit room from me.

Only *this* kind of dirt I cannot dish.

It crosses a line that even my skewed moral compass cannot abide.

'Come on, Ash, what gives?'

I raise my eyes from my untouched pint to see

Jackson grinning at me from the other side of the bar. 'Where'd you come from?'

'We're short-staffed tonight. I'm helping out.'

'A bit beneath you, wouldn't you say?'

'Nah, I kind of enjoy it.'

He scans the darkened corners of the room, the various people making out, and barely raises a brow. And why would he? This is his life day in, day out. This is his club—Blacks—complete with sex on tap, catering to the British elite. The upper crust. A circle to which I once wholeheartedly belonged and now wouldn't piss on if it were on fire.

These people have money. Enough to pay for the exclusive membership and the non-disclosure agreement that comes with it. Anything goes within these walls—within reason—and no one on the outside is any the wiser. Including my client. But the presence of my target—*her*—tells me there's more to Coco Lauren than what the world sees. What the press witnesses. And that's what I need to tap into, to expose, if I'm to get what I need and deliver what my client demands.

'Jesus, you need something stronger than a pint, judging by the look of you.'

I barely acknowledge his observation. Truth is, what I need is something that gets her to step out of line, outside of this safe haven where I can't say anything without compromising my friend's business.

He backs up and snatches a bottle from the side with two shot glasses, smacking them down between us. 'You never come here, so I repeat: What gives?'

The truth will only piss him off, and I'm not about to lie, so I stay quiet and his eyes narrow, his powerhouse of a frame turning rigid. If he wasn't my oldest friend I'd think he was about to punch me.

'You'd better not be here on the clock...'

'Hey, easy.' I raise my palms. I knew he'd be suspicious, and he has every right to be—because he's right. I *never* come in here. 'The twisted secrets of this place are safe with me.'

He continues to study me and I know he's warring with what he knows of my work and what he knows of me. I know he doesn't like how I earn a living; we agree to disagree. As far as I'm concerned, these people deserve what they get.

Just like the princess teasing me with her long bare legs, cute little arse and a face that's bordered by a blonde low-swinging bob. She projects such innocence to the outside world, but not now, not in here.

As if on cue she stands and bends over the table to whisper in the ear of her female companion. I clock the feline curve of her body, the gentle swell of her hips, the delicate arch to her back, and then her friend turns and they kiss. Not just a peck. A deep, tongue-sinking kiss that has a spasm of heat ripping through me.

I straighten against it. *Fuck.*

I've seen her dressed for swanky lunch dates, the gym, charity galas and shopping sprees, and now I get to see her half-naked, with an intent that screams one thing: *sex*.

And in surroundings such as these, with soft

lighting, plush grey sofas and the perfect balance of glass and warm wood, she's lending a sophisticated charm that you could lose yourself in. It's only the debauched goings-on here that make it more than just a hip wine bar, and she's smack-bang in the middle of it. Adding to it.

I don't want to see the appeal. The allure. The legs that go on for ever. And that kiss that sears the air, my skin, my blood.

'Ah, now I see…'

Jackson's enlightened murmur snaps me out of it. I pull my gaze back to my pint, chug back a gulp.

'It's a woman that brings you my way—now it makes sense. It's about time.'

I almost choke on the bitter drink. 'Hardly.' He's close, and yet so far off the mark. 'I can't say I care for your choice of clientele.'

He laughs. 'You don't need to care—not for sex. You ought to try it some time…a bit of no-strings fun. Celibacy doesn't suit you.'

'Really?' My brow lifts. Never mind him punching *me*, I'm going to swing for him across the bar, to hell with the doormen flanking the place.

He laughs harder as he pours clear liquid into both shot glasses and slides one across to me. 'Your mistake was letting one get under your skin.'

'One?'

'You know who I mean—Jess.'

I throw back the shot and wince. The harsh hit douses the burn of her—my ex, the woman who left the second my family lost it all. 'Yeah, well, I'd take a woman out of my local over one from here any day.'

'That's not what your face was telling me a few seconds ago.'

I glower at him—but, hell, he's right.

I drag my mind back to the job, to what I should be focusing on.

Coco is clearly at home here, her open affection with the other girl and the show they're putting on for the guy across from them makes that obvious. Nothing in my research suggested she swung that way, but Philip Lauren—my client, her half-brother—had suspected it.

'I'm not sure I'm her type.'

Jackson grinned. '*Everyone's* her type if they can deliver in the bedroom.'

Heat unfurls deep within my gut. I can't pinpoint the cause. Desire, envy, anger… She's just like my ex, I try to tell myself. Only, Jess's vice was money. Coco's is sex. Just as her brother had said.

'How often does she come in here?'

'Depends. You asking for you, or for work?'

'Does it matter?'

It really didn't. It wasn't like I'd put his livelihood at stake. It was the reason her brother was giving me shit. He expected me to have uncovered something by now, and the one thing I'd uncovered was the one thing I couldn't divulge.

'I've promised I'm taking your secrets to the grave regardless.'

'Glad to hear it.'

He's talking to me but his eyes are on her, just as mine were. His expression is thoughtful, almost concerned. And I'm listening, my ears attuned to whatever has him looking so intent.

'It used to be once a fortnight, occasionally once a week, but lately it's been more.'

'More?'

'Yeah.' He looks back to me. 'She's probably been here twice this past week alone.'

'And that bothers you?'

'Not so much bothers me, but you know... This place serves a purpose, and whatever that is for her seems to me she's needing it more and more.'

'It's sex, Jackson. Perhaps she's just on heat.'

I'm purposefully harsh, flippant, but I don't want his concern. It doesn't pay for me to care, to soften towards her, but I can feel it happening. As each day goes by, each new discovery only adds to the appealing enigma that is Coco Lauren.

'It's more than that for people like her.'

Jackson's like a dog with a bone. He's not letting this go. Maybe she's ensnared him too. Not that I'm *ensnared*—unable to douse the attraction more like.

'They come here to get away from it all, and if she's upping her visits, something's bothering her.'

'You sound like you care.'

'She's nice, that's all.' He gives a shrug and his eyes drift back in her direction. I let mine do the same, watching as she walks in the direction of the ladies' room, her hips swaying provocatively. I feel the telltale ripple of heat through my groin and clench my jaw.

'You could be good for her, you know.'

Jackson's tone has a sincere ring to it that makes my blood run cold, as effective as a cold shower ever would be. Never would I go back to a woman like that. They have a knack for taking you to your knees and I've no interest in risking that again.

'If you haven't forgotten how to do it, that is?'

'Shut it, Jackson, or regardless of your bouncers I'll take you down right now.'

I shake my head and neck the minuscule drink. He's hit a nerve and he knows it. Hell, maybe that's why Lady Legs is having such an undesirable effect on my libido.

Who are you kidding? The reason you haven't had sex in an age is because you can't find anyone who does it for you. That is, you couldn't until you started this job, until her...

I look to the closed lavatory door and beat back the thought.

You're here on business, not for sex. And if you were looking for sex it wouldn't be with one of these hoity-toity bitches who remind you so much of Jess.

I'm wired and it's driving me crazy.

Usually I can lose myself in this place. Forget the trappings of my life on the outside and have fun. It takes the edge off—just enough to go back to it and do it all again. Smile, perform, play the part to perfection.

But not now. Not with Granny so sick.

She's the closest thing to a mother I've ever known, and since losing my father two years ago she's been my world.

Nothing can bury the pain. I aim for distraction, pure and simple. But not even distraction is enough tonight.

Caitlin murmurs something in my ear, her dainty tongue tracing its delicate ridge, and I watch as the eyes of the up-and-coming footballer opposite—what was his name? Ryan? Reece? Ricky? I don't know, he's new—turn to saucers. He's out of luck, though. I'm not in the mood, and no amount of Cait's expert attentions are going to do it for me. Not tonight.

I push out of my seat to rise. I take pity on him and give him a view as I lean in to make my excuses to her and kiss her full on the mouth. She tastes of strawberry, the remnants of the daiquiri she's been sipping, and I linger a second longer, urging my body to obey, to want, to overtake this pain with the numbing heat of desire. But…nothing.

With a smothered sigh, I head to the bathroom, triggering a text to my driver to collect me in ten. I'll hit the hard stuff when I get home, knock myself out in my own private domain. I'm not even fearing the hangover that's bound to ensue. Anything to beat off the impending pain of loss that's hanging over me.

A quick pit stop, a sweep of red across the lips and I re-enter the room. Caitlin's chatting to Jackson at the bar and the footballer's long gone. The fact that

I'm not struck with the slightest hint of disappointment tells me I've done the right thing.

The sigh comes full force now and I move off—just as a wall appears in front of me and I smack right into it. A wall of hard, lean muscle that smells oceanic and male, all fresh and inviting, not like the expensive cloying cologne most guys here favour. No this is more natural, more… Just *more*…

My eyes trail upwards from where our bodies are still pressed up against one another. A black shirt, open at the collar, an honest hint of hair… How unusual. A square-set jaw, ample stubble… Nice. A full mouth, firm yet sensual, *very* nice. A strong nose, not too big, not too small. And eyes—

Oh, my God.

I start to lower my lashes, but I've never stood down in my life and force my eyes open. Wide.

Fierce blues pierce me, the coloured rims almost drowned out by glittering pupils. I swallow. At least I think I do. But my throat's still closed tight as my cheeks start to heat. Part of me is aware I should step back. The other part is more than aware that he hasn't made any attempt to either.

I wet my lips and manage, 'Hi,' feeling glad when it's not the squeak I feared.

His eyes rake over my face and then he seems to come alive on a breath. 'Apologies.'

Stepping away, he rubs a hand over the back of his head and my palm tickles like it's mine that's grazing over the dark buzz cut. And then he moves off and the connection is gone, the spell with it.

What was *that*?

Distraction, that's what.

'Wait.' I reach out to touch his arm and feel heat permeate my fingertips, solid muscle flexing beneath the shirt. 'I'm Coco.'

He hesitates as he looks back to me, his eyes still piercing, still ablaze. It's like there's a war raging in his head—he looks angry, even. But instead of being scared I'm drawn in. My body is well aware that this is what I need right now and I can't let it go.

'I know who you are.'

It's a simple statement, but there's an edge to it. I almost want to say it's contempt, and curiosity toughens my spine as I retract my hand and smile. 'You say that like it's a bad thing.'

'Look, princess, you're just not my type.'

I laugh. The sound tinkles, high and easy. I'm already having fun. More fun than I've had in a long time. 'Really…?'

'Really.'

He makes no attempt to leave, though. *Interesting.*

I cock my head to the side, let my gaze travel over him slowly, more brazen this time.

'I hardly think I'm yours either,' he adds, his tone rough and teasing at the electricity already thrumming in my veins.

I lift my eyes to his as I say, 'Let me be the judge of that.'

A pulse dances in his jaw and I wet my lips as I step closer, reaching out to toy with the first fastened button of his shirt. His chest stills beneath my fingers but his face is set hard. If not for the slight flare to his nose and that tripping pulse point I'd think the chest thing was a figment of my imagination.

'You going to tell me your name, or am I to guess?'

His throat bobs and I can sense his need to clear it. I'm not naive when it comes to sex. Sex and attraction. His body is giving me all the signs, even if he doesn't want me to see it.

'It's like that, is it? Hmm… Let me see…' I smile as I ponder and watch his eyes flicker back at me. Am I amusing him? I *want* to amuse him… 'What about… Reginald? Penfold? Archibald…?' I mock pout at his flat expression and catch the slightest twitch to his lips. Definitely amused. 'No? What about Terrence? Bert? Ernie—no, Arnie…? Ooh, yes… Arnie… I can definitely see a bit of Schwarzenegger in you…the whole *I'll be back* thing?'

I tuck my chin in as I deliver my best Terminator impression and my ridiculous comedic act—which, to be fair, makes me look like I sport a double chin— is totally worth it as he rewards me with a grin he clearly doesn't want to give.

'It's Ash.'

He takes firm hold of my fingers, which have just made tantalising contact with the exposed hairs of his chest, and my moment of triumph dampens as I sense the rejection coming.

'And I have to go.'

'Don't be a party pooper, Ash. We were just getting to know one another.' I take another step forward and my breasts brush against his chest as I breathe, my fingers still trapped in his warm, firm grasp.

'And as I said, you're hardly my type.'

He looks away and I follow his line of sight. He's looking towards Caitlin at the bar and I realise what he means.

'She's a friend of mine…a *close* friend.'

He turns back to me. 'So I saw.'

I frown just a little. Is he jealous? Or is Caitlin his type and he means it when he says I'm not? She's the opposite of me—a fiery petite redhead, free and easy. Normally I'd offer to share—to enjoy a debauched night of fun as a threesome. It's something we've done many a time before. But I don't want to. Not this time. Not with him.

I realise he's staring at me, his striking blue eyes penetrating my mind, and suddenly I feel naked… exposed. Like he's reached inside me and can read the very heart of what makes me tick. Which is nonsense. Utter nonsense.

I plaster on my superficial smile—the one I save for the cameras—and his eyes adjust to the change he's seen in me. 'If you're not interested,' I say, stepping away, 'far be it from me to force you.'

I start to pull my hand from his grasp and walk. It's time to go home and do what I intended all along. Now I can add his rejection to my list of things to forget.

'Wait.'

He firms his grip over my fingers and I pause mid-stride. Part of me—the part that felt every millimetre of exposure beneath his gaze—knows I should keep on going. But the devil in me, the pain, needs the distraction more. I look back at him and raise my brow in question.

'I've changed my mind. Let's grab a drink—somewhere else, though. For all Jackson is a mate of mine, his beer sucks.'

'Somewhere else?'

I genuinely hesitate. What I have in mind requires the sanctity of Blacks—this club. These four walls keep everything private. It's why I come here. To let my hair down, to beat off the stress, do whatever I so desire without judgement. Without exposure to the press. Without threat to the great house of Lauren.

'There's a pub not far from here…serves proper craft beer.' He gestures to the bar, where the footballer has returned and is trying his luck with Cait again. 'Bring your friends.'

I chew my lower lip. Would it hurt? Just this once?

But it would only take one photo, one loose tongue, even, and the press would pounce. My reputation would be in pieces and Granny's trust—*love*—would be irrevocably lost.

No, while Granny still lives, I'll be the Coco Lauren she believes in, no matter if it's not the whole story.

Guilt churns away in my stomach—but, hell, I *am* that Coco Lauren in all the ways that matter. Not that she'd see it. She would never approve of my pleasure-seeking side, never understand that I have no interest in relationships and the disappointment that they bring.

No, she would simply tar me with the same brush as my mother and be done with it.

And no one is worth taking that risk for, Coco, no one...

CHAPTER TWO

I LOOK AT her chewing anxiously over her lip and feel something twist inside me. This case is bugging me. There's a doubt I can't shift. A sense that this job is messed-up—that *I'm* messed-up for playing a part in it.

Something just isn't right.

And seeing her hesitate, spying the vulnerability in her glittering green gaze, not to mention the way my body refuses to chill around her, I know I should be ending this now. Walking away from both her and Philip Lauren.

But I've never called it a day on a job before. I've always been careful about which projects to take on, who I go after, who I work for…

But this time you were blinded by the memory of Jess, far too quick to judge.

The idea of another spoilt little rich girl getting her just deserts overrode my good sense. Because that's what Coco is—Christ, *Coco*. Even her name got to me. Dripping with arrogance, money, affluence. Everything I hated.

Or so I thought…

It's not hate that has me standing here hanging on her every word, laughing inside at her sudden play-fulness, on fire at her flirtation and delicate touch. No. It's this dogged attraction I just can't shake.

That's not why you're suggesting going elsewhere, though…

I pull her back to me with the hand that's still clutched over hers.

No, you're doing this to get her out of her safe haven. To expose her.

So why does it feel so wrong and so right all at once?

'I'd rather stay here.'

She says it nervously, her lashes fluttering as she stares up at me, her breath making her chest brush against mine once more, her lips teasingly parted.

I've only to duck my head and I could taste her, just as she tasted her friend not ten minutes ago. The urge burns through me. Fire at the memory, fire at her proximity, at the daring shade of her lipstick, all drawing me in.

And then she runs her tongue over her lower lip and my restraint snaps. I forget everything—work, my purpose, my age-old hate. All sense homes in on the gentle swell of her lips as I dip to sample.

Just sample, nothing more.

Nothing that will get out of hand or cut too deep.

But as I sweep my lips over hers, my taste buds come alive. She's all sweet and strawberry-like, tan-talising, inviting… And then I hear it, her tiny moan, so slight but definitely there, and it ripples down my ear canal, through my blood, right down to my disobeying cock.

I want to groan at the force, groan at the control I can feel slipping away. *This isn't you. This isn't what you do.* But it emerges as a growl, low in my throat, beating back the judgement.

To hell with it.

She shifts, her free hand travelling down my chest and around to my back as she encourages me closer, her message clear. And then her tongue brushes brazenly across mine and I give up on my sampling. I want it all—every last bit.

I spin her into a darkened recess carved out of the wall. The round table occupying it is the perfect height for her arse to rest as I lift her onto it. She hooks her legs around me, encasing me, hauling me closer. I can feel her heat through my jeans, feel her skirt bunched up to her hips as I rake my fingers down her thighs.

What are you doing? You're in public, anyone can see.

But isn't that the point? You need to get her somewhere you can use it? And with other people—her redhead friend, for starters...

My gut twists tighter, contending with the pulsing heat, and it's a sickening contrast so marked that I gain a second's clarity to tear my mouth away. 'Come with me?'

She shakes her head, her green eyes blazing into mine as her hands take advantage of our parting to unfasten my shirt just enough to slip her fingers within.

'No, I want you here.'

'Why?'

She strokes my skin, her fingers burning a fiery trail down my torso that has my cock pressing harder, eager for satisfaction. Eager for it *now*—not in twenty, thirty, forty minutes. However long it takes to get her somewhere I can use it.

She smiles, all sultry and appealing as fuck. 'Don't *you* have a side you like to keep hidden?'

A side? Christ, I feel like my whole twisted self should be locked away right now.

'Don't tell me the great Coco Lauren fears a little bit of gossip?' I try to sound light, but the words are tight, my teeth gritting against the heat racing through my veins. Desire and my endgame at war.

'This kind of gossip has the power to hurt those that I care about, Ash.'

She says it softly, sincerely, and for a second she's exposed, giving me a glimpse of pain so obvious I feel it against my will.

'Like who?' Because surely she's talking about herself? Protecting herself. Surely, she's aware that this makes her vulnerable to people like her brother. Not that I truly understand his goal.

'People I love.'

My body tenses, the twisting sensation deep inside me increasing tenfold. And then she shakes her head, as though clearing it, and hooks her hands around my neck, her touch searing my skin even as I try to stay focused.

'But I don't want to talk about it—just take my word for it...'

She moves in to kiss me and I pull back, knowing it'll be my undoing. I sense I'm on the cusp of something, of understanding, of getting to the bottom of Philip's intent. Why I want to is beyond me. I should be running from her, from *this*, from the entire job that has me questioning everything, and instead I'm pushing.

'How can gossip of this kind hurt? You're single, available, an adult—'

'And I'm a Lauren—born of a scandalous mother. Believe me, *this* kind of gossip has the power to sow the seeds of my downfall.'

I can feel her withdrawing but I don't stop. Not yet. 'You fear the public backlash? The loss of your golden halo?'

Her eyes flash and her skin pales just enough to tell me I've hit a nerve. 'No, the only eyes I care about are my grandmother's.'

'Scared she'll disinherit you?'

She frowns up at me and I know I've pushed too far. Maybe even said too much. But then everyone would assume she has an inheritance; they just wouldn't all know its value, like I do.

What I don't expect is the sudden movement of her hand as her palm makes for my cheek. I grab her wrist a split second before it collides with my skin and face off the fire in her gaze.

'Apologies.' And I mean it—I do. *Damn it*, why do I care?

Her eyes tremble as they stay fixed on mine and I feel the need to explain. I can't stop myself. 'I meet spoilt little rich girls who put money above love and family all the time.'

'Just because we're born into money…'

She tries to pull her wrist free but my fingers are locked. The contact heats me as her eyes project the same fire.

'It doesn't make us all cold-hearted bitches.'

'No, it doesn't.' It's like she's throwing my own deductions back at me and I almost laugh at the irony of it. 'But if you're so worried about this side of you getting out, why risk it?'

'Because I need to live my life too—because right now she's dying, and I don't know which way is up…'

Her voice cracks a little, her fire dwindling. And, God help me, my gut turns over as I stay locked in her gaze. I knew this too. That her grandmother was sick. I just hadn't anticipated her caring this much.

Now who's the heartless bastard?

I can't speak. Nothing can get past the chaos she has evoked within me.

She wets her lips, takes a shuddery breath. 'Because I thought you were the man who could take that pain away, be my distraction just for a second, just for now.'

Her eyes glisten as they waver over my face and then she backs away from me, shaking her head as my body reels from her admission.

'I can see I was wrong. You're not my type after all…'

She starts to walk, trying to pull free, but I yank her back to me. I'm not even thinking. It's impulsive— a need to take it all away, just as she hoped I would. Because I can't face her pain a second longer. I can't deal with the sickening guilt that comes with it either.

I claim her mouth and force all the guilt out, hanging on to her startled whimper, the swift surrender of her pliable mouth and the heat of her hands as they thrust inside my shirt. She rakes her nails over my chest and I feel a heady sting as she pierces the skin, wild, hungry, desperate. Heat surges through my body. My cock is more than willing to be the distraction she demands.

And what about you? Do you really want to go there with her? She's your fucking target, for Christ's sake!

But she's a target who doesn't deserve to be. This little exchange off the back of all that I've already witnessed is enough to prove that.

But if she's not like Jess—a woman I despise— doesn't it actually make her all the more dangerous? All the more to be avoided?

She bites down on my lower lip and tugs. Pleasure-pain drowns out the inner voice of reason as her fingers move to my belt. *Fuck*, she's undoing it.

'We shouldn't…' I manage against her lips.

'We should.' She nods, her breath coming in short pants. *'Now.'*

I can sense eyes upon us. Does she know we're being watched?

Of course she does—you're in Blacks.

But in that moment I feel like I'm the only person in her world. The way she's looking at me, drowning in me, makes power surge through my veins, and I can't stop my hands from sliding higher, my thumbs caressing the soft flesh of her inner thighs. She feels so perfect; her eyes, her breath, the arch of her body are all so responsive to me.

You don't deserve what she's giving you...

She parts my belt, unfastens my button, my zipper. My cock strains ready and then she slips her hand inside my briefs, her warm fingers taking hold. I freeze. I can't breathe, can't move. I grit my teeth and squeeze my eyes shut just for a second, just enough to regain some control, and when I open them again, she's grinning up at me, her eyes alive with mischief. So much better than the pain seconds before...

She pumps me once and my balls contract—*shit*.

'And there I was, believing I'm not your type...'

She moves over me now, her eyes dropping to take in the sight of her hand gripping me. Masterfully working me. My thighs tremble... My groan is strangled in my throat.

I'm fucked.

She sweeps her thumb over the tip of my cock, sweeping up the pre-cum as more appears. I breathe, ragged, losing it. She runs one scarlet-red nail over my slit.

'Fuck.'

She looks at me from beneath her lashes. I'm so ready to be inside her, so scared I'll shoot my load before I even get there…

'Mmm… I wonder if you taste as good as you look, Ash.'

Oh, Christ, no.

I shake my head, the move negligible with my body pulled so taut, my fingers tight upon her thighs.

'How about I find out?'

She slips forward, forcing me back a step to give her the space to drop to her knees, and I stare at the wall ahead of me, my brain screaming at me to stop her as my cock eggs her on, bucking in her grasp.

She gives a pleased little laugh—and then I feel it, the delicate point of her tongue, sweeping over the sensitised head and my eyes drop. I'm lost to her and all she can do.

Her lashes lift, her eyes lock onto mine and she grips the base of my cock, steadying my length to trace a teasing path around her mouth with my very tip. Like I'm her fucking lipstick.

Holy mother of God.

I fling my hand to her hair and pull her away. Just for a second…just until the wave passes. The wave that's pushing me too close to the edge.

'You know what I think?' she says, looking up at me. 'I think I'm *exactly* your type.'

The words hit home. Harsh, true. She *is* my type. She's everything I've wanted and evaded for so long. Her haughty air, her elegant poise, her perfect fuck-me-now lips.

I bring her back to my cock. 'Less talking.'

I don't need a reminder that I'm destined to walk the world alone because I let my dick pick 'em, thus exposing me to the worst of the female species— the ones who will always feel themselves superior. *Hell*, she *is* superior to me. Because I'm the villain of this piece. I'm the one out to expose her, to break her, all for the money her brother is willing to pay me. And she—

She sucks over me and my mind quits, only a moan breaking through my consciousness. It's not me. It's not her. It comes from someone close behind me. Someone watching. It shouldn't turn me on—none of this should. And still I fork my fingers through her perfect bob and hold her there. Watch as she takes me deeper with every thrust, her cheeks hollowing as she sucks, her eyes bright as they reach inside mine, her soft, feminine scent sailing up to me.

I am fucked. I can't stop this—no matter what I want, or what is right.

I'm going to take all she's willing to give—take it and walk away. Just as Jess would deserve, just as Coco—

Damn it, she isn't Jess.

And that's what's eating at me, even as heat starts to streak through my limbs.

You're the one to be despised. Not her. You're the one blinded by your own pain, your own past, taking it out on her. You're the nasty piece of work.

I groan over the realisation, squeeze my eyes shut,

throw my head back. My balls contract, my release is imminent, and—

Fuck, I should warn her. But pleasure steals my voice, my ability to move. I can only grip her head tighter and try to breathe, try to stave it off. And then I'm gone, my hips jerking forward with the force of my release.

Heaven flows through my entire body, my head falling forward as my eyes open to take her in, wide with shock, with desire, with all manner of mixed-up emotion. And then there's her hum of satisfaction, reverberating around my length as she takes my all. She's not quitting and I don't want her to. She's taking my every last drop, forcing out reality and making me want more. *So much more.*

I soften my hands in her hair, caressing instead of holding. I drag in a breath and then my brain rips through the haze—*you fucking idiot*—and sends guilt and hatred hot on its tail.

And it's not her I loathe. I know that with ice-like clarity now.

It's me—all me.

Something flickers in his gaze, and for a second I worry that it's regret I can see. I don't want Ash's regret. I want the fire back. The same fire that has me all wet, aching, needier than I can ever remember. It's the perfect antidote for life. Powerful, all-encompassing, a perfect distraction.

I release his cock and put right his underwear—but I don't zip him up. I'm not done yet. Not if I have my way. I lick my lips as I stand and take pleasure in his touch as he tilts my head towards him, his thumb and finger gentle on my chin.

'You're pretty talented.'

'Call it practice.'

His eyes flash and his fingers flex. *He didn't like that*...

'I'll bet you've had plenty of practice too.' I throw it back at him and run my teeth over my bottom lip. I want to push him. I want to toy with his obvious conflict. I want this twisted game to go on for however long he will play it. 'I bet your tongue is skilled in so many ways—or do you use your fingers more?'

I take hold of his hand upon my chin and slowly lower it down my body. My breasts prickle inside the confines of my bra as he travels through the valley between them and over my exposed midriff, which has me sucking in a breath.

He isn't stopping me, but that war is back. I can see it in his gaze. At any moment he's going to back away and leave, and the very idea is making my heart beat that little bit faster and urging me on.

I lift myself up on tiptoes and lean into his ear, my free hand working my skirt up, my other hand drawing his hand down. 'Feel how wet I am…just for you.'

I slip his hand inside my lacy knickers, press his fingers into my wetness. His breath hitches in my ear, a curse hot on its tail.

Better. So much better.

My lips lift in victory as I dare to lean back, to

meet his eye, and slowly I circle my hips over his touch, my hand still tight on his.

You're not going anywhere, Ash, not yet.

His lips are deliciously parted and I love it, taking advantage to sink my tongue inside his mouth and coax his own into action. He comes alive at last, his fingers moving of their own volition, his mouth crushingly sweet as he takes control.

He slips his fingers deeper, enters me as his thumb grazes my clit and I buck on the spike of pleasure that runs through me, the continued onslaught of his mouth catching my sigh of ecstasy.

I raise my hands to his shoulders and cling to his body for support, my lower half on a shameless ride of its own.

I struggle to catch my breath as his thumb works me to fever pitch, his mouth endless in its brutal exploration of my mouth. I tear my lips away, press my forehead into his shoulder and remember the audience taking in our brazen display, enjoying what they can see, what they can hear.

I look to where his hand is buried in black lace. His movements are quick and dizzying, his fingers in deep. He's skilled, all right, and I'm seconds away from combusting. My nails bite into his shoulders, my body tenses up and I fling my head back to look at him, to register the blazing heat of his gaze.

'That's it—come for me, princess.'

His words, his hand, his skill… Every muscle floods with heat, my insides are wound so tight, and then I burst from the inside out.

'Fuck...' My eyes clamp shut, my body spasms and he locks his arm around my waist, holding me tight. He won't drop me. I won't fall. It's perfect—perfect and safe.

His thumb rolls over me, slowing against my heightened sensitivity, and then he palms me, his hot heat pressed against my wetness until my body eventually stills and my breathing calms.

My head falls forward, he withdraws his hand and reality seeps in.

Nothing's changed. Life is as it was before. But for those blissful few minutes it was gone, and for that I am grateful.

Slowly I raise my lashes and calm my expression. He doesn't need to join me on the comedown. He doesn't have to shoulder what I do.

'Thank you,' I whisper.

He curves his hand around my behind beneath my skirt. 'You're welcome.'

And then he releases me to fasten his trousers. He steps back, his attention off me. So off me that I'm floundering.

I look away and smooth out my skirt, suddenly awkward, sheepish. Do we just say goodbye? It's what I would normally do. But I don't want to. Already the chill is taking over and the distance is building between us. I want the warmth back.

What's the likelihood of us seeing each other again? I've been coming here for years and never seen him, regardless of his claim that Jackson is a mate. Maybe he's not from London. Maybe he's just visiting.

So many questions burn through me and I can't give voice to a single one.

Regardless of his actions, he said I wasn't his type. Would that still be the case now we'd had our fill?

He's very still and I risk a look. He's staring at me, but I can't read him. He's impenetrable, cold. While his blue eyes seem to pierce me, strip me bare. My confidence is in tatters. Obliterated with the surprising force of my orgasm and his sudden detachment.

Perhaps it's because I could see myself wanting more.

More like what?

A date. A normal, everyday date, like any normal, everyday woman would want.

But you're not one of them. Never have been... Never will be.

The growing chill reaches my heart and I shiver.

'I should go,' he says, smoothing a hand over his hair.

I nod, still speechless, my messed-up thoughts keeping me tongue-tied as I wrap my arms around myself.

He starts to walk and then stops. My heart flutters, my head lifts, I'm hopeful. But then he continues on and I watch him leave…cold, sober, sad.

I turn back to the ladies' room, my head swimming with what's gone down.

You sure you want to let that go…?

I'm already spinning on my heel and heading after

him, but as I break out onto the pavement and scan the street all I see are the doormen. There's no sign of him. Not even a lit-up car about to leave. Where in the hell *is* he?

I look to the doormen, who are doing their best not to notice me. 'Did you see where he went?' I say, and they give me a brief look.

'Who?' one says.

'The guy that left just ahead of me.'

'Afraid not.'

I think he's lying. In fact, I know he's lying. Maybe it's the fact that I'm on the wrong side of the non-disclosure agreement now I'm outside the building that means he won't tell me anything.

I'm about to ask again when I hear a car door open behind me, down the street, and my heart soars. I turn towards the sound.

Maybe he's seen me... Maybe he's coming back for—

'My lady?'

It's my driver. Hope vacates my body, the chill returns, and I wrap my arms around my middle and head towards him. The sinking feeling inside me is ever more pronounced.

It was foolish, anyway. I've read of infatuations that start with such a spark. I've read it in my mother's diary, have been able to feel my mother's lust and then love for my father through the pages. But I always thought such a thing out of my reach. Every boy, teen, man has taught me that aside from sex I'm good for one thing only: *money.*

No, make that two things. Money and a title. I have them both. And because of that I'm destined to become a spinster.

My tombstone:

Lady Coco Lauren
Lived and died
Single and alone

Why did one chance meeting with a stranger make me hope for something more?

CHAPTER THREE

THREE DAYS HAVE gone by since my momentary lapse in judgement.

Momentary lapse?

Monumental fuck-up, more like.

I swear I can still hear her moans ringing in my ear, taste her on my lips, my fingers… I've only to close my eyes and I see her dilated gaze looking up at me, her skin flushed pink, her body moving with sheer abandon in her quick-fire orgasm, my fingers buried deep—

Fuck. There my dick goes, tightening inside my jeans, painful and persistent, nagging for release.

What the hell's got into you?

Stupid question.

She has.

Her taste, her scent, her flirtatious little mouth. She's got under my skin, exposed my inner desires. Making her come while others watched on, her sucking me off, me losing control…

And not only that she's fucked with my job, making me cross a line that I'm struggling to come back from. Making me question everything.

But here I finally am. After three long days of battling my conscience, her insane appeal and every crazy doubt she has instilled, I'm back with it and tailing her. Because I have to. I'm a fucking PI—it's what I do. I don't fall for princesses, and I don't give a fuck. I really don't. I learned that lesson well, and no amount of honesty from her lips is going to change that.

But I can almost hear my inner laughter, mocking me. As if it knows that I'm here because I can't stay away.

It's two thirty in the afternoon and I'm standing in the shadows at an outdoor charity gala for the local children's hospice, my eyes hidden behind shades and once more on her.

I wear a baseball cap, a nondescript hoodie and jeans, my casual clothing blending right in with that around me. But she shines above everyone. Her hair is tied back, highlighting her radiant smile, her effortless grace. She wears a soft pink sweater, white skinny jeans and a pair of trainers. Nothing special, but on her...

To her right is a child in a wheelchair, with no hair and pale, tubes travelling from her nose and arm to a bag of liquid high above. Coco ducks down to talk to her, her smile natural and vibrant, and the girl nods and murmurs in return, her own lips lifting.

They talk a little more and I see Coco's PA start

to get edgy as she watches from the sidelines, her eyes flitting between the watch on her wrist, the tablet she has tight in her hand and the pair talking.

It seems Coco isn't adhering to the schedule, and as I look back to her I can see why. She has the girl laughing now, and the joyous noise is lighting up all those around them. Hell, even *my* insides lift. She doesn't care for her schedule—she only cares for the girl.

And then she stands and turns. For a second I think she spies me, and then I realise she's wiping her eyes. She does it so discreetly, so smoothly, that any ordinary onlooker would probably miss it—but not me. I've come to know her gestures, her smiles, her laughs, those that are forced and those that ring true.

She's crying.

My gut twists and sinks, and I double back.

Guilt. That's what this is. Guilt and another emotion I haven't felt in so long it's almost alien to me now. I don't want to acknowledge it. I just want to get as far away as possible and that means telling her brother I'm out.

You're going soft, comes the mental gibe. The same one that has plagued me since we crossed the line at Blacks. And it's backed up by the sensible argument that I've been blinded by what we did, what we shared. That ultimately she's still the spoilt little rich girl I once had her pegged as—that her brother has her pegged as.

But it's bollocks.

I've followed her enough to know she cares about

these charity projects. Not the front—not the face of it. She cares about these people. And she works hard. She barely stops—moving from one event to another. Even those lunches seem to be more a function of her public role rather than for her pleasure.

No, the only time I've truly seen her do something for herself is at Blacks. That was for her. *All* for her. And I loved being able to give her that. Loved it too much.

And there was her total honesty, her love for her grandmother, her need to bury the pain.

My chest tightens as I fist my hands. I have no choice but to bring this to a close. Even if it could ruin my reputation. Philip Lauren isn't the kind to take my withdrawal lying down, and the more anxious he becomes, the more his nasty side shines through.

How the fuck I didn't see this side to him in the first place, I don't know.

Liar. You didn't see it because you didn't want to; you were too interested in taking down another Jess. Another hoity-toity, good-for-nothing rich girl who only has love for herself.

And more fool me… I couldn't have been more wrong.

I deserve the pain that plagues me now, the sickening guilt, but the least I can do is tell Philip where to stick it. He'll likely do his damnedest to see Livingston Investigations closed down as a result, but I'm not afraid of him or the threat. My PI work exists for a reason: to bury my past and save others from similar fates. It isn't my bread and butter. I have property up and down the country that gets that for me.

Not that I'll roll over in the face of Philip's anger—far from it. I might even have some fun with it. And if I can convince him there's nothing to tell, maybe he'll just walk away from whatever this vendetta is and leave both her and my business alone.

I take my mobile out of my back pocket and send him a text.

We need to meet. Friday. Usual place. Seven o'clock. Don't be late.

I smile as I pocket my phone. It'll certainly give me some satisfaction, watching the guy stew on it as I tell him what I really think of his sister and all that I've learned.

Well, almost all—I'll leave out the finer detail that starts with Blacks and ends with our brief spell of fun.

If only I could forget about it...

Okay, I've officially hit stalker level.

It's been a week since I went all gaga over Tall, Dark and Handsome, and despite several visits to Blacks, he's been a no-show. Which is as I expected, if I'm honest. So last night I swallowed my pride and confronted Jackson. He was his friend. He'd know where Ash lived, and with some gentle persuasion he'd tell me.

What I didn't expect was a grin as wide as the Thames is long and the information that Ash's home address is just around the goddamn corner. It was obvious Jackson was matchmaking, and that gave me hope that whatever this connection between Ash and me is, it's powerful enough for his friend to believe in it too.

So here I am, at six thirty on a Friday evening, nervously toying with my bag as I stare at the exclusive warehouse development before me. It doesn't look like much from the outside, but I'm not fooled. This postcode doesn't come cheap, and whatever's hidden on the other side is going to be just as exclusive...*rather like the man himself.*

And here's another dose of truth: I didn't expect him to be this well-off either. His rough, honest edge hinted at something more normal, something more ordinary—something I wanted to reach out and hold on to so bad.

All I have to do is ring the damn bell and, fingers crossed, he'll be at home and willing.

So why I'm still standing here, ten minutes after my driver opened the car door to let me out, I don't know.

Derek's probably watching me from the car and wondering exactly the same thing. I must look like I'm losing my mind.

I pull my handbag tighter over my shoulder and scan my clothing. Today I'm dressed in black skinny jeans and a free-swinging white shirt—perfectly innocent and a complete contrast to the debauched ideas taking centre stage in my brain. My underwear is bang on, though. It may be white, but the crotchless panties and the revealing lace bra communicate exactly what I'm after.

I take a breath and look to the frosted glass of the double front doors ahead that give nothing away, at the brick archway above that appears far more daunting than it should, and butterflies kick up inside my belly.

What are you doing?

Fuck it, I'm doing what I want—screw the judgement and the doubts. I head for the door. Reality can be pushed away for a night at least. I deserve this. A bit of fun…a bit of—

The door swings open as I reach for the buzzer beside the entrance—the single, solitary buzzer. *Christ, does he own the whole lot?* And then he's there, filling the opening, and I'm gaping like a fucking fool.

'Coco?'

His surprised expression all but does me in. He's even more handsome than I remember, his jaw still unshaven, his eyes just as piercing beneath his dark angled brow, all rugged, rough and—

His brow quirks.

Fucking get with it, Coco.

I straighten, my hands tight over the strap of my bag as I cling to it for solidarity when my legs want to give way.

'Hi,' I say—like this is totally expected, like I *haven't* just stalked the bejesus out of him. 'I thought we could do dinner…if you're free?'

I struggle to hold his eyes. He's doing it again: reading me and all my fucked-up mental chaos. I lower my gaze but stand firm. He's wearing a deep blue shirt and dark denim jeans. Very smart. And as I breathe in, I get the welcoming scent of freshly applied cologne. He looks and smells date-worthy.

Oh, Christ, was I asking him on a date?

My eyes flick back to his and I see my double take reflected back at me.

'How did you find me?'

Not quite the response I was hoping for...

'Jackson gave me your address.'

Fire sizzles beneath my cheeks. *Please, God, let my make-up do its job and stop me from looking crimson.* I'm blonde, I'm freckly, I go red at the drop of a hat.

'It's not like I tailed you or anything. I'm not some stalker.'

I swear his skin pales. *Shit.* He thinks I *am* some stalker.

'Jackson thought you could do with me swinging by.'

'Jackson should mind his own bloody business.'

He scans the street, clearly on edge, and I feel the situation rapidly running away from me.

'Look, it's okay if you're busy.'

'I am.'

'Going somewhere nice?' I try for a smile and gesture to his outfit. He has the same number of buttons undone at the collar, the same hint of hair...

'You shouldn't be here, Coco.'

I realise I'm staring. Right at his chest. My palms are tickling with reignited memories. I pull my gaze back to his face and swallow past the desire-shaped wedge taking up camp in my throat. I hear his words, register their negativity, but there's also his tone, and the pulse working like crazy in his jaw…

Is he really freaked out by me turning up? Or is he fighting the same forceful attraction?

Please let it be the latter.

'No, you're probably right…' I take a breath and give him another smile, wanting to test the water. 'But I can't get our last meeting out of my head.'

His mouth tightens, his throat bobs. He says nothing, but his eyes tell me he's reliving it too and I push on, my confidence returning. 'I thought maybe we could…you know…see each other again?'

'*See* each other?'

It rasps out, but his tough-guy exterior is at odds with the widening of his eyes. The rabbit-caught-in-the-headlights look makes him seem boyish and I give a soft laugh.

'Don't worry, Ash. I'm not asking you for a relationship…or even a real date…' Although the truth was I'd take the date. 'Only sex.'

I straighten on the last word, my chin jutting just a little, like I'm trying to convince him as well as myself.

'You mean more distraction?'

'Yes, if that's what you want to call it.'

'It's what *you* called it.'

'I did.' I step closer and he tenses, backing away.

'I'm not about to go all clingy on you, if that's what you're worried about. I'm not like that.'

'That's not what I'm worried about.' He shakes his head. 'You shouldn't be here,' he says again.

'No? Where *should* I be, then?'

His eyes move over me, hesitant, probing. 'Seeing a counsellor, a professional—someone who can help you deal with what you're going through.'

I laugh. I can't help it. *Is he for real?* 'I don't need a therapist.'

'I didn't say you did. I'm just telling you I understand.'

He says it like he knows it. Like he's lived it with me. And confusion, a sudden surge of sadness, has my temper sparking. 'How can you possibly understand? I came to hook up with you again, not to be lectured. But of course you won't get that, will you? Since I'm just a spoilt little rich girl?'

'No, Coco, that's not... You're not...' He rakes his fingers over the back of his head, turning away in frustration, tension thrumming off him in waves. 'You just shouldn't be here.'

'*Why?*'

He stares back at me, the nerve in his jaw pulsing. He looks like he wants to say so much and yet nothing is coming.

'Ash, what—'

'You need to go.' He raises his palm to me and avoids my eye.

'Are you going to tell me the other night wasn't

fun?' I'm going to make him acknowledge this, if nothing else. 'Because *I* thought it was.'

His eyes flicker in my direction, that nerve in his jaw ever more pronounced.

'I particularly loved the feel of you in my mouth.'

He sucks in a breath and damn if his cheeks don't heat. The sight has my belly tripping out and the telltale warmth is quick to spread, killing off the sadness, the confusion, the anger. He's like my on-and-off switch and I'm not ready to give up on him.

'Coco, don't do this.'

'What?' I say in mock innocence. I let my eyes drift over him, wetting my lips. 'Or did you prefer sinking your fingers into me?'

'*Coco.*'

He's so tense, and I'm getting off on it now. Goading him, pushing him where I want him.

'I'm not the man you think I am; you can't play those games with me.'

'Games?' My smile is seductive, calm, the perfect front. 'Who's playing games? I'm being a straight shooter and telling you exactly what I want.'

His breath shudders out. 'Go home, Coco. Before we do something we both regret.'

'*Regret?*' I frown. 'How can we possibly have regrets? We're just two strangers hooking up. What's wrong with that?'

'*Everything's* wrong with it.'

'Am I missing something? Do you have a girlfriend—or a *wife*?'

He's shaking his head at me but I feel like I'm

missing something huge and I can't begin to imagine what.

'Is that your car?'

His sudden change in tack has my frown deepening and I follow his gaze to where Derek waits for me.

'Yes.'

'Come on. I'll walk you.'

Hell, no.

My laugh is harsh, almost manic. I glare back at him, confusion morphing into anger at his condescension.

'Forget it. I'm not a child. I don't need you to hold my hand. You don't want me—that's fair enough. But don't patronise me while you reject me.'

I spin on my heel and force my stride to be steady as I head for the car. I won't give him the satisfaction of racing off and letting him see how his words, his contradictory behaviour have hurt me. And I certainly won't let him see the tears that come from nowhere.

Because they aren't about him. They're about everything else. His rejection has only served to trigger the whole damn lot.

'Coco…' he calls after me. 'I'm sorry—I didn't mean to upset you.'

And now he's offering out pity? I shake my head. *No fucking way.*

I've heard enough. I don't turn. I don't break stride. I head to my car and get in. I don't dare look back at him until I'm safely locked away behind the privacy glass and the car is moving. Then I look and I see him standing there, confusion in his eyes.

'Where to, my lady?' Derek asks.

The last thing I want is to go home like this. I spent the morning with Granny, chatting with her doctors, the nurses, trying to mask the pain, to be strong. This foolish seduction was to have been my solace, my hope. Now that has failed, and I'm even more messed-up than before. The tears were living proof.

'Blacks...please.'

CHAPTER FOUR

WATCHING HER DRIVE away was hard. *Really. Hard.*
But I'd done the right thing, so why did it feel so
wrong?

*Because you want her. Like you've only ever
wanted one other: Jess. And that's why you need to
get as far away from her as possible.*

But, fuck, there's something about her—that tantalising contrast of vulnerable, innocent do-gooder
and hidden temptress.

Philip Lauren's words come back to me full force:
she's no innocent and I want you to prove it.

Yes, I can prove it all right—but not to that bastard.

No, tonight I walk away from him, the job, her.
Definitely her.

She spells trouble. Messy, heart-screwing trouble.

I squeeze my temples with my thumbs and fore-
fingers. With Jess I was young, foolish and naive. I
wasn't foolhardy enough to let it happen again. Nowhere close.

But Coco Lauren...

Damn it, I should have turned away the second

my gut told me to. I swore I would never let anyone get close after Jess. My job has become my lifeline—it's pulled me out of the darkness, given me the drive to move on. I'll never forget, I'll never forgive, but I won't dwell on it either. And I sure as hell won't let myself care about another woman again.

I take a breath and head for my car, reconsidering my choice of vehicle almost immediately. I need the motorbike. A hair-raising blast on two wheels to clear my head before I face off the other Lauren and put this madness behind me once and for all.

But the ride doesn't work.

I'm still mentally delivering my walk-away mantra half an hour later, as I meet the man I'm unfortunate enough to call my client.

'Seriously, Livingston…?' Philip Lauren eyes my casual get-up with distaste and it only makes me grin.

We're in a high-end bar—the kind that insists on a blazer—and the fact that my outfit has already pissed him off is a bonus. 'Don't get your knickers in a twist, Lauren, I don't expect to be stopping long.'

He visibly balks. His princely expression is pained. I swear even his blow-dried golden locks stand perfectly on end at my disrespect. But I don't have time for it. Nor do I care.

'Ah…' His eyes spark now, as though he's had some grand revelation. 'So you have what I need, then?'

I lean back in the rock-hard Chesterfield armchair and raise my leg so my ankle rests over my

knee, all casual and to him increasingly disrespect-
ful, I'm sure.

'Nope.' I flick a hand at him. 'There's nothing
to give.'

His eyes narrow, his cheeks streak. He's angry.
And my gut loves it.

'Look, Mr Livingston, I'm paying you good
money to dig this dirt.'

He lowers his voice on the last word, leaning in as
he scans the nearby tables, not wanting to be overheard. But I don't even flinch.

'There's no dirt to dig.'

He shakes his head fervently. 'Like hell there
isn't.'

He's so certain. Desperate, even. And not for the
first time I wonder at his goal, the endgame, why he's
so eager to ruin his sister. What does it matter to him
that Coco likes her sex on the wild side?

'What makes you say that?'

'A leopard doesn't change its spots, and a whore
like her *definitely* doesn't.'

His words hit me like a slug to the stomach and
I fight to keep my expression neutral. The slice of
pain coming from my tightened right fist tells me
I'm losing the battle, my nails piercing the skin of
my palm. I unclench it slowly and rub my jaw, as
though I'm considering his words and not staving
off the need to kill him.

'If you're so sure, why do you need the proof?'

'Because without proof I can't get my hands on
what I need.'

'Which is...?'

'None of your goddamn business.'

He quiets when he sees our drinks approaching and the waiter slipping me a questionable stare.

So I don't fit into your la-di-da club? So sue me.

I happily stare the waiter down, and to my amusement he almost spills the drinks as he sets them down before scurrying off.

'I don't pay you to ask questions,' Philip Lauren pipes up again. 'I pay you to get evidence of her sexual proclivities.'

'And I'm telling you there's nothing to report. She's above reproach.'

He laughs and leans back in his chair, whisky in hand. 'You're lying. What I can't work out is why...'

I shift in my seat and take up my own drink for a swig. 'What makes you so certain?'

He eyes the glass in his hand, all thoughtful. 'She and my wife boarded together in their teens.'

'They were friends?'

I want to know more; I can't help it. I'm not one for digging into my clients' reasoning. They give me a job and I deliver. But this case is different. I *need* to know.

'To an extent.'

He lifts his eyes back to mine and they flash with an angry fire that tells me he isn't letting this go—that, whatever his reasoning is, he will keep pushing until he has exactly what he needs. It wouldn't be hard for another PI to retrace my steps. I followed her movements and discovered her visits to Blacks pretty quickly. A few enquiries in the right places and he'd soon have what he needed.

'But that was years ago. Maybe she's changed, maybe she's saving herself for marriage or destined to become a nun—who knows?'

He laughs again. 'You're funny, Livingston. I'll give you that.'

I'm not trying to be funny. I'm trying to put him off—to bring an end to this mission he's so determined to see through. I don't want to care. I don't want to protect her. But I can't stand by while her brother desecrates her reputation for his own gain.

'There's no way she could have changed,' he says, sobering, and his voice is so serious I wonder if he's trying to convince himself of that fact—if his need for her to be as he suspects far outweighs whether he considers it true or not. 'She's just being very careful about it.'

'Doesn't matter how careful she's being. If she was at it—' I hate the words as they form, feel acid riding high in my throat. There's guilt at my lie, at my part in her potential downfall, as well as anger at his conviction. 'I would know. I'd have the evidence.'

'Or maybe you're not as good as everyone says—yourself included.'

He gives me a shit-eating grin and I want to swing for him. He's fucking lucky we're in public. I take a breath instead, flexing the fist that is so determined to ball up, and ask the other question that's itching to be answered.

'Tell me, why is it you want to ruin your sister's

reputation so much? I mean, I have a brother—I get how annoying siblings can be—but this…'

'Again, it's none of your business.'

'There's clearly no love lost between you…not on your part at least.' I see the flash of something—possibly guilt—and jump on it. 'So, tell me, does she *really* deserve this?'

He downs his whisky in one. His eyes water at the hit of booze and lines mar his face, ageing his perfect veneer.

'I don't have to sit here and listen to you question my reasoning, Livingston. I'm paying you to get me evidence, and if you can't do that, then I'll find someone else who can.'

My neck prickles. So much for hoping he would let it go.

But why is it your problem what he does after you're gone? Just walk away and forget you ever met him. Met her.

'Suit yourself.' I start to rise, to leave, to get the hell away, but he shoots up, halting me halfway to standing.

'Wait—just hear me out.'

I look at his pleading gaze. Is he going to open up? Do I really want him to if it means I have to stick around? But what if it means understanding his intentions towards Coco?

I'm already dropping back into my seat, my inner messed-up stance driving my decision.

He lowers himself once more and forks his fingers together on the table, leaning in again. 'Truth is there's no one better than you at this. I know that. You know that. And I *need* this. Believe me, it'll be worth your while.'

'I charge a flat fee. We've—'

'Double. I'll pay you double.'

I don't react visibly, but inside the adrenalin rush has my every sense on high alert. My fee is already substantial—to double it would be laughable. No amount of information is worth that.

Questions hammer ever more acutely through me. What does he hope to achieve? How low will he sink? How much danger is Coco in?

'I mean it, Livingston—man to man now,' he insists.

I swallow back the rising bile. In my mind he lost his man status the second he showed his true nature.

'You get me that evidence and I'll pay you double— maybe more if it's juicy enough and you can deliver it in the next two weeks.'

I have to swallow again and force my hands to relax their death-grip hold over the arms of my chair. 'Why the rush?'

'Time's running out.'

'Why?'

'You need to stop asking so many questions.'

'And *you* need to try answering some.'

'I'll tell you what you need to know and no more.' He reaches into the inside pocket of his blazer and pulls out a folded piece of paper, which he slides across to me. 'Try this place. I hear she's a regular…'

I take the sheet and bite back a curse. I know what

I'm going to see before I even unfold it. But seeing *Blacks* in scrawled handwriting has my gut in knots.

I throw back my drink and pocket the piece of paper.

'Well?' he presses.

I get to my feet and look down at him just long enough to say, 'Consider it done.'

Then I walk away, recounting what I know now.

Time isn't on Philip Lauren's side and he won't stop until he has what he needs. And if he knows about her presence at Blacks then he already has contacts who, with the right persuasion, will give up what he's asking for. Hell, he might even try to gain access himself—not that Jackson will let him anywhere near the place once I've spoken to him.

I'm Coco's last hope. So long as I'm on the job and he's not going elsewhere I can ride this out.

And if he does decide to employ another PI, they will fail, because I'll see to it she stays out of trouble.

And what about you?

Seems I'm destined to walk straight back into trouble…

But in my case, who said trouble couldn't be fun? If keeping her safe means sharing more of what she asked me for earlier this evening, out of the public eye—or, more specifically, out of her brother's eye— then where was the harm?

Yeah, you just tell yourself that…

I slam open the door before the doorman can do it for me.

I just need to keep a lid on it for a little bit longer. I've done it for ten years; I can do it for umpteen more. And once the danger has passed I'll walk away with a clear conscience. I will have kept her safe, and that's all that matters.

I pull out my phone and fire off messages to my researchers. I want to know all there is to know about Philip Lauren. I want to get to the root of his desperation and understand the exact timescale I'm working to. I should have done it sooner, but I had no cause to investigate Philip Lauren when he first came to me.

I see Coco in my mind's eye, see those bright green eyes, too generous by far—too generous and too vulnerable and getting to me more than they should.

Shit.

But I can't walk away—not yet.

In fact, I'll start with her. There must be so much she can tell me herself, if I can coax her into talking a little. And as for Jackson's potential membership leak…that needs flagging now.

First Blacks—then Coco.

'Come on—spill.'

Cait elbows me as she says it.

'You're not jealous that I went off with Ricky, are you?'

She laughs, knowing she's way off the mark. We don't have that kind of relationship. We're more friends than lovers—have been since we went to boarding school together. Our messing around came more from being shafted by the opposite sex than anything else. Sex with each other is safe, fun companionship. She's hot. And she doesn't kiss and tell. Neither do I. It works.

She also knows me better than anyone. And she knows my mind is on six feet, two inches of dark, broody hotness.

'Have you seen Jackson tonight?' I ask. I want to quiz him about Ash. I want to understand him better…try to make sense of his rejection.

'*Not* the question I expected…' She sips at her espresso martini—tonight's drink of choice—as she looks to the bar and nods. 'Jackson was here earlier, doing his thing. I think he teases us on purpose—all that macho muscle and daring cheek.'

She winks at me.

'I'm telling you, I would *so* be on him if he'd shake off that no-dating-the-clients rule. It's criminal, really.'

She frowns into her drink and then her eyes light up as she looks back to me.

'Don't tell me you're after him as well as Tall, Dark and Sexy… What was his name again?'

'Ash,' I supply swiftly, and her grin is back, her brow hitting the roof.

'Ah, yes, *Ash*,' she drawls. 'Now, *that's* the man I expected you to be talking about.'

I shake my head. 'Nothing to tell. He bailed when I offered a repeat.'

'Really?' She pins me with her astute blue gaze. 'Then the man's a fool and—' Her eyes leave me and widen. 'Well, speak of the devil—or rather devils…'

Every nerve ending pricks up. 'What?' I ask. Even though I know.

'They've just stepped in and… Oh, yes, he's spied us…or rather *you*.'

She gives a flirtatious little flutter of her fingers in their direction.

'Cait.'

'Oh, hush—you need to get laid and I need to see the spark back in your eye. That guy can do both.'

Heat creeps into my cheeks. 'Cait, I—'

'Ladies…pardon my intrusion, but I believe I owe this one a date.'

Ash is so close I can feel his body heat penetrate my left-hand side. Cait is now staring in wide-eyed amusement. I don't know whether to turn and smile or blank him entirely. The latter is what I *should* do, for refusing me earlier, but my body has a mind of its own and it turns to him. My eyes are quick to follow as they rise to his… Warm, friendly, apologetic, even.

'You do?'

He smiles and my blasted insides soar, uncaring that he patronised and humiliated me earlier this evening. 'I do. Can we start over?'

I look back to Cait. Her eyes are still wide.

'Hey, don't be looking at me—this is up to you… Not that I mind sticking around, though, if you like…'

She looks him up and down, blatantly happy with what she sees, and I kick her beneath the table. The move earns me a grin as she scoots over, glass in hand, and rises out of the booth.

'Didn't think so. She's all yours, Ash.'

But as she straightens, she fixes him with a glare, her free hand reaching out to poke him in the chest.

'Mark my words, though, buster: mess with her and it's me you'll answer to. I may be small, but believe me, *I can bite.*' She punctuates the last three words with a jab of her finger and then turns and walks away.

Ash watches her go, clearly bemused, and it frees me to look at him—*really* look at him.

You'd think after all we've shared I'd be immune to him by now. Instead my eyes rake hungrily over him, taking in the same clothes he wore earlier, only now his sleeves are rolled back, his forearms deliciously bare, flexing muscle exposed and worthy of salivating over. My mouth does just that.

What the hell is wrong with you? my wounded pride mentally admonishes. *Do you really want to go another round with him?*

'Got your fill?'

Shit. Caught staring. A great start at keeping your cool.

I pride myself for my front—it's never let me down before. I depend on it to get me through each day, to be the perfect Coco Lauren. But it's nowhere now. It's taking a fucking holiday. Maybe that's what I should be doing—hitting a deserted island until I can get this craziness under control.

Or you could go for the far less extreme coping strategy of not giving a fuck?

I smile to hide my mental roller coaster and decide to adopt my trademark Coco Lauren tone—the one I've perfected—and I'm sure as hell going to wheel it out now if it kills me.

'Yes, you can leave now.'

I take my barely touched martini and sip it, the bittersweetness sliding smoothly down my throat as I fix my sights on Cait, now sidling up to the bar.

'Okay, I deserved that.'

I don't react. I keep my eyes on Cait and count to ten. *One, two, three…*

'Can I get you another drink?'

Four, five, six…

'An espresso martini?'

Seven, eight, nine…

'Coco, please…'

I don't know whether it's the gentle way he says my name or the fact that he has the gumption to slide into the booth that makes me look at him.

'I don't need another, thank you.'

He scans the bar, smoothing his hand over his hair. He looks nervous now. I like him nervous. It creates a shift in power that I can work with.

'Why are you here, Ash?'

His blue gaze returns to me, all soft and alluring. And, God help me, my clit pulses—instant, acute. I exhale over it, crossing my legs beneath the table and clamping my thighs tightly together. *Behave.* He doesn't need to know the effect he has on me.

'Cat got your tongue?' I raise my brow, arrogant and assured.

No, I'm not going to turn into a hot, gooey mass inside. I'm not.

He runs his teeth over his bottom lip—*definitely* nervous—and I *definitely* like it.

'I came to see you…to apologise for earlier and to…' he opens his palms out to me '…talk.'

I take a small, steadying breath as I smile over my glass. 'Talk?'

His gaze falls to my mouth as I take a sip and I purposely sweep away the remnants with my tongue. If I'm going down, I'm taking him with me.

'*Just*…talk?'

'To begin with, yeah…'

I'm rewarded with a flash of perfect white teeth and a grin that makes my belly flip, upping the low, incessant ache inside me.

'What can I say? I'm an old-fashioned guy.'

The door to the club opens and his grin stills, his eyes flicking in its direction.

'Waiting for someone?' I ask, turning to see a couple walk in.

'No.' He's looking at me when I turn back, but then his eyes flit to the bar, where I can see Jackson talking to his staff.

'You been here all evening?' he asks me, but his eyes don't leave the bar.

'Since leaving your place?' He nods and I frown. This feels like some strange interrogation all of sudden. 'Yeah, is that okay, *Mother*?'

His eyes come back to me, sharp at first, but they soften as he smiles. 'Sorry, I was momentarily distracted.'

He leans forward on his elbows, giving me his full attention now—a fact my hyped-up body positively purrs over and is more than willing to forgive the little interruption for.

'How about we take this conversation back to my place?'

I laugh, surprised, delighted, confused. 'Is that your best chat-up line?'

He laughs too, the sound deep and husky and so fucking erotic he might as well have strummed his fingers over my clit.

'You answer my question and then I'll tell you whether it is or not.'

My laugh is real and easy now, and my fingers run through my bob as my body loosens up. I don't understand his power over me, this dizzying attraction coupled with his ability to put me at ease so readily, but I'm happy to go with it if he gives me a little truth first.

'What's changed?' I ask.

'Since earlier?'

Like he needs to ask... 'Yes.'

'Let's just say I've had a few hours to consider my options.'

'Options?'

He shifts in his seat and leans even closer, all serious now, and I'm completely hooked, barely aware of the glass in my hand.

'I can walk away from you—abstain from all the delights the gorgeous Coco Lauren has to offer...' He draws his words out, slow, thoughtful, and his eyes are doing their thing again, penetrating my very soul and projecting the heat of such delights.

Then he leans back, and his severity morphs into playfulness as he gives me a cocky grin.

'Which, let's face it, would keep your heart in one piece and avoid the devastating heartache that's sure to ensue when I up and leave you.'

I laugh derisively. 'Oh, believe me, there's no risk of that. My heart is not up for grabs.'

His eyes drop to my lips, the playfulness gone as quickly as it came. 'So you say. In which case, how about we get out of here and stop wasting time?'

'And I thought you wanted to *talk*?'

'Oh, I still want that, princess. I like to know who I'm letting share my bed.'

My laugh turns awkward. 'I'm sure you know enough already, thanks to the Great British press.'

He's quiet for a long moment, like he's waiting for me to say something more—but what? It's true. Not a month goes by without me featuring in some article or other.

'Is that really all there is to know about you?' he asks quietly.

The worry mounts, the hairs pricking at the back of my neck.

'What about the person beneath the public image? Your family? Your dreams? What does the great Coco Lauren want aside from "peace, love and harmony"?'

He's quoting me, from an article published in a gossip magazine last month, and I cringe inwardly. It was a family photo shoot, taken before Granny got too sick to perform for the camera. In it, my pristine white dress is respectable, to the knee and chosen by Granny especially. The string of pearls around my neck was a gift from her. A sedate French manicure, simple white heels and a silky-smooth bob. All just so. The picture of Lauren perfection.

And a total contrast to the girl sitting here now.

My cheeks blaze at the falsity of it, of me, and a sudden spark of anger hits—how *dare* he make me feel like this?

'What's your point, Ash?' My tone is like ice and his eyes narrow.

'I didn't mean to upset you.'

'No? Just like you "didn't mean to" earlier this evening?'

'Hell, no.'

He reaches out, combing his fingers through my hair and holding me there as he leans in. I want to break out of his hold, but already desire is drowning out the anger, more potent the closer he gets.

'I just want to know the real you.'

The real me...

My breath flutters over my parted lips, and then he's there, working them further apart, his tongue gently probing.

'I find you fascinating...'

He sweeps inside, his nose nudging mine as he

encourages me to angle my head so he can delve in further.

'I want to get to know you better…'

My heart sings at his words, and my mouth is quick to follow his bidding. People don't usually want to know me. They want what I can give them. Money, status, connections.

And what if he's just trying to get you into bed?

A giggle erupts and he breaks away to frown at me. I can't help it. I'm heady on his words and the ridiculous mental argument they've sparked. What does it matter whether or not he means it? I only want him for sex, for distraction. There's no getting hurt here. No feelings—just fun.

'Are you trying to wound my ego?' he grumbles.

I laugh a little more. 'I think your ego is impenetrable.'

'Believe me, no ego survives a girl erupting into giggles when you kiss her.'

'Then let me make it all better…' I say softly, leaning in to do just that.

The door opens again behind me and his body instantly tenses, his eyes dart.

It's my turn to frown at him. 'What—'

'Hold that thought,' he says, 'and let's get out of here.'

I'm about to ask what the rush is but he's already out of the booth, his attention on Jackson at the bar. The guy gives him a nod and then Ash offers his hand to me.

'But I haven't finished my drink.'

I'm used to doing things on *my* terms, whether I'm doing it for the public or for me. I'm the one in control. And the fact that I'm losing it more and more in Ash's company is freaking me out.

Admit it—don't you like it...just a little?

'I'll make you another,' he says.

My eyes narrow as I take a leisurely sip of my drink, making him wait. He really is itching to leave. I'd like to think it's because he wants me that badly, but I'm not convinced.

'Are you going to promise me one as good as this?'

'Better.'

I give a soft laugh, loving his confidence. 'Very well.' I slip my hand into his and feel my entire palm come alive at the contact. 'You have a deal.'

I rise up, hooking my bag over my shoulder as I make for the main entrance, but instead he tugs me the opposite way and I frown at him in surprise.

'My car's in the basement.'

'I didn't realise there was parking here.'

'It's Jackson's private garage.'

'Oh.'

I follow him, giving Cait a little wave as I go. Her grin is all-knowing, and then her attention goes back to the bar and more specifically to Jackson. I watch them for a second longer, their easy conversation evident from across the room and I shake my head. The poor guy is going to get eaten alive one of these days.

'You laughing at me again?'

'Your ego suffering again?'

Now he laughs and I follow him out, his husky rumble working its magic over me.

CHAPTER FIVE

'MY GOD, ARE all these Jackson's…save for yours?'

I look at her as she surveys the underground garage, where the line-up of sports cars is impressive even to me. 'It's a weakness of his—he can't resist a new toy.'

Her excited green gaze sweeps to me. 'So, come on, then—which of these babies is yours?'

'Just over—'

'No, actually don't tell me. I want to guess.'

I stop and look at her. 'Okay…' I string the word out, curious at her reasoning.

'I think a car can tell you a lot about a man.'

I fold my arms across my chest and work hard not to look in the direction of any particular car. This is going to be interesting.

Her heels clip against the concrete floor as she starts to walk, looking at each car with open appreciation. Occasionally she dips, caresses a bonnet and then looks to me. It shouldn't be provocative, but with every stroke of her delicate fingers, every dip and rise that she performs, my cock gets harder—to the point that my jeans are suffocating. I adjust discreetly, not taking my eyes off her.

She's teasing me. I think she's about to declare a vehicle as mine and then she moves on and gives me a little shake of her head, her bob swinging and making my palms itch with the need to fork my fingers through it.

She pauses before a blacked-out Range Rover now, private plate, nondescript. It means something to the owner—I know it does, because Jackson takes great delight in explaining this to anyone who asks.

'This one,' she murmurs, turning to face me and resting her hip against it. 'It's big and strong and...' She looks me up and down. 'Safe.'

I bark out a laugh. '*Safe?* Christ, you really know how to kick a man when he's down. You might as well declare me boring.'

She's not wrong, though. I have the exact same model in my garage back at home.

She walks towards me, her heels doing their musical clip again, her body statuesque and so fucking appealing in her white shirt and tight jeans.

'For the record,' she says, pausing before me, reaching out her hand to make tantalising contact with my chest, 'there's nothing boring about being safe.' She strokes her palms upwards, hooking them over my shoulders. 'In truth, I happen to find the sense of security when I'm in your arms quite a turn-on.'

And then she curves into me, her lips brushing over mine, and I'm lost. In her touch, her kiss, her words… I like it that she feels safe with me. I *want* her to feel safe.

She wouldn't feel that way if she knew the truth, though…

I squeeze my eyes shut and cut off my conscience. It doesn't matter what brought us together—what matters is that I'm doing right by her *now*. I wrap my arms around her and pull her tighter against me, my hardness pressing between us almost painfully.

Then tell her the truth—all of it. Let her deal with the threat her brother poses.

I kiss her back, pushing out the foolish idea. I can't do that until I understand what's at stake, what's really going on. And I can't do that until I *know* she's safe. She's all lightness and goodness, and Philip's none of that. God knows what he'll do if he's confronted by her when his desperation is at its peak. And that's exactly what would happen if I tell her—she has the guts to go straight to him and have it out.

Yeah, and what about the shitstorm that will hit when she learns the truth about you? You sure you're not running from that too?

I kiss her harder, desperate not to feel the aching truth of it. All I want is this. This moment. Her body curving into mine…her desire.

She sighs into my mouth. The heady sound provokes a growl of my own and I break away before I lose the last of my control and take her here in the garage, where anyone could see us.

'Come on.' I grab her hand and pull her along, past the Range Rover she picked out.

'But…' She stops, pulling back a little. 'It's not yours?'

'No.' I grin at her. 'This is mine.'

I come to a stop before my motorbike and her mouth gapes.

'You're kidding?'

'Why so surprised?'

'I'm not—well, I am, a little…'

'Is my ego about to take another hit, Coco?'

She laughs nervously, the sound so cute and edgy I want to kiss her all over again.

'No, this bike is all you.'

My chest puffs like a proud fucking peacock; it doesn't matter that I know it's ridiculous to be so pleased at her simple statement.

She strokes her hand over the sleek black frame, her teeth worrying over her bottom lip. 'I've just never been on one before.'

'I'll look after you,' I say, knowing just how true those words are, although guilt pricks all the same.

'I know.'

She flicks me a quick look that tells me she means it too and I struggle to add, 'It's not far to my place anyway…as you already know.'

Her cheeks flush, and the contrast with her over-bright green eyes and her blonde hair makes her appear more fairy than princess. My mind races with all that I want to do to her, to do with her. And all that I wish I could tell her and can't.

Christ.

I throw my focus into action, reaching for my leather jacket and holding it open for her. 'Wear this.'

She hesitates a second before obediently slipping her arms in. Her scent reaches up to me, all soft and floral. I've only had one whisky—courtesy of Philip Lauren—but standing here with her so close I feel punch-drunk.

She turns to face me as she zips up the jacket, and I'm more than just punch-drunk. I feel winded. She looks small, dwarfed by the black leather, but it's not that—it's the hit of possessiveness that comes over me.

'I must look a sight,' she says, suddenly coy, and I realise I'm practically scowling at her—*idiot*.

'Believe me, that's the least of your problems right now.'

She frowns. 'How so?'

I can't answer her. Putting a voice to my thoughts will make them far too easy to act upon.

I take up my helmet and she forgets her question, delivering another instead. 'You're not putting that on me?'

'Too right I am.'

'And what about you? Where's yours?'

'I only have one, and there's no way I'm risking anything happening to your cute little face.'

I expect a laugh, or a rebuke at my overprotectiveness. Instead she drags her teeth over her lower lip, her cheeks flushing deeper. She *must* be used to compliments. People must throw them at her like confetti. So why does it feel like she's hearing them for the first time with me?

The idea pulls at my chest. I focus on putting the helmet on her instead and tightening it. Really. Well. 'You okay in there?'

She nods and tries to smile, the cushioned front to the helmet giving her a hamster expression.

I grin. 'Suits you.'

'Something tells me I don't want to ask why.' Her voice is muffled by her squished cheeks, and I laugh. I can't help it. I laugh even harder when she tries to scowl at me, her green eyes shooting daggers before I slip the visor down.

'Come on.'

I swing my leg over the bike and gesture for her to get on behind me. She places her hand on my forearm as she clambers on and scoots in close, her arms tight around my middle. I try to take a breath, but my chest feels closed in.

She leans her head over my shoulder. 'Ready when you are, bad boy.'

I turn to look at her and curse the visor that hides her eyes from me. 'Bad boy?'

'The car was big, strong, safe…but this bike is badass.'

'If I'm so badass, why are you trusting me to take you back to my place?'

It's a genuine question.

She shrugs and rests her head against my back. Doesn't matter that she's wearing a great big helmet. I feel the gesture like we're skin-to-skin.

'Jackson considers you a friend,' she murmurs, 'and that's good enough for me.'

I shake my head in amusement, bewilderment and a sea of other emotions that I know starts with deception and ends in a twisted, tangled mess around my heart.

I kick the bike into life, pulling back on the throttle and letting its roar fill the garage as well as my head. But I can't shift the weird warmth, the heat that has nothing to do with sex and everything to do with her readily bestowed trust.

Coco would be the end of my life as I know it if I let her—of that I'm certain.

Just as well Philip Lauren's timescale is short, because keeping a lid on this is proving harder by the second.

I've never understood the fascination with motorcycles. The idea of being so vulnerable on two wheels and at speed puts the fear of God in me. But with Ash between my thighs, and the engine reverberating through me, it wasn't fear I felt—nothing close.

I clench him tighter and he calls back, 'You okay?'

More than okay...

But it's impossible to speak. Instead I nod against his shoulder and hold on as he takes us the short distance to his home. It's the quickest few minutes of my life and I find myself wishing he lived a hundred miles away just so we could stay like this for longer.

We sit quietly, the engine idling, as we wait for the garage door to roll up. I'm so lost in the feel of him, of pressing him close, I don't register the inside of the garage as he takes us in.

It's the engine cutting off that wakes me up and I straighten, creating some distance between us and realising just how tightly I was holding him.

'Sorry,' I blurt.

'What for?' He kicks the stand down and I set one foot tentatively on the floor to steady myself.

'For almost squeezing you to death.' I slip off the bike and fumble over the helmet fastening. My fingers are shaking, my thighs buzzing with the lasting effect of the engine.

He climbs off and turns to me, his fingers nudging my own away as he stares through the visor. 'I'd die a thousand times over if I got to go out like that each time.'

His voice is husky, his eyes wicked, and I swallow back the instant hit of lust.

He pulls the helmet up and over my head and I shake my hair out, feeling the air rush over my scalp, teasing at nerve endings already alert at his proximity, his words. I barely finish the move and he's tossing the helmet to the ground, his fingers forking through my hair, bringing me up to the fierce onslaught of his mouth.

Fireworks erupt in my belly; heat uncoils through my every limb.

I'm vaguely aware of the garage door rolling down amidst the rush of blood in my ears, punctuated by our fierce grunts as we rip at each other's clothing. He has his jacket off me, my bag has hit the deck, his fingers are undoing the buttons of my shirt as I tug his own from his jeans.

He rides my mouth, desperately deepening the kiss as he strides forward, taking me back against the hard wall of the garage, imprisoning me between brick and lean, hard muscle. He drops his hands to mine and lifts them above my head, lacing his fingers through mine, pinning them there before breaking the kiss.

I whimper, wriggling against him. I don't want his mouth to leave; I don't want my hands trapped. I want to feel him. *All* of him. But then his mouth is travelling down my neck, searing my skin with its dampened trail. My shirt hangs open and my body arches against the wall, offering my lace-covered breasts to the arrival of his mouth.

He breaks away long enough to stare down at me, to heat me with his look alone. His eyes are dark and hungry.

'You are so beautiful…'

Sheer pleasure radiates out from my core—seeing him, hearing him so sincere, so choked, feeling his arousal pressing between us, hard, eager… Knowing it's real, that he feels it as badly as I do, is exhilarating.

I clamp down on my bottom lip to stop a strangled whimper from erupting and then he's parting my mouth again, his tongue forceful, his mouth ravenous. I squeeze my thighs tight, nursing the budding ache, but it's driving me crazy. I need more.

I lift my leg around him, locking him against me,

seeking out the friction I need. My jeans pull taut, a thick, unyielding layer that frustrates as much as it teases.

'*Ash...*'

'What, princess?'

He drags his mouth against me as he speaks, his hands raking down my arms to slip beneath my shirt. He cups my breasts, his thumbs rolling over their hardened peaks, already erect and pressing. He works them both, caressing, tweaking, groping. I struggle for air, struggle to keep on kissing him back as the pressure builds through my middle.

My hands drop to his hair, half pushing him down, half holding his mouth to mine. I want it all—his hands, his mouth everywhere.

He tears himself away, resuming his hand's tantalising path down my front, over the swell of one breast, continuing to stroke, to toy, and then his teeth surround one peak and he nips at it. I cry out, pleasure streaking through my veins, my clit pulsing wildly as I clench around the ache. He does the same to the other, alternating between his fingers and his teeth, again and again.

I lower my gaze to take it all in. He's a badass all right, and I'm fucking loving it. My mind fills with carnal imaginings...the things he'll be up for in bed and out of it.

I take in our surroundings. The whitewashed garage walls, the bright overhead lights, the motorcycles, the cars...*the fucking great big Range Rover.*

'I *knew* it.'

He gropes my breast hard and nips at the exposed skin just above the strip of lace with his teeth. 'Knew what?'

'You own a big black muscle car.'

He laughs, the sound ragged with desire. 'So what does that make me? A big, *safe* badass?'

'Hell, yeah.'

He tugs at my shirt, stripping it from me and flicking it aside. His force triggers a fresh swell of heat and then one hand slips to my bra clasp, undoing it with an ease that tells me he's done it many, many times before. A strange prick of jealousy erupts, and I quickly shake it off. I don't do jealousy. He's not mine to be jealous about.

And then all thought dissipates as the cool garage air sweeps over my bare breasts and my bra hits the floor at the same time the hot cavern of his mouth surrounds one peak, sucking me in.

My head drops back and my *'Yes...'* is a breathless pant.

'So fucking perfect.' He brushes the words against my nipple as he releases me, his palm lifting my breast to offer its peak to the flick of his tongue. He rolls his thumb over the protruding flesh, then his tongue. He shifts to the other, sucking it in, his tongue playing before releasing me.

I'm losing my mind on sensation. I tilt my pelvis and ride my body higher against him, my jeans biting almost painfully into my flesh. I just want... I just need...

'Ash...'

He pops open the button of my jeans, then the zip, smoothing his hands around to my sides to shove the restrictive fabric down. I lower my leg to ease his way and he stops the second he can slip his fingers inside.

'*Fuck*, Coco…' He straightens and looks down at me, at where his fingers gently probe. 'Crotchless?'

His voice is a croak, his face strained with tension, his eyes disbelieving and so fucking keen. I'm not sure if it's a question or a statement but I nod anyway.

'Easy access.'

'*Fuck.*'

He slips his fingers through the opening designed for just that. He parts my lips, running his fingers upwards; the second he strikes my clit, I whimper. He rolls over me, his touch so soft he's hardly there. I bite into my lip as I move with him, asking for more. Deeper, harder, faster…

'There are so many things I want to do to you right now.'

I can hear it in his voice: the carnal promise, the ideas merging with my own. He slips back down to my opening, spreading me with his fingers as he dips inside.

'Like what?'

He lets go of a ragged breath and plunges his fingers in deep, his mouth sweeping over mine to steal one rough kiss. 'Like this…'

He pulls me with him to the front of his bike

and places my hands on the handlebars, angling me forward.

'You are beautiful,' he rasps with appreciation, his hands soft as he strokes the curve of my back. 'You know that, don't you?'

Do I? I don't know anything other than the quiver of anticipation running through me and the promise of release, the heat of his palms as he strokes my skin, the crazy stream of sensation along my breasts as they fall heavy in the cool air, my nipples sensitised from his thorough exploration.

'*Don't* you?' he insists, lowering his hands to the waistband of my jeans and working them down my thighs.

'Yes.' I'd say yes to anything in that second.

'Better.'

He smooths his palms over the curve of my arse, his appreciation drawn out, teasing. My skin prickles in his wake. And then he dips low, between my legs from behind, and I moan, *'Yes, more, yes.'*

He dips inside me like he's savouring me. 'So wet.'

I hum as my body sways, the sweet heat of his invasion urging me to spread my legs wider, wanting more. His other hand joins in the attentions, curving around to my front, strumming my clit as he moves within me. I feel a spasm of sheer pleasure deep inside; he has my G spot.

Fuck, yeah.

The pressure is acute, compounded by the perfect rhythm on my clit. I'm panting and crying out at once. It's so good. So intense. I'm going to come—but, no, not yet… I want him with me. I want to tell him to stop, but I can't.

'Come for me, princess. Let go.'

My body rides him of its own accord, its movements rigid and fraught with the tension spiralling through my limbs. I widen my stance again, my jeans cutting further into my thighs an added sensation. Punishing. Powerful. *Yes.*

I lift my eyes to the bike and catch my reflection in the sleek black metal, my mouth slack, my breasts bare, and then I'm coming so hard I fear I'm going to fall.

I drop forward, the cold shield of the bike is sharp against my skin, and then his hands are on my hips, pulling me back against him. I rise and hook my hands around his neck, pressing my arse into his hardness, teasing him as the waves taper off, my limbs fill with sated bliss.

He shudders, his breath ragged as he clamps my lower body tight against him. 'You're so fucking beautiful when you come.'

I turn my head into him, press my lips to his jaw. 'I want you inside me—here, now.'

His cock pulses, his body rocking with it. 'I won't last long.'

'I don't need you to.'

I love that he's honest about it…that the effort it's taking for him to hold himself back has his entire body vibrating against mine. I kiss him again and snuggle my head under his chin as he slips a hand inside the back pocket of his jeans and retrieves his wallet. A condom comes next, and then the wallet joins my bag on the floor, the empty condom packet too.

I lean forward as he unfastens his belt, the jangle of the buckle and the pop of buttons filling my ears, my body reheating with anticipation. I look over my shoulder, desperate to take him in, not wanting to miss a second of his slipping restraint. His cock is bare, pulsing in his grip; his teeth are gritted, his neck corded.

I've done that to him, and I smile as I take hold of the handlebars once more, my arse rubbing against his length and making him hiss through his teeth. I love it that he's so desperate, so keen, and the wetness slips between my legs, coating my underwear. I couldn't be more ready for him.

Slowly he rolls the condom down and grips the base of his cock hard. I nudge back, purposely positioning him in the valley of my arse, telling him without words that I need him now. He grips my hips, steadying me, but he doesn't do what I ask. Instead he slips one hand around my front, beneath the lace, straight to my clit, which is so sensitised in the aftermath that I buck and cry out.

'Patience, Coco.'

'If you want patience you've got the wrong woman.'

'Is that so?' he murmurs, his eyes falling to my arse. 'Guess I'll just have to teach you.'

He flicks over my clit again, but this time he

doesn't stop. It's fierce, brutal, and yet my toes curl, my thighs tighten, and I know I'm going to come again.

'Ash... Ash...'

He keeps up the pressure over my clit as he takes himself in his hand, probing inside the slit of my underwear.

'I love these,' he says. 'White, so fucking innocent, and yet they're so not.'

He rocks against me, the tip of his cock nudging at my opening. He does it again, teasing inside, his hiss of breath as erotic as the movement itself. And then he thrusts so hard, so deep, that he has to use both hands on my hips to stop me from collapsing over his bike.

My nipples brush the cold metal, the headlamp presses against my clit and his cock nudges my G spot. Such a multitude of sensation all at once that my head spins on it, my body hanging on the precipice of release.

His fingers bite into my hips, his tension vibrating through their lengths. His thrusts turn short and jagged and he growls low in his throat. He's so close, but so am I. Every thrust of his body, treats my nipples, my clit, my G spot to a delicious jolt of friction.

My legs tense up and I stop breathing. I give myself over to the mind-obliterating power of it and then I hear him cry out, his release bringing my own.

Together we rock, the movement long, deep. His arms wrap around my middle, pulling me against him, holding me tight. The warmth of his body seeps through his shirt, heating my back as he trails a hand over my front, over the goosebumps now appearing.

'Are you cold?' he says against my ear.

I shake my head. I can't even speak. I would have let him do anything, have anything, in the heat of what just went down. It should scare me. But I'm too content for fear.

I hook my hands behind his head once more, feel his buzz cut tickling my palms. 'I'll take that cock-tail now.'

He presses a kiss into my neck. 'I'll take that talk too.'

A man who truly wants to talk—to me, about me…the real me…

The unfamiliar prospect should unsettle me, but with his arm around me, his hand worshipping my front, his back heating me through, I'm anything but unsettled.

CHAPTER SIX

I'M SURPRISED I can hold my hands steady as I craft her the perfect espresso martini. It's a damn good job I could do it in my sleep. My hours as a mixologist in London's high-end bars have taught me well. It was fun, even if the reason I was there wasn't.

'You really can mix a drink,' she says as she leans on the industrial chunk of wood and aluminium that forms the centre island of my kitchen.

She looks too cute, her white shirt buttoned just enough to be decent but not so much that I can't drink in her cleavage every time I look up. Her hair is delightfully ruffled from our antics, her eyes intense as she watches me work; her lips are worked clean of lipstick and they sport a dusky pink tone that reminds me of the inside of a strawberry. And just as tasty.

My cock twitches inside my jeans, gearing up anew, a reminder of just how 'cute' I find her.

I want to say that it's my need to protect her making these feelings more intense—the same kind of protective instinct that had me seeking justice for my family all those years ago. But I'm not convinced.

After all these years I've spent avoiding her type, I'm now powerless to deny I want her in every which way I can have her. I want Coco.

Which is absolutely fine, I tell myself. *You can have her and then walk away.*

She's in this for the sex, and I'm in it to help her, enjoying what she's so willing to offer at the same time.

So why does it feel wrong?

Because you're lying to her. You are becoming the kind of person you despise. The kind you seek to bring down.

I shake the drink. Hard. Fast. I don't want to think about it any more. I just want to be—

'And there I was thinking you were making it up—some corny chat-up line to get me to come home with you.'

Eyes alive with teasing, she takes up a handful of nuts from the bowl I put out earlier and pops one into her mouth.

I grip the shaker tighter. 'I don't make things up.'

Unless I'm on the job, which I am now...kind of...

I feel the brutal force of my confession wash over me, my skin prickling even though it's warm in here.

You've not lied to her, my conscience tries to reason. *You've merely omitted to tell her everything. That's different.*

I pour a little of the mix and then shake again... Pour, shake.

Concentrate on the drink.

'So come on—tell me,' she says. 'How did you learn to do this?'

I almost breathe a sigh of relief, grateful for the question, even if it does mean talking about the past. It beats the internal moral debate and self-loathing that came before it. And, hell, I know everything about her—she deserves to know something of me.

The idea soothes my torment.

'Jackson and I worked the bars together when we were younger. He was plotting his empire and I— well, I just needed to bring in some cash.'

'Sounds like fun.'

'It was.'

If I didn't think about all the shit going down at home: my family's assets being seized, our bank accounts frozen, my university degree forgotten since we had no money to pay for it.

She spins on the bar stool and takes a good look around the room, the high ceiling, the industrial-inspired lighting with black cabling and copper dome lights, the raw wood cupboards against exposed brick walls. It's all designer, high-end, and I anticipate her question before she even asks.

'Something tells me it's not what you do now, though. So what is it, Ash? Software engineer? Financial genius? Entrepreneur?'

My neck prickles with the impending lie that I don't want to tell. 'This and that.'

'This and that...?' Her brow lifts as she mimics me. 'How very specific... Hmm, let me think...'

I can't help but smile. Does she know her nose wrinkles like a rabbit's when she's thinking?

I turn and open the cupboard in which I keep the coffee beans. Taking a couple out, I place one on top of each drink and offer her a glass.

She takes it from me with a cheeky grin. 'It certainly looks the part.'

And then she sips it and I'm lost in the movement. I almost forget the tricky terrain she has hit with her questioning, but then her eyes are open again, pinning me with their inquisitive stare.

I look away and take up my own drink, needing the hit of alcohol, the confidence to navigate what's coming.

'If not for all this I'd say you were in the military—or the police, even…' She tilts her head to one side and her shirt slips a little, stopping at the curve of her shoulder and teasing me with a hint of collarbone that I want to follow with my fingertips, my tongue.

'What makes you say that?' I ask, dragging my eyes back to hers.

'There's your physique for starters.' She gives me a coy smile. 'You're too fit for a desk job.'

I give a short laugh. 'I think there are plenty of businessmen who'd beg to differ.'

She waves a dismissive hand. 'I've met plenty of businessmen and none of them are your Christian Grey variety.'

'Christian Grey?' I frown.

'*Fifty Shades?* You know—Christian Grey, the sexy billionaire who'd have your knickers around your ankles and you tied to a bed quicker than you could beg for it.'

'Well, I'm safe. Knickers aren't part of my wardrobe.'

She rewards me with a laugh that has something inside my chest expanding so fast I can't breathe and my ears straining to capture every last note.

'I don't think you'd be his type either,' she murmurs, her eyes sparkling in the golden light of the kitchen. 'But it's not just that—you have this aura about you…a protective vibe. Like I told you earlier, it's a security thing… Oh, my God, that's it!' Her eyes widen excitedly. 'You're a bodyguard!'

I laugh awkwardly. Christ, how I wish I was that right now. No secrets, no lies…

'Not a bodyguard, then…'

She pouts at me, nose wrinkling anew.

'I give up.'

'You want me to tell you?'

She smiles and nods.

I'm not going to lie. I can't. Truth is there's actually no harm in me being honest. To an extent at least. She doesn't need to know it all. Not yet.

Yes, and it's all about protecting her, not yourself, from what it will do to her, to you, to your relationship.

Relationship? There is no fucking relationship.

'I'm a private investigator.' I say it over the internal rant, louder than it needs to be, and she chokes mid-sip of her drink, her eyes popping out of their sockets as goosebumps streak across my body.

'You're *not.*'

I swallow back the rising panic and the need to confess all, my guilt working its way to the surface. 'What's wrong with being a private investigator?'

I hate myself even as I say it.

'Nothing.' She straightens and wipes her lips with the back of her free hand. 'I'm just surprised.'

'I deal in property too,' I add quickly, suddenly feeling inferior to Her Ladyship in front of me and foolish as fuck for telling her the truth. What does it matter that my job is beneath her? Why do I care?

'So being a PI pays well, then?' she asks, her eyes once again travelling over our surroundings.

'Well enough—but it's the property that really pays…the investment. I do the PI work to help people.'

'*See*—I knew it.'

'Knew what?'

'That you *helped* people. Whatever it is you do, I knew there had to be an element of that in there.'

I smile then, my chest lifting and burying the fleeting sense of inferiority. I do help people. That's why I became a PI and that's why I still am one. There's nothing wrong with my motives. I just misjudged this one case.

'What got you into it?'

'The PI work?'

'Yes.'

She nods eagerly and my smile tightens, my chest falls with the memories I'd like to leave in the past.

'You don't have to talk about it—not if you don't want to.'

'No, it's fine.' I force myself to relax. If I want her to open up to me, the least I can do is the same in return. 'It's a long story.'

'I have all night.' She slips from the bar stool to stand before me, her fingers gentle as they stroke across my brow. 'I want to know what makes your brow do that and take it away.'

I can't breathe past her touch... A weird sensation is lifting inside me.

You're supposed to be helping her, not the other way around.

I chained my demons down a long time ago. The last thing I expect is for them to rush to the surface on her command. But here they are—and more. She's making me *feel* again...something I thought I was long past.

And if I feel, how can I be sure I'll be ready to walk away when the time comes...when she no longer needs me... What if I find I need her instead? What then?

Fuck.

For the first time I see a crack in the solid exterior that is Ash and I'm not letting it go.

He's exposed me in so many ways already, and to see that he's not immune, to see that my playfulness has brought us to this point—I can't let it lie even if I want to.

It's disconcerting to feel this bond with someone I've only just met. I'd blame it on the fierce attraction still burning strong if not for the fact that I've been there, done that. This is something more. It's deeper than sex. And if I understand him I stand more chance of understanding this. Because I've never dared love, never dared risk my heart before. I want nothing less than what my parents had.

Maybe I *can* find that here.

'Let's go and sit down,' he says.

He doesn't balk from my touch, but he doesn't smile at it either. He's all serious and unreadable, but I feel his acceptance, know that I'm about to get what I pressed for.

I lean into him as he curves an arm around my back and leads me into the living area. It has two floor-to-ceiling glass windows made up of square panes and to the left hangs a painting of a dream-scape, its style very familiar.

'Is that… Is that a *Cleveland*?'

His lips quirk at my obvious appreciation. Or is he just happy that we're off-topic temporarily?

'He's a friend of mine.'

'No way—he can't be.'

He grins now. 'Don't ever say that in front of him. He already has an epic ego and he'll never let me live it down.'

'Wow…' I look back to the painting, to the mix-ture of reds and blues swirling to create stunning shadows and light, shapes that could be trees, clouds, cliffs, water—whatever you want them to be.

'It's called *Illusion*.'

His voice has turned gruff and I feel his eyes on

me. My cheeks warm under his attention. 'It's glorious.'

He doesn't shift focus, and his appreciation is very much on me as I continue to study the piece of art and try to keep at bay the heat simmering just beneath the surface. It would be so easy to roll with it, to get down and naked right here before the masterpiece, but I'd be no closer to understanding what makes this man tick, why my body feels instinctively drawn to him, appreciated and protected by him.

'I'll be sure to pass that on when we next meet.' He reaches out to stroke my hair behind my ear and my lips part just enough for me to breathe.

I turn to look at him, at the heat in his gaze, and swallow. 'Shall we sit?'

He cocks his brow. '*Not* what I was thinking.'

I roll my eyes to break the mood. 'You have a one-track mind.'

'Judging by your colour, I'm not the only one.'

He's not wrong, and I laugh, but I make my legs obey and head for the sofa, knowing he'll follow.

I sink down into the dark cushioned softness, its deep back inviting me in further, and I feel my muscles practically sigh at the comfort. Christ, when did I last just sit, relax, do nothing, think of nothing? I close my eyes, only for a second, and I enjoy it.

The sofa shifts with the arrival of his weight and when I open my eyes he's watching me.

'Don't get to sit down much, hey?'

I give him a small smile, but my head stays resting on the sofa back as I tilt it to face him. 'Such is the life of a busy socialite.'

He doesn't smile. Instead his mouth thins, his eyes narrow. 'Is that all you think you are?'

I shrug softly. 'It's what I am, and I do what good I can with it. My grandmother was—is—the same. She saw it as a great privilege to have inherited the Dukedom. It was no small feat for my great grand-father to get the patent amended to allow his solitary heir, Granny, to inherit, heaven forbid a woman, a non-Royal at that, should be a duchess in her own right.'

'It's about time that whole nonsense changed any-way.'

I nod, relieved that he sees the rules of succession within the peerage as outdated and sexist as I do. 'True, but it's rarity meant extra press exposure and greater interest from the public, which Granny was able to work in her favour to help the causes close to her heart. She has done so much with her role and paid her dues thrice over.'

'And now you want to do the same? Even though your brother will be the one to inherit the title?'

'Yes. Just because he will be the Duke of Rush-ford it doesn't mean I can't continue the work that I do. Our private fortune is to be split equally and I'll carry on using it to help others.'

'But don't you want more? For you?'

My blood fires with irritation, sending my back ramrod straight, the peaceful moment gone. 'What are you trying to say?'

He riled me when he touched on my public persona back at the bar, so I'm surprised he's dared to go there again.

'Nothing—I don't mean to upset you.'

There's the apology again, and I can see he means it, his eyes turning soft with concern, but my hackles are up and the need to defend myself is riding high.

'I'm just trying to understand what it is you do… what you want to do in the future. What drives you?'

'I want to help people, and with my family's money and connections I can do that. I don't have a degree, a career, a fancy job title. I'm me. Just me.'

He nods. 'I get that—totally. And, yes, you do a lot of good. I know you have your charities and your fundraising efforts. I just meant what do you want for *you*, personally?'

'Oh…' My temper flares, his question poking at an age-old nerve. 'I get it. You think someone my age must want to get married, have children, settle down. Is that it?'

His brow lifts. 'Perhaps…'

I shake my head. I've had this conversation a thousand times over. With Granny, with Cait and, more frequently, with the press. I usually give my well-rehearsed answer, that I haven't yet met the right man to sweep me off my feet. I don't add the truth, that I've met enough to know he doesn't exist.

Although now, staring into Ash's eyes, I find that resolve wavers. Maybe it's that realisation that has me blurting, 'I want the impossible.'

He frowns. 'The impossible?'

'I want what my parents shared—a whirlwind passion and the love that stems from it.' I look into my glass at the frothy topping and smile even as my cheeks burn with my confession. 'You can laugh… It's fine.'

'I'm not laughing.'

No, he's not. He sounds so goddamn sincere I can almost believe that he thinks the same and is feeling the same—it encourages me to explain.

'My mother died when I was two,' I say. 'I only have her diary to go on, but let's just say she was good with words. She loved my father and he never stopped loving her. The day he died he gave the diary to me—said I should learn what I could from her, that she was the role model I should aspire to.'

'I'm sorry.'

I look at him, surprised. 'Why?'

'For the loss of your parents…for not having them with you now.'

I smile wistfully. 'Life would be quite different.'

'You wouldn't have your brother, for a start.'

There's an edge to his voice that startles me, and he looks away, leaning forward to place his drink on the low-slung table before us as he clears his throat.

'At least you have him,' he adds, deadpan now.

My laugh is sudden, harsh, wiping out my concern over his outburst seconds before. 'We're not that close. I think my stepmother fears I might lead him astray.'

I shake my head and brush her away from my mind.

'Why would you say that?' he asks.

Why? There are so many reasons why—starting with my mother and ending with me. 'Because of my mother…who she was, what she did for a living.'

'What does it matter what she did or who she was? You are *you*.'

I don't miss the fact that he doesn't question what my mother did, that he already knows. He's more aware of my family than I would ordinarily expect for a typical guy. Which explains why he knows of that magazine article too. But I won't hold it against him. Why *shouldn't* he know what the press are so quick to dish out?

'If only it were that simple,' I say.

'I can't imagine what life must have been like for you, growing up with a stepmother who sees you in that way. It must have been lonely.'

He reaches over, his hand soft upon my shoulder, his thumb gently caressing, and I lean into the comfort he offers, grateful for it.

'It would've been if not for Granny.'

And it will be again when she's gone.

The pain hits me full force and I take a shuddery breath, trying to let it go.

'You're very close?'

I nod, struggling to talk. 'She's been good to me. Life…life isn't going to be the same when…when…'

I can't finish the sentence, let alone the thought.

My fingers shake as I raise my glass to my lips and blink back the tears that threaten. 'She has only weeks—maybe two months at most. The doctors don't seem to know.'

His hand reaches around me, drawing me in, and his other hand takes my glass from my unresisting fingers to place it on the side.

I don't realise I'm properly crying until I'm against his chest, the dampness of my tears seeping into the fabric of his shirt.

My body shudders with the sobs I've kept trapped inside for so long, and the heaviness eases as I let go. I breathe in his scent, his warmth, his comfort, tuck my hands beneath my chin as I curl into his lap.

Granny's words—*stiff upper lip, girl; never show people you're weak or they'll flock like vultures*—run through me, mock me. But being with Ash isn't part of a show, an act. It's real, *I'm* real and it feels good.

I snuggle down deeper against him and just let go…

If he's a vulture, I'll happily build an aviary to keep him.

CHAPTER SEVEN

I HOLD COCO to me, one hand smoothing over her hair, the other on her back. My heart pounds in my chest, so hard I fear she'll hear every beat for what it is: my guilt, my deception…and something more.

I care about her. There's no use denying it. It's as real as she is in my arms.

I'm starting to get answers too. I'm willing to bet that the Duchess's imminent death is the reason Philip Lauren is so desperate to discredit his sister. It's clear the standard to which Coco believes she has to live her life, her grandmother demonstrated it by example and the slander Philip is after will pull her apart in the eyes of the Duchess. Heaven knows what would happen then. Whether the Duchess would, or indeed could, put family ties—love—over reputation and title.

I want to dig deeper, ask Coco more questions, but I can't just yet. The way she's sobbing suggests she hasn't cried in a long while, and *this* I can do: hold her while she lets go.

'We're not supposed to be talking about me.' She

sniffs eventually, and then gives an unladylike snort that makes my lips quirk.

I bow my head and press a kiss to her hair, the scent of her shampoo teasing my senses and calming my pulse. 'No? What are we supposed to be talking about?'

She wipes her eyes with her sleeve and looks up at me, her big green eyes glistening and wide with so much emotion that it reaches inside me.

'You,' she says simply. 'Why you became a private investigator.'

I give her a small smile. She's right, and I owe her this. I owe her a piece of me in return.

I settle back into the sofa, pulling her with me, my eyes staring unseeing at the window ahead and the dark outdoors beyond.

'When I was at university, a business deal my father was involved in came under scrutiny. It was serious. He was facing a long prison sentence. Our bank accounts were frozen, our assets seized. It was a living nightmare, the kind you so desperately want to wake up from—only you can't.'

She presses up off my chest. 'Was he guilty?'

'Everyone thought so, but it didn't make any sense. My father was a good man…honest, kind; he brought my brother and me up in the same vein. Especially after Mum died. He'd always gone above and beyond. Then his best friend, Clive—he was my godfather too—started sowing seeds of doubt in our minds, telling us Dad hadn't been right since

Mum had passed, that he'd been gambling, drinking, the works…'

I shake my head, remembering those conversations; the nausea that would come, the disbelief and the split loyalty.

'I trusted Clive. He'd always been there for us and I figured he was trying to protect us, prepare us for what the future might hold.'

'But he was lying?'

I look at her. 'Yes—every last word. I overheard him on the phone, talking about the deal to a man I later discovered was his lawyer. I heard enough to start digging. I couldn't go back to university with it hanging over us; I couldn't even afford to go back. I worked in bars to keep some money coming in and I looked into Clive and his dealings. He had no reason to suspect me; made it easy for me, really.'

'What happened?'

'I gave every last scrap of evidence I could find to my father's lawyer and it was enough to get the case thrown out and Clive convicted.'

'Your poor father—it must have destroyed him, being betrayed like that.'

'You could say that; he was certainly never the same. He'd lost his wife and his best friend in the space of a few years. Jake and I were all he had left.'

'Jake?'

'My brother.' I clear my throat, clear the strain from my voice. 'My father retired not long after— got a fishing retreat up in Scotland. He just couldn't face the rat race any longer.'

'I'm sorry.'

I hold her tight against me, press her head into my chest and breathe…just breathe. I haven't talked about it in so long, haven't let the pain back in. Seeing the man you've admired for so long broken by the people he loved most…it's another reason not to let anyone get close.

I should be remembering that, not getting all cosy and exposed with her. But it's too late for warnings.

'Your father's lucky to have such a clever son.'

I laugh softly. 'And your granny is lucky to have someone who loves her as you do.'

She scoffs gently. 'I'm not sure *lucky* is the word she would use.'

I tilt her chin up to me, her green eyes lock with mine and I almost forget what I want to say as the need to kiss her beats into my consciousness.

'What makes you say that?'

'You know that Austen quote—"a single man in possession of a good fortune, must be in want of a wife"?'

'Vaguely.'

'Try it in reverse.'

'Ah…she expects you to be married off.'

She rolls her eyes with a sigh and slumps back against me. 'Has done for years. She can't understand why I haven't brought someone home to meet her yet.'

'No one?'

'No. Anything like that demands public attention,

and it's hard enough working out whether a relation-ship is going places without having press scrutiny on top. Besides, every guy I've ever met has shown his true colours eventually.'

'What's that supposed to mean?'

'They want what I can give them—money, title, the works. They're not interested in *me*.'

'I don't think that's fair.'

She laughs against me. 'Don't judge people by your standards—you're an exception.'

'I am?' It's so quiet, my own surprise at her knee-jerk remark takes my breath away.

And then she looks up at me again, her eyes nar-rowed as she considers me.

'I think so. The second you met me, you told me I wasn't your type.'

My lips lift. 'And you're taking that to be a *good* thing?'

She reaches up to cup my jaw, her thumb brushing over my lower lip, her eyes tracing the move. 'Yes. You meant it when you said it. I get the feeling you don't go in for people like me; you like life a little less complicated.'

'And what about you? What do you—'

She cuts me off with her lips, my question an-swered before I even ask it. She wants *me*. And, Christ, I want her.

I know I have to come clean and tell her the truth—it's too big a lie…*a secret*. But not yet—not until I'm sure of the facts. Not until I'm sure she can't get hurt, sure that her reputation is safe and her brother is dealt with for good. *Then* I can confess. *Then* she can face off Philip and deal with him.

And then she can face off you too...

My blood runs cold—fear, guilt, *what ifs* plaguing my mind—and I kiss her all the more, pushing them away. Her fingers slip beneath my shirt, her exploration rough, hungry, desperate. I return it all twice as hard, twice as needy.

She moans against my lips and I stand, taking her with me.

'Where are we going?' she asks as I pull her along.

'Bed.'

I want her to know how special she is. Not because of her money, her family name—none of it. Only because of *her.*

I turn the lights on low when we reach the bedroom and stop before the bed. I turn her to face me, my eyes locking with hers, and silently I undress her. My fingers are soft and unhurried as I take my time over her and I love it that she lets me.

Her shirt floats to the floor, her bra too. I unfasten her jeans and slip my hands beneath her knickers, smoothing them down her legs, her soft calves, her dainty feet with those delicate red-tipped toes. She steps out, her fingers soft on my shoulder for support, and then I toss them aside and rise back up. She stares up at me...so trusting, so beautiful.

'Let me show you how special you are,' I say into her eyes, and I pull my own shirt over my head, letting it fall to join hers. 'Let me show you it's about you.'

I dip to taste her lips, a sweep of my tongue against hers parting her lips further and taking the whimper that she utters.

'It's not about your name…'

I stroke my hands up her sides, my palms gentle as they cup her breasts, my thumbs rolling over the peaks already tightening against my touch.

'It's not about your status…'

I whisper a path along her jawline to her ear.

'Your money…' I scrape my teeth over her earlobe and she shudders into me. 'Your title…'

I lift her up and she wraps her legs around me.

'This is about you.'

I take her to the bed and lay her down softly.

'*You*, Coco.'

Her eyes glisten and blaze all at once and my chest is fit to burst with the crazy swell of emotion spilling over. I kiss her until it eases, until I can breathe fully, but instead it grows, and she's kissing me back now, pleading for release.

I force myself to slow down. 'Patience…'

'I don't do—'

I silence her rebuke with another tongue-sinking kiss and she moans.

'We've covered that one,' I say, breaking away to sweep along the collarbone that had teased the hell out of me earlier to the curve of her shoulder.

She wriggles and rakes her nails down my back, demanding more. I nip at her skin in return. She tries to unfasten my jeans and I grab her hands, forking my fingers through hers as I press them back on either side of her head.

'Stay.'

She looks like she's going to argue, so I instruct her before she can.

'Every time you move your hands, I'll stop.'

She bites into her bottom lip.

'Understand?'

She nods.

'Let me…'

Let me love you was the shocking phrase that rode my tongue, ready to leap out, and I flick my gaze away in order to regain control.

This isn't love. I hardly know her.

Not true. You've lived in her shadow for weeks…

But I am done with that emotion. I only care because of the part I've played to date, working for her brother's money. It's just my guilt, intensifying everything else.

I can't breathe. The world halted with his words…

Let me…

*Let me…*what?

I'm still trapped in the heat of his look. It doesn't matter that his eyes have fallen away. He's still got me. Immersed in the passion I can read. The passion and something more—something visceral that calls to a part of me I've never dared expose before. A part that makes me vulnerable.

He lifts his head and my lashes flutter as I search

his depths, reaching for that same look, that same connection, waiting for his words to come.

'Let me…have this.'

Have this?

It's not the mammoth confession I've surprised myself into wanting. It's simple. It's all I should expect. And it's enough. For all he's done for me in the short space of time I've known him, helping me to feel real, to be me, I'd let him have anything.

I nod and raise my head to his, dutifully keeping my hands pinned, forked in his. He meets me halfway, his kiss soft, tender, and he doesn't stop until I slacken beneath him, my fingers relaxing. He releases one hand to cup my thigh, his palm hot and searing against my skin as he bends my leg. He releases the other hand and does the same with my other leg, spreading me open beneath him, and then he rises.

'Stay,' he commands again, his eyes on fire as they trail down my body.

Anticipation has fire licking through my loins and I nod, my mouth slack as I wait…and wait.

His finger trails a path down my front, around each mound. 'You are so perfect…'

My subconscious wants to scream, *I'm not! I'm so far from it.* But I can't speak. I am so caught in his spell as I lie there, open to his gaze, his touch. He traces my navel and my belly tightens. Beneath, my clit is waiting for that first touch.

But it doesn't come. Instead he backs away and lowers his head. 'I bet you taste perfect too.'

I let out a moan and then he's there, his fingers parting me for the arrival of his mouth, and my belly launches into my throat, the surge of sensation making my body arch as my head presses back, my hands twist to claw at the quilt.

'Fuck...' I curse, my eyes squeezed tight.

He is a master, a true, bona fide expert, with the kind of skill that's born of experience. And, Christ, I'd know. I've given and received enough times. Jealousy claws its way back in but he sucks over me, banishing the unwelcome thought.

He's all flicks and sips, his tongue rough, his stubble rougher. *Oh, hell.* I pull at the bedding, my thighs straining to close, but his hands are there, pressing them wider, and his growl of contentment is working over me.

'Ash...*Ash*...'

I'm practically pulling myself up the bed, the intense streaks of pleasure impossible to control, his mouth unrelenting—and then I am shattering, the explosion inside so intense, so fierce, I can't breathe for it. And even then he doesn't stop. But I'm too sensitive—it's too many waves, too much.

I start to pant, one hand flying to his head, clawing at him, as my lower half bucks with every sweep of his tongue. And then I feel that heated tension rebuild and I can't believe it—it's not possible... Just... not...*possible*! And then I'm not only at the peak, I'm riding above it, and the resurgence of pleasure is so startling, so acute, I can do nothing but grip the back of his head and stare as the sensation builds to an almighty crescendo and then I am convulsing, wild, lost, euphoric.

I rock forward, both hands hugging him to my pussy as I ride it out. Wave after wave. And then he rises up and I pull him to me. I feel raw, exposed, *wanted*, and I throw it all into a kiss. I taste myself on him and tongue him deeper, unable to get enough. His arms surround me and I'm trembling, struck dumb by what just happened. By all of it. By him.

He lies down and takes me with him, our mouths still joined. And I realise I'm not sure I can ever get enough of this—not ever. I want a future. I want it all.

I slow the kiss and break away, waiting for his eyes to meet mine.

Ask him. Just ask him.

The words hang in my throat. I'm scared of rejection. Scared of acceptance.

'I know we said this was just about sex…'

I feel his chest still, spy the sudden tension around his eyes and curse my big mouth.

'Yes.'

I swallow and force my eyes to hold his. 'Well, what about we give this a shot? Try the odd date? I have a charity ball tomorrow night. You could come. It might be fun.'

I'm losing him. I can see it in the crease between his brows, the shutter falling over his expression. And those bloody tears are returning. Now that he's

opened the floodgates, it appears there's no stopping them.

I drop my head to his chest, my ear coming to rest
over his heart, and I listen to it race beneath me. 'It's
okay. I'm more trouble than I'm worth.'

His hand upon my shoulder tightens. 'Don't say
that. Don't *ever* say that.'

That passion is back in his voice—so why the
shutter, why the rejection that he has yet to put into
words?

'It's just… It's just in my line of work, I need to
keep out of the public eye—you know, under the
radar. No one's going to hire a PI whose face is rec-
ognisable to the masses. It'll ruin my business.'

I close my eyes and breathe through the pain. He
makes a fair point. I know he does. And he's not
rejecting me—not really.

*He's not promising you anything more either. In
fact, he's telling you it can never be.*

But I only have myself to blame for wanting more,
for lowering my guard and letting him in. I only have
myself to blame for tearing my heart in two.

'We can have this, though, can't we?' I say softly.
'At least for a little while?'

He lifts my chin and looks down into my eyes.
The passion I could hear in his voice now flares in
his depths.

'For as long as we want it.'

He seals his words with a kiss and I close my eyes.
A solitary tear escapes to trail down my cheek but I

kiss him harder. I kiss him to block out the sadness. I kiss him to forget the pain. I kiss him to make the present matter more.

I kiss him until he's making love to me and we are as close as two people can be.

CHAPTER EIGHT

I WAKE TO the realisation that I'm not alone—to the realisation that I am more at home in my bed than I have ever been. And I know it's because she's here, her naked body wrapped around mine.

She's snoring softly, fast asleep, and I lie still, not wanting to wake her. Not wanting this moment to end. Even though I know it has to.

A woman like her has a schedule that doesn't stop for the weekend, no matter how much I wish it could. How much I wish reality could be different. How much I wish we lived in a world where she and I stand a chance. But I'm no fool.

The second she learns of my contract with her brother, it will all come to a swift and crushing end.

Won't it?

It has to end—that's a given. But maybe it would be better all round if my involvement with her brother never came to light. If I can see him off with nothing and keep her reputation intact we can just go our separate ways. No harm, no foul.

My chest tightens, my hold around her with it,

and I force myself to relax. It's the only way it can
end. Any other possibility leads to her being hurt,
and that far outweighs my own concerns.

I ease out from beneath her and set her down on
my pillow. She mumbles in her sleep and for a second
I fear she'll wake. I stay stock-still. I can't face her
yet. Not with the war of emotions so clearly written
on my face. Instead she pulls my pillow further down
beneath her head and breathes deeply, her body relaxing, her face blissfully at peace once again. And
I'm so lost in that look, her beauty, everything she
has come to mean.

You need to move. Now.

I slip from the bed and quietly move around the
room, pulling on some workout gear and heading
downstairs to my gym. I need to work this out of me,
focus on pounding the treadmill, the punchbag—
anything but the chaos inside.

Not that it works. I'm just as messed-up over an
hour later, having showered, donned some tracksuit
bottoms and sorted breakfast: freshly brewed coffee and an array of whatever I could muster on a
tray before me.

But as I walk through my bedroom door, I find my
feet rooted. She's awake and stretching, her beautiful
body naked from the waist up. She freezes when she
spies me, her eyes widening, her arms still in mid-
air, and then slowly she brings them down.

'What?' she says, clearly spying something in my
expression—not to mention the fact that I haven't
moved or said a word.

Way to go in freaking her out and failing to hide it. And you're supposed to be an experienced PI, for fuck's sake.

I walk towards her and plaster on a smile. 'I'm just struggling with the realisation that there's a beautiful woman in my bed.'

She rolls her eyes and wrinkles her nose in that cute little rabbit move which has my gut flip-flopping—

Your gut? Who are you kidding? Your heart, more like.

'Please don't tell me you're one of those.'

My eyes narrow. 'One of those…?'

'Yeah—one of those men with a woman-free bed.' She goes all dramatic and flutters her hands. '*"Yeah, I'm gonna shag you until you walk like John Wayne, but I won't let you into my bed unless you are the one."* That kind of man.'

She waggles her brow and laughs as she says it, and the move cracks me up too.

'No, I'm not one of those.'

Her laughter dies from her eyes and I see what my admission has cost her. *Shit.* I recall what she asked of me last night about wanting more. Did she want to be the one? Did I want her to be?

Stupid, dangerous question.

But I can give her my honesty. About this at least.

'Truth is I'm not averse to bringing women home…' I see her swallow, her cheeks pale a little, and I push on. 'I just haven't had the inclination in a long time. In fact, if you must know, I can't even remember the last time I got laid.'

I laugh on the last. It's awkward, but it's honest, and her smile, the warmth reigniting in her cheeks, makes it worth it.

'Well, in that case, I'm honoured.'

She's suddenly gone all shy and, God help me, I'm falling so quickly and deeply that my heart pulses in my chest and tells me exactly what I'm feeling for her. It doesn't matter how impossible it all is—it's there. My absolute love and affection for a woman who's been in my life for weeks but doesn't know me from Adam.

I return her smile—although mine is more of a grin—to hide the chaos within, and slide the tray onto the bedside table.

It can't be love—not yet, it can't.

'So, my lady, we have options: coffee, juice, granola, toast and eggs—oh, and fruit. So what's your poison?'

'You.'

My heart leaps and I don't look at her straight away. I know if I do she'll see too much. *Christ*, she probably already has.

'But you'd best make it quick as I have a brunch date with Granny and she doesn't take kindly to tardiness.'

Ah, fuck it—breakfast can wait.

My heart, though… That's another matter. But I'll deal with that when she's safe from her brother.

And from me.

* * *

I let myself into the house and my well-practised mask falls into place.

Our housekeeper gives me *the look* as she bustles into the hallway—the one that says, *Out all night again?*—but I simply beam at her. 'Morning.'

She shakes her head, but her face softens a little as she smiles back. 'I'll bring brunch up shortly.'

'Thanks, Sue.'

I take to the stairs, my mood a weird mix of light and dark. On the one hand I've had the best sex of my life—no, the best *night* of my life. On the other hand I can't keep having it for ever and at some point it has to end.

But that point isn't now, and maybe that's why the lightness is winning out.

I walk along the galleried landing and down the east wing of the house to Granny's room. I can hear voices. It's Philip. *Great.* He won't waste any time before remarking on my night out.

'She hasn't come home again,' he's saying.

'She's a grown woman. I don't expect her to always be here.'

'It's not the fact that she's out all night—it's what she's doing that has me—'

I push open the door and he stops abruptly, turning in my direction.

'You were saying, Philip…?' I say smoothly.

'Ah, so good of you to return, Coco.'

He turns back to Granny, who's sitting ramrod straight in bed, the mountain of cushions at her back helping to keep her there. Her eyes narrow on me, sharp as ever, and then return to Philip as he bends to kiss her forehead.

'I'll call in later to check on you.'

'I have cards with Grace at three,' she returns shortly, sounding like she's delivering an admonishment rather than stating a simple fact.

It's just how she is. *Cards* is code for *treatment*. She does both in tandem. Another Lauren seeking distraction.

'Make sure you don't interrupt then.'

He nods and then walks towards me. 'Where have you been this time?'

He leans in to peck my cheek as I offer it to him on autopilot.

'None of your business.' My response is tight, delivered under my breath, and even though Granny is now staring out of the large balcony window, I know her ears are attuned to us.

I don't give him time to rebuke me. I stride past him and drop a kiss to her paper-thin cheek, my hand gentle on her shoulder, feeling only bone.

'Morning—how are you feeling?'

The door closes behind me, signalling Philip's departure, and I feel my chest ease just a little.

'Old,' she quips, and then she turns to look at me and frowns. 'So, come on—where were you?'

'Out with a friend.'

She thumbs the newspapers strewn across her bed. She already has one open at a page portraying me in an article about one of the charities I front, making preparations for tonight's ball.

She traces the picture with her forefinger. '*Just a friend?*'

I lower myself to perch on the edge of her bed. 'Just a friend.'

She looks back at me and I see her jaw is working. Something is bothering her, and her weight loss is making any sign of tension more pronounced.

'That "friend" put this colour in your cheeks?'

She waves a frail finger at my face, her eyes sparkling as she says it, and I can't help but smile, my guilt shining through.

She makes a low humming sound in her throat and folds her hands on her lap. 'You need to be careful, though, child. You have the weight of the world looking on. And the name of Lauren to protect.'

I have heard this speech a thousand times, and I practically say the words along with her.

'You'll never be far from scandal. Not with a mother like yours. And I need you to be. I need you to be above reproach. And, heaven help him, your brother needs it too.'

Adrenaline spikes in my blood and I have to work hard to keep my face neutral. It doesn't matter how many times they throw my mother at me; it still hurts. My mother loved my father; he loved her back. Whatever she did before then I don't care about. But Granny does. And he chose badly, according to her.

'Philip can look after himself.' I focus on the bit I feel comfortable arguing with.

Her frown deepens, her eyes sad. 'Not when he's led around by that mother of his—and don't get me started on his spendthrift wife. That Clara won't be happy until she has them penniless, and the estate doesn't come cheap. It will need to be maintained, looked after, invested in when I'm gone and—' She breaks off and winces, the breath shuddering through her.

'Please stop worrying. The doctor says you—'

She waves a hand at me, her head shaking as she coughs. 'Dr Know-It-All can zip it. I'll stop when I'm six feet under.'

'*Jesus*, Granny.'

'Language!' she admonishes. 'I need to know I can trust you—that you will take care of things. Philip, or rather those women, won't be able to do anything with regards to the private estate without your say-so. Look out for him, guide him as much as you can, keep him on the straight and narrow and above all uphold our good name, I'm counting on you, Coco.'

She looks to the newspaper page again, rearranges it, then rearranges it some more.

I want to say, *It's just a name—what does it matter? Surely happiness should come first.* But the last time I tried that argument I was sixteen and she refused to speak to me for weeks, persuaded my father to cut off my allowance and vetted anyone who came within a six-foot radius just in case they were corrupting me.

No, I've been brought up to project perfection. To be everything Granny believes my mother wasn't.

How different would my life have been if my mother hadn't been killed in a car accident when I was just a baby? Would she have brought Granny around eventually?

Not for the first time I wonder about giving Granny my mother's diary. Would it make her see my mother as I do, as Daddy must have? I only have to read it to see all the good in her. She had a naughty streak, for sure—her diary makes that clear too—but she was a good person. A person worthy of my father's love…a love that never waned.

But it's private—something my father entrusted to me and me alone.

'Can I ask you something, Granny?'

She looks back at me. 'Of course, child.'

'Why did you dislike my mother so much?'

She's so still and for a second I don't think she's heard me, or she's blanked out, her meds doing something weird, but then she blinks and looks towards the window.

'It wasn't that I disliked her. She just wasn't right for your father—for the Laurens. She was too wild, too young. She was eighteen when Robert brought her home after they eloped.' She shakes her head. 'He *knew* we'd never accept her—not with her… her *occupation*—so he ran away. He figured we'd have no choice but to accept then, that we'd rather not have a divorce on our hands. The press had already had a field day over us—imagine adding a divorce to it.'

'But they were in love,' I say. 'What did it matter that she was a stripper?'

Granny's eyes dart to mine.

'What?' I say, seeing the horror in her gaze. 'It's what she was.'

'Do you have to *say* it?' Her tone is hushed, as though we're in a public room with a judgemental audience listening in. 'How can you ask me that? You're twenty-four—you've been brought up to be a Lauren through and through. You of all people should know that it's not acceptable.'

I shake my head, sadness overwhelming me. 'It doesn't mean that she wasn't a good person, or that she loved Daddy any less.'

I'm a good person and I attend the very kind of clubs you abhor, dear Granny, but it doesn't mean I love you any less.

'Love is for fools,' she quips. 'Look at your brother and the way Clara takes advantage of his love.'

'But at least my parents were happy; you can't say the same for Daddy's second marriage.'

She balks at my mention of it, such is our shared dislike of my stepmother, but I'm not giving in.

'If we go by your standards, that marriage should have been perfect. She had her own money, her own status, and look how unhappy they were.'

Granny's eyes cloud over, and I know some of my words are sinking in.

'And you know why, don't you?' I push on.

She looks back to the window, like it will save her from where I'm heading.

'Granny...?'

She waves a hand at me to stop and it trembles. She looks so weak, so frail, the strength she's mustered to sit up straight seeping from her body as she starts to hunch. I know my father's death weighs heavily on her, that she has always struggled to come to terms with outliving her only child. And I know that talk of his misery in later years will make that pain more acute, but I can't stop. I need to say it.

'Because he never got over my mother—just like you never got over Grandpapa.'

She blinks rapidly and I know she's fighting back the weakness of tears—that even in front of me she doesn't feel able to show that level of humanity. It frustrates the hell out of me, and my own emotions are bubbling so close to the surface that I want to scream them free.

'Yes. And the pain of loving someone,' she says quietly, 'only to lose them, is a burden I wouldn't wish on anyone.'

'*Really*, Granny?' I can't hide my impassioned disbelief. 'You'd really rather never have known that happiness with someone than go through the pain?'

She doesn't answer. She's still focusing trance-like on the window.

'You were so lucky to find what you did with Grandpapa,' I say. 'And Daddy was so lucky to find it with my mother. I'd give anything for that.'

She looks back at me, shaking her head, her eyes bittersweet. 'For ever the romantic, aren't you? I've always worried it will get you in trouble.'

She reaches out to cup my cheek, her bony hand cold against the heat of my skin.

'You have such a big heart…but you have your mother's wild streak in you too.'

'Is that such a bad thing?' I ask softly.

There's a rap at the door that saves her from answering and I push off the bed to open it, knowing it will be Sue with brunch. There's no use fighting this out with Granny. I don't even know what I'm fighting for. To clear my mother's name? To lift the shackles of the Lauren name? I mean, Christ, it's the twenty-first century—who gives a toss about family reputations any more?

I look back at Granny as I pull open the door for Sue. Above Granny's bed is a painting of my great-great-great-grandmother, all prim and perfect. I can see myself in her, I can see Granny in her and I realise that this is what it's about. A legacy that exists long after we're gone, a part of us that travels through the generations.

That's why I can't fight her.

Because I get it.

But I want to live my life too. I want to be happy.

Why can't I have it all?

I smile at Sue as she brings in the laden tray and my mind is catapulted back to another tray, another person offering it up, and my body warms. My heart swells.

I'm an old romantic, Granny's right, and now that I've found a man worthy of loving, have had a glimpse of happiness with him, a glimpse of what the future might look like, I'm going after it.

I just need to make him realise he wants it too and then we can work out the rest together—his job, the public, all of it.

CHAPTER NINE

COCO'S BEEN GONE an hour, tops, and I've been staring at my computer screen, revisiting everything I know of her...of the Laurens. The Duchess's illness, guesstimates of the estate value, including their private wealth, and the business Philip continues to run. Facts, figures—tangible things that I can work with.

But none of it eases the weird angst inside me. I'm edgy beyond reason, and if I stop focusing for a second Coco fills my vision, taking over and making it personal—*too* personal.

I open up an article I have bookmarked and there she is, looking exquisite in a slinky silver number, attending a red-carpet event. Just beneath is a picture of her parents, Robert and Elizabeth Lauren, taken when they were a similar age to what Coco is now.

I keep on reading, even though I've read it multiple times before. It feels more important now—more crucial to my understanding of her and what Philip can hope to gain.

It makes for tragic reading. The sullied reputation of her mother, the open disapproval of her parents' marriage as a result and the sudden death of Elizabeth in a car crash. And her father's second marriage was reputed to have been fiery at best.

I imagine what Coco's life has been like—trying to avoid censure, the kind of slander her mother suffered, coping with the derogatory press coverage of her father's second marriage. Hell, it even makes me feel sorry for Philip, who grew up through it all.

It doesn't excuse his behaviour now, though. Or his mission to ruin her.

And I can say that because I've been there. I lived through it when my father was arrested. It was the biggest case of fraud the country had seen in years and my father was splashed through the media—us too, for a time.

I still don't understand why her brother wants to taint their family name with more scandal. Maybe it's for blackmail purposes or maybe it's something far simpler. I know I said it outright to Coco, but does her brother hope that by ruining her reputation he can somehow get her pushed out, disinherited, cut off? That would explain the timescale pressures, with the Duchess so sick.

My eyes fall from the screen as I shake my head. I can't get my head around it.

She's gone through enough already. Losing her parents. Soon to lose her grandmother. How can her brother be seeking to ruin her too?

I press my fist to my mouth and breathe through the rage clouding my brain; rage doesn't get me any closer to finding answers.

I look at my phone. How long has it been since I instructed my researchers to dig up everything they could on Philip? Thirteen hours at most. Hardly long enough. But a quick chase-up won't hurt.

I snatch it up, but it illuminates before I can do anything, ringing through the quiet.

Philip.

I fight the urge to throw the damn thing down and take another controlled breath before putting it to my ear.

'Philip.'

'Where did she go last night?'

'Hello to you too.' I sit back in my seat, my eyes on the screen, on her. 'She was already under the radar by the time I left you.' That was no lie.

'Have you checked out that club?'

'I swung by.'

'And?'

'And you can't just walk into a club like that and get details—it's going to take time.'

'For fuck's sake, Livingston, I've paid you a fortune already and you've got me sod all.'

'Like I said last night, I can walk away from this and you can find yourself some other—'

'No, no, it's fine. Just watch her. She has a charity gig tonight at the Savoy. Why don't you follow her after? She'll have had a few drinks… She'll be looking for a good time.'

I clench the phone tighter, my hand pulsing around it. I hate the way he says it. But is he right? Would she go to Blacks? Or would she come to me?

The latter was the safest option…for her.

Yeah, you're only thinking of her.

I ignore the mental gibe and focus on my next move. I have her number. I could text, arrange to meet…

'Livingston? You there?'

'I'll be there.'

I go to cut the line, not wanting to listen to his plummy, irritating-as-fuck tone any more, but then I stop.

'And, Philip?'

'Yes?'

'Get off my back or you'll definitely be finding yourself someone else.'

I hear his blustering down the line and my smile is cold as I hang up. People like Philip Lauren respond to a firm hand. The firmer I am, the more he will listen. The second I look weak, he will pounce.

Then I launch Coco's contact details and send a text.

Why don't I pick you up from the event tonight… bring you back to mine? Ash

Her response is swift.

Midnight. Savoy. Don't be late. My dress will turn to rags.

I smile at her *Cinderella* reference.

You could be in a bin liner and I'd still want you. No need to worry about the pumpkin. I'll bring my

big, strong, safe car around the back. Tradesman's
entrance. ;-)

I can't believe I've just added a wink to a text.
I'm still questioning it when her response pops up.

Great. See you then. PS did you get my number
from my fairy godmother?

Shit. I think fast.

I won't tell Jackson you called him that. He might
bar you.

I'm rewarded with a laughing emoji and an *X*.
I fire an *X* in response and lean back in my chair,
realising I'm grinning like a bloody idiot.
But I don't care.
She's safe from Philip for another night and that's
what matters.

I've never been more glad to leave an event in my
life. I'm like a kid on Christmas morning, giddy and
hyper as I sweep through the remaining guests and
make for the doors. I've already had a text from Ash
saying he's here and I can't wait to see him.
I know how I look. I'm wearing my favourite
silver dress—low at the back, high at the front, but
with a daring split to the thigh to make up for it.
I feel sexy, and I know that's because of him, the

way he makes me feel, the things he says, the way he looks at me.

And he listens. *Really* listens. He's not just eyeing me, pondering what he can get. Christ, part of me wishes he was—then I could coax him into something public, something more certain. But I'm not going to debate that now. I'm going to enjoy what I can have: him, naked and beneath me.

I have to ask a passing waiter for directions to the tradesman's entrance and I expect his brow to hit the roof. I mean, I'm giggling like a schoolgirl as I ask. I could blame the champagne but it's not that. I'm drunk on Ash and what the night has in store.

He points me in the right direction and I'm off, as fast as a person can travel on heels as high as mine. Even the weight of 'will we or won't we have a future together' has left me. All I care about is the here and now—and he is definitely *here*.

I thrust at the bar that's holding the double doors shut and burst out onto the street. His car is there, neon headlamps shining, and my heart soars into my throat.

Yes.

I shove the doors back into place and the car door opens. He steps out and I lift the skirt of my dress as I walk faster than the front slit will allow.

He's a silhouette against the lights, his tall, imposing frame so *him*. It's starting to rain, but I barely notice as I come to a stop in front of him and tilt my head back to meet his eyes.

'Hi,' I say—and his lips are on mine, feverish, urgent.

The rain starts to pick up, its patter as rapid as my pulse, ruining my hair, my make-up, but I couldn't care less. All I think about is him, his hands hot on the bare skin of my back, his heat mixing with the wet specks of rain as I kiss him harder. He's all minty fresh and delicious and I want more. I want it all. He's missed me. I can feel it. Just as I've missed him.

The rain starts to pound, pelting the car, the ground, us. He wraps me tighter against him and breaks his mouth away.

'Come on—before we get caught doing something we shouldn't.'

I laugh, delirious on the rush he's kicked up within me, and hurry in step with him to the passenger door. He pulls it open and helps me in, before closing it and racing around to his side. I get a brief glimpse of him in the headlamps: rakish stubble, shorn hair, strong jaw, glinting gaze, rain running down his face and dressed all in black… I smile.

The second he jumps in, I lean across and kiss his cheek. 'Thank you for coming.'

He catches my face in his palm, holding me there, his eyes ablaze and all the more intense with the rain beading on his lashes.

'Any time.'

He strokes away the dampness on my cheeks as I inhale his words. *If only it could be.*

He sweeps over my lips with his thumb, his lips, then settles back into his seat, running a hand over his face and hair to dry it off before buckling himself in.

I do the same. 'You think you could do this every night?' I'm only half joking.

He grins as he puts the car in Reverse. 'For as long as you want me to.'

I give a soft smile. I can't imagine never wanting this—him at my beck and call.

Ten minutes into the journey and neither of us has spoken further. The rain is lashing down, the wipers are beating it back, making him frown with concentration. I haven't wanted to distract him and, to be honest, I'm enjoying the view.

'What?' he suddenly says, flicking me a look.

'Hmm…?'

'You've been smiling like the cat that got the cream ever since you got in.'

I reach out and place my hand on his thigh, squeezing softly. 'It kind of feels that way.'

His leg tenses beneath me and I see his jaw pulse. 'You need to move your hand before I have to pull over.'

I laugh, the sound husky and loaded with the imaginings that have been keeping me company so far, and he looks at me briefly, shaking his head.

'How was the ball?'

'Are you trying to distract me?'

'Yes.'

I pout and pull my hand away. 'It was good. I think we stand a chance of raising more than we anticipated.'

'That's good.' His eyes are fixed ahead now, as he drives. 'Did your brother go?'

My laugh is harsh this time. 'My brother would see it as a waste of his time. If there's nothing in it for him, he doesn't see the point.'

He nods, his fists flexing around the wheel. 'You're very different?'

'We share our father's DNA—that's as close as it gets.'

He has successfully managed to kill my mood. Especially since I have no intention of returning home tonight, and that will lead to further questions from Philip tomorrow. In front of Granny, of course.

'If he had his way he'd see me out of his life for good.'

I expect him to scoff. Instead he frowns at me, serious, concerned. 'That's a bit extreme.'

'Not for him. He'd probably have me dead if it wouldn't dirty his hands too much.'

'That's ridiculous—you can't mean that.'

Did she? No, she guessed not. But... 'He'd see me thrown out of the family without a penny—I know that much.'

'What makes you think that?'

I shift in the seat and smooth out my dress. I feel his eyes flick to my exposed thigh, to the slit that won't be tamed now I'm seated, and he swallows as he looks back to the windscreen. His obvious desire warms me, helps to beat back the chill of our conversation. Cait is the only one with whom I've ever really discussed Philip and his obvious dislike of me.

'He puts a lot of effort into picking apart my flaws for Granny's benefit. Take this morning, for example. The fact I hadn't returned home last night was his topic of conversation when I arrived to visit her.'

'You're a grown woman.' His fists flex around the steering wheel again as he presses himself back in the seat. 'What business is it of his?'

'It's not my lack of homecoming that bothers him. It's what he thinks I've been up to with my time. He'll do anything to have my reputation pulled apart in Granny's eyes.'

'But *why*?'

I shrug. 'To get me written out of her will, pushed out of the family, named and shamed... Take your pick.'

'But your grandmother loves you,' he says softly, clearly finding my reasoning hard to believe. 'Surely she wouldn't take his snide remarks as a reason to cut you off?'

I look out of the passenger window as I consider his question. 'She loves me in so much as she can, but she'll always put the Lauren name first. The family heritage.' I blow out a breath as I turn back to him. 'It sounds crazy, but it's true. "A Lauren must be above reproach."'

I mimic her voice as I quote her and smile. He doesn't return it.

'Sounds cold to me.'

My smile fades. 'It's not her fault. She's a product of her time. It's not Philip's either—not really. He grew up in my shadow; our father always sided with me…doted on me. I was his last connection to my mother and… Well, Philip's mother also struggled with the same inferiority. She was never good enough either. But that was made worse by her nature.'

'Her nature?'

'She's always out for what she can get—Clara too.'

'Clara?'

'Philip's wife.' I grimace as I say it. I can't help it. Her callous, money-grabbing ways are so obvious to everyone but Philip. 'I think he'd grant her anything to keep her happy, to keep her love, if you can call it that.'

'And you really excuse Philip's behaviour because of them?'

I shrug. I know it's hard for him to accept—for anyone to accept, really—but we grew up together. I saw my brother's suffering first-hand and I see his continued suffering now.

He meets my eye briefly. 'So what will you tell them when they ask where you've been tonight?'

'Same as this morning. I stayed at a friend's… And I'll tell them that every night this week if you'll have me.'

CHAPTER TEN

WHEN COCO SAID *every night*, I didn't believe her. I took it as some sort of ploy to get the conversation off Philip and onto us.

But it's now Thursday, five days since the charity ball, and it's the seventh night we've spent together in a row.

I trail my hands along her bare side as she curls into me and presses a kiss to my chest.

'I think you know my every sweet spot,' she murmurs sleepily, and my lips find her hair, breathing in her familiar scent as I kiss the ruffled mass.

'I should hope so.'

It's one thirty in the morning. She'll be up again in five hours. Just like she has been every weekday morning, so that she can get back home, hit the gym and visit her grandmother before she starts another rammed day.

She doesn't rest unless she's sleeping—a fact I've ribbed her about—but she simply shrugs it off.

'Now, sleep,' I say, stretching out my free arm to tap off the bedside lamp.

She's gone in seconds. There's a telltale twitch to her body, a steady rhythm to her breathing. I'm not, though. The longer this goes on for, the bigger my lie—*no*, my omission—gets.

I tell myself I'm looking after her, putting her best interests first. But the more I care, the more I know my reasoning is twisted. Because, yes, I'm doing this for *her*, but I can't deny how much it works for me too. How much I'm enjoying our time together. No matter how borrowed that time is.

And I know it is. Philip is getting twitchier by the day. There's only so long I can keep stringing him along. But I'm getting closer to understanding him. I have enough information to understand the poor state of his finances now, and to know that his wife's spending habits are exacerbating the situation.

I know the family business is struggling too, and that he's under pressure to resign. It appears that Philip has a loose tongue, and the information his golf buddies have been privy to over the years has benefitted them greatly—his company not so much.

How he didn't see the pattern, I don't know, but it's enough to see that pressure to resign becoming an insistence. And Philip won't want that. To be forced out of the company his father left to him would be the ultimate humiliation. And it's the kind of ammunition I need to ensure he stays the hell away from Coco.

And the guy doesn't need her money, surely. Yes, it doesn't come cheap managing the estate he stands to inherit with his title, but there's the Lauren money too. The private wealth, investments, property, including the London residence in which they spend the majority of their time alongside their ailing grandmother. That house alone is worth a fortune even by today's standards. But it truly begs the question: Why sink so low as to go after his sister's money anyway? If that truly is his aim as Coco seems to surmise.

Maybe there's more to it than just money? Resentment, perhaps? By her own admission she was always her father's favoured child, and her parents' marriage was happy, full of love. The same can't be said for the household Philip was raised in.

Or maybe a guy like Philip can never have enough money.

I'd certainly seen enough of that in my time. Clive was a prime example.

But what did it matter at the end of the day? I'm almost ready to turn the tables on Philip. To fight dirt with dirt and get him off Coco's case.

Then I can tackle the truth of what this is between us and whether we have a chance—because it's getting harder by the day to imagine life without her in it.

'What's wrong?'

Her voice startles me, and I realise I'm gripping her tightly. I force my hand to relax, my body too.

'I thought you were asleep.'

'I was.'

Her head moves against me and I can just make out her eyes in the darkness, looking up at me.

'And then you seemed to stop breathing. What's wrong?'

'Nothing.'

'I don't believe you.'

'Nothing for you to worry about at any rate.'

'If it's bothering you, then it bothers me.'

I can hear how much she cares in her voice and guilt claws through my chest.

Just bide your time. You can tell her when she's safe.

I nudge her lips with my own. 'It can wait. Now, go back to sleep. You've another full-on day tomorrow.'

She groans. 'Don't remind me. I'm not sure what's worse—the fact that I have back-to-back meetings or a family dinner to contend with.'

The family dinner gets my vote.

'Just tell your brother you can't make it.'

'I can't. He wants to discuss Granny's care and we're all going—his wife, his mother… I want to be there and make sure they're doing right by her.'

She falls quiet but her fingers are toying with the hair on my chest, betraying her active brain. Is she worrying about the meal? Her grandmother's health? The future?

'Ash?'

'Hmm…?'

'Pick me up after? I should be done by ten at the latest.'

I smile at her soft request. 'Of course.'

Whatever she's thinking about, worrying over,

the fact that she still wants me there at the end of it makes everything feel okay, even though it shouldn't.

Dinner is all one would expect from a Michelin-starred restaurant, but I'm not really tasting anything. The starter was swallowed in silence, the main amidst a smattering of small talk. Clara looks bored beyond measure and I'm doing my utmost to ignore my darling stepmother. I'm eager to get the night over with, so I can make my excuses and hurry back to Ash.

I'm more tired than usual too, and I know I have our nightly antics to thank for that, but dealing with the force that is my brother and the women flanking him is always hard work. His mother even now is raking a critical eye over me and sending the hairs on the backs of my exposed arms prickling. I rub them and do my best to ignore her.

'Are you cold?' Clara asks me, frowning at the move.

'A little.'

His mother sips her wine and offers me a disparaging smile. 'Perhaps if you dressed more appropriately you wouldn't be.'

'You ought to know,' I snap, regretting it as soon as it's out.

My dress is an elegant sleeveless black number, down to the knee, nothing indecent about it. She's just getting at me. But fighting with my stepmother never did me any favours. Normally I can ignore her, but not tonight. This meeting has me on edge and I want it over.

'But we're not here to discuss my attire, are we? We're here for Granny. So why don't we get that out of the way and then we can all get back to our lives?'

'Goodness, you make it sound like it's such an inconvenience, having to talk about your grandmother.' My stepmother looks to Philip. 'Doesn't she, darling?'

'Yes.' His eyes narrow on me. 'Have you someplace else you need to be, Coco?'

I feel my cheeks colour. I know they're baiting me, and I shouldn't rise to it, but it's so hard. Especially having endured them for over an hour already, with their mundane sniping at people about whom they have the pleasure of gossiping.

'It seems you're rarely at home these days,' he continues. 'And I've heard some interesting tales on the grapevine as to what has you so occupied.'

Is he serious? Could he know about Ash? Or is this just another gibe? A continuation of his questioning over my whereabouts in front of Granny?

Both his mother and Clara look from him to me, smiles that send my blood cold playing on their lips. I try to ignore them.

'I've been home enough to spend time with Granny—that's all that matters.'

'You've been just as doting as ever.' He nods, overly sincere. 'As have I, for that matter. But it isn't enough—hence this meeting.'

My sudden panic about Ash morphs into a greater fear now. 'What do you mean?'

'I don't think her living at the London residence any longer is a good idea.'

'But it's her favoured home. It's close to her on-cologist, her friends, the h—'

He waves his hand to cut me off. 'You misunderstand me. I think we need to convince her that a hospital—a specialist hospice unit—would be a better place…more comfortable—'

'Is this your doing?' I blurt at my stepmother, my stomach churning over. There's no way my brother would have come to this conclusion alone. He's not *that* heartless.

'Calm down, Coco,' my brother orders. 'It benefits us all to know that Granny is taken care of properly 24/7. She can't even tackle the stairs on her own any more.'

'So? We'll convert a room downstairs for her—one that gives her access to the garden and the—'

'Don't be ridiculous, dear. Which room are you suggesting? The drawing room? The garden room? The library?' My stepmother shakes her head, her perfectly coiffed hair unmoving. 'All that medical equipment will ruin the house; you'd need handrails put in, and there's no bathroom downstairs for her to use. And all for the sake of—what? A month? Maybe two?'

I don't want to listen to her. I don't want to listen to any of them.

'But she wants to be at home—she's *asked* to stay at home.'

'Yes, but our summer soirée is next month and how can we possibly consider holding that with your grandmother under the same roof...or not, as the case maybe.' She sips at her wine, calm as you like, and looks pointedly at Philip.

I stare at her in disbelief. She can't be serious. She wants to put the location of the Lauren annual bash above... No, it cannot be. 'You're not serious?'

'Of course, we can't exactly hold it somewhere else, we always have it in London,' Clara chips in. 'It's convenient to all. Not to mention it's a family tradition.'

'And we know how your grandmother is about tradition,' my stepmother adds.

'*Christ*, have some bloody compassion,' I snap.

She doesn't even smart. 'Compassion only makes one weak, and we know how she feels about *that* too.'

Philip doesn't say a word, only eyes his glass as he rolls the stem of it in his fingers.

'Philip, seriously, you know this isn't right?'

'*Philip* will do what is best for him and his soon-to-be title, he will be the Duke of Rushford and, as such, he needs to start taking the lead at these functions. The soirée is the perfect beginning.'

'But...but she's not even dead yet.'

Philip's eyes lift to mine, a crease between his brows. There's a twisted kind of torment in his face and it betrays his inner fight with what is right and what he is being told.

Clara reaches across the table, her hand resting on his wrist and drawing his attention. 'Come on, darling, it's time you did what you were born to do: take control.'

She runs her teeth over her bottom lip and looks at him adoringly. I can see the power-hungry glint in her eye. She doesn't love him. She only loves what he can give her, and he has fallen for it. Fallen for what I myself have always sought to avoid.

'Please, Philip,' I say, calling his attention back to me. 'Don't do this.'

'It will suit Granny better to be cared for in a specialist unit.' There is no emotion to his voice as he drags his eyes to mine. 'It would be better—easier—if you talk to her, convince her it's the right thing to do.'

I shake my head. I can't listen to any more, can't witness the manipulation that's so obviously in play.

'No, I won't do it. It's her home. She has a right to die there.'

My eyes start to sting and blur, turning them into blobs rather than people. I plant my napkin on my plate and stand. I won't give them the satisfaction of seeing me cry.

'Sit down, child,' my stepmother hisses. 'Dessert is just coming—you're making a scene.'

I blink back the tears and give her a scathing smile. 'I hope for your sake that Philip doesn't learn by your example, because if natural order has its way, there'll come a time when *you'll* be the dying one and he'll be shovelling *you* off to an alien environment against your wishes.'

'Well, really…' she huffs but I'm already looking to Clara now.

'And as for you, I'm not blind to what you are. One day the veil will lift and Philip will see it too, then you'll get what you deserve.'

Her gasp of outrage fills my ears as I turn away and I take some comfort from it. I've hit my mark. But I can't bring myself to say anything more to Philip. I need to be gone.

I need Ash.

My distraction.

It used to be Blacks. Now it's him.

I get that I've only swapped one kind of escapism for another, and that this one has the power to hurt me down the road, but right now I can't worry about that.

I just need him.

I know Coco's upset. Her message tells me so by its urgency.

She's asked me to pick her up two streets down from the restaurant and here I am, parked up and waiting.

I'm surprised she's not here already. And then I spy her, scanning the road for cars, for me. She's pale, sad, her eyes glistening and killing me even from this distance. She sweeps a shaky hand through her hair as she weaves through the pedestrians, the evening rush thick as ever in London.

I reach for the door handle, ready to go and get her, too impatient to wait for her to find me—and then freeze. My eyes zone in on someone else a few beats behind her.

Shit.

My blood runs cold.

Eric Bower.

My number-one rival. I lean back in my seat, as though at any moment he's going to look straight at me and piece it all together.

I try to tell myself it's just a coincidence—that the fact he's walking in the same direction means nothing. But it's bull. Everything about his overly casual stride and wandering eye tell me he's on a job. And what are the chances he's after someone else in the vicinity?

Coco pauses and pulls out her phone.

Bower turns to scan a florist's window.

No, it's no coincidence.

Fuck you, Philip.

I punch the edge of the steering wheel and start the ignition, pulling out into traffic before she can see me. The system in my car announces an incoming text message, and I know it's from her even before I instruct it to read it out loud.

Where are you? I'm here... X

My head drops and I grimace, frustration, anger, guilt making me clench the steering wheel tighter. I try to ease the tension in my shoulders, tell myself

I'll be there for her soon. But I hate it that I've just abandoned her when I know she needs me.

I pull over as soon as I'm out of sight, much to the displeasure of the people in the car behind me, and they honk, but I'm already taking my phone out, my brain racing. Where's safe? Where can I meet her and not have Bower on her tail?

I grip the back of my neck as I think. Blacks—it has to be. Philip already knows she goes there. So long as I stay out of sight and get her to come to me we'll be fine.

I fire off a reply.

Change of plan. Something came up. Meet me at Blacks?

I can't breathe as I wait for her response. What if she tells me to go to hell? But why would she? To her, I've just been held up. I haven't run away because her brother has a second PI on her tail.

Her response is swift.

Okay. XX

The *XX* pulses, stabbing up at me from the screen. Projecting guilt and affection in one.

Time is running out. It won't take long for Bower to know what I know, even with me being careful. We tap into the same resources; it only takes one misplaced word, a flippant comment, and he'll figure things out.

Worse still, it only takes her appearing at my home when I don't expect it—just like she did that Friday night—with Bower on her tail and our relationship will be outed.

I toss the phone onto the passenger seat and pull back into the traffic. I just need to keep things under my control a little while longer and then I can worry about what comes next.

But how, with Bower so close?

Get out of London. Take her away.

It's possible. I have the resources to sneak her out and I have the perfect place too. I'm long-overdue a visit there myself.

But would she come?

I don't like how disappointed I feel at Ash's change of plan.

I know it's not his fault that I've become dependent on him to keep reality at bay. But the second I get his text asking to meet at Blacks instead, the tears escape and I'm drawing attention. The kind I don't need—the kind I'm usually good at keeping at bay.

I pull my coat up around my ears and pick up my pace, heading for the Underground, where I can blend into the background easily enough.

I'll be with him soon; I can lose myself in him and he'll make everything feel okay again.

But for how long?

You can't keep seeking distraction; you have to face reality sooner or later. Granny's dying and you can't change it.

I close my eyes over the pang of pain and realise that's not all I'm running from.

It's my feelings for him too. The risk that he won't feel the same way, that I won't be able to convince him to give us a shot. My feet stall and my heart pulses as my stomach turns over. What if I have to let him go?

I shake my head and focus through a teary haze. *Shit.*

I'm being watched. Several passers-by frown in my direction, and a guy's trying to look like he's not, but I see him watching me anyway. Probably a reporter, looking for his latest scoop.

Fuck.

I must look insane, with my mental argument written on my face, and tears too.

I take a breath and move.

Get to Blacks. To Ash.

The rest can come later—much later. Alone, if I have to.

CHAPTER ELEVEN

'THREE VISITS IN one month?' Jackson's brows almost hit the overhanging glassware as I approach the bar. 'This has to be a record, Ash.'

I'm in no mood for his teasing and he clocks that quickly enough. He says no more as he turns away and pulls down two shot glasses and goes for a bottle.

'Save it.' I hold my palm out to him as I slide onto one of his swanky high-backed bar stools. 'Not tonight.'

He turns back to me and rests his elbows on the bar, leaning in to look at me properly. 'Jesus, what is it this time?'

'I need your help.'

'You're telling me? I thought you were finally getting some…putting a smile back on that grim face of yours—you certainly looked—'

I shake my head and he stops short. 'What do you need?'

'You found your leak yet?'

'No. People talk—it might simply be a case of

Chinese whispers getting out of hand—but I have my people looking into some of our newer members.'

'Sounds wise.' I pull out my phone and pull up a photo of Bower. 'You had any enquiry from this guy? The name's Bower—Eric Bower?'

He frowns at the screen. 'No. Should I have?'

'He's a PI. I think that bastard Philip Lauren's hired him.'

He cocks a brow. 'In addition to you?'

I nod. 'I wouldn't give him what he needs so he's obviously decided to get someone else on the case.'

'Why do I get the feeling it's not occupational pride that bothers you?'

I swallow. I wish I'd taken up his offer of a drink. I need the hit. I also need something to do with my hands, which are constantly fisting and flexing. But not only do I need to drive, I need my wits about me to ensure we're not tailed.

'She doesn't deserve any of this.'

'No,' Jackson says. 'I tried to tell you that.'

'Yeah, well…consider me told.'

'You're more than told,' he says, squinting into my eyes like he can see right through me. 'You're falling for her, aren't you?'

I shove up from the stool and turn away from him. 'Don't be ridiculous.'

'I haven't seen you this on edge since… Well, since that shit went down ten years ago.'

I flick him a look. I want to flip him the bird too, but, hell, I know he's right. Not that talking about it, thinking about it, is going to help right now.

'Look, she's coming here soon. Do me a favour and send her down to the garage on the quiet? I don't know whether you have a leak or not, and I hope for your sake you don't, but…'

'You don't want to risk it getting out?'

'Yeah.'

'No problem.' He straightens and gives me an assured grin. 'Get yourself down there; you won't be disturbed unless it's her.'

'Thanks, mate, I owe you.'

'And for what it's worth, Ash…' he says.

I've started to head off but I look back at him, knowing I should probably keep on going.

'I'm happy for you. She's a great girl.'

'And she could do a lot better than me.'

He shakes his head, but I'm gone, heading towards the private access that leads to the basement car park. The same way I took her out of the club the other night. Can that really be only a week ago? So much has changed since then…and yet nothing.

I'm still the man hired to dish the dirt on her—on the face of it, at least. But now my focus has changed, my goal is reversed, and navigating that while trying to protect her is messing with my head. Not my heart. Because I can't be in love with her—not yet. Falling, yes. Getting in deep, yes. But in love…?

I slam open the door and sprint down the stairs, wishing I could keep on running, sprint until my lungs burn, until that's all I can think of. Not this crazy confusion and the fear that it's sparked.

No one falls in love this quickly—*no one.*

* * *

Blacks is bustling when I get there and sweep inside, my feet eager to take me to him. Eager to get me out of the public domain, away from the fear of exposure, of saying or doing the wrong thing when my emotions are riding so high.

I enter the main bar area—the place where I first saw him—my eyes desperately scanning, but he's not there. Disappointment fires anew and I take out my phone to send him a text.

'Coco?'

I look up to see Jackson heading towards me, smiling.

'Hey.' I try to smile back but I know it's shaky, and my voice is trembling in its simple greeting.

'Ash is waiting for you downstairs.'

My heart skips. *He's here. Thank God, he's here.*

'This way.'

He gestures for me to follow him. 'Thank you.'

He walks me to the door that leads down to his private parking garage and opens it for me. 'Give him my regards.'

'Will do.' My smile is real now, my voice solid.

Not even my heels can stop me racing down the stairs, and as I burst out into the car park he's there, leaning against the bonnet of his car. He straightens as soon as he sees me, his reassuring form like a welcome beacon, and I run to him.

I don't care about putting up a front, about manners or dignity, only that he's here, and I can let go.

His brow furrows, his eyes question, but he holds

his arms out to me and then I am in them, and I'm kissing him with all the passion and the emotion that's overflowing inside me. And I pray he doesn't stop me—not until I'm ready.

But he isn't stopping. His hands fork in my hair and his mouth is as hungry as my own. He spins me so I'm pushed up against the car, his hands raking feverishly beneath my coat as I grapple with his clothing.

This is what I need. This all-consuming passion that blots all else out. I have no idea how private this garage is. But I'm guessing only Jackson has access, and he's upstairs, and I don't want to stop to ask.

'I've missed you,' I say against his lips.

'I've missed you too.'

The confirmation, the resonance of his tone with mine—it's everything and more.

'Nothing hurts when I'm with you.'

He stills, his hands midway to cupping my breasts. 'What's happened?'

'I don't want to talk about it—not now. Make me forget, Ash.'

He presses his forehead into mine, his blazing blue eyes burning through me. I drop my hand to the bulge in his jeans and squeeze. Air hisses between his teeth.

'That's a dirty move—'

'Too many words.' I cut off his retort with my tongue, dipping inside his mouth, grazing his teeth.

His growl is feral as he pulls my thigh up, exposing the lace tops of my hold-ups and his fingers graze over the detail, his eyes too. 'You have no idea how much I want you right now.'

'Then take me.'

His eyes lock with mine. 'Here?'

I nod—swift, fierce. 'Please.'

His lip quirks. I can see he wants to, *feel* he wants to.

'Do you have protection?' he asks.

Fuck.

'No.'

He clamps his eyes shut and I can feel him forcing his body to stand down.

'But I'm clean.'

He opens his eyes at my assurance, stares into me like he can't believe what I'm saying.

'I'm on the pill…and we have to be tested, don't we, to be members here?' I look up to the ceiling, to the club above. 'You?'

'Coco…' He shakes his head like he's battling some momentous decision.

'I *trust* you.'

His eyes burn into mine and take my breath away. There is so much there. And I'm not just talking heat, desire. I'm talking pain. For what, I don't know. I just know that sex will make it stop, for him and for me, at least in the now.

I cup his jaw in both hands, stroke my thumbs over his stubble. 'I *need* you.' I hook my leg around his waist, pull his hardness up against me and stroke my body over him. *'Now.'*

He drags in a breath, ragged and raw. His eyes fall

to where our bodies meet, where I continue to ride his clothed hardness, and his hands take hold of my hips, gripping me tight.

'What are you doing to me?'

'This.' My hands fall to his jeans, popping open the button. 'If you'll have me.'

His head is shaking. 'I'll always have you.'

My breath catches… My eyes sting. But now isn't the time for tears. 'Good.'

I slide down his zipper, my teeth scraping over my bottom lip as I reach inside his briefs and pull him out. He's hot, thick and throbbing.

Oh, yes.

He ducks his head, takes my mouth with his, and I pump my hand over him, loving how his entire body trembles, his breath shudders, his lips lose traction with mine.

He thrusts his hands up my thighs, my dress bunched within his grasp, and I tilt my pelvis higher as I lower his cock to me, slipping aside my thong as I go.

I'm so wet his head slides in with ease, slipping past my clit, parting my lips, and inside… I throw my head back as I accept him in one blissfully sharp thrust. He's so perfect, so hot and hard as he fills me, and I clench around him tight.

'*Coco…*' He groans, his body stilling, his length buried within me.

I open my eyes, stare up at him. He's trying to fight, to keep control.

'Let go with me, Ash.'

I move over him, one hand pulling his head down, bringing his mouth to mine, the other pressing down between us, my fingers forking either side of his cock, buried deep within me, enjoying the feel of him there, coated in my wetness, before I pull back to circle over my clit.

I whimper into his mouth, my body shuddering around him as I let ripples of ecstasy work their way from my core to the tips of my toes. He lifts me against him, draws my other leg up and around him as he presses my body back against the car and finds his rhythm, swift and fierce, driving me crazy.

I raise my free hand to his face, run my thumb over his lips, and he dips his mouth over it, tongues it, sucks it back as his eyes lock with mine. All heat and fire. No pain. Not now.

He nips at my palm with his teeth and then flicks his head back, his neck cording with tension. His climax is coming and I'm wrapped up in his pleasure, my fingers picking up their pace over my clit.

'Fuck, Coco...*Coco*...' His eyes lock back onto mine, his thrusts turn jagged, and I grip him tighter between my thighs.

'Yes, Ash.'

Pleasure explodes through me, through him. His release is hot and pulsing, so raw and intense within me. His groan echoes off the brick walls and I cling to him, my head dropping into the crook of his neck, my body unwilling to let him go, my mind unwilling to let the outside world back in.

I listen to his heart pounding, to the rasp of his

breath as it starts to steady and slow. He lowers me
to my feet and I can feel him slip out. *No.*

I look up at him, regret clear in my face as I say,
'Now I wish we were in bed.'

He gives a soft laugh as I scoop tissues from my
jacket pocket and help him out with the mess.

'Lucky no one walked in on us,' I say, making
conversation while I scan the car park for a bin.

'Jackson said he'd keep it secure.'

He takes the tissues from me and walks off to
the corner of the garage, clearly knowing his way
around. I watch him go, admiring his firm behind in
his jeans, the sheer masculinity in the breadth of his
shoulders, the severe cut of his hair. A fresh ripple of
desire runs through me, centring around my heart.

He gets rid of the tissues and turns back to me,
his stride faltering as he cocks a brow at me. 'What?'

I smile. I can tell he's read it all on my face. 'Nothing.'

His smile is tentative, questioning, as he closes
the distance, pulling me against him once I'm within
reach.

'Nothing?' he says, looking down into my eyes.

'I was just so sad earlier…' I stroke his cheekbones, his hair, raking my eyes over his face and
seeing all that I'm falling for looking back at me.

'And now?'

'It's still there, but it's easier when you're with
me.' He squeezes me against him tighter. 'Does that
sound weird?' I ask.

'No, it makes perfect sense.'

Does that mean he feels it too? Is that why he understands? I wish it could be that. I really do.

'Are you going to tell me what's wrong?'

'Yes…but let's get out of here first. I could do with a glass of wine in good company.' I smile at him. When I contrast him to my company not one hour ago, I'm doing him a disservice. 'Make that *great* company.'

I sweep my lips over his, a gentle kiss before moving away, but he pulls me back.

'Coco?'

'Hmm?'

His eyes are so sincere they tug at me, pulling on strings I've never felt before.

'Just…'

I stare up at him, lost in his open expression, and then he shakes his head and grins.

'Nothing. It can wait.'

CHAPTER TWELVE

My brain is whirling on the drive back to my place.
The vehicle is keeping my hands busy but my mind
is so occupied by her.

She seems more settled than she was before. So
settled that I think she's likely to fall asleep before
we make it back. She's half curled up in the seat, her
head turned to the side, her eyes flickering between
me, her hands and the outside world.

But, Christ, when I first saw her, saw the trace
of tears in her over-bright eyes, her smile so genuine, so relieved, I was unable to speak. I could only
open my arms to her and hold her, kiss her back as
she kissed me.

And then those three simple statements: *I've
missed you... I trust you... I need you.*

I tighten my grip on the wheel as the words repeat
through my brain, burning deep, as I remember my
hunger, so possessive as I staked my claim.

I haven't... I've never... Not since Jess—not since
that relationship—have I trusted anyone enough to
go without protection. It's huge. Monumental. But it

felt so right, so natural, and now inside me my confession is bursting to get out.

I almost told her, there in the basement car park. And what a disaster that would've been, hot off the back of what we'd shared. She might have legged it back up top, out onto the street, where Bower would have been lying in wait, ready to get whatever detail he could to report back to that bastard Philip Lauren.

No, the timing hadn't been right. But, damn it, I want this all out in the open. I want to be there for her fully—no lies, no omissions.

I look across at her, see her eyelids heavy as she struggles to stay awake, and I stroke back the hair falling over her face. She gives me a small smile, which I return, and then her eyes are closed and I drop my hand back to the gear stick.

'Nearly there,' I say softly.

She gives a nonsensical response and cosies up deeper into her coat. She truly is at ease with me. And I would be the same if not for what I've kept from her.

I look back to the windscreen and focus on the drive, on something I do have control over in that second.

Just have faith. It will all come right in the end...
Yeah, because life's kind like that...

But if I can just get her away from here, confront Philip Lauren when she's safe from any immediate backlash on his part, deliver the threat of what I can do with the information I've gleaned and get him to call off Bower.

Because she doesn't deserve it. She doesn't deserve any of it.

And you don't deserve her…

I clench my jaw tight. That's something she will have to decide for herself, once she has all the facts and I've come clean.

Because I will…just as soon as she's safe.

I wake to the invigorating smell of coffee, the sound of cooking in the kitchen, and I roll over.

Ash's lingering scent cocoons me, and his quilt is warm and soft against my bare skin. To wake up like this every morning, not to feel alone any more…

I clutch the bedding to myself and smile into the sheets. Perhaps things aren't as complicated as he initially thought; perhaps he will change his mind about me, about us.

It felt that way when he stopped me from getting in the car last night. When he pulled me back against him and then changed his mind and said we'd talk later…

Only I'd fallen asleep.

I remember him cutting the engine, stirring enough to respond to his voice, and then he carried me here. I wanted to wake up—wanted to tell him what had happened, have him tell me it would be okay, tell me what it was that he'd stopped himself saying in the underground garage. But it was too easy to curl up under his quilt, just like I'm doing now, and let him surround me, comfort me.

And when I woke in the quiet of the night, hot and

uncomfortable, still clothed in my bra and thong, I stripped them away, and the instant my naked body curled into his, he stirred. We made love—nothing frantic, no words… Just eyes closed, mouths tasting, touching, all sensation. We savoured one another until we were sated and then let sleep claim us once more. So idyllic, so—

'Morning, sleepyhead.'

I turn at the sound of his voice—*wow!*

My mouth opens on a breathy sigh. He's walking towards me, tray outstretched, and steam is rising from two coffee mugs and a mountain of scrambled eggs. But it's not the offering that has me gaping— it's him. His sheer masculine beauty.

He's naked down to the teasing V at the base of his abs, just a pair of lounge pants hanging low, and he's barefoot, with a sexy-as-fuck grin that's as heated as I feel.

'Morning.'

It's a little gasp, and his grin widens.

'You can't be out of breath already; we haven't even started on the morning sex yet.'

'Is morning sex on offer?'

He slides the tray onto the bedside table and looks down at his crotch. I follow his eye and the sight of the tentlike bulge forming has my belly contracting.

'Guess I needn't have asked.'

'Guess I needn't bother to answer.'

'Not with words, at any rate…' I reach out and take hold of him through his clothing.

'Jesus, Coco.'

But his body bucks into my grasp, telling me just how welcome my touch is.

'The food will get cold…'

'I'm not putting this to waste,' I say, climbing up onto my knees and slackening the waistband of his pants. They fall to floor and I smile up at him as I wet my lips. 'Are you going to stop me?'

His eyes flare with anticipation. 'I can't say no to you.'

I kiss his very tip and air hisses through his teeth. His curse is fierce as his hands fork through my hair and cup the back of my head.

'Good,' I say softly, and then I press him between my lips, take one deep suck.

He's so fucking hard, and I'm already wet at the sight and feel of him, my clit throbbing fiercely with the power I hold.

He rocks and I take him further, my fingers lifting to cup his balls. His sharp intake of breath tells me it's what he wants, what he needs. And then I pull back slowly and release him with a pop, loving how his muscular frame flexes at the move and he drags in more air.

'Lie down,' I say softly.

He does just as I command, stepping out of his trousers and lying down beside me. All the while his eyes are locked in mine, lost in mine. I climb on top of him, one hand pumping his throbbing length, the other dipping between my legs, scooping up my wetness. I'm so ready for him, and I don't want to wait a second more. I slide his cock back, use his head to separate my folds and then I sink down, taking his all.

'Christ, Coco. *Yes*...' His hands drop to my thighs, his fingers biting into my skin. 'What I would give to wake up like this every morning...'

I undulate over him, hear his words chiming with my thoughts from seconds before. 'Me too.'

I ride him faster, harder, dropping both hands to his chest as my movements become more jagged. And then he rises up, holds me tight against him as I rock, rock, rock... There's that perfect hit of friction, his sheer size filling me, his body engulfing me, and then I'm gone, my head thrown back as I cry out.

I'm soaring, my body rigid and pulsating. And then he cries against me, shuddering with his own release, his forehead pressed against my clavicle, his mouth pressed into my skin. I feel so close to him in that moment, with his cock buried deep, his head so tight against me, his arms enclosing me. The need to cry is back, but it's full of happiness.

I wet my lips, find my voice. 'How's that for a good morning?'

His breath moves down my front and he breaks away just enough to say, 'The best.'

And then he's pulling me back against him again, delivering a kiss to my skin before pressing his cheek to my chest.

We stay like that for what feels like for ever, and yet I'm still disappointed when he pulls back to look up at me, his hands raking through my hair.

'Your breakfast will be cold.'

I sweep a kiss over his lips. 'It'll still be perfect.'

He laughs softly and lifts me away. Dutifully, I sit back against the headboard, give him the chance to disentangle himself from the covers, and then pull them up just enough to cover my breasts.

I give him a wicked grin. 'I'm ready to be fed.'

'You'll be waiting a little while, then; a man needs to recharge.'

I laugh. 'You *know* that's not what I meant.'

'That's a shame.' He rises off the bed and offers me the tray. 'I'll be back in a second—don't eat it all without me.'

And then he pulls his lounge pants off the floor and heads into the bathroom. To clean himself up, I'm sure. But there's a look on his face a split second before he turns away—that same pain I read in the underground garage.

He's suffering too. And I don't know why.

CHAPTER THIRTEEN

I ENTER THE BATHROOM, walk straight up to the cold tiled wall and press my head against it. I feel sick. I love her. I know I do. There's no denying it now. I don't want to wake up another morning without her here in my bed—*our* bed.

So much rides on the truth coming out and I'm scared. I haven't been fucking scared in years. I haven't felt the pain of loss in a decade, and I have no idea how I'll come out of this in one piece if she rejects me.

I take a breath and push away from the tiles. Standing here isn't going to help.

I clean up and pull on my bottoms. I take one last check in the mirror and then, happy that I don't look like the fucked-up idiot I feel, I return to her.

She's like a blushing bride, sitting up in bed after a night tangled in the sheets with her man, eagerly scoffing a piece of toast. And there goes my nausea again. Over a potential future that I want so badly and fear I can't have. The kind of future I haven't wanted since Jess upped and left.

'This is so good.'

She has her mouth full as she says it and I feel a tickle dance over the fear. My laugh is giddy and light and everything I need in that moment.

'I'm glad Her Ladyship approves enough to forget her finishing school manners.'

'I didn't attend a finishing school. How old-fashioned do you think I am?' Her cheeks flush deeper, her eyes glisten bright as she places a hand over her mouth. 'But, yes, she does approve.'

I walk to the bed and climb in beside her, taking a coffee mug off the tray still on her lap. I can't face eating. I'm scared the nausea will make a return pretty swiftly.

'You ready to talk about what happened yesterday?' I ask, lying back against the headboard and raising the mug so I can breathe in the familiar aroma, using it to gain a sense of calm.

She chews her food slowly, raking a hand through her hair as her eyes lose their spark. I wish I'd waited until after breakfast, but if I have my way I'll be taking her home to pack a bag and then getting the hell out of the city.

'My brother…my stepmother—' She swallows like it pains her to do so, her tears instant and crippling. 'They want me to convince Granny she would be better off in a hospice under twenty-four-hour care.' She shakes her head and starts to tremble.

Oh, God.

I take the tray from her lap, slide it out of the way and pull her into me. She comes easily, her head tucking beneath my chin, the tears, the sobs, racking her body as she lets go.

I rock her and hush her softly, murmuring words of encouragement—*It'll be okay... It'll be okay*— but will it, when all is said and done?

The fraud-filled boulder swells large in my chest, suffocating, heavy. I close my eyes and force myself to breathe through it.

'I don't want to do it—it's not fair, and it's not right,' she rambles through her tears. 'They just want life to continue like nothing's wrong... They don't care that being at home is a comfort to her...that it's important... They only care what effect it has on their plans, on their stupid summer soirée.'

'You don't need to do anything you don't want to,' I whisper into her hair, my lips brushing over its softness. 'You don't.'

'But I'm just tired of it—tired of trying to act like everything's okay, like I can cope, when it isn't and I can't.' She sniffs and looks up at me, wiping her nose, her eyes, with the back of her hand. 'I *never* fight with her.'

'With who?'

'My stepmother. It's not worth it. But last night I got so angry I walked out on them—created a scene, according to her.'

'I'm sure you didn't create a scene.' Wet strands of hair cling to her blazing cheeks and I brush them back as I try to reassure her. 'And even if you did, what does it matter? You have every right to be upset.'

She folds herself back into me.

'Granny wouldn't approve. Laurens don't cause a scene. Laurens need to be above reproach. Laurens don't show their feelings. Laurens sport a stiff upper lip at all times.'

It comes out in a controlled flurry as she channels her grandmother, letting rip the pressure she's permanently under. I can feel her physically cracking under the words and I'm taken over by a need to protect her, to take her away, to give her a break even for a few days.

'It's not healthy to bottle everything up.'

'But I *have* to. I have to keep up appearances. I'm not going to let her down—not while she's still here.'

'Then let me take you away—give you time to recover, regain your strength.'

She's looking up at me, wide-eyed, shaking her head.

'I can't go away—not with her so sick.'

'A few days won't hurt.'

'But what if my brother has her kicked out while I'm gone?'

'He won't.'

'You can't know that.'

I can, because I'll have people watching him. But I can hardly tell her that.

'Does she have a close friend? Someone you trust who could come and stay for a couple of days?'

'There's Grace… She's been visiting quite a bit; she'd come if I asked her.'

'There you go.'

'But you said we have to keep under the radar—your job, my…my notoriety…'

'You don't need to worry about that. The place I have in mind is quiet, peaceful. We'll hardly see a soul.'

She sighs softly and puts her arms around me, cuddling in. 'It sounds perfect.'

'It is.'

Her head-shake is softer now. 'But it doesn't feel right, leaving when she's so ill…'

'I'm talking a few days at most—a chance to recharge. You owe it to yourself and you owe it to your grandmother to look after your health too.'

She goes quiet and I wonder if I've lost her, if the idea is too much. I hold my breath as I wait.

Eventually she nods and gives me the lightest squeeze. 'Okay.'

Okay. I mentally repeat that as I relax and press a kiss to her head, staying there as I breathe her in and think.

The first part of my plan is in motion. I hope the rest can come my way as easily.

Although, I don't need easy—I just need her.

If she'll still have you when the truth is out…

'Where are we going?'

I packed as he instructed—warm clothing, enough for a couple of nights away—but I haven't actually asked until now. I think part of me is stunned that I'm actually doing it. I'm not impulsive. I don't just pack up on a whim. But one look at Granny's face when I told her I'd been invited away and I knew it was the right thing.

She actually smiled and squeezed my hand, said it was a lovely idea and told me that she and Grace were looking forward to the peace and quiet. Ever a Lauren, ever controlled, ever in charge.

I even saw Philip—albeit briefly. But it was long enough for me to make my thoughts clear once more on his attempt to move Granny elsewhere.

When I told him I'd be gone for a couple of days, he smiled. I don't want to think about what that smile meant, but I have assurances from Grace that she'll tell me if anything untoward happens in my absence, and I don't think Philip would dare—not if he wants to avoid the fuss I'd kick up on my return.

I shake off the negative direction of my thoughts and look at Ash in the driver's seat. He still hasn't answered my question.

'Come on—where are we going?'

'It's a surprise.' He smiles at me as he says it and then looks back to the road. 'You should lie back, chill… Although, don't get too comfy—we'll be getting out soon.'

'You have *met* me, right? I don't "chill".'

His smile becomes a grin. 'It's time you learned.'

I harrumph and look out of the passenger window at the rain, which won't stop falling and is making the afternoon feel much later than it is.

'I'm beginning to wish I'd said we could go away for longer—then you'd have had us in the Bahamas, or anywhere but here. It's so grey and miserable…'

'It won't feel as bad when we're up in the air.'

'When we're *what*?' I turn to him. 'What do you mean?'

His grin is still there, riding strong. 'You'll see.'

Less than an hour later, we're standing on a private airfield with a small aircraft before us and no pilot.

'Ash, what's going on?'

'You ready for some fun?'

'Fun? In that?' I point a shaky finger at the thing, which looks more like a large child's toy.

'Don't tell me you're afraid of flying.'

I spit out the rain that's gathered over my lips and pull my hood further forward, tugging my coat tighter around my neck. Our bags have already been taken on board and I know it's just me he's waiting for.

But seriously...?

'No, not afraid of flying. But that... In *this*.' I fling a hand around me at the weather.

'It's quicker this way—no traffic.' He holds out a hand to me. 'Come on. We're getting soaked.'

I slip my hand in his, but I don't move.

He gives me a little tug. 'Trust me.'

I take in the zippy-looking aircraft, bright shiny red, and I'm still convinced it's more toy than vehicle, but I trust him—I really do. I give the ground one last longing look and then climb into the cockpit, looking for a way into the back.

'Sit down,' he calls up.

'Here?' I say, pointing to the two seats that look far too pilot-worthy for me.

'Yes.'

I can tell he's enjoying this; his eyes have the playful glint to them that normally precedes a cheeky make-out session, not a flight. I sit my arse down as he closes the door. My gaze sweeps over the multitude of instruments…screens, buttons, joysticks, levers…

Oh, crap.

I'm so distracted I don't realise I've lost sight of him outside, but then he's back, and the door is opening on the other side as he climbs in right alongside me.

My eyes widen. *'You're* flying it?'

He shakes his head, eyes still dancing. 'My ego really isn't safe around you, is it?'

I can only smile as butterflies kick up in my belly. I'm nervous—I can't deny it. But as he slips into pilot mode and starts chatting to someone I can only assume is air traffic control while navigating his phone and what looks to be a flight plan, I admit to becoming awestruck.

He catches me staring and gives me a lopsided grin as he speaks into the headset. He passes me a similar contraption to wear. Then he helps to strap me in, his hands brushing over me, and all the time there's a look of concentration on his face that I find as sexy as his come-to-bed look.

If not for the fact that he's talking, I'd pounce—and, judging by the flash in his blue eyes as he settles back into his seat, he knows it too.

I force myself to behave and let him get on with

piloting, but I have so many questions. Like, how he learned to fly, *why* he learned, whose plane is this…? But they can wait—at least until we're airborne.

And even then I'm mesmerised. As we hit what he tells me is cruising altitude, I can't take my eyes away from him—the way he navigates the various controls, watches the screens, the gobbledygook he speaks into the headset. He's so confident and in control.

Who'd have thought flying could be a form of foreplay?

I've never understood the fascination with a man in a pilot's uniform before, but now I'll be right up there with heart eyes.

'Flying is in the Livingston blood.'

His voice pipes up through my headset and subconsciously I touch my fingers to the ear pad, my cheeks flushing at my inner ramblings.

'My father learned for fun, but his father was a pilot in the RAF, and *his* father before that. There's nothing quite like taking to the skies and getting out of the rat run below.'

I smile as I imagine him as a child watching his father in awe, just as I'm watching him now.

'You want to try?'

He eyes the joystick—if that's even what it's called—and I laugh, shaking my head. 'I'm happy to watch.'

'Maybe some other time?' he asks, hopeful, and my body warms.

My smile is all the answer he needs.

CHAPTER FOURTEEN

I PULL THE plane into the Livingstons' private hangar, my body abuzz.

I *knew* she'd love it. The second the Scottish Highlands had come into view, her attention had turned to the landscape, pleasure written across her face.

'That was pretty special,' she raves as I cut the engine, her eyes still bright, her cheeks warm and rosy. She already looks more relaxed, happy.

'I'm glad you enjoyed it.'

I unfasten my harness and lean across to help her do the same. Our hands collide and her eyes shine into mine as she wets her lips. I don't know whether it's an intentional move to pull me in but I'm there, kissing her. My lips are soft upon hers, nothing urgent or desperate. We have time together now. No risk of the outside world looking in, no interfering. Just us.

Her mouth parts willingly, her excited little whimper encouraging me on. I smooth a hand through her hair, my thumb across her cheek, and keep on kissing her. Soft, tender, loving… Its effect is all the more powerful below my waist, around my heart. I don't want to pull back, and I don't want to—

Rat-a-tat-tat.

She freezes. The sound comes from the glass behind me.

So much for no interfering, no outsiders…

But you chose this place—and he's no outsider.

I let out a breath and press my forehead to hers.

'Who's that?' she whispers like he'll overhear.

I shake my head and smile. 'The guy who gave me the flying bug.'

Her lips part…her eyes widen. 'You brought me to meet your *father*?'

Yeah, I guess I did.

Not that I thought about the magnitude of that at the time—only that it was the right place for her. *She's* thinking about it, though; I can see it in her face.

'Is that okay?'

'Yes—no. Yes.' She smooths out her jeans, her hair, her cheeks. 'You could've warned me.'

I grin, understanding her hesitation and adoring her all the more for it. 'You look perfect.'

She does. My father is going to love her. My mother would have too.

My head spins with the realisation, my heart pulses, too big for my chest. Fear is quick on its tail. If I have to give her up will I have to endure what my father did when he lost Mum? Is it the same kind of grief?

'I don't believe you…not when you're looking at

me like that.' She presses herself back in her seat like she's trying to hide from my father, who's rapping on the glass again. 'What's wrong?' she asks.

'Nothing at all.' I snap myself out of it, snatching a quick kiss to prevent any further protestations from her. 'But we'd best open up before he tries to clamber in and meet you himself; this is going to be fairly novel for him.'

'Novel?' she says as I lift her door handle and push it open.

'You'll see.' I turn to open my own door and spy Dad's grinning face through the glass.

Here goes...

The door lifts up. 'It's about time, you kids.'

Kids? Really?

'Hey, Pop.'

I clamber down and give him a hug, pounding his back as he does mine and whispering, 'Behave, okay?'

His eyes flash mischievously. 'Always.'

'Er...gentlemen?' Coco's voice is faint as she leans through the cockpit. 'Fancy giving a lady a hand?'

I start to move, but Dad's like lightning as he heads around the plane. 'I've got this, son.'

I laugh. 'Never seen you move so fast!'

He shoots me a look and I hear Coco's tantalising giggle.

Yes, he's going to love her, all right.

I climb back into the plane to get the luggage as I hear Dad introduce himself.

'Peter Livingston—at your service.'

She laughs a little more. 'Coco Lauren. It's a plea-sure to meet you.'

She climbs down, with his aid, and I meet them a few moments later, plane locked up and bags in hand. He's telling her about the other plane in the hangar—his Cessna, the one I learned to fly in.

'She's old, but perfectly adequate, and she'll give that flash Cirrus a flight for its money.' He jerks his thumb at my Cirrus and laughs. 'It's all fur coat and no knickers, that one.'

'Dad!'

Coco is in giggles, and I swear I'm blushing. *Bloody hell.*

'You can't say that.'

'You can't say anything these days… It's a won-der we're not all mute!'

She actually snorts now, and I'm about to bollock him and demand he shut it entirely, but my eyes land on her and I'm rooted. She's glowing. Radiant. Ev-erything I wanted her to be by taking her away, and we've only been here five minutes.

Dad catches my eye and smiles. There's so much to read in his expression. Approval is high up there and it swells within me too, to the point that I have to clear my throat to speak.

'Can we at least get to the house before you scare her off for good?'

His smile simply grows. 'Sure can—the Land Rover's just outside. Not afraid of dogs are you, Ms Lauren?'

'Coco, please—and, no, I love dogs.'

'They're going to love you.'

Dad moves off. Coco gives me a glowing smile and follows in his footsteps, and I'm still rooted, staring after them. It feels so *right*, having her here. All I need now is my brother, Jake, to turn up and the family circle will be complete.

The thought brings with it such warmth, such contentment. I know what it is because I've felt it before. There was the time before we lost Mum, and there was the time with Jess, but this is different— more profound, more real. And if it's this strong, then surely she feels it too? Surely it can survive the truth?

Surely *we* can survive it?

My God, his father looks like him...or rather Ash looks like his father.

And they're cracking me up. They're like a double act, with Ash the unwilling participant, and it's priceless.

Peter is whizzing us cross-country in his Land Rover, which looks older than me and smells fresh of wet Border collie. And he's using the trip to point out several of Ash's firsts. That's where he did his first stand-up wee; that's where he learned to ride a bike; that's where he face-planted in a cowpat... It's a brilliant tour, steeped in Livingston history. And made all the more entertaining by the colour creeping so high in Ash's cheeks that he looks sunburned.

I smile at him, sitting there in the front passenger

seat, while I grip the grab handle for dear life and
take a face licking from Dotty, the youngest and most
boisterous of three collies.

'You okay back there with them?' Ash asks, stroking the head of Dolly, the eldest collie, deemed sensible enough to sit upfront.

'Absolutely.'

My jeans have taken a beating, muddy paw prints
galore, but my raincoat has protected my baby pink
cashmere jumper from the worst. Not that I'd care
if it hadn't. This is fun. *Real* fun. Even with his father's daredevil driving.

'How far is the house?' I ask, feeling in part to
blame for Ash's heightened colour and thinking it
might spare him any further embarrassing commen-
tary if we discuss something else.

I look at those endearing streaks in his cheeks and
my stomach flips, failing to land right when we're
propelled over a mini swell in the rugged terrain.

'Just over the crest of this hill,' his father pipes
up.

I lean forward to gaze through the windscreen
at the sharp incline ahead and laugh. 'You call this
a *hill*?'

Both men grin as they look at one another.

Clearly what constitutes a hill in Scotland is not
the same as for London. But, seriously, it's essentially a mountain—and naturally beautiful with it.
All green and rocky crags, with the occasional track
carved out.

'Have you been to the Highlands before?' his father asks.

'No.' It's a squeak, and my grip is tightening even more as we hit a particularly bumpy patch. I fear being catapulted to the other side of the Land Rover, regardless of the seat harness.

'Ah, then you're in for a treat. You should come back in the summer, when the heather is in bloom and it's a blanket of purple out there.'

'She's not even stayed once yet, Pop.'

Ash's eyes flit to me, and the hope in his eyes chimes with my own.

'I can imagine I'd like that a lot.'

'My mother was from up here, and although she married an Englishman, her heart never left,' his father says, his voice unaffected by the rattling around us, although my insides feel like they're about to clamber up and out of my body. 'She would bring us here holidaying when I was a boy, and I bought this place not long before Ash was born. It was a bargain back then.'

We reach the crest as he says it, the car finally hitting an actual road and going quiet, smooth. I relax—only to have my lips part in surprise at the enchanting view ahead.

'It was our country retreat until I'd had enough of the city life altogether. Then it became my home.'

'But is it…? Is it meant to look like a castle?' My words are almost a whisper, as if speaking any louder will break the spell of what I can see.

'I think the wealthy trader who built it in the nineteenth century fancied himself a bit royal...' His father gives a hearty chuckle. 'And, considering the moat he fashioned around it, I'd say he was none too popular either.'

He turns to look at me briefly.

'Just don't expect much on the inside, though. It's only me and the dogs now, so I stick to the west wing. Easier to keep clean that way.'

'West wing—got it.'

Ash raises his brow at me. 'He's not kidding either, the place needs a lot of work in parts, so don't expect anything too grand.'

I nod, beaming. Truth is I'm already in love with the place.

Even as we get closer and I can make out the crumbling walls, the odd piece of scaffolding and the greenery growing where windows should be, it's still majestic. Still gorgeous in its own unique way— from the little stone bridge that crosses the water to the imposing structure itself, with its four pointed fairy-tale turrets.

'I love it.'

Ash looks at me as I say it and smiles. I'm so grateful to him for doing this. For realising I need this. I hold his gaze, spilling my all into that one look as the car slows to pass over the bridge, and the moment shatters in the bouncing excitement of my four-legged companions, who are now clambering up. Dotty chins me in the process. I laugh as I tickle her, and we look out of the window together.

The colours are beautiful. The sun is starting to set, and the water is rippling with the golden hues of the sky and the rolling hillsides.

I can almost imagine London away altogether. Is that why his father came here?

I think back to what Ash told me about his family past, the reason for his father's early retirement, and I have my answer.

His father pulls the car up and cuts the engine. 'Home sweet home.'

We all pile out and the dogs scurry off to investigate. 'Mary has made up your usual room, son. Do you want to take Coco on up and then come find me when you're done?'

'Sure, Pop.'

'Thank you,' I say.

His father beams at me and then walks off in the same direction as the dogs.

I turn to Ash. *Mary?* I mouth.

He smiles. 'Housekeeper—of sorts. She lives in the neighbouring village and comes to sort Dad out every once in a while. Her husband farms the land here.'

'It's good he has some company.'

'I think he's quite happy in his own, truth be told.'

We both watch him playing with the dogs and I wonder if we're thinking the same: Does he ever get lonely?

'Come on,' Ash pipes up. 'Let's get in before we freeze.'

I'm surprised to find tears pricking once more,

and I blink them back before he can catch them. I don't want him doubting his decision to bring me here. Not when I'm so happy to be here with him in his family home.

'Lead the way.'

CHAPTER FIFTEEN

WE ENTER THE house through the kitchen and I show Coco the lived-in areas of the ground floor: the living room, the dining room, the library—Dad's favourite room.

As we enter the entrance hall, her gasp is audible. 'This isn't grand?'

She raises her brow at me and twirls on the spot, captivated by the high-ceilinged room, with its imperial staircase, ornate features and parquet floor. But I'm one hundred percent hooked on her and her obvious pleasure.

'I feel decidedly underdressed.'

She laughs as she says it, but my head is already undressing her, wrapped up in her free and easy presence. 'That can be arranged.'

She stills and looks at me, and the very second our eyes collide, I know she's wanting the same.

'But your father...?'

'Is busy.'

I drop the bags to my feet and close the distance between us, pulling her in for a kiss that's all the deeper for the interrupted one in the cockpit. She curves into me, her soft sigh telling me she's as keen as I am.

'You ready to see my bedroom?'

She lifts her lashes, her cheeks colouring. 'It feels kind of weird. I've never stayed under the same roof as my... Well, you know... A boyfriend's parent.'

She blushes further as she puts a label to me— hell, my whole insides are blushing over it, loving it and wanting more.

'I promise you, this house is big enough that he won't hear a peep—unless, of course, I make you scream.'

She bites into her lip as she eyes me. 'Now, there's a thought.'

Heat surges south and I turn away to grab the bags before I drop her to the parquet and say to hell with any potential audience.

'This way...'

She starts after me and then stops. 'Wait—my shoes...'

'Keep them on. This place can get chilly. If it makes you feel better, you can leave them outside the bedroom; it'll save me the job of taking them off you when we get there.'

She laughs. 'Thank you, Ash.'

I frown at her. 'For what?'

'For bringing me here. It truly is perfect.'

Her voice is so soft, her eyes are the same, and there's so much emotion clouding her gaze. I curse the fact that my hands are full of baggage instead of her.

'You're welcome.'

She does take her shoes off outside the door, and I do the same, gesturing for her to go in.

She turns the knob on the door and pushes it open.

'The light pull is just to your left.'

She pulls on it and her face lights up with the glow from a central chandelier. 'Wow!'

'You like it?'

'What's not to like?'

She pads in, tracing her fingers over the antique furnishings, the window seat with its full-height drapes and then the four-poster bed.

She curls her fingers around a bottom post and smiles at me, all coy. 'This could be fun.'

The heat pulses in my groin.

Fuck.

I release the bags and kick the door closed. She straightens as I stride towards her, her smile growing, and then my arms are around her and I keep moving, walking her to the bed, onto her back, my mouth on hers, hard, urgent. My saving grace is that she's right with me, her mouth just as hungry, her hands just as fierce.

There are too many layers—our coats, our sweaters—but they're coming off. Our hands are ripping them away from each other. Our jeans are next, and our underwear, and then she shivers.

'Are you cold?' I manage to ask.

'No.' She shakes her head, her mouth finding mine and kissing away any doubt. 'I want you.'

She wraps her legs around me. I feel my cock

probing at her hot, slick warmth and I pull back, pinning my hands on either side of her head as I stare down into pools of green, dilated with desire.

She has her hands on my neck, her fingers brushing over the hairs at my nape. She wets her lips, suddenly hesitant. 'What is it?' she asks.

'You,' I say.

A delightful little crease forms between her brows.

'I'm losing myself in *you*.'

Her lashes flutter, her eyes glisten. 'I feel the same.'

I hope so.

I feel the alien prick of tears and kiss her until the sensation passes, until the burn subsides.

'Now, Ash, please.' She moves against me, pulling herself close, submerging the head of my cock in her alluring, tight heat.

'Look at me, baby.'

I need her with me—need her to see everything she has come to mean as I sink inside her.

She opens her eyes, stares up at me.

'Thank you for letting me take you away.' Slowly I enter her, savouring the feel of her surrounding me, the way her skin colours, her pleasure radiating out. 'Thank you for letting me give you this.'

She shakes her head, hooking her hands around my neck. 'I'm the one thanking you.'

She stays with me, her eyes on mine, even as I fill her completely and her head threatens to rock back. She stays locked on my gaze, clenching me tightly.

The pulsing heat is calling to me, and my eyes are trying to close as pleasure overtakes my body, my mind. I force them open. I need this. The connection. The security of it. I need it to get through what is to come. To have faith that it will all come good.

'Tell me you're mine,' I urge.

She nods her head, her eyes flashing with sincerity.

'*Tell me*. I need the words…'

'I'm yours, Ash.'

My chest swells with the bittersweet happiness of knowing what I have now and what I risk losing. I squeeze my eyes shut against the pang, scared that she will see, and when I open them again she's there…

'*Always*, Ash.'

Always. Always. *Always*.

I focus on that, rocking into her with every echo, claiming her as mine, wishing away all else. I drop to kiss her and together we rock, kiss, devour, our eyes locked together, sharing it all.

And when we come it's in harmony. Everything's perfect, exactly how it should be.

No truth can take this away. It can't…

I'm shaking. The truth of my words is tearing through me as my limbs soften around him and the waves of pleasure fade.

I love him.

I *love* Ash.

It doesn't matter that I've only known him weeks,

that we agreed there could be no future. I have fallen for him.

And if what I read in his face, in his demands, is true, he loves me too.

I grip him tighter to me. Uncertainty is creeping in. It was he who said there could be no future. He who put his job before us. Will he still?

His head lifts, and his eyes scan my face as he strokes back my hair.

'I have a few things to do. Why don't you freshen up and meet me downstairs in a bit?'

I offer him a small smile, my brain a confused rambling. *Just tell him. No, let him tell you first. Don't make a fool of yourself. You're getting high on his kindness.*

And then he's pressing himself up and off me, and heading to what I assume is the bathroom, and I'm no closer to working out where to begin this conversation because I don't want to lose what we have now.

But what if he can't give me more?

I hope a shower will clear my head, make me think straight, but I'm just as confused as I make my way downstairs an hour later. I follow the sounds of movement and the delicious scent of spices, but when I get to the kitchen it's only his father I see.

'Ah, Coco—excellent timing.' He looks up from the pan he's stirring, an apron tied around his waist, his cheeks flushed from the billowing steam.

'How so?'

I grin. I like him—a lot. I can't for the life of me

imagine him in a boardroom, though; he seems far too chilled and exuberant.

'I could do with a little helper. Ash has had to disappear to make some calls, but he shouldn't be too long. I hope you like curry.'

I breathe in the spicy aroma and nod. 'Smells delicious!'

'Good. Good…' He pops on a pan lid and stirs another two pans simultaneously. 'Ever made naan bread before?'

I laugh as I edge closer and see what he has cooking. 'No, I've never even baked—unless you count the cooking I did at school…and let's just say my home economics teacher thought I was beyond help.'

'Nonsense. Everyone can bake so long as they have the right teacher.'

It's Ash. He's back.

I turn to him. My smile is instantaneous and giddy. I'm so happy to see him again it's ridiculous. He comes straight to me and wraps his arms around my waist, pressing a kiss to my forehead. I hear the dogs patter in behind him.

'Enough of that, son. Those naans aren't going to roll themselves. Dotty—down!'

He pushes the young collie back as Ash pats my behind with a grin and slips his hand in mine to lead me to a counter dusted with flour.

'*You* know how to do this?' I say.

He positions me in front of him, his warmth radiating down my back as he takes up the dough and starts to break it into smaller balls.

'What have I said to you about my ego?'

His father chuckles and I follow suit, turning my head to look up at him.

'I'm just in awe of your skills.'

'Why do I feel like you're teasing me?'

'I'm one hundred percent serious,' I reply softly, holding his eye for a beat before taking up one of the small balls he's created. 'Right, show me the way.'

We work together, rolling out the naans and cooking them under the grill while his father tends to the bubbling pans and the dogs curl up together in the corner, having decided spice is not their thing.

It's all so easy, so relaxing, and the time just flies by. *This* is what being in a family is like. A normal family. No pretence, no walls—just existing. It's how my mother would have had it—how my father would have been had she survived.

The thought makes me sad and happy in one. Sad for losing it…happy to have found it here.

After dinner, once we've cleaned the pans and taken our wine into the library, I excuse myself to pop to the bedroom and check my phone. I want to check on Granny. There have been no calls or texts and, taking that as a good sign, I head back downstairs.

As I approach the study I can hear Ash talking, and my stride slows of its own accord.

'After Jess I just didn't want to go there—didn't want to risk going through it again.'

'Your mother never liked that girl… She saw right

through her from day one. I only wish you'd had the same insight.'

'Mum was always a good judge of character.'

'Well, I wouldn't go that far. Clive had her as fooled as the rest of us. *She* was the one who suggested he be your godfather.'

'Yeah, well...lucky for us we saw through his act.'

'*You* saw through it, you mean.'

The room falls silent and I can hear the crackling of the fire. I can't make my legs work. *Who's Jess?* I know all about Clive, but Jess... He's never told me about her.

'She reminds me of Jess.'

My heart skips a beat at his father's remark. *What?*

'She's *nothing* like her.' Ash is so vehement as he says it.

'No, no—not when you get to *know* her. But her appearance...the air she has about her.'

Ash blows out a breath so forceful I can make it out from this distance. 'Yeah, well...she's not.'

'Lucky for you, hey?' His father is all jovial now. 'Seems you picked right this time. She's lovely, Ash, truly lovely.'

'I know.'

'So why so serious, then? You look like you have the weight of the world on your shoulders when you should be walking on air.'

'It's not that simple.'

'Of course it is. Love can be that simple if you just let it in.'

'Like I did with Jess?' Ash says, and his cynicism,

the realisation that he once loved this girl, whoever she was, strikes through the very heart of me.

I press back against the wall, my hand over my chest as I try to ease the chaos beneath. I almost want to walk the other way, to forget what I've heard. It's made me realise how much I don't know about him. How much I *do* want to know and understand. Is this the pain I glimpsed? Is his heart still broken over *her*?

'*She* wasn't worthy of your love, but…'

I close my ears off and cough as I head to join them, knowing that to listen to any more isn't right. If I want answers, Ash can give them to me.

'Ah, Coco—again your timing is impeccable.' His father rises out of his chair before the fire; Ash does the same. 'I'm about to call it a night.'

'Don't leave on my account.' I feel like he's leaving because of me, and considering he rarely has company, I don't want that.

'I've had a busy day chauffeuring and catering— amazing how it can take its toll.' He grins at us both and looks like he'll say more, but then he simply shrugs and whistles to the dogs, who immediately spring to attention and trot to his feet. 'I'll see you both in the morning.'

'Night, Pop.'

'Goodnight, Peter.'

'You can call me Pop too, if you like.'

He gives me a wink and off he goes, leaving me blushing in his wake.

'He means it affectionately.'

Ash looks awkward, uncomfortable. Has he guessed I was eavesdropping, or is he still reeling from the conversation with his father?

'I know.'

I wait for the door to close before taking up my wine glass and heading over to the chair his father had been sitting in. Ash tops up his own glass and sits opposite me, but his attention is on the fire. He's distant. Thoughtful.

'Who's Jess?' I ask.

His eyes snap to me. 'You heard?'

'Sorry.' I grimace. I don't want him to think it was intentional. 'I couldn't help overhearing the tail end of your conversation, but it kind of feels like something I should know.'

'I don't talk about her at all if I can help it.'

'But you can tell me anything—you know that, right?'

He studies me, unblinking, long and hard.

'Ash?' I press softly.

He comes alive, the air shuddering from his lungs as he leans his elbows on his knees, his eyes falling to the glass he's cupping in his hands.

My gut twists. Did he love this Jess *that* much? He looks so broken…torn apart. Maybe I don't want to hear this after all. Maybe—

'We met at school. She was the popular girl every guy wanted and every girl wanted to befriend.' He gives a harsh laugh I don't recognise. 'I guess you could call me the male equivalent… I was smitten, so was she, and we were together right through school, university… I thought that was it—she was the one.'

I sip my wine, hoping it will ease the sickness inside, but instead it burns a path all the way through me. 'The one?'

His eyes flick to me. 'I was coming to the end of my gap year and she'd been doing a placement in Paris. She flew home and I surprised her in Arrivals with a diamond ring.'

'You proposed?'

He nods his head, his eyes on his drink. 'She said yes. It was sorted. We agreed we'd complete our studies and then have a grand wedding in the summer, start our lives in earnest.'

'What happened?'

'Clive happened.'

I frown at him, not putting two and two together and fearing it's because my heart is breaking with every word he says.

'The second my family's money left the equation, she walked.'

I shake my head. 'I don't believe that. No one would be that shallow.'

He scoffs. 'You'd think that, wouldn't you? Hell, I thought so too—until I ended up falling foul of it.'

'But that's *sick*.'

He shrugs. 'It wasn't just the money—it was the scandal too. She didn't want to be tarnished by it.'

'But you cleared your father's name, proved he was innocent, recouped some of the money.'

'Oh, yeah, I did all that.' He leans back in his

seat now, slumped, almost defeated. 'And she came back, all right—told me she'd made a mistake, that she loved me, begged me to understand.'

He rubs his fingers over his jaw, his eyes lost in the memories, and then I remember the night we first met—the night he told me I wasn't his type.

'That's why you were so harsh when I first met you?'

He frowns in confusion.

'When you said I wasn't your type?' I explain, softening my words with the hint of a smile. It's about all I can muster when my heart is losing control in my chest.

He cocks his head, his eyes sweeping over me. 'You reminded me of her, yes.'

'I'm sorry for that.'

'Don't be sorry.'

He places his drink down on a small side table and moves to kneel before me, his eyes soft as they gaze up at mine.

'It turns out I do have a type; *you* are my type, *she* was my type, but that's superficial…' He cups my jaw and strokes my skin. 'You see, underneath, you're nothing alike. And what I feel for you… It's more. It's real. I…' My breath hitches and he shakes his head. 'I'm not very good at this.'

I bow my head towards him, dizzy on the meaning of his words, the promise of him feeling more, the promise of his potential love…

'On the contrary,' I say, brushing his lips with my own. 'I think you're better than you know.'

And then I'm kissing him with every ounce of the love I feel inside. Because he loves me, and I love him, and we have all the time in the world to tell each other how we feel, to carve out a path together. To find a way to make our lives converge. Because I'm not turning my back on this. Not now that I have it.

CHAPTER SIXTEEN

I CAN'T SLEEP. Coco has her head on my chest, snoring softly, but I'm staring into the darkness plagued with *what ifs*.

I almost told her everything. When we were sitting before the fire and I was so lost in my thoughts, thinking of ways to explain that wouldn't impact the plan I have underway back in London.

But then she asked about Jess—a topic I could easily cover now that my past no longer has any hold over me. Thanks to her. Thanks to Coco and my love for her, I realise that what Jess and I had was never love.

But you can tell me anything—you know that, right?

Her words haunt me. The one thing I really wanted to confess I couldn't—not yet.

Soon though—very soon.

Philip Lauren will be waking up to a special delivery package today, and I expect a phone call soon after. A barrage of abuse. And then his rational side will have to win out. Or so I hope.

Then I can make real time for this—for her.

I press my lips to her head, letting my breathing ease and hoping for sleep to come and take away the *what ifs*.

I wake to the incessant buzzing of my mobile phone and an empty bed. Ash isn't far, though. I can hear the shower running in the en suite bathroom and I smile, my mind already visualising him naked and all soaped up.

I reach for my phone on the bedside table. I should hurry and join him—the sliver of light coming through the curtains tells me I've overslept as it is. But then, what's the rush? The day is ours and it feels so good.

My phone stops ringing as I pick it up and I have to activate it again to see the notifications.

Three missed calls: Grace, Philip, Grace.

Granny.

I sit bolt upright as the world around me spins. Something's happened. Something bad. My hand soars to my throat as I try to breathe through the panic.

Calm down. You don't know for sure. There could be any number of reasons why they would need to ring...

No, there's only one.

With fuzzy fingers that are far too slow to do what I want, I call Grace back.

Pick up, pick up, pick up.

It goes straight to voicemail, just as the ping of

a message arriving comes through. It's a voicemail from Grace.

'Coco, darling, it's Grace. Don't panic, but your grandmother has been taken into hospital with suspected pneumonia. She's in the ICU. I don't... I'm not... I think you should come as soon you as you are able. Philip will send you the details. Take care.'

My stomach heaves... My skin prickles from top to toe. Here I am, playing happy holidays with Ash, worrying over the state of my love life, when Granny's fighting for her life. It feels like some twisted punishment for letting go, for being selfish enough to think of myself. How could I have thought leaving was okay?

I throw back the quilt. I need to get home—now. I need to tell Ash.

I don't even dress. I head straight for the bathroom, opening the door.

Ash's dawning smile dies the second he sees me. 'Coco...?'

I can't find my voice; I'm trembling all over. I grip my upper arms and start to rub them, shaking my head.

'Coco?'

He slams off the shower and walks towards me.

'It's Granny.' I swallow as I look up at him. 'She's been rushed into hospital.'

He inhales softly and reaches for his robe from the back of the door, wrapping it around me and pulling me in close. 'Do you know what's happened?'

My teeth rattle. 'Suspected pneumonia.'

'Okay.' He's so calm, so composed, and already I take comfort. 'We'll get dressed and go. Do you think you can get your stuff together while I let Dad know?'

I nod, so grateful that I don't even have to ask to leave. He just *gets* it.

He turns away to grab a towel. 'Do you know where she is?'

I shake my head. 'Grace says Philip is going to send me the details.'

'Okay.' He wraps the towel around his waist and comes back to me, his hands firm and reassuring on my arms. 'Go and message Philip, then get ready.'

I nod up at him and move away to do as he instructs, but my mind is racing. Guilt, fear, sadness... What will I find when I get back to London? Just how bad is it? ICU means bad.

When Ash returns to find me staring unseeing into my bag, he does it all for me. His calm and controlled manner is everything I need, and as he puts his arm around me to draw me towards the door I feel his strength, his warmth, seep into my body. I know that with him by my side I can face this.

I can face anything life throws at me so long as we're together.

I'm so focused on Coco and her pain that nothing else matters as I drive to the hospital. She's sported a haunted look ever since she came to me in the bathroom, and I've never felt so powerless in all my life. Nothing can take away her pain; I can only be with her and get her to her grandmother's side as quickly as possible.

But her silence—it's killing me. She's barely said a word between saying goodbye to Dad, the plane ride and now the car journey once more.

The hospital is only minutes away now. I'm worried that she feels guilty at having gone away, and if so, that's down to me.

I mean, *Christ*, if her grandmother dies and Coco's not there, that's on my head—that's worse than everything else put together.

My hand pulses around the wheel and I realise my knuckles are white. I try to ease my grip, not wanting her to see how anxious I am, but as I look at her I see she's fixated on the passing world, her body stock-still, her eyes distant.

I suppress the ragged sigh that runs through me. I feel desperate, pained, anxious, and so full of love for her it's unreal.

'Thank you for doing this,' she suddenly says into the quiet.

Thank you? Christ.

I want to do so much more. I reach over and take her hand in mine. Her fingers are like ice and I don't want to release them. I want to give her my body heat, my comfort. I want to take away her pain.

The car grumbles, demanding a gear change, and I give her a gentle squeeze before taking my hand away.

My mind turns to Philip. I know the package was delivered this morning—what I don't know is whether he'll have opened it. From what I can make out he's been at the hospital since their grandmother was admitted in the early hours, and it's likely he'll still be there now. Which means I run the risk of being seen dropping Coco off, of having our relationship blown.

But it all seems so insignificant now. It doesn't matter that her grandmother's death is expected. When it comes to the cold, hard reality of it, life and love come first.

Will Philip see it that way?

Was my package unnecessary?

I navigate the hospital's one-way system, looking for the drop-off bay, and she turns to me.

'Park up.'

'I'll drop you at the door,' I say softly. 'You can call me, and I'll come and pick you up later.'

Her eyes widen. 'But—' She breaks off, shaking her head as she looks away.

'What is it?'

She doesn't say anything. I reach over and touch her thigh. 'Coco…?'

'I thought…'

She looks back to me, her eyes wavering over my face, trembling with a fresh well of tears.

Shit.

'Can't you come with me…please? I don't want to go in alone. I don't—' She breaks off again and hugs her arms around herself. 'Sorry, I shouldn't ask. Of course you can't—'

'I will.'

The words are tight, my heart tighter. I can't say no to her. Not when she needs me. But Philip will be there…

Fuck Philip. You love her and she needs you.

My jaw pulses and I look to the road, changing direction with carefully controlled force and heading for the car park.

Whatever waits for me on the other side of those doors, I deserve it.

She has to come first.

Always.

But can I warn her?

How do I do that without making this trip all the more devastating?

I look at her, sitting across from me, and her wet smile of gratitude pulls me apart.

'Look, I'm not sure what's going to happen when we get in there,' I try. 'Your brother… He might… Well, he might say some things about me…about us.'

She flings a hand out and squeezes my leg, her head shaking. 'I don't care what Philip has to say. I only care that you're here, by my side.'

Because you don't know.

I shake my head, my fist pulsing around the wheel.

Just tell her.

I pull the car into a parking space and cut the engine, but I'm slow to turn to her, slow to gather my thoughts. 'I'm sorry, Coco. I'm sorry for—'

'I know you are. But you're here and that's all I need; now, let's go.'

Her hand is already on the door handle, her eagerness to get in there clear, and I tell myself it'll be okay. That I'll have all the time I need to make it up to her.

If she lets you anywhere near her again...

Ash is my saviour. He talks to the reception staff, gets the necessary directions to the ICU, and his arm is a constant around me, a welcome hold that gives me heat, strength, courage.

I know the ICU is bad news. And I think in some way that impedes my step, as if seeing her there will confirm my fears. Even though I always knew it would come to this, I thought we had some time. But not now—not while I was away.

'What if she's not conscious?'

I think the words come out, but it's not until Ash speaks that I know they have for sure.

'Let's just wait and see what they say, hey?'

'But what if I don't get to say goodbye? What if she goes and I haven't told her that I love her? What...?'

I can't talk any more as the tears take over and Ash pulls me into him, stopping us altogether. He kisses my head and cups my jaw, encouraging me to look up at him.

'Remember what she always told you? "Stiff upper lip"?' He mimics me and I laugh through my tears as I nod. 'So, come on, get those Lauren genes going and put up a front she'd be proud of. You can tell her all those things whether she's sleeping or not, just as soon as you get through those doors.'

I smile. It's pathetic, but it's there, and he brushes his thumbs over my eyes, sweeping away the tears.

'Good girl. Now, come on…let's—'

'What the actual *fuck*?'

I freeze mid-sniff, sense Ash turn rigid, his face losing all colour as he looks past me to the doors we're about to go through.

I turn to see Philip gawping at us. 'Calm down,' I say. 'This is—'

'I *know* who he is, Coco.' His eyes are pinned on Ash, unmoving. 'What the fuck are *you* doing here?'

I frown, unable to understand his words. What does he mean? How can he possibly *know* who Ash is?

Before I can say anything, Ash is pushing me back behind him, forming a human shield, his hand palm-out to Philip.

'Easy, Lauren—let's talk about this later, not here.'

'Not here?'

Philip's brows rocket, spit forming with his words. I've never seen him this angry.

'I'm a bloody fool. I don't know why I didn't see it sooner. Are you two in cahoots? Is that what this is? You turning the tables on me?'

He's not making any sense. 'Ash?' I say to his back, but he doesn't even turn. *'Ash?'*

Now he looks at me, his eyes hard, impenetrable.

My brother starts to laugh, a wild, hysterical cackle.

'Oh…she doesn't *know*.' He shakes his head. 'My God, have you been playing us both? Getting Lauren money every which way?'

'Ash?'

It's a squeak now. My stomach is turning over. Bile is creeping up my throat and making it hard to breathe, to move, to think.

'Coco…'

He turns in to me, his hands reaching to cup my upper arms, but I'm stumbling back, breaking away. 'What does Philip mean?'

My brother sneers. *'I'll* tell you what it's about—'

'Shut the fuck up, Lauren,' Ash throws at him. 'This is our business.'

Philip steps towards him. 'Funny, that. Last time I checked I was *paying* you to dish the dirt on her.'

His words wash over me like ice and fire all at once. I think of Ash's job. I think of what he's paid to do. Then I think of the Ash who has made love to me, protected me. I can't make them merge and my head starts to spin, my stomach lurches, and I know I'm going to vomit as I double over with a retch.

'Coco…'

Ash bends to me, his hand gentle on my back, but I thrust him away. His touch burns me with betrayal.

'Go! Get out of here! I don't need you! I don't need anyone.'

I push past them both, fighting through the tears to make out the route to the ladies' room.

'Coco, please let me explain—'

He's hot on my heels but I can't… I can't… I can't deal with this now.

I push through the lavatory door, but Ash doesn't give up—he's in there with me.

'Get out,' I say, turning to him and backing up against the sinks.

'Please, Coco, I—'

A toilet flushes and an elderly lady steps out. She takes one look at me and the tall, foreboding man and swipes him with her handbag.

'The lady said get out! We may be living in the modern age, but the ladies' room still means it's for ladies, you brute.'

His eyes look to me pleadingly. He's barely aware of the woman shoving her little hand at him, her bag making repeated contact with his chest.

'*Please*, Coco, you have to hear me out.'

My eyes water with a fresh wave of tears and I can't even see him properly. He's just a blurry outline as he relents to the pressure of my impromptu bodyguard and backs out.

I once saw him in that role. A bodyguard. A good man, exposing bad people for the benefit of the weak and vulnerable.

I had been the bad person in his eyes.

Philip was the good.

I turn to the sink as I hear the door open and then swoosh closed. There's a muttered 'Good riddance. *That* showed him, love. Now, are you okay?'

I shake my head. How can I be? I've avoided getting seriously involved with anyone because money is always the endgame—my family's money and status. I fell for Ash because I thought he was different.

Turns out he wasn't different at all. He was after Lauren money, just as every guy had been before him. And I was fool enough to fall for it.

'If it helps, I think he looked fit to cry himself,' says my rescuer.

My head just keeps shaking, as if I can magic it all away, pretend it isn't true.

Only, it *is* true.

And there's no explanation he can give that will take away the reality that he's being paid by Philip to dish the dirt on me. And, boy, have I given him plenty.

CHAPTER SEVENTEEN

I LOOK UP at the hospital entrance across the road, my hands thrust in my pockets. It's been a week since I was last here, my world in tatters at my feet as I was forced to walk away.

Not a second has gone by without me thinking of her; even my dreams tease me with a mixture of reality and fantasy, happy and sad. But I can't take it any more.

I know her grandmother has recovered enough to be admitted to a ward and is making good progress. She may even get to go back home. I've gleaned all this by getting hold of her friend Grace's number. I haven't used my network of contacts and I certainly haven't gone to Philip. My life as a PI is over, my taste for it ruined by my thoughtless prejudice, epic misjudgement and the devastating consequences it has had on the one person I have come to love so much that every second without her physically hurts.

And that's why I'm here—to tell her. To be honest, to bare my soul if I have to—it's all I have left to give, if she lets me get that far.

I watch the doors—watch the people milling in and out, the smokers who look like they're at death's door, getting another fix, the friends and relatives taking a patient out for a stroll—and then I see her, her blonde bob dancing as she walks, head down, her eyes on her phone, focused and not breaking step.

A quick flick of the eyes up to check the road is clear and then she's crossing it, a few strides down from me. I try to call out and my voice is stuck, nerves closing my throat over. I start after her as a vehicle comes tearing around the corner, speeding for the entrance, just as she steps off the pavement.

'Coco!' I grab her arm and pull her up against me as the vehicle screeches to a halt, doors flying open, people shouting. But it's all tuned out as I lose myself in those green eyes that I've missed so goddamn much. 'You shouldn't walk and text.'

She shrugs her arm out of my hold. 'What the hell are you doing here?'

I swallow, my hand falling helplessly to my side. 'Please…can we talk?'

I know she wants to deny me; I can see it in her narrowed gaze, the hard set of her jaw. But then she turns and starts to make for the car park.

'You've got until I get to my car.'

I let go of a trapped breath and fall into step beside her. 'I meant over coffee…somewhere more private.'

She laughs, harsh and loud. 'What? So you can try to seduce your way into my trust like you did before? Tell me, Ash, how many unsuspecting souls have you seduced to get the information you need?'

I pale under the assault of her words…at how low she thinks I'll sink. 'I've *never* slept with a target before.'

'A *target*?' She repeats it thoughtfully, derisive. 'So that's what I am?'

'No, not you—not now.'

'Oh, *wow*—lucky for me.'

Her voice is so high-pitched, so angry, and she picks up her pace, her fingers trembling as she rakes them through her hair and clutches her bag tighter over her shoulder.

'How long were you following me?'

I shake my head, not wanting to tell her but knowing I have to. 'I don't know…a few weeks.'

'Every day?'

'Most days.'

'The charity galas, lunch dates, hospital visits, shopping trips? There you were, in the shadows?'

She shudders and it resonates down my spine like a chilling trickle. This is going badly—worse than even my garbled imaginings.

'Please, Coco, forget everything you think you know about us—how we met, what you think I did or lied about… Coco.' I reach for her arm but then think better of it. 'Coco, stop—just for a second— and look at me.'

She stops, but she doesn't turn.

'*Please*, Coco.'

My voice shakes, desperate, fearful. But I have to do this—I have to tell her. Even if she walks away again, at least she'll know the truth.

Slowly she turns, her tormented green eyes lifting to mine. I don't dare close the gap between us, scared of having her move off again. At least she's looking at me now. And I know I look like shit, but I don't care. I hope it will help show her what this is doing to me.

'Spit it out, Ash.'

She raises her chin and wraps her arms around herself.

'I love you.'

It trembles out of me, and it feels so good to say it, but she doesn't react. Not even a blink. Did she not hear?

'I *love* you, Coco.'

Her lashes flutter, her eyes water, and I push on.

'I love you like I've never loved anyone in this world. I love you more than you can possibly begin to imagine. I didn't set out to hurt you. I set out on a job, where everything was black and white. He was good; you were bad. You were like Jess.'

Her head shakes, her nostrils flare. 'Don't think I haven't figured that much out.'

'But you're not. *Christ*, I knew that before I even met you in the club. I'd been tailing you for weeks, falling in love with you a little bit each day.'

She looks away. 'Now you just sound like a stalker.'

'I know.' I rake my hand over my hair. 'But I mean it. I followed you and discovered the real you—the person with a heart so big you spend your days seeing that other people are happy, and to hell with your own happiness.'

'Then why didn't you just tell Philip that and *piss off*?' Her eyes spear me, fresh tears welling, and her cheeks streak red. 'Why did you have to get close to me? Why did you have to make me care about you? *Why?*'

Oh, God, this is crushing me. I want to reach for her, pull her in, make everything all right. But I know she'll run even if I dare.

'I didn't make you care about me. The person you ended up caring about is still me—how I've been with you is all real, all *me*.' I take a breath and plough on. 'That night in the club when you... propositioned me... I would've walked away had you been anyone else but you—I would have been able to. But I couldn't. I knew it was wrong, but I couldn't stop myself.'

She snorts out a laugh and wipes the back of her hand across her eyes. 'So you're blaming your dick now?'

'No, I'm blaming my goddamn *heart*!'

She sniffs, her eyes widening over my outburst. But, hell, I'm going out of my mind. Why can't I get it through to her that I love her?

'I couldn't leave you—not when I understood that Philip would stop at nothing to ruin your reputation. I knew that if it wasn't me then another PI would be hired to tail you—a fact Philip proved when he did exactly that—and there was no preventing what they'd find. Your presence at Blacks, the things that go on there... Another PI wouldn't be as bound to their own loyalties as me.'

'You mean your friendship with Jackson?'

'Yes.'

'So really I have Jackson to thank that you didn't dish the dirt?'

I shake my head, frustration mounting, my pulse racing.

'I stuck around to *protect* you—don't you get it? I kept him from getting what he needed even though I knew I was falling for you—falling for you and having to lie at the same time, hating myself for it even as I loved you.'

Her head is shaking rapidly. 'That's not love, and that's not honesty. Trust—you should have *trusted* me with it.'

'I couldn't. I was scared. So scared of what you would do. Scared that you would go straight to Philip and have it out with him. And you're too good for that. Whatever you said or did, he would always sink that bit lower, be that bit more devious. I couldn't risk it—not until I knew I could protect you, build up some information of my own.'

'*No!* You should have told me—given us the chance to deal with it together.'

She's right. I know she's right. And the real truth of it hits me like a blast of icy air.

'I was scared I would lose you.'

She says nothing. She's frozen still and I push on, my voice a mere whisper.

'I was so scared that the second I confessed you would despise me, hate me for who I am and what I did.' I reach out to cup her cheek, the impulse too strong to fight. 'I was scared that the love blazing in your eyes…' I sweep away her tears with my thumb and see exactly what I feared staring back at me '…would die.'

No, no, no.

I swallow back the rising tide of pain, blink back the tears that threaten. 'I know I was wrong—I see that now—but it doesn't mean I don't love you. You have to believe that… *Please* believe that.'

Her eyes close and she raises her hands to her ears, shaking her head. I can feel her entire body tremble beneath my touch. I'm losing her…

'Coco—'

'Don't… I can't… Don't…' She breaks away from me, her step jerky, and then she turns and runs.

I watch her go, knowing I can't follow and feeling the world shatter around me.

'Just do one thing?' I plead after her, the sound choked over the wedge in my throat. 'Speak to Philip—ask him what I told him.'

Her step falters as she looks over her shoulder, one brow raised in disbelief. 'And you trust *him* to tell me the truth?'

'No…' I take a breath. 'But he's the only hope I have left.'

I stare at my father's study door—now Philip's—my body immobile. I've found myself here more times than I can count over the past week, but this is where my courage leaves me and I end up walking away.

Ever since I saw Ash outside the hospital, saw his tortured expression, his hoarse protestations of love have hounded me every waking hour. I didn't let myself believe him—I couldn't. To do that would run the risk of opening myself up all over again, and I'm not over his first betrayal. How can I possibly hope to survive another in the future?

Problem is I can't kill the spark of hope—the idea that maybe I won't have to survive another betrayal because there won't be one, because if he loves me half as much as I love him, then our future could be as perfect as any life can be.

Because I do love him—if he's the man I got to know, the man whose relationship with his father is so heart-warming, the man whose bond to Jackson is so loyal, whose love for me kept him at my side whenever I called. I'm not blind to the fact that he came into the hospital, knowing that he ran the risk of running into Philip, because *I* asked it of him.

He did it for me. And so I owe him this. I owe it to myself too.

Just ask Philip.

We've barely spoken since the day he outed Ash. The day he outed his own devious plan too. Even now my skin prickles over his deception—anger, hurt, betrayal all coming to the fore. I need to deal with it all. I need to do this.

I take a breath and rap against the door.

It opens before my hand even drops to my side, but it's not Philip. It's my stepmother.

'Oh, it's you.' She looks me up and down, says it like I'm a piece of shit on her shoe. I so don't care.

I blame her for the way Philip is. Her, our father, Clara... They all had a hand in it.

No one forced him, though...

I give her a sickly-sweet smile and stride past her. Philip is at his desk, studying some paperwork, and I turn to look at his mother. 'Would you mind giving my brother and I some privacy?'

'I was leaving anyway.'

Her voice is unusually high-pitched as she looks towards Philip, and it makes me wonder what I've actually walked in on.

'These walls are beginning to make my skin shrivel.'

Philip's eyes shoot up, spearing her from across the room. 'In that case, maybe it's time you found yourself somewhere else to live. Perhaps you and Clara could bunk up together, Mother. You get on so very well and she'll be looking for someone else to feed off now that I've told her it's over.'

What? It's over. Him and Clara. Really?

The first ripple of hope, of excitement runs through me as his mother pales on a sharp intake of breath. I wait for her to retaliate, to hit back as soon as she's over her shock, but instead she gives a meek 'Yes...well...perhaps I should.'

'Excellent!' His eyes go back to the papers as he lifts them up. 'Don't take too long about it.'

She says nothing, her disbelieving gaze frozen on her son, and when she realises he's finished with her she flicks me a look.

'I think you can go,' I can't help saying.

I want to laugh, but that would probably take things too far. Instead, I take great delight in her heightened colour and wobbly exit.

As the door closes I look back to Philip. What the hell have I missed? I've seen her treat him in all manner of ways—trample, push, goad, belittle, the works—it's partly why he's like he is, and it's why I can't hate him for what he did. But never have I seen him stand up to her.

And as for him and Clara…?

I find my anger towards him floundering, a surprising swell of admiration building. How long have I itched for him to fight back? And not at me, but at the real purveyors of his misery.

'What?' he says.

I realise I'm staring, lips parted, eyes wide. 'Can we get her back in here and do that again?'

He takes a shaky breath and tosses the papers down, reaching for the almost empty whisky decanter on his desk and pouring a double measure. 'Look, Coco, I don't know why you're here, but I'm tired, fed up and trying to get my head screwed on straight, so if you want to lay into me please just get it over with. I deserve it—and more.'

I study him closely. He looks like he's barely slept, worry lines mar his perfect features, and the glassy state of his eyes suggests he's had several drinks already.

'What's going on?'

'What *isn't* going on?' he mutters, taking a swig and turning in his chair to look at me. 'Clara told me what a fool I'd been not to see what was going on under my nose with you and Ash, told me it just proved what a mug I was. This was after she'd informed me that Granny's deterioration was a blessing in disguise as it meant her and Mother could resume their party preparations without the worry that she would still be here.'

His voice cracks and he breaks off, his eyes falling to his glass as he clenches his jaw. His pain is so obvious and I know it has nothing to do Clara and everything to do with Granny's health.

'As for Mother…' He shakes his head as he says her name, his mouth twisting derisively. 'She's spent the last hour listing every one of my useless qualities to ensure I take full responsibility for *her* crappy existence too, as well as informing me of my failings as a husband and a future Duke, that letting Clara go is an epic misjudgement, that my darling wife makes the perfect Duchess.'

He laughs now. 'And, oh, how I know Clara agrees. She only married me for my title, you know. It's so obvious now. My title and my money.'

'I'm sorry.'

He looks at me. 'No, you're not.'

'I am.'

It's the truth. I know he won't understand it, but I am. I lived his childhood with him. I was aware of the pedestal on which I sat while he took all the shit that was thrown at him by our father as well as his mother.

He shakes his head. 'You shouldn't be.'

'Don't get me wrong, I'm still livid at what you did—what you tried to do. I still can't get my head around it.'

He pinches the bridge of his nose and squeezes his eyes shut. 'You and me both.'

'Are you saying you've had some wonderful epiphany—that you can miraculously see the horror of it all?'

His eyes stay shut and he shakes his head again. 'I wish I could go back and undo it—the whole damn lot. Go back to before Clara…before…'

He swallows hard, his skin deathly white. He looks like he's going to be sick, and even though I don't want it to I can feel my anger ebbing away.

He wets his lips, and looks at me, lost, pained. 'Is that why you've come? To have it out? To give me what I deserve?'

I straighten my spine. 'That—and I want to know what Ash told you about me.'

He gives a gentle scoff. 'As if you don't already know.'

'I want to hear it from you.'

He shakes his head again, one corner of his lip lifting. 'Fuck all, if you must know…' He leans back in his chair. 'I should've known the guy was smitten. He's supposed to be the best in the industry—it never occurred to me that he would fall under your *perfect* spell too.'

'Don't say that.' The way he drawls out the word *perfect* makes my skin crawl. 'I'm not perfect.'

'On that we must agree to disagree.'

'Is that why you hate me so much? Is that why you felt I deserved it?'

He stares at me, the silence long and strained.

'The truth is I never hated you. I *envied* you. Ash told me nothing because there was nothing to tell— because you didn't deserve it.' His voice cracks and he clears his throat, visibly trying to recover. 'But me, on the other hand…'

He leans back in his seat to open a drawer in the desk and pulls out a manila envelope. He tosses it onto the desk before me.

'What's this?' I pick it up, my eyes still trained on him.

'You might as well take a look…' He rubs his jaw, the movement awkward, shaky. 'He's probably told you it all already.'

I go to open it, but stop. It just doesn't feel right. 'What's inside?'

'You really don't know?'

'I'm assuming it's information relating to you?'

He smiles at me but his eyes are dead, wet at the corners. 'It's all my dirty laundry. Seems he was making sure I wouldn't take any steps against you. Judging by your expression, you had nothing to do with this bonus investigative work?'

My stomach twists. 'I'd never do that to you.'

He sits forward in his chair, knocking back his drink with a wince. 'No, you wouldn't, would you?'

His eyes meet mine, red-rimmed and swimming. I want to reach for him, tell him it doesn't mean he can't change, be a better person, free of the women who have tormented him for years. But I'm rooted. Unsure.

'I don't blame him, you know.' He's reflective as he says it. 'He was right to fall for you, to protect you... *Christ*, I'm glad he did.'

My eyes narrow. 'You are?'

He rakes his hand over his face. 'I don't think I could've come back from that.'

'From what?'

I want him to spell it out, to acknowledge his intent. I need to hear it from his lips, to have it out in the open and believe that he regrets it, that there's hope for us.

His eyes and his hunched-up body tremble.

'From ruining me?' I press, so softly it's a wonder he hears. But his shuddery breath, the awkward nod of his head, tell me that he has.

'I am sorry, Coco. I know it's not enough, and I don't even know if I can ever make it up to you, but...' Another breath and his eyes lock with mine. 'But I'm going to try.'

A lump forms high in my throat and I lift my chin and nod. 'I believe you, Philip. I don't need to read this.' I close the envelope without looking inside and place it back on the desk. 'We can talk when you're ready. I'm still your sister—your blood—and I don't want to lose you.'

He eyes me, disbelieving. 'How can you mean that? After all I've done?'

'Believe it.' My eyes prick as the truth hits me.

'Soon you'll be all the family I have left, and…and I don't want to lose that.'

He's across the room before the first tear falls, his arms around me, hugging me tight.

'It's not too late?' he whispers against my hair. 'For us?'

'No,' I assure him on a small sob. 'It's not.'

I only hope the same applies to Ash.

CHAPTER EIGHTEEN

I PULL OPEN the fridge for a beer. 'Bollocks.' The shelves are practically bare. No beer, no nothing.

I slam the fridge closed and snatch a glass off the drainer, a bottle of whisky next. It's not my preferred drink, especially at four in the afternoon, but needs must. And I definitely need it. I need to block out the sight of her walking away, her anger, her pain, her hate...

I'm all out of hope. She must have spoken to Philip by now. And if she has he's either lied or it wasn't enough to convince her.

I can't even blame him. This is all my fault. *Mine*.

I fucked up the best thing that's ever happened to me and now I have to face the consequences. Only I don't know how to. I don't know how to live without her.

I pour a glass as I head into the living area, where the painting on the wall teases me with the memory of her appreciation. I make a U-turn and head back to the kitchen. Not that that helps either. *Fuck*.

She's everywhere.

I slap the whisky glass down on the centre island and pour. Wishing the painful memories away. Wishing *her* away.

Maybe I should've taken Jackson up on his offer of a night out. The guy's been hounding me all week. And we could go somewhere new. Somewhere devoid of memories. Somewhere I can get hammered and forget. Even if it's only for a few hours, it has to be better than this.

Yeah, like you'd really wish yourself on him right now.

I deserve to wallow in my own sodding misery.

I take a swig of my drink and close my eyes, feel it burn down my throat and contend with the punishing ache inside.

Better.

Then the doorbell goes and my phone starts to flash up at me from the counter.

Piss off.

It's Jackson. Won't the guy just give up?

I ignore both and take another swig.

There's an incessant banging on the door now, every knock like a physical blow to my already aching head, and I wince.

Seriously, Jackson, piss off.

He doesn't, and it's driving me crazy.

I stride to the front door and yank it open. 'Jackson, will you just fu—'

The curse dies on my lips. I can't believe my eyes. This has to be some twisted trick, the booze soaring to my head…

'Ash?'

Coco frowns up at me, her beautiful green eyes flashing with what looks so much like concern. Not anger, not pain, not hatred.

She's wearing jeans and the same soft pink sweater she wore to Dad's. Memories warm me, slaughter me, but she's here. It has to mean something.

Her frown deepens. 'Ash…?'

My throat is so dry I can't speak. I wet my lips and run a hand over my face, stopping to grip my jaw as my eyes narrow and focus, still disbelieving.

'Coco?'

Her lips quirk just a little. 'Can I come in?'

'Sure.'

My voice sounds so fucking weird, so distant, but I can't function past the crazy flutter taking off inside me. I step back to let her past and her familiar scent wafts up to me, messing with my head, telling me she's real, that this is happening.

'I'll have one of those.' She nods to the drink still in my hand.

'Sure,' I repeat, swinging the door closed and making my way trance-like back to the kitchen, my ears attuned to her soft footfall behind me.

She's here. She's here. She's here.

I set my glass down and get another one for her, then reach for the bottle and start to pour. But I'm shaking so much the liquid sloshes outside the glass.

'Ash…'

She places her hand over mine. She's right alongside me, her perfume in the air, her presence radiating down my side.

Slowly I set the bottle down and look at her. It really isn't hate I see. 'I'm so sorry.'

'I know you are,' she whispers.

I go to pull her in. I need to hug her, feel her, believe that she believes me. But she steps back, shaking her head, and my stomach plummets. My hands fall helplessly away.

'But…?'

Her throat bobs, her eyes lift to mine. 'I can't… When I think about it…the idea of you following me—*all that time*—and not once telling me…' She shakes her head again, her palm pressing into her chest. 'It hurts… It really hurts. I feel sick with it.'

'I *know*.' Hearing her say it, seeing the flash of pain, of disgust, I feel sick too. 'I would do anything to change what I did. To go back and do it differently. I'd do anything not to have caused you this pain.'

'I know you would.' She breathes in deeply. 'Philip said the same.'

'You spoke to him?' My heart spasms in my chest. 'About what he did? About me?'

She nods, her hand shaking as she reaches out and picks up the glass of whisky I poured for her. I stay quiet as I watch her take a sip, my eyes desperately searching hers, looking for a sign—any sign of what is to come.

'He had his reasons—I know he did; I think I understand more than he knows.'

She swallows and takes another breath, her eyes locking with mine.

'I know about the research you did into him too— the case you built against him to protect me.'

'He showed you?'

'He tried to, but I don't want to know. I think he's hit a turning point and I'm hoping we can repair things.'

'*Repair* things?' I frown at her, feel a flare of anger, even jealousy, that she can think to forgive him while we…we flounder…

'Our relationship,' she confirms softly.

Her eyes narrow on me, reading it all, I'm sure. I shake my head. 'Are you crazy?'

'Are you being a hypocrite?' she snaps, and I realise she's right. 'You want me to forgive *you* for what you did, but not my brother?'

'I don't know.' I rub the back of my neck, cling to it as I try to make sense of what I'm thinking, of how I feel. 'I know this mess is my fault, but I blame him too—for what he wanted to do to you.' My body vibrates with anger at the very thought. 'To the woman I love.'

The pulse flutters in her neck, the glass shakes in her hand.

'I know what he wanted to do, and I know why. But his marriage is over, he's finally seen sense where Clara and his mother are concerned, and once Granny is gone…' She swallows as her eyes glisten over and she raises her chin with reignited strength.

'We'll only have one another, and I'm not giving up on him yet.'

My blood runs cold.

Only have one another.

'And what about me? Can't you have me too?'

'I want to,' she says, and I can see she means it, but I can also see the fight in her. 'I want that so much—to be able to act like it never happened, to bury it.'

'Then give me a chance to make it up to you,' I plead, my voice a husky mess of desperation as I reach a hand out to her. 'Let me love you like I've wanted to for so long.'

She exhales sharply as she looks to the heavens, a solitary tear escaping and crucifying me on its path.

'I *want* to—so badly. But I don't know how we do that when you still… When you're still…' She looks back at me, her free hand gesturing wildly. 'When you're still doing that to other people. The whole PI shit. I get why you did it, why you chose to before, but now…'

I step forward, unable to stand the distance any longer. 'That side of me is long gone.' I reach out to cup her arms and this time she lets me. 'I've already quit the business—there's no way I could carry on.'

Hope flares in her eyes as they widen. 'You have?'

'*Yes.* I didn't realise how messed-up I'd become, how blinded by the past I've been—not until you… Until I almost…almost…' I can't finish the sentence—it hurts too much. 'I hate myself for what I did, and I know I don't deserve you, don't deserve your forgiveness, but the idea of living without you, of walking away…'

My voice fails me, my eyes close as the sob rising in my throat gets too much, and then I feel her palms on either side of my face, her touch soft, soothing.

'I don't want you to walk away, Ash.'

I hear the words, hope pulsing in my chest, and I open my eyes, take in her blazing beauty.

'You don't?'

'No.' She shakes her head. 'I've wrestled with so much pain these last two weeks, every day, without you, feeling lost…empty. I can't go on like that.'

I almost don't want to ask the question, but I have to if we're to stand a chance at a future. 'Can you forgive me?'

She studies me quietly and I can't breathe as I search her gaze.

'Yes,' she says eventually, so softly I can barely hear it.

But it's there, and my chest soars, tears prick, making my vision swim as I look down at her.

'Can you… Can you love me?'

She looks to my mouth and runs her thumb over it, her lips coming next. She kisses me—a single featherlight sweep of her mouth—but I'm rigid, stock-still. Hope upon hope is building.

'I have no choice in that, Ash. I *do* love you.'

My breath leaves me in a rush, so ragged. I'm so happy hearing those words, seeing the truth of them once more alive in her bright green gaze. It's all too surreal, too perfect, too dreamlike.

'You do?'

'Yes, Ash, I do.'

I press my forehead to hers, pull her body tight against me. 'Do me a favour?'

'What?'

'Kiss me again so I know this isn't a dream?'

'I think we can go one better than a kiss…'

She rakes her fingers down my front, easing them beneath my sweater. Her fingertips over my bare skin make my stomach contract.

'We have so many lost nights to catch up on.'

'Coco…'

I can't speak any more, can only claim her mouth with all the hunger, all the love, all the pent-up pain I can now let go of because *she is here*. And she loves me. Just as I do her.

She yanks my sweater over my head and I grip the hem of hers, but she presses her palms into my chest, stopping me from going further. I drag in a breath, my eyes burning into hers.

'Tell me again,' she says, her eyes bright with desire, her cheeks flushing pink.

'I love you, Coco Lauren!' I grip her by the waist and lift her onto the counter, her resultant laughter music to my deprived ears.

'And if you let me…' I step between her thighs, drawing her against me '…I will show you just how much every day and every night for the rest of our lives.'

I seal my vow with my lips upon hers and start to show her…one stroke, one lick, one kiss at a time…

CHAPTER NINETEEN

I LOOK DOWN at the leather-bound book clutched in my hands and smile. I know this is the right thing to do now. I know I need Granny to understand my mother—her good heart and her love for my father. I also need her to know that I've found my happiness too. That I am in love and loved in return.

I turn to look up at Ash beside me.

'You okay?' he asks, his arm around my waist giving me a gentle squeeze.

'Yes. It's the right thing to do.' I've already marked out some pages in the diary—the ones that shine with my mother's love. 'Will you wait for me downstairs?'

'Sure.'

He presses a kiss to my brow and I breathe in his scent, his love, his support.

'Thank you.'

And then I turn to face Granny's bedroom door and give it a gentle knock.

'Come in,' she calls from the other side, her voice still perfectly controlled, even though I know each day becomes more and more of a struggle for her.

I blink away the tears that form and step out of Ash's embrace to open the door and walk inside.

She's propped up in bed, her eyes bright with her love for me, and the sense of doing right swells. 'Granny, I'd like to read you something...'

EPILOGUE

Eighteen months later

'IF YOU'D TOLD me I'd be wearing a skirt I would have said no—you know that, right?'

Philip fluffs out the sides of his kilt as he says it and I can't help erupting into a giggle.

'Who would've given me away, then?'

'I could've done it just as well in trousers.'

'And you wouldn't have been half as dashing.' I waggle my eyebrows at him. 'Haven't you seen the ladies eyeing you up?'

'You are joking.'

'Not at all, and you're quite the eligible bachelor now. You should make the most of it.'

Now he grins, his eyes seeking out one redhead in particular, currently slow-dancing with Jackson in the recently refurbed ballroom of the Livingston Castle.

'Oh, no, you don't. Cait's off-limits.'

He flashes me a cheeky look. 'Surely as your maid of honour she should be top of my list.'

'You're not the best man.'

'Best man, brother…' he shrugged '…same difference.'

'Philip!'

'Oh, dear, that's her warning tone…'

I turn at the sound of Ash's voice and feel the warmth of his hand through the white lace at the base of my spine.

'What have you done now?' he asks Philip.

'He's setting his sights on Cait.'

Ash gives a hearty laugh, his eyes dancing. 'I think that's a great idea.'

I frown up at him.

'See?' Philip blurts. 'Even your husband agrees.'

'Really, Ash?' I'd stamp on his foot if I could find my feet beneath my dress. Instead I fire him a glare. 'Not helpful.'

He shrugs. 'What's the worst that could happen? Although, he might have Jackson to get through first…'

'The question is,' Philip says, as he considers the couple on the dance floor, 'does she want a bit of rough—no offence to your mate—or does she want Prince Charming?'

'Prince Charming?' Ash mimics, choking on his giggles now, and I elbow him in the ribs.

'Right, Livingston.' Philip straightens and offers out his hand. 'Fifty I get the girl.'

I stare between them in disbelief. 'Don't you—'

'You're on,' Ash interjects, shaking his hand, his grin rivalling Philip's own.

'No time like the present to get started.'

My brother extracts his hand, rearranges his cravat and makes for the dance floor.

'Philip Lauren...' I wait for him to look back at me. 'You dare mess her around and it'll be me you answer to.'

He chuckles. 'Keep your knickers on—I wouldn't dare.'

I watch him walk off and I can't be angry. I'm too happy.

Happy that I've married the man I love.

Happy that I have the brother I always wanted.

Happy.

Just happy.

Ash leans into my ear. 'Now, about those knickers...'

A shiver runs through me. 'You're just trying to distract me from your bad behaviour...'

'No, Mrs Livingston. If I wanted to do that, I'd do this...'

He scoops me up in the air with ease, the abundant layers of my dress creating a cloud between me and his face.

'Ash!' I bat them down and laugh and glare at him all at once. 'Put me down!'

'Only when we're alone.'

He's already heading for the double doors that lead out into the hallway and the guests are parting before us, laughing, cheering and offering up smiles and salutes with their glasses.

My cheeks flush red as I plaster on a smile. 'Ash, what will they *think*?' I say between my teeth.

'That I'm desperate to have my wife all to myself.'

'Ash!'

'What?' He looks down at me as we enter the hallway. 'Aren't you keen to find out whether I'm a true Scot in a kilt?'

I frown. 'A true…?'

He wouldn't be…not all day!

'Are you?'

He grins. 'You'll see.'

* * * * *

AN HONOURABLE
SEDUCTION

BRENDA JACKSON

To the man who will forever be the love of my life, Gerald Jackson, Sr.

To all of my readers who asked for Flipper's story. This one is for you!

To the Brenda Jackson Book Club/Facebook fans. Over 4,000 strong and after fourteen years, you guys still rock!

'Many waters cannot quench love; rivers cannot sweep it away.'

—Song of Solomon 8:7

Prologue

The Naval Amphibious Base
Coronado, San Diego, California

"What kind of trouble have you gotten into?"

David Holloway, known to his Navy SEAL team-mates as Flipper, glanced at the four men surrounding him. They were like brothers to him. More than once they'd risked their lives for each other and they would continue to have each other's backs, on duty or off. That bond was what accounted for the concerned looks on their faces. He wondered how they'd known he'd been summoned to the admiral's office.

"Let's hope I'm not in any trouble, Mac," Flipper said, rubbing a hand down his face.

He had to admit he was wondering what was going on, just like they were. Usually, you were only summoned to a meeting with the admiral when you were getting reprimanded for some reason, and he never got into trouble. At least he *rarely* did. As the son of a retired SEALs commanding officer and the youngest of five brothers—all Navy SEALs—he knew better.

"Maybe there's an event on the base and he wants you to escort his daughter now that you're the single one among us," Coop said, grinning.

Flipper didn't grin back. They'd seen Georgianna Martin, the admiral's twenty-three-year-old daughter. She was beautiful, but they'd heard the horror stories from other teammates who'd been ordered to take her out on dates. According to them, those evenings had been the dates from hell. The young woman was spoiled rotten, selfish as sin and had an attitude that sucked. That's why Flipper didn't find Coop's comment at all amusing. He hoped that wasn't why the admiral wanted to see him.

It didn't surprise Flipper that it was Mac who'd asked if Flipper had gotten into trouble. Thurston McRoy—code name Mac—was older than the other four men on the team, who had all started their careers as SEALs around the same time. Mac had been a SEAL five years before the rest of them. Mac seemed to like to think he was the big brother looking out for them, almost like he figured they couldn't take care of themselves. He was forever giving them advice—even when they didn't ask for it.

In addition to Mac and Flipper, their SEAL team included Brisbane Westmoreland, code name Bane; Gavin Blake, whose code name was Viper; and Laramie Cooper, whose code name was Coop.

Flipper checked his watch. "Since I have a couple of hours to spare before meeting with the admiral, let's grab something to eat," he suggested.

"Sounds good to me," Bane said.

Less than an hour later, Flipper and his four teammates shared burgers, fries and milkshakes at one of the most popular eating places on base. They decided to sit outside at one of the café tables in the front instead of inside where it was crowded since it was such a beautiful May day.

No one brought up his meeting with the admiral again or the notion of him taking the admiral's daughter on a date. He was glad. Instead, the guys had more important things to talk about, namely their families.

Bane's wife, Crystal, had given birth to triplets last year and he had new photos to share, so they passed Bane's cell phone around.

Viper's wife, Layla, was expecting with only a few months to go before Gavin Blake IV would be born. Viper was excited about becoming a father, of course.

Like Bane, Mac had plenty of photos to share; he was married and the father of four.

And Coop had a two-year-old son he hadn't known about until he'd run into his old girlfriend about six months ago. They'd reconnected, gotten married and were now a happy family.

Earlier in the week, the teammates had gotten word from their commanding officer that next week was the start of a four-month leave. For Flipper, that meant heading home to Dallas and he couldn't wait. His mother had a birthday coming up and he was glad he would be home to celebrate.

"I don't care what plans you all are making for your leave, just as long as you remember my mom's birthday celebration. I understand you not showing up, Viper, with a baby on the way. The rest of you guys, no excuses."

"We hear you," Bane said, grinning. "And we will be there."

When Viper ordered another hamburger, everyone teased him about being the one to eat for two instead of his wife. And then everyone talked about what they planned to do with their four months off.

It was two hours later when Flipper walked into the admiral's office. He was surprised to find Commanding Officer Shields there as well. Flipper saluted both men.

"At ease. Please have a seat, Lieutenant Holloway."

"Thank you, sir," he said, sitting down. He was used to being under his commanding officer's intense scrutiny, but there was something in the sharp green eyes of Admiral Norris Martin that was making him feel uncomfortable.

"You come highly recommended by your commanding officer here, Lieutenant Holloway. And the reason I asked to meet with you is that we need you. Your country needs you."

Flipper was happy to step up. He was a Navy SEAL, and the reason he'd enlisted, like his father and brothers, was to protect his country. "And what am I needed to do, sir?" he asked.

"Our investigators have provided intelligence and a preliminary report that says acts of espionage are happening in Key West. Someone is trading valuable government secrets to China."

Flipper didn't respond immediately.

The one thing he hated was a traitor, but he'd discovered that for the right price, a number of American citizens would perform acts of treason. He understood that. However, what he didn't understand was why he'd been singled out for this meeting. He was part of a SEAL team. He didn't work in naval intelligence.

Confusion must have shown on his face because Admiral Martin continued, "The report was given to me, but I don't believe it."

Flipper raised a brow. "You don't believe a report that classified documents are being traded in Key West, sir?"

"Oh, I believe all that, but what I refuse to believe is that this suspect is guilty of anything."

"Is there a reason why, sir?"

"Here is the information," said Commanding Officer Shields, speaking for the first time as he handed Flipper a folder.

Flipper opened it to find a picture of a very beautiful woman. She looked to be around twenty-four, with dark, sultry eyes and full, shapely lips. Then there was her mass of copper-brown spiral curls that flowed to her shoulders, crowning a cocoa-colored face. A pair of dangling gold earrings hung from her ears and a golden pendant necklace hung around her neck.

He knew he was spending too much time studying her features, but it couldn't be helped. The woman was strikingly beautiful.

Reluctantly he moved his gaze away from her face to check out the background of the photo. From the tropical vegetation captured by the photographer, she seemed to be on an island somewhere. She stood near a body of water that showed in the corner of the eight-by-ten photo. Scribbled across the bottom were the words:

Miss you, Godpop 1
Love, Swan

Swan? It was an unusual name, but it fit.

He moved to the next document in the file. Attached to it was a small family photo that showed a tall Caucasian man with sandy-brown hair and brown eyes standing beside a beautiful woman who closely resembled Swan. Her mother. In front of the couple was a beautiful little girl who looked to be around eight.

Flipper studied the child's face and knew that child had grown up to be the gorgeous woman in the first photo. The shape of her face was the same, as were her eyes. Even as a child, she'd had long curly hair.

The family photo was clipped to a profile of the young woman. As he'd guessed, she was twenty-four. Her name was Swan Jamison. She was an American, born in Key West. Presently, she owned a jewelry store on the island. That was all the information the document provided.

Flipper lifted his gaze to find his commanding officer and the admiral staring at him. "I assume this is the person naval intelligence believes is the traitor."

"Yes," Admiral Martin said. "She's my goddaughter. I am Godpop 1."

"She's my goddaughter as well," added Commanding Officer Shields. "I am Godpop 2."

Flipper's gaze moved from one man to the other. "I see, sirs."

Admiral Martin nodded. "Her father was part of our SEAL team and our best friend. His name was Andrew Jamison."

Flipper had heard that Commanding Officer Shields and Admiral Martin were part of the same SEAL team a number of years ago.

"Andrew was the best. He lost his life saving

ours," said Commanding Officer Shields. "He didn't die immediately, and before he died, he made us promise to look after his wife, Leigh, and his daughter, Swan." The man paused and then said, "Over twenty-eight years ago, when we were taking some R & R in Jamaica, Andrew met Leigh, who was a Jamaican model. They married a year later, and he moved her to Key West, where our team was stationed. After Andrew was killed, Leigh returned to Jamaica. When Swan graduated from high school, she returned to the Keys and moved into her parents' home."

"How old was she when her father was killed?" Flipper asked.

"She was fifteen," Admiral Martin said. "Swan was close to her dad. Leigh was so broken up over Andrew's death that she didn't want to live in the States without him, which was why she returned to Jamaica. She passed away two years ago."

Flipper's commanding officer then took up the tale. "Leigh sent for us before she died of stomach cancer, asking us to look out for Swan after she was gone. We would have done that anyway, since we always kept in touch with both Leigh and Swan. In fact, Swan rotated summers with us and our families even after Leigh returned to Jamaica. We took our roles as godfathers seriously. We were even there when Swan graduated from high school and college."

"Did Swan have any American grandparents?" Flipper asked.

He saw both men's lips tighten into frowns. "Yes. However, her paternal grandparents didn't approve of their son's marriage to Leigh," said Commanding Officer Shields.

"So they never accepted their granddaughter." It was more of a statement than a question.

"No, they never did," Admiral Martin confirmed. As if it was a topic he'd rather change, the man added, "We've been given some time to find out the truth, but not much. Luckily, Swan's Godpop 3 has a high-level position at naval intelligence. Otherwise, we wouldn't know about the investigation. We have thirty days to prove Swan is not a traitor and identify the person who is. That's where we need your help. Instead of releasing you to go home as we're doing for the other members of your team, we are assigning you to a special mission, Lieutenant Holloway. You are being sent to Key West."

One

Key West, Florida

Swan Jamison was beside herself with excitement
as she opened the huge box on her desk. Although
it contained only her jewelry-making supplies, the
package served as affirmation that while rebuilding
was still taking place in certain areas, the majority
of the island had recovered from the hurricane that
had hit eight months ago.

"Anything for me?" Rafe asked, sticking his head
through the office door.

Her shop was in a very trendy area so she could
capitalize on the tourists visiting the island. To help
with high operating costs, she leased out one of the

large rooms in the back. Rafe was her tenant, who'd converted the back room into a tattoo shop. On some days, he got more customers than she did.

"Nothing for you, Rafe, just supplies for me." She checked her watch. "You're early today." Usually he didn't open up until noon.

"I have a special appointment at ten thirty and I need to ready my ink." And then he was gone. Rafe didn't say a whole lot except to his customers.

The door chime alerted her that *she* had a customer. Jamila, who worked part-time and usually only in the mornings, had taken time off for a day of beauty—hair, nails, pedicure, bikini wax, the works. Her boyfriend worked on a cruise ship that was due in port tomorrow. Swan was happy for Jamila and happy for herself as well. The cruise ships always brought in tourists who wanted to purchase authentic handmade jewelry.

She walked out of her office as a man perused her jewelry display case near the door. That was good. While he checked out her jewelry, she would check him out.

He had a nice profile. Tall, broad shoulders that looked good in a T-shirt and a pair of muscular thighs that fit well in his jeans. He had diamond-blond hair that was neatly trimmed and his hands were the right size for his body.

There was something about the way he stood, straight and tall, that all but spelled out *military man*. And the way his legs were braced apart, as if he had to maintain his balance even on land, spelled out *navy*.

Too bad. She didn't do military men. In all honesty, lately she hadn't done men at all. Too busy.

And then there was the issue of Candy's divorce. Swan knew she shouldn't let what had happened to her best friend darken her own view, but Swan was known to claim whatever excuse suited her and that one did at the moment.

And speaking of the moment, she had looked her fill. She needed to make her first sale of the day. "May I help you?"

He turned and looked at her, and every cell in her body jolted to attention.

Wow! She'd seen blue eyes before, but his were a shade she'd never seen. They were laser blue; the intense sharpness of the pupils captured her within their scope. And his features... Lordy! The man had such gorgeous bone structure! There was no way a woman had ever passed by him and not taken a second look. Even a third, while wiping away drool.

"Yes, you can help me."

And why did he have to sound so good, too? The sound of his voice—a deep, husky tone—made her throat go dry.

"All right," she said, walking over to him. She knew she had to get a grip. Her store had been closed for two months due to the hurricane, and now that the tourists were returning, she needed to catch up on sales.

"And how can I help you?" She didn't miss the way he was looking at her. She saw interest in his eyes. There was nothing wrong with that. She took pride in her appearance because she had been raised to do so. Leigh Rutledge Jamison, who'd been a Jamaican model, had taught her daughter that your appearance was everything.

Pain settled in Swan's heart. She missed her mom so much.

"I'm looking for a gift for someone."

Swan nodded as she came to stand beside him. Not only did he look good and sound good, but he smelled good as well. She glanced down at his hand and didn't see a wedding ring. He was probably buying a gift for his girlfriend or soon-to-be fiancée.

"What do you have in mind?"

"What do you suggest?" he asked her.

"Well, it depends," she said, looking into those gorgeous eyes.

"On what?"

"What the person likes. I make jewelry from stones, but as you can see, there are a number of them, in various shades, colors and styles."

He smiled and Swan felt a tingling in the pit of her stomach when a dimple appeared in one of his cheeks. "I honestly don't know what she likes. Her tastes change from year to year. It's hard to keep up."

Swan nodded. "Oh. Sounds like the two of you have known each other for a while."

His smile widened even more. "We have. I would have to say I've known Mom all my life."

"Your mom?"

"Yes. Her birthday is next month. I was passing by your shop and thought I would drop in to see what you had."

A racing heart for starters, Swan thought. So the woman he was thinking about buying jewelry for was his mother. "Well, I'm glad you came in. Let me show you what I have."

"All right. There looks to be a lot of nice pieces."

She appreciated the compliment. "Thanks. I made most of them myself."

"Really? Which ones?"

She led him to the area set aside for Swan Exclusives. "These. Most of the stones come from India, Argentina and Africa."

He leaned in to look. "You did an excellent job."

Whoever said flattery, especially coming from a good-looking man, would get you anywhere knew just what they were talking about. "Thank you."

"I'm David, by the way. David Holloway." He offered her his hand.

She took it and tried to ignore the sensations that suddenly flowed through her from the contact. "Nice to meet you, David." She quickly released his hand. "And I'm Swan."

"The name of the shop."

"Yes."

"It's a unique name."

"Yes, my parents thought so. On their first date, my father flew Mom from Jamaica to New York to see *Swan Lake*."

"Some date."

"Yes, he was trying to impress her."

"I take it he did."

Swan chuckled. "Yes, because he actually flew them there. He had his pilot's license."

"Now I'm impressed."

She didn't like bragging about her father but there were times when she just couldn't help it. "He served in the air force—that's where he learned to fly. And then he went into the navy after deciding he wanted to be a SEAL. That's when he met Mom, while he was a SEAL. She hadn't known about his stint in the air force until the night he rented a plane to fly them to New York."

Why was she telling him all this? Usually she wasn't chatty. "What about this one?" she asked as they moved to another glass case. "I call this piece *Enchantment*."

"Why?"

"Look at it," she suggested, leaning closer to the glass. He followed suit. "This is one of my favorite pieces because the teardrop gemstone necklace is pretty similar to my very first piece." No need to tell him that she'd made that one for her own mother.

"It is beautiful."

Something in his tone made her glance over at him, and she found him staring at her and not at the jewelry in the case. His eyes held her captive and their gazes met for a minute too long before she broke eye contact with him.

She swallowed. "So are you interested…in this piece?" She wanted to ignore the way her stomach seemed to be filled with all kinds of sensations, but she could not.

"I'm interested in a lot of pieces, Swan, but I'll start with this one."

Swan Jamison was even more beautiful than the photograph he'd seen last week.

The photographer hadn't fully captured the rich creaminess of her skin. And the shade of red lipstick she wore today seemed to make her lips plumper, more well-defined. Luscious.

He had read the dossier on her. He knew his commanding officer and Admiral Martin were operating based on a personal connection with her. He was not. If Miss Jamison was guilty of any wrongdoing, he would find out. And if she wasn't the one handing out classified data to China, then he would discover who was.

"So you want to buy this particular piece?"

Her question brought his thoughts back to the present. "Yes."

"Wonderful. I think your mother will like it."

"I'm sure she will. What about earrings?"

She lifted a brow. "Earrings?"

"Yes. Do earrings come with the necklace?"

"No, but I can make you some."

He'd been hoping she'd say that. "When?"

"It will take me a couple of days. The cruise ship docks tomorrow, so the shop will be busy. Two days from now will work for me, unless you need them sooner."

"No, I can wait. My mother's birthday is next month."

He would have an excuse to return to her shop.

Flipper watched her open the case and pull out the necklace. He knew his mother was going to love it.

"If you don't mind, please complete this ticket," she said. "And I will need full payment for the earrings before I make them."

"That's no problem," he said, taking the document from her.

After he completed the form, he handed it back to her. She glanced at it. "So you're from Texas?"

"Yes. Dallas. Ever been there?"

"Yes, once. I thought it was a nice city."

"It is. I was born and raised there."

"And what brought you to Key West?" she asked him.

"Work, at least for the next thirty days." That wasn't a total lie.

"Hurricane relief?"

"Something like that."

"You're military?"

"At one point but not now." He would let her think he was no longer military.

"I knew immediately."

He lifted a brow. "How?"

She shrugged. "Military men are easily recognized, at least by me."

"Because your dad is military?"

"He *was* military. Dad died years ago in the line of duty."

"I'm sorry." Flipper was always sorry whenever a fellow soldier lost their life.

"Thank you. Your package will be ready in two days, David. Your mobile number is on the form you completed. If I get to it sooner, I will call you."

"Two days is fine. I'll be back."

"'Bye, David."

"'Bye, Swan." He then turned and walked out of the shop.

As much as he wanted to invite her out to lunch today, he knew he couldn't rush things. He needed to earn her trust, even though he had less than thirty days to prove her innocence and determine who had no qualms about making her look guilty.

Swan was cheerful that night as she let herself into her home. Sales today had been better than normal. A tour group from New York had converged on the island and they'd come to spend money. She'd been happy to oblige.

Opening a jewelry shop had been a risky business move, but one that had paid off. She'd earned a degree in business management from the University of Miami and returned to the island after college to work as a manager at one of the elite hotels on the island. She'd enjoyed her job but had felt something was missing in her life. She hadn't been using her jewelry-making talent.

She'd promised her mother on her deathbed that she would find a way to use that talent.

Even after taking care of all her mother's funeral expenses, there had been more than enough money left to buy a little storefront. It had been a good investment because of its location. Some days were busier than others. This had been one of those busy days.

Now she was ready to wind down for the evening. She pulled her hair back in a ponytail and eased her feet into her favorite flats before heading to the kitchen for a glass of wine. As she did so, she couldn't help but think about her first customer of the day.

David Holloway.

He was a cutie, she had to give him that. And the memory of those eyes had stayed with her most of the day.

David Holloway had come into her shop to buy a birthday gift for his mother. How sweet. His mother was lucky. A lot of men didn't even remember their mothers' birthdays. She'd dated quite a few of those men and never developed lasting relationships with any of them. She figured if a man didn't treat his mother right, then there was no hope for a girlfriend.

As she opened the French doors to step out on the patio, she again remembered those blue eyes and how she'd felt whenever she'd looked into them. No man's eyes had ever made her feel that way before.

The effect was unsettling.

Okay, so what was wrong with her? Cutie or no cutie, she normally didn't get caught up over a man. She dated when it suited her, but she would admit that no one had suited her lately. At least not since her best friend, Candy, had left Key West to go live in Boston. Candy had refused to live on the island with her ex and his new wife—the one he'd married before the ink had even dried on the divorce papers.

Refusing to dwell on how shabbily Donald Knoll had treated Candy, Swan looked out at the water. It was calm tonight. When she had evacuated due to the hurricane, she hadn't known what to expect when she returned. Between her home and her shop, there had been some damage, but not as much as she'd feared.

The thought of losing her home had been devastating. This was where her father had brought her mom after they'd married. This home held so many childhood memories—of her father leaving on his missions as a Navy SEAL, of how happy she and her mother would be whenever he returned.

But then he hadn't returned.

Swan felt a knot in her throat as she recalled that day. She'd never seen that sparkle in her mother's eyes again. Swan recalled her mother telling her once that when you met a man who could put that sparkle in your eyes, then you knew he was a keeper.

Swan often wondered if she would ever find her keeper.

She had plenty of time. Besides, she needed to rethink her opinion about men first. If what Don had done to Candy wasn't enough to keep her single, all Swan had to do was remember William Connors, the businessman she had met while working at the hotel.

At the time, he had convinced her he was a bachelor without a care in the world but claimed that he wanted to make her Mrs. William Connors one day.

For some reason, Candy hadn't trusted him. She had a friend who worked for a private investigator check him out. Swan had been devastated when the investigation revealed there was already a Mrs. William Connors, along with three Connors children.

William had been playing her. He had been a lesson well learned. Her only regret was that she'd shared her body with him. She'd been young, naive and impressionable. He had been her first and he should not have been.

She was not naive now and she went into relationships with caution and even a little mistrust. Her mother once told her that being mistrustful wasn't a good thing. Swan knew she would have to learn how to trust again.

She took another sip of wine. Unfortunately, she hadn't gotten there yet.

* * *

"So how did things go, Flipper?"

"Have you met her yet?"

"Does she have a traitorous face or just a pretty one?"

"Do you think you'll be able to prove she's innocent?"

Flipper heard the questions coming at him nearly all at once. While unpacking, he had placed his mobile call on speaker to engage in a five-way conversation with his SEAL teammates.

"I think things went rather well, Mac. And yes, I met Swan Jamison today, Viper. I went into her jewelry store to purchase Mom a birthday gift."

Flipper eased open the dresser drawers to place his T-shirts inside. "She doesn't have a traitorous face or just a pretty one, Coop. The woman is simply gorgeous. Beautiful beyond belief. And yes, I hope to prove she's innocent, Bane, because Commanding Officer Shields and Admiral Martin truly believe she is."

"What do you believe?" Viper asked.

Flipper leaned against the dresser for a minute and thought about Viper's question. "Too early to tell."

"Did you ask her out on a date?" Coop wanted to know. They could hear Coop's two-year-old son, Laramie, chattering in the background.

"No, not yet." Flipper's attraction to her had been instant. He'd felt it the moment he looked into her face. Discussing her now wasn't helping matters.

All it did was force him to recall what a beautiful woman she was—a woman he would have to spend time with in order to discover the truth.

"Then how do you plan to see her again if you don't ask her out?" Mac wanted to know, interrupting Flipper's thoughts.

"I ordered a pair of earrings to go with the necklace I bought for Mom. She has to make the earrings and I'll make my move when I pick up my purchases in two days."

"And if she turns you down?" Viper asked.

"Not an option. I now have less than thirty days to get this all straightened out."

"We should be there with you, watching your back," Bane said.

"No, you guys are just where you need to be, which is home with your families. I've got this."

"Well, some of our families don't appreciate us being home," Mac grumbled.

Flipper rolled his eyes. They'd all heard the complaints from Mac before. After every extended mission, their teammate went home to an adjustment period, where he would have to get to know his wife all over again and reclaim his position as head of the house. Sometimes the adjustment didn't go over well. Mac had a strong personality and so did Mac's wife, Teri. "Do we have to send both you and Teri into the time-out corners?"

"Hell, I didn't do anything," Mac exclaimed.

Flipper chuckled. "Yeah, right. You better get

your act together, Mac. No other woman is going to put up with your BS."

"Whatever. So what did you notice about the place today?"

Mac was changing the subject and Flipper decided to let him. "Everything matched the architectural report I was given. Even with the repairs due to the hurricane, there were no major changes. Front door. Back door. High windows. Glass storefront. No video cameras outside. There are several rooms in back. One is being used as a tattoo parlor. I didn't see the person who runs it. I think I'll go out tonight and do a little more investigating," he said, sliding into a black T-shirt.

"Be careful, Flipper," Viper said. "Although you might not have seen any video cameras, that doesn't mean there aren't any."

"I know. That's why I'm wearing my Pilf gear."

Everybody knew how much Flipper liked digital technology. In addition to all the futuristic developments the military used, Flipper had created a few of his own high-tech gadgets behind the scenes. Some had been so impressive the federal government had patented them as Pilf gear to be used by the military. Pilf was the name Flip spelled backward. On more than one occasion, Flipper had been offered a position with the Department of Defense's Research and Development Department and had turned down each offer, saying he loved being a Navy SEAL more.

"We don't give a damn if you plan to parade around naked tonight, Flipper. Be careful."

He knew Mac was in his big-brother mode. "Okay, Mac. I hear you and I will be careful."

"Call to check in when you get back to the hotel tonight," Bane said.

"It will be late and I wouldn't want to wake up any babies, kids or a pregnant woman. I'll text everyone."

A short while later, wearing undetectable military gear under his clothing, Flipper left his hotel using the stairs.

Two

Two

Two days later, Swan didn't leave the shop for lunch. Instead she accepted Jamila's offer to bring her something back from the sandwich shop on the corner. Although she'd tried convincing herself her decision to hang around had nothing to do with the fact that David Holloway would be returning today to pick up his items, she knew it did.

And her anticipation was so bad that every time the door chimed, her heartbeat would kick up a notch, only to slow back down when someone other than him walked in. She checked her watch. The shop would be closing in an hour. What if he didn't make it before closing time? What if…?

The door chimed, and her heart nearly stopped when David Holloway walked in.

She'd told herself the man hadn't *really* looked as good as she remembered from that first day, but now she saw that he did. In fact, today he looked even better than she remembered. Maybe it had something to do with the unshaven look. Men with a day-old beard had sex appeal. But it could also be his tan, which indicated he'd probably spent the last couple of days lying in the sun.

If he'd been at the beach, there was a good chance he hadn't been there alone. But didn't he say he was in the Keys working?

Why did she care?

She quickly dismissed all those questions from her mind as she continued to watch him walk toward her in a strut that had blood rushing through her veins. His blond hair and blue eyes seemed brighter against his tanned skin. He was deliciousness with a capital *D*.

But then that capital *D* could also stand for *dangerous* if she wasn't careful. Or it could stand for *delusional* if she didn't get control of her senses. Right now, she would play it safe and claim the capital *D* stood for *David*. She couldn't allow herself to think any other way for now, no matter how tempting.

She smiled. "Hello, David."

"Hi, Swan."

"Your tan looks nice."

He chuckled. "So does yours."

She grinned. "Yes, but mine's permanent."

"I know and I like it."

She didn't say anything to that because she understood what he was implying. He was letting her know he had no problem with interracial dating. She didn't have a problem with it either. Neither had her father, although his family had had conniptions about his marriage to Swan's mother. She pushed that thought to the back of her mind, refusing to dwell on an extended family that had never accepted her or her mother.

She reached behind the counter and retrieved a box. "I hope you like the way the earrings came out." She opened it to show him the final earrings.

"Wow!" He ran his finger over the stone that came closest to matching the color of his eyes. "You're very gifted."

"Thank you, and I believe your mother will love them."

"I'm sure she will. I think I've outdone my brothers this time."

She closed the box and placed it, along with the one containing the necklace, into a shopping bag. "You have brothers?"

"Yes, four of them. I'm the youngest."

"My goodness. Any sisters?"

"Not a one. Three of my four brothers are married, so I have sisters-in-law. They are the best."

"And the fourth brother is still single?"

"He's divorced but has a beautiful little girl. And

she's my parents' only granddaughter. They have six grandsons."

"Sounds like a nice family. Is your father still alive?"

"Yes, Dad is still alive. He and Mom own a medical supply store."

She nodded as she offered him the bag. "Here you are, David. Thanks again for your business."

He accepted the bag. "Thanks. Now that this is taken care of, there's something I want to ask you, Swan."

She lifted a brow. "What?"

"Would you go out to dinner with me tonight?"

Normally Flipper was good at reading people, but he was having a hard time reading Swan. He definitely needed to remedy that. Although both Commanding Officer Shields and Admiral Martin were convinced of her innocence, the jury was still out for him. He had to remain impartial and deal with the facts, not speculations.

For two nights, he'd searched the area around her shop. Getting inside without triggering her alarm hadn't been easy, but he'd done it. Once he'd picked up the location of the interior security cameras, it was a small matter to make sure he stayed out of their range and within a certain perimeter until he could deactivate them and do what he needed to.

"Go to dinner with you?"

"Yes."

She was apparently mulling over his invitation in her mind and he would give her time to do that. He had no problems studying her while he waited for her answer. Today she looked even prettier than the other day. He figured it had to be the lighting in this place.

"Yes, David. I'll go to dinner with you. You name the restaurant and I'll meet you there."

She wasn't going to give him her address and he had no problem with her being cautious. Little did she know he already knew where she lived and had visited yesterday while she'd been here at her shop. She had a beautiful home on the ocean. Inside it was as neat as a pin with no clutter. She'd even made up her bed before leaving.

"I noticed a restaurant off the pier. Summer Moon. I've heard only good things about it since I've been here." And he knew the place was within walking distance from her home.

"Everything you've heard is true. Summer Moon is fabulous and one of my favorite eating places. I'd love to join you there. What time?"

"What about seven? Will that be a good time for you?" He figured since it didn't get dark until close to nine, he wouldn't have to worry about her walking to the restaurant in the dark. After dinner, he would walk her home or put her in a cab regardless of the fact that she lived only a few blocks away.

"Seven is perfect."

"Good. I'll see you then."

* * *

Swan watched him walk out of the shop.

David had the kind of tush that made a woman want to squeeze it…after doing all kinds of other things with it.

She jumped when fingers snapped in her face. Frowning, she looked at Jamila. "What did you do that for?"

"To keep you from having an orgasm in the middle of your shop."

Swan rolled her eyes. Jamila, the attractive twenty-two-year-old green-eyed blonde, evidently thought reaching a climactic state was that easy. "It would take more than ogling a man for that to happen, Jamila."

"I don't know. Your eyes were about to pop out of their sockets and your breathing sounded funny."

"You're imagining things."

"Denial can be good for the soul, I guess. So who is he?"

Swan and Jamila had more than an employer-and-employee relationship. Their friendship had started when Jamila first moved to the island a couple of years ago and patronized Swan's. It didn't take long to discover that Jamila liked nice things and decided Swan's was one of her favorite places to shop. Last year, Jamila had been looking for work after she lost her job as a day cruise ship captain.

As far as Swan was concerned, it hadn't been Jamila's fault when an intoxicated customer had tried coming on to her and she'd kicked him in the balls. Surgery had to be performed and the man had sued the ship company. They'd settled out of court but not before firing Jamila for all the trouble she'd caused.

Jamila had gotten an attorney herself so she could not only sue her former employer for an unfair firing but also sue the intoxicated customer. To avoid negative publicity, her former employer wanted to settle out of court with her as well. The intoxicated customer was also trying to settle since the woman he'd been with on the ship hadn't been his wife. If things worked out in Jamila's favor, she wouldn't need a job at Swan's much longer.

"He is a customer who came into the shop a couple of days ago to buy a gift for his mother."

"His mother and not his wife?"

"He says his mother."

Jamila snorted. "Men lie all the time."

How well she knew, Swan thought. Then she wondered why Jamila was men-bashing today. This wasn't the first comment of that type she'd made since arriving to work. Her boyfriend had come to town a couple of days ago with the cruise ship, right? So what was going on?

Swan decided not to ask. She didn't want to hear another sad story about a man that would ruin her date tonight with David. It was a date she was definitely looking forward to. She figured going out to dinner with him wouldn't be risky as long as she kept things in perspective.

She knew what could happen if she let her guard down when it came to a man.

Flipper deliberately arrived at Summer Moon early so he could see when Swan arrived. His stomach felt floaty the moment she turned the corner from the street where she lived.

Be still, my...everything.

She was wearing a printed sundress and a pair of high-heeled sandals, but what caught his attention— and was still holding it tight—were her long shapely legs that seemed to go on forever. He would love to see where they stopped under that dress. He forced that thought to the back of his mind.

But the closer she got, the more that thought wiggled back to the forefront. He shouldn't let it. He was on assignment and she was the subject of an investigation. He shouldn't see her as temptation. Letting his guard down around her could be a dangerous and costly mistake. He had to keep his head screwed on straight, no matter how innocent she seemed and how beautiful she was, and she was definitely one gorgeous woman.

Men, even some with female companions, were giving Swan second looks, and Flipper tried to downplay his anger. He had no right to be upset about other men checking her out when he was checking her out himself. The best thing to do to control his crazy reaction was to stop looking at her, so he glanced down at his bottle of beer and thought about the reports he'd finished reading a short while ago on her employee and her tenant.

Jamila Fairchild had worked for Swan for a year. He knew all about her former job as a captain of a day cruise ship, why she'd gotten fired and her litigation against not only her former employer but also the man who'd caused the ruckus in the first place. Naval intelligence hadn't left any stone unturned in Ms. Fairchild's report and she'd come up clean. Flipper would verify that she was.

Then there was Rafe Duggers, the tattoo artist. Although his parlor was located inside Swan's shop, there was a back door for his customers to use without entering through the jewelry shop. Flipper hadn't gotten a chance to look around the tattoo parlor and he intended to do another visit in a few days. Rafe was too squeaky-clean to be true.

No wonder naval intelligence was trying to point the finger at Swan. After all, it was her shop and they had somehow traced activity as originating there. But how? When? He hadn't found anything.

He had searched Swan's office, the small kitchen in the back, the bathrooms and another room that she used as a workshop where she made her jewelry. He'd come up with nothing, even after checking out her computer. So what were the grounds for accusing her?

Flipper's mind flicked back to Swan and he stood when the waiter escorted her to his table. "Hello, Swan. You look nice."

"Thanks and so do you. I was trying to be early and you still beat me here," she said, sitting down across from him.

"I was thirsty," he said, sitting back down and indicating the beer. Now that she was here and sitting directly across from him, he was more than thirsty. If he wasn't careful, he could have a full-fledged attack of desire. She had a pair of beautiful shoulders and her skin appeared soft and smooth to the touch.

Then his mind drifted to wanting her and he quickly snatched it back. "You walked here. Does that mean you live close by?" he asked, deciding it was best to keep the conversation moving.

"Yes, not too far," she said. He knew she was deliberately being evasive.

The waiter handed him another beer and gave them both menus. "What would like to drink, miss?" the waiter asked her.

"A glass of Moscato please."

When the waiter left, she glanced over at Flipper before picking up her menu. "You're not working so hard that you're not enjoying the Keys, are you?"

"I'm doing a bit of both. I admit the ocean is beautiful tonight."

She smiled. "I think it's beautiful every night."

He nodded as he took another sip of his beer, straight from the bottle. "So are you a native or a transplant?"

"A native. I was born and raised right here on the

island in the same house I live in now. My mother never made it to the hospital before I was born."

He raised a brow. "She didn't?"

"No. Mom came from a part of Jamaica where the belief was that when it comes to delivering a baby, a midwife is better than a medical doctor. My father promised to find her a midwife here. Otherwise she would have insisted that I be born in Jamaica and he didn't want that. He wanted me born in America."

"So he was able to find a midwife?"

"Yes, but I was born a few weeks early and the midwife wasn't here."

"So who delivered you?"

"My dad, with the help of three of his closest military friends. They were stationed at the base here and were visiting, watching a football game at the time. Needless to say, over the years I've gotten four different versions of what happened that night. My mother didn't remember a thing other than it took four men to deliver me. Although Godpop 1 claims my father passed out trying to cut the umbilical cord."

Flipper laughed. He then asked, "Godpop 1?"

"Yes, my father's three closest friends, the ones who assisted that night, became my godfathers. That's how I distinguish them. Godpop 1, Godpop 2 and Godpop 3."

Flipper nodded. No wonder the three men felt such strong ties to her. "You're lucky to have three godfathers. I don't have a one."

"Yes, I'm lucky," she said, after the waiter set

the glass of wine in front of her. "They were my and Mom's rocks after we lost Dad, especially when my grandparents showed up at the funeral trying to cause problems."

Then, as if she realized she might have shared too much, she asked, "So what do you plan to order?"

Swan thought David had picked the right place for them to have dinner. When he asked for recommendations on what to order, she suggested Summer Moon's crab cakes and, as usual, they were delicious. The mango salad was superb, and after dinner they enjoyed listening to the live band.

When the band played their last song, she glanced over at David to discover him staring at her. The intensity in his gaze nearly scorched her and she took a sip of her wine. "Thanks for dinner, David."

"Thank you for accepting my invitation. The place is about to close. Are you ready to go?" he asked her.

"Yes." Because she knew he would suggest that he walk her home, she added, "If you still have a little bit of energy, I'd like to treat you to something."

He lifted a brow. "What?"

"A laser show that officially kicks off the summer season. It's a short walk from here." Since it was in the opposite direction from where she lived, she would have no problem catching a cab back later—alone.

He smiled as he beckoned for the waiter to bring their check. "Then by all means, let's go."

Once the show began, it didn't take Swan long to decide that David was wonderful company. She could tell he was enjoying the laser lights as much as she was.

She attended the event every year and it seemed the displays only got better and better. Each year, they honored a different state and tonight that state was New York. The New Yorkers in the crowd showed their happiness with whistles and shouting. And when a huge display of the Statue of Liberty flashed across the sky in a brilliant variety of colors, Swan caught her breath.

After that, the showrunners took the time to honor the servicemen in attendance with a flag salute. She couldn't hold back her tears as she remembered how much her father had loved his country and how, in the end, he'd given his life for it and for her.

David must have detected her weepy state. He pulled her closer to his side.

"Sorry," she said. "I get all emotional about our servicemen and servicewomen, especially those who sacrifice their lives."

"You sound very patriotic."

She pulled back and looked up at him. "Of course I'm patriotic. Aren't you? You did say you used to be in the military, right?"

"Yes, I'm very patriotic," he said, wrapping his arms around her. She wished she didn't think the arms around her felt so strong and powerful.

"I thought you would be, but you said I sounded patriotic as if you thought that perhaps I wasn't."

"I apologize. I didn't mean it that way. I'm glad you're so patriotic."

She nodded, accepting his apology. Scanning the area around them, she said, "They are serving complimentary wine coolers over there. Let's go grab a couple."

"Sure thing." He placed his hand on the small of her back.

The contact sent a rush of desire through her that was so strong she had to force herself to breathe. Swan quickly glanced up at him and noticed he'd been affected by the feeling as well. However, he hadn't removed his hand.

Instead, he pressed his hand more firmly into her back and she felt him urging her away from the crowd and toward a cluster of low-hanging palm trees. Once they stood in the shadows, he turned her in his arms, stared down at her for a long moment and then lowered his mouth to hers.

The moment their lips touched, he slid his tongue inside her mouth, and she recalled her thoughts from earlier that day. He was delicious—and dangerous— with a capital *D*. And it wasn't just because he tasted of the beer he'd consumed at Summer Moon, but because he tasted like a hot-blooded man. All the sexiness she'd seen in him was reflected in his kiss.

When she began kissing him back, he wrapped

his arms around her and deepened the exchange by crushing his mouth to hers.

She didn't mind his eagerness. In fact, she welcomed the pleasure of his hunger, his taste, which was getting more provocative with every stroke of his tongue. It had been a while since she'd been kissed, and certain parts of her were reminding her of just how long it had been. Not only that, those certain parts were goading her to keep up with the forceful demands of his mouth. She hadn't been kissed so thoroughly or possessively before in her life. Or so passionately.

Swan wasn't sure how long they stood there kissing. It wasn't until they heard the sound of fireworks that they disengaged their mouths. She glanced up as more fireworks exploded in the sky. Instead of looking up, David trailed his tongue along her neck and collarbone with wet licks.

"Say you'll go out with me again, Swan."

There was no way she wouldn't say it. She looked at him and saw deep desire in the eyes looking back at her. "Yes, I'll go out with you again."

"Good."

And then he lowered his head and kissed her again.

Flipper had tried everything possible to get to sleep. He'd counted sheep, counted backward, rolled his eyes for a full thirty minutes and had even tried hypnotizing himself. None of those things helped.

He couldn't remember ever feeling this tight with need. So here he was, close to four in the morning, and still wide awake. Nothing he did could erase the taste of Swan from his mouth and the act of kissing her from his mind.

The kiss would complicate his mission, but it hadn't been an act. It had been the most real thing he'd done in a long time. He had wanted that kiss. Needed it. It had been inevitable.

Sitting across from her at dinner and watching the movement of her mouth had caused a throbbing need to erupt in his gut, making him rock hard. There had been no way to ignore the delicious heat of carnal attraction spiking between them.

And the patriotism he'd seen in her eyes when she'd gotten teary-eyed in support of servicemen, and then when she'd told him about her work with the city to find lodging for homeless vets, hadn't helped. Neither had the fact that she'd looked stunning and had smelled irresistibly hot tonight.

Kissing her had made his entire body feel alive. Had revved up his passion to a degree that his libido had him tied in knots and had his pulse tripping. He could feel himself riding the fine edge of intense desire heightened by more sexual energy than he'd felt in a long time.

While kissing her, he hadn't cared that they could have been seen in spite of the low-hanging trees. He'd been beyond the point of caring. He'd been tempted to drag her to the ground right there.

Damn. How was he going to clear her of anything when the only thing he'd wanted to clear her of was her clothes?

He had access to women whenever he needed them. There were always women who went bonkers for men in uniform and he had no problem engaging in one-night stands. Those types of relationships had always been the way to go for him. He liked being single, coming and going as he pleased, with no one to worry about but himself.

It had been a long time since any woman had kept him up at night and that wasn't cool.

Grabbing his phone he texted the message: If anyone is awake. Call me.

Within seconds, his phone rang. It was Bane. "What's going on, Flipper?"

"Why are you up?" Flipper asked his friend.

"Feeding time. Crystal and I rotate."

"Oh? You're breastfeeding now?"

"No, smart-ass. The trio are on bottles now. What are you doing up?"

Flipper stretched out across the bed. "I couldn't sleep. I tried everything. I even tried to hypnotize myself."

Bane chuckled. "I guess it didn't work."

"No, it didn't work."

"So why can't you sleep, Flip?"

He wasn't one to kiss and tell, no matter who the listener was, so he said, "I still haven't figured out anything about the situation down here and the CO and the admiral are depending on me."

"Maybe they're going to have to accept naval intelligence's report that she's guilty."

"I don't think so." Flipper paused. "She cried tonight."

"What do you mean, she cried?"

"Today was the first day of summer and there's an annual laser show to commemorate the change in season. One of the laser displays was a salute to New York, where they did an awesome light replica of the Statue of Liberty and American soldiers. She got emotional and cried. Dammit, Bane, a person who is betraying their country doesn't cry for those in the service. Call me a sucker for tears but I don't believe she has a traitorous bone in her body."

"Then it's up to you to prove it. What about those two people who hang around her shop?"

"The woman who works for her and the tattoo guy? Both seem clean. But I will dig further. I have to."

"Okay, but make sure while you're digging for answers that you're not burrowing yourself into something you can't handle."

"What do you mean?"

"I think you know what I mean, Flip. You were sent there to prove her innocence—not to prove she has a passionate side. Remember that. Good night."

Flipper clicked off the phone and rubbed a hand down his face. Little did Bane know that after the kiss with Swan tonight, Flipper was driven to do more than prove her innocence, or her passion.

He wanted to possess Swan completely.

And he had a feeling the desire wasn't one-sided. He'd seen the look in her eyes during dinner. He'd felt how her body had responded to his touch. He was certain the same sensations that rushed through him had affected her, too. Kissing her had been inevitable, something they both wanted and needed.

The genie called desire was out of the bottle and Flipper honestly didn't know how to get it back inside.

Three

Swan pushed away from her desk and took another huge gulp of ice-cold lemonade. It had been that way for her all day. Instead of concentrating on the online orders she needed to fill and ship out, her mind was wrapped around that kiss from last night.

All she had to do was close her eyes to remember every single detail, specifically every sensuous lick of his tongue inside her mouth. Even now, the memory sent multiple sensations coursing through her body, causing pleasure the likes of which she'd never encountered before.

She looked up at the sound of a knock on her door. "Yes?"

Jamila stuck her head in. "Mr. Make-you-have-an-instant-orgasm is back."

Swan didn't need to ask Jamila what she meant or who she was talking about. "Any reason you can't wait on him?"

Jamila smiled naughtily. "I could use the pleasure but he specifically asked for you."

Swan nodded. "I'll be out in a minute."

"Okay, I will let him know."

Swan reached over and took another gulp of her lemonade. She didn't want to admit it, but after that kiss last night, David could become an addiction. Besides putting down a gallon of lemonade, she'd been twitching in her seat most of the day, thinking that if his tongue could do that to her mouth, then Lordy…she could only imagine what else he would be able to do…

She quickly stood, refusing to go there even as a naughty part of her mind wished that he would. Leaving her office, she rounded the corner and stopped.

David stood in the middle of her shop wearing a pair of khaki shorts and a muscle shirt. The sight of his muscled abs and strong legs made Swan bite back a groan. Just when she thought he couldn't get any sexier, he'd proved her wrong.

He must have heard the sound of her footsteps because he turned and smiled.

As if on cue, she smiled back. "Hello, David, you came to make more purchases?" Hopefully he would take the hint that she didn't expect him to just drop by without a reason.

"Yes. I'm buying jewelry for my three sisters-in-law and would love for you to offer suggestions."

Swan couldn't help but smile since she liked making sales. What store owner wouldn't? "I'd love to help you pick out pieces of jewelry for them."

An hour later, Swan stood at the cash register to ring up all of David's purchases. With her assistance, he'd selected some really nice pieces, with a number of the stones chosen specifically because that's what he'd said they would like. Then he wanted earrings to complement the necklaces, which he paid for in advance. They decided to select stones for the earrings tomorrow since they'd spent a lot of time on the necklaces today and her shop would be closing in less than an hour.

From their conversation, she knew the Holloways were a close-knit family. He'd even pulled out his phone to show her pictures of his young niece and nephews.

"No pressure for you to marry?" she asked when he tucked his phone back into the pocket of his shorts.

"None. My parents have been married for more than forty years and are still very much in love. They make sure their kids and grandkids know that. They believe we will know when it's time for us to marry without any pressure from them. We'll be the ones to have to live with the people we choose. They just want all their children to be happy."

She nodded. "I like the way your parents think. I want to believe that, had my parents lived, they would have a similar philosophy. Dad used to tell me all the time that he wanted me to grow up and be whatever I wanted to be and do whatever I wanted to do, and that he and Mom would always have my back."

She suddenly felt a deep sense of loss. "Appreciate your parents, David. You never know how truly great they are until they're gone. But in all honesty, I think I've always known I had great parents."

At that moment, he did something she wouldn't have expected from him—he reached out and took her hand. "They sound great and I know they're proud of your accomplishments."

"Thanks." That was a nice thing for him to say. To avoid thinking about just how nice he was, she slid the bag with his purchases toward him and gave him the credit card slip. He signed it and gave it back to her.

"How would you like to go to happy hour at Danica's with me?"

After talking about her parents and missing them like crazy, she could use more than just an hour of happiness. She would love to be able to have a lifetime of that feeling.

It wasn't that she was *unhappy*, because she wasn't, but there were times when she wondered if maybe there was more out there for her than what was currently in her life. Perhaps she was short-changing herself on some things. What those things were, she had no idea.

"I would love to go but good luck getting a table at Danica's. They have the best hot wings and are always crowded, *especially* for happy hour. I think the entire island heads over there at five."

"Since I know you don't close your shop until five, how about if we meet over there at five-thirty? I guarantee we'll have a place to sit."

"Um, sounds like you might have connections, David Holloway."

"We'll see." He took the bag and turned to leave, and just like before, she watched his movements until he was no longer in sight.

"Wow. You do have connections, don't you?" Swan said, sliding into a stool at the bar. "I've been here a number of times and the best seat I've ever gotten is at one of those tables outside."

Flipper smiled. Like at Summer Moon, he'd arrived early and was waiting for her. He liked seeing her stroll down the sidewalk looking as beautiful as ever.

Today she was wearing a pair of shorts and a pretty top. Her legs were long and shapely and he could imagine them wrapped around him while...

Whoa, he didn't need to go there. Ever since that kiss, he'd been trying *not* to go there—no matter how tempted he was to do so. Quickly, he changed the direction of his thoughts.

"I know Danica personally," he said, trying hard to keep his naughty thoughts in check.

She lifted a brow. "Really? How?"

There was no way he would tell her the whole story. Danica was the godmother of former SEAL team member Nick Stover. Nick had given up being a SEAL a few years ago to take a job with Homeland Security after his wife had triplets. Instead of the whole history, Flipper gave her a modified version. "Her godson and I used to work together."

"Oh." The bartender chose that moment to take their drink order.

"I know you used to be in the military at one point but what do you do now?" she asked once the bartender had walked away.

Flipper had expected that question sooner or later and had a prepared answer. "I travel a lot and my job deals with ocean marine work. I guess you can say I'm a specialist in that area."

"Sounds interesting."

He chuckled. "Trust me, it is."

The bartender set their beers in front of them along with a huge plate of hot wings. They dug in.

"Your assistant at the store seems nice," Flipper commented. "I hope she didn't get offended when I asked specifically for you."

"No, very little offends Jamila, trust me."

"You've known her a long time?"

If his question seemed odd, she didn't mention it. "We met a couple of years ago when she moved to the island. The first time she came into my shop she nearly bought out the place. Like you, she has a huge family living up north and wanted to buy holiday gifts for everyone. Thanks to her, I made my month's quota in that one day. She earned a friend for life."

Flipper took a long swig of his beer. What Swan had just told him was interesting. Based on the naval intelligence report he'd read, Jamila didn't have any family. No parents, siblings, aunts, uncles or cousins. She'd been adopted and her adopted parents had been killed in a car accident in her last year of high school. And they hadn't lived in the north but out west in California.

Why had Jamila lied?

"So you hired her that day?" he asked, grinning, trying to make a joke of what she'd told him.

"No, she had a job as a ship captain at one of the day cruise companies in town. When things didn't work out for her there, I hired her on part-time."

He'd read the report and knew why Jamila had been let go and knew about her pending lawsuits. There was a big chance both cases would be settled out of court in her favor. "Is the reason she's part-time because she's a student?"

"Sort of. She saw how much money Rafe makes and—"

"Rafe?" He knew who Rafe was, but Swan didn't know that.

"Yes, Rafe. He rents space in my shop where he operates a tattoo parlor. He's good and always has a steady stream of customers. Some are so pleased with his work that they recommend him to others. I've known people to fly in just to use his services."

She took a sip of her beer, grinned and added, "Jamila decided to give him some real competition by becoming a tattoo artist as well. I have to admit she's pretty good. But Rafe doesn't seem worried. He even allows her to assist him sometimes. I guess you can say he's taken her under his wing. I think that's nice of him."

Flipper took another swig of his beer. "Yes, that is nice of him. Real nice."

Later that night, as they waited for a car at the taxi stand, Swan turned to face David. "I had a wonderful time this evening."

Once again, she had enjoyed his company and hated that their time together was about to end. It didn't come as a surprise to her that the sexual chemistry between them was more explosive than ever. The kiss they'd shared the night before had ignited something within her. From the way she'd noticed him looking at her, she believed something had ignited within him as well.

More than once, her smooth bare legs had brushed against his hairy ones. The sensual contact had sent a gush of desire through her.

The first few times it happened, she'd pulled

away. But finally, she'd decided not to pull her legs back and he'd given her one of those *I know you did that on purpose* looks and she had smiled innocently and sipped her beer.

He had initiated the next physical contact and she could envision his mind at work trying to decide how to push her sensual buttons. She doubted he could push them more than he was already.

"I'm glad I got to meet Ms. Danica. After all the years I've been living here, this was my first time meeting her. She's nice."

"Yes, she is."

"And I definitely appreciate this," she said, holding up the bag of hot wings the older woman had given Swan to take home.

"I think she appreciated how much you enjoyed them."

She chuckled. "You're probably right."

"What do you have planned for later?" he asked in a deep, husky tone that seemed to have dropped a purposeful octave.

He had taken her hand when they left Danica's to walk to the taxi stand. The feel of his fingers entwined with hers had stirred something within her, something that grew with every step they took. She was aware of every detail about him as they walked together. Because of his long legs, more than once he had to slow his pace so she could keep up with him.

Swan could have walked home but figured he would suggest walking there with her. She was still cautious about letting him know where she lived. When she left Jamaica to begin living on her own, her mother had drilled into her the danger of letting a man know where you lived too soon. In her heart, Swan felt David was safe, but still...

"It's near the end of the month and I need to work on the books for my accountant." No need to mention she had tried doing that very thing today at work and hadn't been able to concentrate for remembering their kiss from last night.

"How about dinner tomorrow night?" he asked her.

She didn't answer right away. Instead, she broke eye contact with him and glanced down at the sidewalk. Hadn't they seen each other enough these last few days? Where was this leading? Wasn't he leaving the Keys in less than a month?

She glanced back at him. "Why? We've gone out twice already. I wouldn't want to dominate your time."

"You're not. And the reason I want to take you out again is because I enjoy your company."

She certainly enjoyed his. "Can I ask you something, David?"

He nodded. "Yes?" Considering her history with William, it was something she probably should have asked David before going out on their first date. She'd discovered the hard way that a man not wearing a wedding ring didn't mean anything these days.

"What do you want to ask me, Swan?"

She met his gaze and hoped she would be able to see the truth in his eyes. "Do you have a wife or a significant other?"

Instead of guilt flashing in his eyes, she saw surprise. "No. I'm not married and I've never been married. I dated a woman for years but because of my frequent travels, she decided to end things. That was over six years ago." He then leaned against a light post and asked, "What about you, Swan? Have you ever been married or is there a significant other?"

"Of course not."

He nodded slowly. "Then I assume there is a reason you thought that maybe I was in a relationship?"

"I needed to be sure."

He didn't say anything. Instead, he looked at her as if tumbling her answer around in his head. "But like I said, I assume there is a reason you needed to know."

"Yes." However, she didn't intend to go into any details.

"Well, rest assured there is not a Mrs. David Holloway out there anywhere. Nor is there any woman wearing my ring. Satisfied?"

"Yes."

At that moment, a taxi pulled up. "Thanks for dinner again." She was about to move toward the taxi when he reached out, took hold of her hand and tugged her to him. He lowered his mouth to hers and kissed her quickly but soundly on the lips.

"I'll see you tomorrow," he said, his words a soft whisper against her wet lips.

"Tomorrow?" she asked in a daze from his kiss.

"Yes, we're supposed to go over designs for the earrings, remember?"

It was hard to remember anything after a kiss like that. "Yes, I remember," she said.

"Then I'll see you tomorrow."

She nodded, and when he opened the door for her, she quickly got into the taxi and headed home alone.

The moment Flipper entered his hotel room he went to the small refrigerator beneath the wet bar and pulled out a beer. Just then it didn't matter that he'd already drank a couple at Danica's. He needed another. There was just something about Swan that was getting to him, touching him on a level he wasn't used to when it came to women. He had truly enjoyed her company tonight.

He and his SEAL teammates had just returned from a two-month mission in South Africa and more than anything he had needed to unwind. He would be home in Texas doing just that had he not been summoned to the admiral's office.

So here he was, and although he was in Key West on official military business and he was supposed to be investigating Swan, he loved spending time with her.

Tonight, when she'd met Danica, it had been

priceless. You would have thought Swan had met a Hollywood celebrity. He had sat there while the two women conversed, immediately as comfortable as old friends.

The sound of Swan's voice had been maddeningly sexy with a tinge of sweetness that had stroked his senses. For the first time since returning to the States, he had allowed himself to uncoil, to loosen up and relax while appreciating the richness of her personality. Her persona was uniquely hers and the sensuality of her very being called to him in a primitive way.

And that wasn't good.

Taking a huge swig of his beer, he switched his thoughts to what he should be focused on—what she'd told him about Jamila and Rafe. Remembering what she'd said, he pulled his phone out of the pocket of his shorts and with one click he connected to his friend Nick Stover.

"This better be good, Flipper. Natalie is taking an art class at the university tonight and I have babysitting duties."

Flipper couldn't help but smile. Like Bane, Nick had triplets and from the sound of the noise in the background, the triplets had him. "Stop whining. Taking care of a trio of three-year-olds can't be too bad."

"Then you come do it."

"Sorry, I'm on assignment."

"So I hear. In the Keys, right?"

He figured for Nick to know that much meant he'd either talked to Bane, Viper, Mac or Coop. "Yes, I'm in Key West."

"While you're there, be sure to stop by Danica's. Give her a hug for me."

"I did that already. Tonight, in fact."

"Good."

"I think she has more photos of the triplets than you do."

"I wouldn't doubt it. So if you can't be a backup babysitter, why are you calling?"

"When you arrive at your cushy job at Homeland Security tomorrow, there are two people I need you to check out for me. I've read naval intelligence reports on them, but something isn't adding up. Call me a suspicious bastard, but after that situation with Bane, when those traitors within the agencies were exposed, I'm not taking any chances."

He then told Nick about the discrepancies between what the reports said and what Swan had told him. "Somebody is lying. Either Jamila lied to Swan or someone falsified the report, and I want to know which it is."

Four

"He's *baaack*," Jamila said.

Swan pushed away from her desk. She didn't have to ask who Jamila was talking about. "I was expecting him," she said in what she hoped was a professional tone. "He needs to look at designs for earrings."

"If you say so. I'll send him in here."

Swan was about to tell Jamila they could use the computer out front, but Jamila was gone after closing the door behind her.

Standing, Swan inhaled deeply. How she had finished the books last night, she wasn't sure. Thoughts of David had been stronger than ever after their night out. When she'd gone to bed, she had dreamed about him. Okay, she'd dreamed about him before, but the dreams last night had been so hot it was a wonder they hadn't burned her sheets. She had been tempted to do something she hadn't done in a long time, re-activate her vibrator.

She drew in a deep breath when she heard the knock on her door. "Come in."

And in walked David, looking sexier than he had the other times she'd seen him. Last night, to stay focused, she had come up with every reason she could think of for why she shouldn't be attracted to him and why a relationship with him wouldn't work.

She'd even thrown in the race card. But of course that was thrown out when she remembered her parents and how happy they had been together. Yet she also couldn't forget how her father's family had ostracized him for his choice in love. Would David's family be the same way? There was no reason to think they wouldn't. And wasn't she getting ahead of herself for even throwing love in the mix?

"Hello, David."

"Swan." He glanced at her desk, taking in all the folders spread across it. "You're busy."

"That's fine. Besides, I need to get those earrings ready for you."

Now that he'd seen her desk, it would make perfect sense for her to suggest they use the computer out front to design the earrings. But now that she had him behind closed doors, she liked it.

Not that she planned on doing anything about having him here.

"Please have a seat while I clear off my desk." Today he was wearing jeans and she couldn't help but watch how fluidly his body eased into the chair. How the denim stretched across a pair of muscular thighs. She quickly switched her gaze before he caught her looking.

"Nice office."

"Thanks." She closed the folders and placed them in her inbox tray. She then glanced over at him and caught him looking at her. She followed his gaze and soon figured out why he was staring.

She was wearing a skirt with a V-neck blouse, and when she'd leaned over to place the folders in the tray, her shirt had shown a portion of her cleavage. Instead of calling him out for trying to cop a view of her breasts, the fact that he was interested sparked a distinct warmth between her legs.

She quickly sat down. "Now if you would roll that chair over here, I am ready." Too late, she realized how that sounded and quickly added, "To look at designs."

He smiled. "I know what you meant."

He rolled his chair behind her desk to place it right next to hers. When he sat down, their legs touched. Moving away would be pretty obvious so she let the denim of his jeans rub against her bare legs.

"Now, then," she said, trying not to notice how good he smelled. "What do you think of these?" she asked, bringing up a few designs on the computer screen.

When he didn't answer, she glanced over at him and found him staring at her. Sitting so close to him, she could look directly into his laser-blue eyes. It was as if his gaze was deliberately doing something to her, causing a surge in her breath and arousal to coil in her core. She saw the dark heat in his eyes and desire clawed at her even more.

"May I make a suggestion?" he asked in a voice that seemed to wobble in a sexual way.

"It depends on what that suggestion is," she heard herself say.

He leaned in a little closer and whispered, "I want to kiss you again. Only problem is that I don't want to stop until I get enough. And I'm not sure I would."

She had been staring at his lips, watching how they moved while he talked. She slowly dragged her gaze back up to his eyes. She saw need flare in his gaze at the same time that anticipation for his kiss thickened the air flowing in and out of her lungs.

"I don't know what to say."

"Don't say anything, Swan. Just bring your mouth closer to mine."

She knew she shouldn't, but she found herself doing it anyway.

Flipper drew in a deep breath when Swan's lips were almost touching his. He flicked out his tongue and she gave a sharp intake of breath when he began licking her lips from corner to corner with the tip of his tongue.

"What are you doing?" she asked on a wobbly breath.

"Since you asked…" He captured her mouth and when she closed her eyes on a moan, he reached up and cradled her face in his hands while he kissed her with a greed he didn't know was in him.

What was there about her that made him accept the primitive part of himself that wouldn't be satisfied until he made love to her? Was it because she crept into his dreams at night and into his every waking thought? Or was it because an arrow of liquid heat shot straight to his groin whenever he saw her? Or could he blame it on the fact that whenever she touched him, he burned? She made him edgy and aroused him as no other woman could.

It was all of those things and more.

Right now, he didn't know how to back away. So he didn't. Instead he accepted the stream of heat in his gut and the crackle of energy passing between them.

Their lips were copulating in a way that sent blood coursing through his veins like a raging river. It was raw, hot and explosive, causing a hot ache to erupt in his gut. It wouldn't take much to lose control and take her here on her desk. At that moment, his entire body was tight with need, totally entranced by everything about her.

The phone rang and they quickly broke off the kiss, drawing in deep breaths of air. He watched as she reached across her desk to press the speaker button. "Thank you for calling Swan's."

At first, no one said anything and then a deep male voice said, "Swan? Are you okay? You sound out of breath."

He watched as she pulled in another deep breath before a smile touched her lips. "I'm fine, Godpop 1. How are you?"

Knowing who she was talking to on the phone was like a pail of cold water drenching Flipper. He was quickly reminded why he'd been sent to Key West. His admiral would have him court-martialed if he knew what Flipper had just done with his goddaughter. If the man had any idea how many times Flipper had kissed her already and how each time he'd wished they had gone even further…

She turned off the speaker so he heard only one side of the conversation, and from the sound of her voice, he knew she was happy about receiving the call.

Feeling a tightness in his crotch from his still-aroused body, he got up from the chair and walked to the window. If she could have this sort of effect on him just from a kiss, he didn't want to think about what would happen if he were to make love to her. Just the thought of easing his body into hers had his stomach churning and caused an ache low in his gut.

Knowing he needed to think of something else, he glanced up into the sky. It was a beautiful day. Monday was Memorial Day and he wondered if Swan had made any plans to celebrate. He'd heard there would be a parade and unlike some places in the States, where stores remained open on Memorial Day, the laid-back businesses in the Keys closed up for one big party.

He liked the Keys. When he retired from being a SEAL, he could see himself moving here to live out the rest of his days. The island was surrounded by the ocean and they didn't call him Flipper for nothing. He loved water. Being in it and being a part of it. Living this close to the sea would certainly be a plus for him. But then there was the question of how he would deal with Swan if he chose to retire here. Even if he could prove she was not guilty of espionage, there was always that possibility she would hate his guts regardless of the outcome, because he had not been truthful with her.

"Sorry about that, David."

He turned, not caring that she could see his still-hard erection. It was something he couldn't hide even if he had tried. Was she sorry they'd been interrupted or was she regretting that they'd kissed in the first place? He hoped it was the former because he doubted he could ever regret kissing her. "I take it that was one of your godfathers?" he asked, knowing it had been.

She was staring at him below the waist, but after

his question, her gaze slowly moved upward to his face. "Ah, yes, that was one of my godfathers. The other two will be calling sometime today as well. It always works out that they all call within twenty-four hours of each other."

He nodded and slowly walked back over to his chair to sit down. "I know you're busy so let's look at the designs."

Had he just seen a flash of disappointment in her eyes? Did she want them to continue what they'd been doing before she'd gotten that call? Didn't she know how close they'd both been to going off the edge and falling into waters too deep to swim out of? Even for him, a SEAL master swimmer.

Somehow they got through the next half hour looking at earring designs. Just as each one of the necklaces were different, he wanted the earrings to be different as well and reflect each one of his sisters-in-law's personalities.

When he was satisfied with his choices, he stood, convinced he needed to rush back to the hotel and take a cold shower. Sitting beside Swan and inhaling her scent without touching her was one of the most difficult things he'd had to do in a long time.

She was so female that the maleness in him couldn't help responding to everything about her. A part of him felt drugged by her scent and the intense physical awareness of her. Even now, desire was racing through his bloodstream.

"I owe you additional monies, right?" he asked.

A couple of the designs he'd selected cost more than what she'd originally estimated.

"Yes. I'll let you know the difference after I finish designing them, when you pick up everything."

He hadn't missed the fact that when he stood her gaze had immediately latched on to his crotch once again. Was she still hoping to see him with a hard-on? If that was true, then she wasn't disappointed. He could get aroused just from looking at her.

And why did she choose that moment to lick her lips? She had no idea that seeing her do such a thing sent the pulse beating in his throat and desire hammering against his ribs.

On unstable legs and with an erection the size of which should be outlawed, he moved around her desk and looked at her. "Yesterday I asked you to go to dinner with me again, but you never gave me an answer."

He figured that seeing how aroused he was, she probably wouldn't give him an answer now either. She surprised him when she said, "Yes, we can dine together this evening."

He nodded. "Okay, you get to pick the place."

She took a slip of paper off her desk, wrote something on it and handed it to him. He looked at it and he must have stared at it too long, because she said, "It's my address, David. I'm inviting you to dine with me this evening at my home."

He broke eye contact with her to glance back down at the paper she'd given him. He looked back at her while trying to downplay the heat rumbling around in his gut.

"Do you need me to bring anything?" he asked her.

"No, just yourself."

Swan glanced around her home and felt the knots beginning to twist in her stomach. She hoped she hadn't made a mistake inviting David here.

Today marked a week since they'd met and if she was going to continue to see him while he was on the island, she couldn't take advantage of his thoughtfulness and expect him to invite her out without ever returning the kindness. However, more than anything else, she needed to keep things in perspective. She needed to remember he was someone she could have a good time with and that's it.

She didn't want anything more than that.

One day, she would be ready to explore her options and consider a future with a man, but that time wasn't now. She liked being single and responsible only for herself.

She knew from Candy that a serious relationship was hard work. And on top of all that hard work, you could assume you had the right person in your life only to discover you didn't. By then, you would have opened yourself up to hurt and pain in the worst possible way.

The thought that a man had caused her best friend that kind of agony bothered Swan whenever she thought about it. Candy loved Key West as much as

Swan did, and for a man to be the reason she had moved away was disheartening.

Swan tried telling herself that not all men were like Candy's ex, Don, or like William. On days when Swan wanted to think all men were dogs, all she had to do was remember her dad.

Andrew Jamison was the yardstick she used to measure a good man. She'd watched how he had treated her mother, had seen the vibrant and sincere love between them. She had not only seen it, but she'd felt it as well. Both her parents had been demonstrative individuals and Swan had often interrupted them sharing a passionate kiss or embrace.

She still felt it here, within the walls of her house and in the very floor she walked on. All the love that had surrounded her while growing up was in this house she now called home.

She was glad her mother hadn't sold it after her father died, when Leigh had made the decision to move back home to Jamaica. Instead, she had kept the house, knowing one day Swan would want to return. It was almost too spacious for one person but Swan knew she would never sell it or move away. This house had everything she needed.

She could see the water from any room, and at night, whenever she slept with the window open, the scent of the ocean would calm her.

Her favorite room in the house was her parents' old bedroom, even though she had not moved into it. It had floor-to-ceiling windows and a balcony she liked sitting on while enjoying her coffee each morning. A couple of years ago, she'd had the balcony screened in to keep the birds from flying into her house, although she loved waking up to the sound of them chirping every morning.

Although neither one of her parents would tell her the full story, Swan knew her father had come from a wealthy family. And she knew he had been disowned by them when he had fallen in love with her mother and refused to give her up. Before dying, Leigh had given Swan a beautiful leather-bound diary to read after her death. That's what had helped keep Swan sane, reading the daily account of her mother's life and love for her father and believing they were now back together.

For weeks following her mother's death, Swan had wanted to be alone to wallow in her pity and read about what she thought was the most beautiful love story that could exist between two people. Her mother had always been expressive with the written word and Swan enjoyed reading what she'd written.

It had made Swan long for such a man, such a love. Maybe that's why she had been so quick to believe in William and why, once she'd found out about his duplicity, she'd been so reluctant to get serious with a man since.

From her mother's diary, Swan discovered her mother's appreciation for her husband's agreement to make Key West their home. The people on the island embraced diversity and tolerated different lifestyles.

Swan had read the account of when her father had been stationed at a naval base in Virginia and had sent for her mother to join him there. In the diary, her mother had written about the hateful stares they would receive whenever they went out together. The unaccepting and disapproving looks. The cruel words some people had wanted them to hear.

Her father hadn't tolerated any of it and hadn't minded confronting anyone who didn't accept his wife. But to avoid trouble, Leigh had preferred to live in Key West, where people's issues with an interracial marriage were practically nonexistent.

However, people's attitudes never kept Leigh from leaving the island to join Andrew whenever he would send for her. Oftentimes, Leigh would take Swan along and they would both join Andrew in different places for weeks at a time.

When she heard the sound of the doorbell, Swan drew in a deep breath. The time for memories was over. The only plans she had for *this* evening were for her and David to enjoy the meal she'd prepared and later enjoy each other's company.

She had no problem with them deciding what the latter entailed when that time came.

"Hello, David. Welcome to my home."

Flipper pushed from his mind the thought of how Swan would feel if she knew this wasn't his first time here. How she would react if she knew he had invaded her space without her knowledge. If she ever found out the truth, would she understand it had been done with the best of intentions? Namely, to keep her from wasting away in a federal prison after being falsely accused of a crime?

He forced those thoughts to the back of his mind as he smiled down at her. She looked absolutely stunning in a wraparound skirt and yellow blouse. "Hi. I know you said I didn't have to bring anything, but I wanted to give you these," he said, handing her both a bottle of wine and a bouquet of flowers.

He had decided on the wine early on, but the flowers had been a spur of the moment thing when he'd seen them at one of those sidewalk florist shops. Their beauty and freshness had immediately reminded him of Swan.

"Thank you. The flowers are beautiful and this is my favorite wine," she said, stepping aside to let him in.

He chuckled. "I know. I remember from the other night." There was no way he would also mention having seen several bottles of Moscato in the wine rack the time he had checked out her house.

He glanced around, pretending to see her home for the first time. "Nice place."

"Thanks. I thought we would enjoy a glass of wine and some of my mouthwatering crab balls out on the patio before dinner."

"Mouthwatering crab balls?"

"Yes, from my mom's secret recipe. You won't be disappointed," she said, leading him through a set of French doors. The first thought that came to his mind when he stepped out on her patio, which overlooked the Atlantic Ocean, was that it was a beautiful and breathtaking view. This had to be the best spot on the island to view the ocean in all its splendor.

He recalled how, as a boy, he would visit his cousins in California and dream of one day living near the beach. Over the years, being stationed in San Diego had been the next best thing. He owned an apartment close to base that was within walking distance of the beach.

However, his view was nothing like this. All she had to do was walk out her back door and step onto the sand. It was right there at her door. If he lived here, he would go swimming every day.

He glanced over at her. "The view from here is beautiful."

"I love this house and appreciate my mother for not selling it when she decided to move back to Jamaica after Dad died. She got a lot of offers for it, believe me. So have I. Mom said being here without Dad was too painful, but she knew I'd feel differently. For me, it was just the opposite. Being here and recalling all the memories of when the three of us shared this place makes me happy."

Hearing how the loss of her parents affected her made Flipper appreciate his own parents even more.

Colin and Lenora Holloway had always been their sons' staunch supporters. Their close and loving relationships had been the reason none of their sons had had any qualms about settling down and marrying. All the marriages had worked out, seemingly made in heaven, except for his brother Liam's.

When Bonnie had gotten pregnant, Liam had done the honorable thing by marrying her. Bonnie had always been a party girl and didn't intend to let marriage or being a mommy slow her down. While Liam was somewhere protecting his country as a Navy SEAL, Bonnie was conveniently forgetting she had a husband.

No one, not even Liam, had been surprised when he returned from an assignment one year and she asked for a divorce. Liam had given it to her without blinking an eye. Since then, Bonnie had remarried, which had introduced another set of issues for Liam. He was constantly taking Bonnie to court to enforce visitation rights to see his daughter because the man Bonnie married didn't like Liam coming around.

Flipper had no qualms about marriage himself, but he had too much going on right now. Namely, resisting the temptation of Swan while he continued his investigation. That was his biggest challenge. The more he was around Swan the more he liked her and the more he wanted to prove her innocence. It was hard staying objective.

"Here you are," she said, handing him a cold bottle of beer. "I figured you would like this instead of the wine."

He smiled. Like he had picked up on her drinking preferences, she had done the same with him. "Thanks. I've never been a wine man."

She chuckled. "Neither was my dad. That's how I knew when it was time for him to come home because Mom would have his favorite beer in the fridge."

He opened the bottle, took a sip and noticed her watching him. He licked his lips, liking the taste of the beer, which was the brand he'd chosen the other night at Summer Moon. When he took another sip and she continued to watch him, he lifted a brow. "Is anything wrong?"

She smiled. "No, nothing is wrong. I just love to watch how you drink your beer."

He chuckled. That was a first. No woman had ever told him that before. "And how do I drink it?"

"First there's the way your mouth fits on the beer bottle. I find it very sensuous."

He tried ignoring the quiver that surged through his veins at the tone in her voice. "Do you?"

"Yes. And then there's the way you drink it like you're enjoying every drop."

"I am."

"I can tell." Then, as if she thought perhaps she'd said too much, she took a step back. "I'll go get those crab balls for you to try."

When she turned to leave, he reached out and

touched her arm. He couldn't help it. The air all but crackled with the sexual energy between them. "Come here a minute before you go," he said, setting his beer bottle aside. "Although I do enjoy drinking beer, I've discovered I enjoy feasting on your mouth even more."

And then he lowered his mouth to hers.

Perfect timing, Swan thought, because she needed this. She'd wanted it the moment he tilted his beer bottle to his mouth and she'd watched him do so. And now he was doing her. Showing her that he was enjoying her mouth more than he'd enjoyed the beer. Just like he'd said.

There was a certain precision and meticulousness in how he mastered the art of kissing. First, as soon as his tongue would enter her mouth, he would unerringly find her tongue, capture it with his own and begin gently sucking in a way that made the muscles between her legs tighten. Then he would do other things she didn't have a name for. Things that made desire flow through her like sweet wine, kindling heated pleasure and burning passion within her.

He rocked his thighs against her and she felt him pressed against her. His arousal was massive. Instinctively, she moved her hips closer, wanting to feel him right there, at the juncture of her thighs.

When he finally pulled his mouth away, she released a deep, satisfied breath. Her mouth was still throbbing and there was an intense ache in her limbs.

Right now, their heavy breathing was the only sound audible, and the laser-blue eyes staring down at her sent a tremor to her core.

She licked her lips when she took a step back. "Ready for a few crab balls?"

"Yes," he said, after licking his own lips. "For now."

Five

He wanted her.

Flipper knew he shouldn't, but he did. All through the delicious dinner Swan had prepared and while engaging in great conversation with her, the thought of just how much he wanted her simmered to the back of his mind. Now with dinner coming to an end, desire was inching back to the forefront. Images of her naked tried to dominate his mind, the thoughts made him shift in his chair to relieve the ache at his crotch.

"Ready for dessert, David? I made key lime pie."

Right now, another kind of dessert was still teasing his taste buds. "Yes, I would love a slice, and dinner was amazing by the way. You're a good cook. My mother would absolutely love you."

Too late, he wondered why he'd said such a thing. From the look on her face, she was wondering the same thing. So he decided to clean up his mess by adding, "She admires other women who can cook."

Swan smiled. "You don't have to do that, David."

"Do what?"

"Try to retract the implications of what you said so I won't get any ideas."

He *had* done that, but not for the reason she thought. He'd done so because it wasn't right for either of them to think something was seriously developing between them. More than likely, she would hate his guts when she learned why he was really in Key West, when she discovered she was his assignment and nothing more. He couldn't tell her the truth, but he could certainly set her straight on what the future held for them.

"And what ideas do you think I wanted to retract?"

"The ones where I would think we were starting something here, the ones that meant I would be someone you'd take home to meet your mother."

He sat down his glass of ice tea, which she had served with dinner. "Any reason why I wouldn't want to take you home to meet my mother *if* we shared that kind of a relationship, Swan?" Although he didn't think he needed to let her know—again—

that they didn't share that kind of relationship, he did so anyway.

"Honestly, David, do I really have to answer that?"

"Yes, I think you do."

She stared at him for a minute. "I'm well aware when it comes to interracial relationships that not all families are accepting."

He chuckled. "My family isn't one of them, trust me. Interracial or international, we couldn't care less. My brother Brad met his wife, Sela, while working in Seoul, South Korea, and my brother Michael met Gardenia in Spain. Like I told you, my parents would accept anyone who makes us happy, regardless of race, creed, religion, nationality or color."

She didn't say anything to that. Then she broke eye contact with him to glance down into her glass of tea. Moments later, she raised her gaze back to him.

"My father's parents didn't. They threatened him with what they would do if he married Mom and they kept their word. They disowned him. Still, my mother reached out to them when Dad died to let them know he'd passed. They came to his funeral but had no qualms about letting Mom know they still would not accept her. They would only tolerate me since I was biracial. They even tried forcing Mom to let me go back with them. That's when my god-fathers stepped in."

Flipper shook his head, feeling the pain she refused to acknowledge, the pain she'd obviously felt because of her grandparents' actions. But he'd heard it in her voice nonetheless.

"It's sad that some people can be such bigots. At the risk of this sounding like a cliché, some of my closest friends are black," he added, immediately thinking of Bane, Viper and Coop. Like her, Mac was of mixed heritage and had a white mother and black father.

"I'm sure some of your closest friends are, David."

He wondered if she believed him. One day, she would see the truth in his words. Then it suddenly occurred to him—no, she would not. There would be no reason for her to ever meet the four guys who were just as close to him as his biological brothers.

"I'll be back in a minute with the pie," she said. Then she stood and left the room.

Flipper watched her leave, feeling that he hadn't fully eradicated her doubts the way he'd wanted to do. That bothered him. He didn't want her to think he was one of those prejudiced asses who believed one race of people was better than another. What her grandparents had done to her father and mother, as well as to her, was unforgivable. Regardless of how she'd tried to come across as if their actions hadn't hurt her, as if they still didn't hurt her, he knew better.

She needed a hug right now.

He pushed back his chair and left the dining room to enter her kitchen. Instead of getting the pie like she'd said she would do, she was standing with her back to him, looking out the kitchen window at the ocean. And he could tell from the movement of her shoulders that she was crying.

"Swan?"

She quickly turned, swiping at her tears. "I'm sorry to take so long, I just had one of those miss-my-daddy-and-mommy moments."

He crossed the room to her, knowing that her tears were about more than that. He knew it and he intended for her to know he knew it. "Not wanting to get to know you—that was your grandparents' loss, Swan."

She gazed into his eyes and nodded. "I know, David, but their actions hurt Dad, although he never said it did. I knew. Mom knew, too. I think that's one of the reasons she loved him so much, because of all the sacrifices he'd made for her. That's why she did anything she could to make him happy so he would never regret choosing her. But it wasn't fair. He was a good man. Mom was a good woman. They deserved each other and should have been allowed to love freely and without restrictions, reservations or censure. It just wasn't fair, David."

And then she buried her face in his chest and cried in earnest. Wrapping his arms around her, he held her, leaning down to whisper in her ear that things would be all right. That her parents had had a special love, one she should be proud of, one the naysayers had envied.

Emotions Flipper hadn't counted on flowed

through him as he continued to stroke her hair and whisper soothing words next to her ear. Inwardly, he screamed at the injustice of trying to keep someone from loving the person they truly wanted to love. It was something he'd never understood and figured he never would. And never would he accept such a way of thinking from anyone.

Swan knew she should pull out of David's arms, but found she couldn't do it. Being held by him felt good. His fingers, the ones that were stroking through the strands of her hair, seemed to electrify her scalp. They sent comforting sensations all through her—and something else as well. A need that he was stroking to fruition. As a result, instead of pulling out of his arms, she closed her eyes and enjoyed being held by him while inhaling his masculine scent.

She wasn't sure how long they stood there, but it didn't take long for her to notice his breathing had changed. But then so had hers. His touch had shifted from comforting to passionate. He was using the same strokes, but now the feelings within her were beginning to build to an insurmountable degree of desire.

Opening her eyes, she lifted her head to stare up at him. The minute she did, she caught her breath at the intense yearning she saw in his gaze. That yearning reached out to her, jolted her with a level of throbbing need she hadn't known existed. She'd heard of raw, make-you-lose-your-senses passion, but she had never experienced it for herself.

Until now.

"David…" She said his name as something burst to life in the pit of her stomach. It made a quivering sensation rise at the back of her neck. He implored her with his eyes to follow this passion, as if letting her know he understood what she was experiencing even if she didn't.

"Tell me what you want, Swan," he said in a deep voice while gently caressing the side of her face. "Tell me."

The intensity in his eyes was burning her, scorching her with the sexual hunger that was coming to life inside her. She wanted more than his erection pressing hard against the apex of her thighs. She wanted him on top of her. She wanted him to slide into her body and begin thrusting in and out. She needed to lose herself in more than just his arms.

Suddenly, she felt emboldened to tell him just what she wanted. "I want you, David. In my bed."

Flipper wanted to be in her bed as well. Lord knows he shouldn't want it, but he did. He would have to deal with the consequences later. He felt too tight and hot to try to fight the demands his body was making. Sweeping her into his arms, he quickly walked out of the kitchen and headed toward her bedroom.

"You think you know where you're going, David?"

He slowed his pace, remembering that she had no idea that he knew the layout of her home. Not only did he know where her bedroom was located, he knew the blueprint of the plumbing underneath her floor. He looked down and met her gaze, grateful she wasn't suspicious. "I figured you would stop me if I went in the wrong direction."

"Yes, I would have stopped you, but you're going the right way."

"Good." When he resumed his swift pace, it didn't take him long to reach her bedroom.

Swan had gotten next to him in a way he hadn't counted on happening. Seducing her had not been part of the plan and he should not have allowed things to get this far. He didn't want to think of the major complications involved, and not just because she was the goddaughter of three top naval officers.

But something was happening that he hadn't counted on. His mind and body were in sync and a rare sexual aura was overtaking him. He could no more stop making love to her than he could stop being a SEAL. For him to even make such a comparison was pretty damn serious.

Instead of placing Swan on the bed, he eased her to her feet, loving the feel of her soft body sliding down his hard one. "If you're having second thoughts about this, Swan, now's the time to say so."

She shook her head and then in a wobbly voice, she said, "No second thoughts, David."

Hearing her affirmation spoken with such certainty, Flipper released a low, throaty groan as he lowered his mouth to kiss her again, needing the connection of her lips to his as much as he needed to breathe. Wrapping his arms around her waist, he pulled her body closer to him as he deepened the kiss, wanting her to feel his erection, the hard evidence of his need for her.

He had never wanted a woman with this much intensity in his life, and he had no idea why Swan was having this kind of an effect on him.

Why she, and no other woman before her, had tempted him to cross a line during a mission. His mind didn't function that way. He had yet to prove her innocence, so technically, she was still naval intelligence's prime suspect, but at the moment that didn't matter. For all he knew, he could be about to sleep with the enemy.

But right now, that didn't matter either because deep down, a part of him believed she was innocent.

What was happening between them was definitely out of the realm of normal for him. He'd known he would have to get close to her, but he hadn't counted on this—his intense desire to do inappropriate, erotic and mind-blowing things to Swan Jamison.

But he wanted her and there would be no regrets. At least not for him, and based on what she'd just said, there would be no regrets for her either.

The moment he ended the kiss, his hands were

busy removing her skirt, followed by her blouse, and when she stood in front of him in her lacy panties and bra, he couldn't help but growl his satisfaction. She looked sexy as hell and the rose-colored ensemble against the darkness of her skin was stunningly beautiful. *She* was beautiful.

He reached up and traced a finger along the material of her boxer-cut panties. This style on a woman had never done anything for him. Until now.

"You should have been a model," he said in a deep, throaty voice, filled with profound need and deep appreciation. She had such a gorgeously shaped body.

"My mother used to be a model. I was satisfied with being a model's daughter."

"And a strikingly beautiful one at that," he said, lowering to his knees to rid her of her panties. He couldn't wait to touch her, taste her and do all those erotic things to her he had dreamed of doing over the past few nights. He breathed in deeply, getting more aroused by the second while easing her panties down a pair of long, beautiful legs.

After tossing her panties aside, he leaned back on his haunches and gazed at her, seeing her naked from the waist down. Her small waist, her stomach, the shape of her thighs and longs legs were perfect. She was perfect.

After looking his fill, he leaned forward and rested his forehead against her stomach, inhaling her luscious scent. He loved the way it flowed through his nostrils, opening his pores and causing his body to become even more erect.

And then he did something he'd wanted to do since their first kiss. He used the tip of his tongue to kiss her stomach, loving the indention around her naval and tracing a path around the area. Then he shifted his mouth lower, licking his way down and enjoying the sound of her moans.

When he came to the very essence of her, he licked around her womanly folds before leaning in to plant a heated kiss right there. It was as if sampling her special taste was as essential to him as breathing. His hands held firm to her thighs when he slid his tongue inside of her, loving the sound of his name from her lips.

Then he went deeper, using his tongue to taste her, claim her and brand her. The latter gave him pause but not enough to stop what he was doing. He'd never claimed a woman as his own and had never thought about doing so. But with Swan, it seemed such a thing wasn't just desired but was required.

And he didn't want it any other way. She was the first woman he wanted to claim. Forcefully, he pushed to the back of his mind what it could mean to make any woman his and decided he would dwell on that aspect of things at a later time. For now, he wanted to focus on the delicious, succulent, enjoyable taste that was Swan.

He took his time, wanting her to know just how much he loved doing this to her. He wanted her to feel the connection his tongue was making with her flesh. However, he wanted her to do more than feel it, he wanted this connection absorbed into her senses, into her mind, into every part of her body.

Moments later, Flipper knew he'd achieved his goal when he felt her fingers dig into his shoulder blades, followed by the quivering of her thighs. Tightening his hold on her hips, he knew what would be next and he was ready.

She screamed his name when she was thrown into an orgasmic state. Her fingernails dug deeper into his skin, but he didn't feel the pain because knowing he was giving her pleasure made him immune to it. What he felt was a desire to take things to the next level, to slide into her body and go so deep it would be impossible to detect where his body ended and hers began.

He finally pulled his mouth away and looked up at her, saw the glazed look in her eyes. Without saying a word, he traced his fingers around the womanly mound he'd just kissed before inserting his finger inside of her. She was ultra-wet and mega-hot and he had every intention of capitalizing on both. The orgasm she'd just experienced would be small in comparison to the one he intended to give her.

Pulling his finger from her, he licked it clean, knowing she was watching his every move. "Sweet," he said softly, holding her gaze.

He slowly eased to his feet and reached behind her to remove her bra. When she stood totally naked in front of him, he feasted his gaze on her. "And I'm about to show you just how sweet I think you are, Swan."

Six

Swan was having difficulty breathing and the blue eyes staring at her made getting air to flow through her lungs even more difficult. Never had she felt this energized from a sexual act. And when David got to his feet and leaned in to kiss her, letting her taste herself on his lips, she felt weak in the knees. But he held her around the waist, holding her up as he kissed her more deeply, making her wish the kiss could last forever.

She released a low disappointed groan in her throat when he pulled his mouth away.

"Don't worry, there's more coming."

He swept her off her feet and carried her over to the bed, placed her on it and joined her there.

"You still have clothes on," she said, reaching out to touch his shirt.

"I know and they will be coming off. Right now, I just want to lie here with you and hold you in my arms."

She smiled at him. "You're not going to fall asleep on me, are you?"

Chuckling, he said, "Asleep? With you lying beside me without a stitch of clothes on? Sleep is the last thing I'd be able to do, trust me."

He'd already pleasured her with his mouth, so she couldn't help wondering what was next. She soon discovered his intent when he reached over and cupped her breasts.

"You are perfect," he said in a deep husky voice.

The words triggered a memory of overhearing her father whisper the same compliment to her mother, after she surprised him with a special dinner after he returned home from one of his missions.

Swan knew she was far from perfect. Those were just words David was speaking. But still, hearing them filled her with joy. Maybe she shouldn't let them, but they did.

Then any further thoughts dissolved from her mind when David eased a nipple between his lips. She moaned at the pleasure she felt all the way to her toes. Just when she thought she couldn't stand anymore, he began torturing her other nipple.

When he finally eased away, she opened her eyes to watch him undress. When he removed his shirt, she saw the tattoos covering his tanned skin on both of his upper arms—huge dolphins emerging from beautiful blue ocean waters. Another tattoo of even more dolphins was painted across his back in beautiful vivid colors. She'd never been into tattoos but she thought his were stunning.

"I like your tattoos," she said.

He glanced over at her and smiled. "Thanks."

When he lowered his shorts, her gaze moved to the area between a pair of masculine thighs. His shaft was massive and marvelously formed. Just the thought of him easing that part of himself inside of her sent her pulse skyrocketing.

"You okay?"

She lifted her gaze to his. She wasn't sure if she was okay. A thickness had settled in her throat when she saw how he was looking at her. Not only did he intend to join his body with hers, she had a feeling he planned to keep them connected for a while.

"Yes, I'm okay."

Swan continued to check him out, thinking he had a mighty fine physique. His body was all muscle and it was obvious that he worked out regularly. A man didn't get those kinds of abs if he didn't.

She watched as he pulled a condom from his wallet and sheathed himself in a way that was so erotic, she felt herself getting wetter between the legs just watching him. Then he was strolling back toward the bed. To her.

"I'm about to make sure you feel more than okay,"

he said, reaching down and easing her up to rest her chest against his. Her breasts were still sensitive from his mouth and rubbing them against his chest caused a multitude of arousing sensations to swamp her.

"What are you doing to me?" she asked in a ragged breath, barely able to get the words out.

"Anything you can imagine," he whispered, lowering her back on the mattress and then straddling her. He stared down at her as he gently moved her legs apart. She felt him, that part of him, lightly touch her feminine folds and then he was rubbing back and forth across them, sending even more sensations racing through her bloodstream.

"Trying to torture me, David?"

"No, trying to pleasure you. Ready for me?"

The movement of his manhood against her was making it impossible for her to concentrate. "What do you think?"

"You're wet and hot, so I think you're ready." And then he entered her in one deep thrust.

She gasped at the fullness and was glad he'd gone still for a minute. This gave her the chance to feel him fully embedded deep within her. It had been a long time for her and her inner muscles were greedily clamping on to him, tightening their hold.

"You're big," she whispered.

"You're tight," was his response. "But we're making this work."

And he did. First he began moving again, gently sliding in and out of her. That only lasted a few seconds before he picked up the pace and began thrusting harder.

She responded by wrapping her legs around his waist. Then he lifted her hips to receive more of him. When he established a slow and deep rhythm, touching areas in her body that hadn't been touched in a long time, or ever, she fought back a scream. She grabbed hold of his hair and pulled it, but he didn't seem to mind.

"Rule number one, Swan. Don't hold back."

Was he kidding? It wasn't a matter of holding back. It was more like she was trying to keep her sanity. David was so powerfully male that he was pushing her over the edge with every deep stroke. Every cell within her vibrated in response to his precise thrusts.

"Hold on, baby. Things are about to get wild."

Flipper had given Swan fair warning. When he began pounding harder, making strokes he'd never attempted with another woman—going deep, pulling out and then going deep again—he felt a quivering sensation start at the base of his testicles and move toward her womb with each and every thrust. He had to hold on tight to her to keep them on the bed. He was determined to show her wild.

Simultaneously, he leaned down to have his way with her mouth, licking it corner to corner and then inserting his tongue inside with the same rhythm he was using below.

What he was feeling right now was more than off the charts, it was out of the atmosphere. When she finally let go and screamed his name, the sound vibrated in every part of his body, especially in her inner muscles. They clamped down on him, trying to pull everything out of him while her hands tightened even more in his hair.

"David!"

She screamed his name again. The sound drove him. He wanted more of her. Wanted to go deeper. Throwing his head back, he felt the veins in his neck strain. There was pain but not enough to dim the pleasure.

And he knew at that moment Swan had gotten under his skin in a way no other woman had.

He began rocking hard into her with an intensity that made him go deeper with every thrust. Then he was the one hollering out in pleasure, saying her name as an explosion ripped through him. Then like a crazed sexual maniac, he leaned in to feast on her mouth and breasts. It was like his desire for her could not end.

"David!"

He knew she was coming again and, dammit to hell, so was he. Marveling at such a thing, he tightened his hold on her. His control had not only gotten shot to hell and back but had died an explosive death as the result of the most powerful orgasms he'd ever endured.

This was what real lovemaking was about. No

holds barred. No restrictions. Every part of him felt alive, drained, renewed. The room had the scent of sex and more sex. But that wasn't all. Emotions he'd never felt before touched him and swelled his heart.

He quickly forced those emotions back, refusing to go there. Knowing he couldn't go there.

The husky sound of deep, even breathing made Swan open her eyes. She was still in bed with David. Their limbs were entangled and his head was resting on her chest as he slept.

This man had been the most giving of lovers. He didn't come until he made sure she came first. He had kissed every part of her body, some parts more than others, and he had stoked passion within her in a way that had made her reach the boiling point. No man had ever made love to her with such intensity.

He had warned her about them getting wild. As far as she was concerned, they had gotten more than wild, they had gotten uninhibited, untamed. She hadn't known she had so much passion within her. He had brought it out and made her do more than own it. He had made her so aware of it that she doubted she could undo what he'd done.

David Holloway had done more than push a few of her buttons. He had turned on all the lights.

That thought made her smile and pull him closer. Feeling exhausted, she closed her eyes and drifted into sleep.

* * *

Flipper slowly opened his eyes, taking in the sight and scent of the woman lying beside him, snuggled close to his body. He was so sexually contented, he could groan out loud. He didn't. Instead he tightened his arms around her.

Things had gotten wild. They had finally fallen asleep after four rounds of the most satisfying love-making possible.

While making love with Swan, he had discovered there was a vast difference in making love to her versus making love to other women. He'd known it before but she had made that point crystal clear tonight.

With other women, he'd usually had one goal in mind—seeking sexual pleasure and making sure she got hers. With Swan it had been about that, too, but it had also been about finding closeness. No other woman had made him want to stay inside her. It had only been the need to replace condoms that had forced him from Swan's side. And then he had been back inside her in a flash…like that was where he belonged. Hell, he was still thinking that way and the twitch in his aroused manhood was letting him know just what he desired.

Flipper was known to have a robust sexual appetite. When you lived your life on the edge, engaging in covert operations as his team did, then you needed a way to release.

Usually, unerringly, he found his release in some woman's bed. He made sure she knew it was one and done. Due to the nature of his occupation, he didn't have time for attachments or anything long-term. Some SEALs did; he didn't. He'd tried it once and it hadn't worked out. Now he preferred being a loner. It didn't bother him that he was the lone single guy among his close friends. To each his own.

So how could one night in Swan Jamison's bed have him thinking things he shouldn't be thinking, especially considering why he was in Key West in the first place?

It had everything to do with the woman he'd had mind-blowing sex with for the past four hours or so. Now he saw her as more than an assignment. Now she was also a woman who had the ability to match his sexual needs one-on-one, something he found invigorating and energizing on all levels. He was a totally physical male and Swan Jamison was wholly, utterly female. Almost to the point that she'd blown his ever-loving mind.

Now she was sleeping peacefully while he was lying here thinking, knowing his honor was being tested. As a military man, he always did what was honorable. On top of that, his mother had drilled into all five of her sons that honor was not just for their country but extended to humans just as much, especially women. Why had that thought settled deep into his mind now?

One reason might be that he'd read the report on her. He knew about those elderly people residing at the senior living complex that she visited on her weekends off and how she'd championed so hard for the homeless. She was working with the mayor to help find funding to build a housing complex for them.

She was a caring person. He'd witnessed her love for her country, for her father, that night at the fireworks and the more he was around her, the more he believed in her innocence.

She made a sound now and he glanced down and met beautiful brown eyes staring at him. Immediately his senses connected with those eyes. She trusted him. He could see it in the gaze staring back at him. Otherwise he would not be here in her bed.

What would she think when she learned the truth? Would she still trust him? He pushed the thought to the back of his mind.

She gave him a beautiful, sleepy smile that melted his insides. Made him wish he had come here to the Keys for a real vacation, a much-needed one. He wished he had entered her shop with no ulterior motive but to do as he claimed, which was to buy his mother a birthday gift. He would still have tried his hand at seducing her, but things would have been different. Specifically, he wouldn't feel as if his honor was being compromised.

"You didn't try my key lime pie," she whispered.

"We can get up and eat some now if you want," he said.

"No, I like being just where I am. We can always eat some later…or even for breakfast."

He leaned down and brushed a kiss across her lips. "Um, breakfast sounds nice. Is that an invitation to stay the night?"

"Only if you want to."

He wanted to. And when he brushed another kiss across her lips, he slid his tongue inside her mouth to kiss her deeply and let her know how much he wanted to stay.

He knew at that moment that his commanding officer and the admiral weren't the only ones with a personal interest in Swan Jamison. He now had a personal interest in her as well.

Seven

The next morning, Swan woke up to bright sunlight flowing in through her window and a powerfully male body sleeping beside her.

Last night was rated right up there with *Ripley's Believe It or Not*. It had been just that spectacular. They'd made love a couple more times before getting up after midnight to eat the pie she'd prepared for dessert. After clearing off the table and loading the dishes into the dishwasher, he'd suggested they walk on the beach.

So at one in the morning, they had strolled hand in hand along the water's edge. It had been a beautiful night with a full moon in the sky. The breeze off the ocean had provided the perfect reason for him to pull her close while walking barefoot in the sand. He told her more about his family; namely about his parents' medical supply company.

Then at some point, they began talking about her company and she found herself telling him just about everything about jewelry making. He was curious about her stones and complimented how beautiful they were and inquired how she was able to create so many pieces.

No man had ever taken an interest in her work before and she was excited that he thought what she did for a living was important. She had found herself explaining the day-to-day operations of Swan's. He couldn't believe how she found the time to handcraft a number of the items sold in her shop.

David also thought it was great that Rafe, through his connections with a huge distributor in California, was able to get some of Swan's more expensive stones at a lower cost and had even helped her save on shipping by including them in the packaging with his ink.

She glanced over at him now as he shifted in bed. He kept his arms wrapped around her while he slept. She studied his features and saw how relaxed he looked.

She drew in a deep breath, still amazed at the depth of what they had shared last night. It had been the most profound thing she'd ever experienced with a man. Making love with David had touched her in ways she hadn't thought possible. He had made her feel things she hadn't ever felt before and those things weren't just sexual in nature. While in his arms, she had felt safe and secure. Protected.

As far as she was concerned, what they'd shared last night was more compelling and meaningful than any other time she'd shared with a man, even more meaningful than the time she'd spent with William. She'd never really allowed herself to fully let go with William. Now she could admit to herself that she'd known in the back of her mind that something didn't add up with him.

Yet she'd been so desperate for companionship after losing her mother that she had wanted to believe William was honest, even though he'd seemed too good to be true. She was glad Candy had become suspicious when he'd never wanted them to be photographed together or when he'd insisted that they spend the night at Swan's place instead of the hotel.

At the time, his requests hadn't bothered her because she hadn't wanted her employer or her co-workers to get in her business. But Candy had seen through all that and knew something in the milk wasn't clean, as she would often say. It had been Candy who'd unveiled her own husband's secret affair with a flight attendant. And once confronted, Don hadn't denied a thing. He'd said he was glad she'd found out because he wanted a divorce.

Pushing thoughts of Don's and William's betrayals to the back of her mind, Swan continued to study David. She couldn't help but recall the number of times he'd made her climax. Now that was simply amazing all by itself.

She was enjoying her time with him, even knowing it wouldn't last. Later this month, he would leave the island and she would probably not hear from him again. She knew that, accepted it. She had long ago learned to live for the now and not sweat the small stuff. Especially those things she couldn't change.

"You're awake."

She couldn't help but smile at the slumberous blue eyes staring at her. The dark shadow on his chin made him look even sexier. "Yes, I'm awake. I guess I should be a good host and prepare breakfast before you leave."

"Um, I've overstayed my welcome?"

"No, but today is Sunday and I have a lot to do."

"Maybe I can help you."

"You don't know what I'll be doing."

He reached out and pushed her hair back off her shoulders so he could completely see her face. "Then tell me."

She gazed into his eyes. "The shop is closed on Sundays and I use my day off to visit Golden Manor Senior Place. My mom used to do volunteer work there when we lived on the island years ago. I would go with her on Sundays to visit everyone. I guess you could say it's become a family tradition that I decided to continue."

"I think that's a wonderful thing you're doing. I'm sure the residents there appreciate it."

"Yes, they do, although those who knew my mom are no longer there. They've passed on. I'm establishing new relationships and friendships."

"Good for you. I'd love to join you."

"You would?" she asked, surprised.

"Yes, and don't worry about preparing breakfast. I'll go home and refresh and be back here within an hour. We can grab breakfast somewhere before heading over. Afterward, we can spend more time on the beach. I enjoyed the walk last night with you."

And she had enjoyed it, too. The thought that he wanted to spend more time with her made her feel really good inside. "Okay, that sounds wonderful."

"I'm glad you think so, and before I leave..."

"Yes?"

He leaned over to kiss her and she knew where things would lead from there. She looked forward to getting wild again with him.

Flipper clicked on his phone the minute he walked into his hotel room. He noted several missed calls since he'd deliberately cut off his phone last night. One was from the admiral, who was probably calling for an update. But first Flipper would return the call to Nick.

"Flipper, should I ask why I couldn't reach you last night?"

"No, you shouldn't," Flipper said, flopping down in the nearest chair.

"You have heard the saying that you shouldn't mix business with pleasure, right?"

Too late for that, Flipper thought, running a hand down his face. Instead of responding to Nick's comment, he said, "I hope you have something for me. There's another angle I want you to check out."

"Okay, and yes, I have something for you. I found out the initial investigation was handed off to a group of civilian investigators, which means naval intelligence didn't rank it at the top at first."

Flipper was very much aware of the part government bureaucracy played in certain investigations. If someone thought a case should be under naval intelligence's radar, then they made sure it got there. "Why?"

"Not sure yet, but first, let's talk about Jamila Fairchild."

Flipper leaned forward in his chair. "Okay, let's talk about her. What do you have?"

"Not what you obviously think. What she told Swan was the truth. She does have a huge family who lives in the north."

Flipper raised a brow. "Then who made the error in the report from naval intelligence?"

"Don't know, but it's worth checking out, although I don't think it's anything suspicious on Ms. Fairchild's end. Especially when I tell you who her family is."

"And who is her family?"

"Her mother's brother is Swan's grandfather."

A frown covered Flipper's face. "The grandfather who disowned Swan's father?"

"Yes, from what I've gathered. But I can find no record of her grandfather ever reaching out to her."

"Interesting."

"Yes, it is. I take it Swan Jamison doesn't know about the family connection."

"No, she doesn't." Flipper decided not to try to wrap his head around this bit of news just yet. Instead he asked, "What about Rafe Duggers?"

"Personally, I think something is going on with him."

Flipper lifted a brow. "What?"

"First of all, certain aspects of his info are sealed."

"Sealed?"

"Yes. I would think if naval intelligence was checking into something related to Swan and her story, they would see that sealed record for her tenant as a red flag. For them not to have flagged it raises my own suspicions about a few things."

That raised Flipper's suspicions as well. Was Rafe a double agent? Someone working undercover? Was someone in naval intelligence deliberately setting Swan up as the traitor? If so, why?

"You weren't able to find out anything about him?"

There was a husky chuckle. "I didn't say that. There are ways to find out anything you want when you know how to do it."

And Nick knew how to do it. He'd been an amazing SEAL, but as far as Flipper was concerned, Nick's natural investigative talents were better served at Homeland Security. "When will you let me know something?"

"Give me a couple of days. In the meantime, don't say anything to anyone about my suspicions about Duggers."

"Not even the CO and admiral?"

"Not even them for now. You mentioned Swan had a third godfather who was someone high up at naval intelligence. Was his identity revealed to you?"

"No, it wasn't but then I didn't ask," Flipper said.

"It wasn't hard to find out," Nick replied. "All you have to do is find out who Andrew Jamison's SEAL teammates were at the time he died and do a little research to determine where they are now." ·

"I take it you've done that."

"Yes, and would you believe Swan Jamison's third godfather is Director of Naval Intelligence Samuel Levart?"

Flipper would not have considered Director Levart in a million years, but it all made sense now. In order for someone to have delayed making formal charges against Swan, that person would have to be someone in power. The admiral had alluded to as much. "Swan doesn't know how favored she is to have three powerful men in her corner."

"Yes, but we both know it wouldn't matter if one of her godfathers was the President. If naval intelli-

gence believes they have enough evidence to pros-
ecute her, they will," Nick said.

Flipper knew that to be true. Now more than ever
he had to find the person intent on framing Swan.
To him, it was beginning to look like an inside job.

"So what else do you have for me to check out?"
Nick asked, reclaiming Flipper's attention.

"It's about something Swan told me." He then
shared with Nick the information about Rafe Duggers's association with some huge distributor in California. "I need you to check that out."

"I will. I know time is of the essence so I'll get
back to you soon, Flipper."

"Thanks, I appreciate it."

"If you're so concerned about me, then why not
return to the Keys and keep an eye on me, Candy?"
Swan asked. She moved around her bedroom getting
dressed while talking to her friend on speakerphone.

"You know why I won't return, just yet. But I did
hear something that's interesting."

"What?" Swan asked as she shimmied into her
skirt.

"I talked to Francola the other day and she said
Marshall mentioned to her that Don is thinking about
moving away from the island."

Swan paused. Francola and her husband, Marshall, had been close friends of Don and Candy's
while they were married. The two couples often did
things together. Personally, Swan didn't care much

for Francola because the woman had been aware Don was cheating on Candy but hadn't told her friend. "I would take anything Francola says with a grain of salt these days," Swan said as she continued dressing.

"I know you still fault her for not telling me about Don and I admit I was angry with her, too, but now I understand her not doing so."

"Do you?"

"Yes. Her relationship with me is not like our relationship, Swan. You and I have been best friends since grade school and we have no secrets. You would have told me about Don had you suspected anything."

"Darn right."

"Well, Francola and I didn't have that kind of relationship. We only met through our husbands, who worked together. Besides, I'm not sure I would have believed her even had she told me. I would have been in denial." Candy paused. "Now, enough about me. Tell me more about this David Holloway."

Swan smiled while putting hoop earrings into her ears. "He's a real nice guy. Thoughtful. Considerate. Handsome as sin." She glanced over at her made-up bed. Although there were no signs of anyone sleeping in it last night, it didn't take much for her to remember all the wild action she and David had shared under the sheets. "And he's great in bed. More than great. He's fantastic."

"Just be careful, Swan. Protect your heart."

Swan slipped her feet into her sandals. "My heart? It's not like I'm falling for the guy, Candy."

"Aren't you? I can hear it in your voice. You like him a lot."

Yes, she did like him a lot. "It won't go beyond me liking him," she said, trying to convince herself of that more so than Candy.

"Can you honestly say that?"

"Yes, because I can't let it. His work brought him to the island and he'll be leaving soon. In less than thirty days."

"Doesn't matter."

Swan knew for her it *did* matter. She only wanted short-term. The last thing she wanted was to do long-term with any man.

Eight

"I enjoyed my time with you today, Swan," Flipper said, looking down at her.

They'd had brunch at Summer Moon before heading to the senior living complex where they spent the next four hours. She assisted the staff by reading to groups of people and even taking a few of the seniors for walks around the complex. Some, she'd explained, had family who rarely visited so she had become like their surrogate granddaughter.

On the flip side, considering what she'd missed out having in her life, he couldn't help but wonder if they had become her surrogate grandparents.

From the moment she walked into the facility, everyone brightened up when they saw her. It was amazing to him. She knew just what to say to elicit a smile or to get them to engage in more conversation. The majority of the seniors knew her by name and he couldn't help noticing a number of the women wearing what looked like necklaces she'd made.

When he inquired about the necklaces Swan confirmed they were her designs but she had taught the women to make them from stones she'd given them. It had taken longer than normal since a lot of the older women's hands weren't as nimble as they used to be.

After leaving the nursing home, they'd grabbed lunch at a sidewalk café before returning to her house where they'd spent the rest of the day on the beach. Later, after ordering takeout for dinner from Arness, they were back at her place.

No matter how tempting Swan was making it for him to stay longer at her place, he would leave when it got dark. The information about Rafe Duggers's sealed records bothered him and he'd decided to poke around in the tattoo parlor later that night to see what he could find.

He glanced over at Swan as she sat across the table from him eating dinner. Earlier today, when he had returned to take her to breakfast, she had opened the door looking fresh and perky and dressed simply in a pair of shorts and a tank top. Seeing her dressed that way reminded him of just what a gorgeous pair of legs she had, as well as how those same legs had wrapped around him while they'd made love that morning and the night before.

When they had gone swimming, she'd worn one of the sexiest two-piece bathing suits he'd ever seen. He had totally and completely enjoyed his day with her. They would be attending the Memorial Day festivities together tomorrow in town, which included a parade.

Because he needed some investigative time, he'd come up with an excuse for why he couldn't see her a couple of days this week. Time was moving quickly and he had yet to find anything to clear her of wrongdoing.

Because of Nick's warning, Flipper hadn't told Admiral Martin everything when he'd called him back yesterday. Namely, he'd left out the discrepancies between what Nick had found out and the actual reports from naval intelligence. Until Flipper discovered what was going on, he would follow Nick's advice and keep that information to himself for now.

"Although I won't be seeing you for a few days because of work, will you still be on the island?" Swan asked.

It was hard not to be totally truthful about why she wouldn't be seeing him. She was the last person he wanted to be dishonest with but he had no choice. His goal had always been to prove her innocence and now that was doubly true. He would check out the tattoo shop tonight and look around in both Rafe's and Jamila's homes this week while they were here at work. Although it had been established that Jamila was Swan's relative, as far as Flipper was concerned, she was still a suspect.

"Yes, I'll still be on the island but I have to concentrate on this project I was sent here to do." No need to tell her that the project involved her.

"I understand how things are when work calls."

He reached up and caressed the side of her face. "We still have a date for the parade tomorrow, right?"

"Yes."

"What about dinner on Friday evening?" he asked her.

Her smile touched something deep within him. "I'd love that, David."

"Good. I'll swing by your shop at closing time Friday and we can go to dinner directly from there. You pick the place."

"All right."

"What time do you want me to come get you for the parade tomorrow?"

"It starts at ten in the morning and we need to get there early to get a good spot. How about if I prepare pancakes for us in the morning around eight?"

"You sure? I wouldn't want you to go to any trouble."

She waved off his words. "No problem. I told you I enjoy cooking."

After they finished dinner, he told her he needed to leave to read some reports for work, which wasn't a lie. She walked him to the door. He leaned down to kiss her, intending for it to be a light touch of their lips.

But the moment his mouth touched hers and she released a breathless sigh, it seemed the most natural thing to slide his tongue inside her mouth and deepen the kiss. Wrapping his arms around her waist, he pulled her tight against him and knew the exact moment the kiss had changed to something more.

It was no longer a *goodbye and I'll see you later* kiss. Instead it was one of those *I need to have you before I go* kind. And Swan seemed to be reciprocating those feelings as she returned the kiss with equal fervor.

The next thing Flipper knew, he was sweeping her off her feet and moving quickly toward her bedroom. When he placed her on the bed, they began stripping off their clothes.

For him, she'd become an itch he couldn't scratch and a craving that wouldn't go away. There was something about making love to her that made every part of his body ache with need. She had imprinted herself on his soul and in every bone in his body and there was nothing he could do about it but savor what they had for as long as he could.

When she was completely naked, his pulse kicked up a notch and his breathing was forced from his lungs when he looked at her. She was beautiful and perfectly made.

He pulled a condom from his wallet in the shorts she'd helped him remove and toss aside. Knowing she was watching his every move, he rolled it over his aroused manhood.

"I want to do that for you the next time."

He looked at Swan. "All right." So she was letting him know she intended there to be a next time for them. He was glad because he wanted a next time, too.

There was a big chance when she found out the truth about why he was here on the island that she wouldn't want to have anything to do with him again. But he forced the thought from his mind.

"You don't have all evening, you know," she teased.

She was right, he didn't and it was a good thing she didn't know why. He moved toward her. "Impatient?"

She smiled up at him. "Yes, you could say that."

"In that case, I can help you with that problem." He leaned in. "I've got to taste you again," was all he said just seconds before his mouth came down on hers.

Swan automatically lifted her arms around his neck the moment his lips touched hers.

Capturing her tongue, David drew it into his mouth. Blood rushed fast and furious to Swan's head, making her feel both light-headed and dazed as his tongue began mating with hers. His technique was rousing her passion to a level that electrified every part of her. Insistent need rushed up her spine, spinning her senses and mesmerizing her with his delectable taste.

He suddenly broke off the kiss and they both panted furiously, drawing deep gulps of air into their lungs.

She rested her head against his chest and inhaled his scent as she continued to catch her breath. She knew she was losing herself to passion again when she felt the hardness of his erection brushing against her thigh, energizing the area between her legs.

Then she heard him whispering erotic details of what he wanted to do to her. His words spread fire through her body and when he gently cupped the area between her legs, she moaned.

"You're torturing me, David," she said, before twisting to push him down on his back so she could straddle him. Before he could react, she lowered her head between his masculine thighs and eased his erection into her mouth.

"Ah, Swan," he growled huskily, gripping her hair. She was fully aware of him expanding and felt a sense of triumph in her ability to get him even more aroused than he already was. The feel of his hands locked in her hair sparked even more passion within her and motivated her to use her mouth in ways she'd never done before.

"Swan!"

She felt his thighs flex beneath her hands before he bucked forward. She wasn't prepared when he quickly switched their positions so that she was the one on her back. The blue eyes staring down at her flared with a passion that sent tremors through her.

Before she could whisper his name, he slid inside her. He kept going deeper and deeper, stretching her in ways she didn't know she could be spread, inch by inch.

"Wrap your legs around me, baby," he whispered in a throaty voice.

When she did as he asked, he began thrusting hard. It was as if his total concentration was on her, intent on giving her pleasure. She felt every inch of him as he rode her hard, not letting up.

"David!"

She screamed his name as he continued to make love to her, throwing her into a euphoric state that seemed endless. He was using her legs to keep their bodies locked while relentlessly pounding into her. Her world was spinning and she couldn't control the need to moan, moan and moan some more.

She was unable to hold anything back when her body erupted into an orgasm so powerful it propelled her toward utter completeness. She screamed his name once again as a deep feeling of ecstasy ripped through her entire body.

Flipper eased off Swan to lie beside her. Pulling her into his arms, his nostrils flared as he inhaled the scent of sex. The scent of woman, this woman. A woman he still desired even now.

He was not new to lust. Been there, done that

and he figured he would be doing it some more. A lot more. With Swan lying in in his arms, snuggled close to him, close to his heart, he knew something had changed between them.

Bottom line, Swan Jamison was not only intoxicating, she was addictive.

"I don't think I'll be able to move again, David."

A smile touched the corners of his lips. He definitely knew how she felt, but he knew he had to move. He had somewhere to be tonight and as sexually drained as he was, he intended to be there.

"Then don't move. Just lie there. I'll let myself out," he said, reluctant to go, although he knew he must.

"You sure?" she asked in a lethargic voice.

"Positive. I'll be back in the morning for the parade and then we have a date on Friday."

"Yes. I'm going to need it. I'll be working late Wednesday doing inventory. I probably won't leave work until around ten."

"With your worker's help?"

"No. The cruise ship comes in Wednesday."

He released her to ease out of bed and put on his clothes. "What does a cruise ship have to do with anything?" He could feel her gaze on his body. He couldn't disguise the impact of knowing she was watching him. He was getting aroused all over again.

"Jamila dates a guy who works on the cruise ship and they only see each other whenever the ship comes to port. She always requests the day off to spend with him. I guess they made up."

He had planned to check out Jamila's house when he'd assumed she would be at work. Good thing he now knew otherwise.

"Made up?" he asked, pulling his shirt over his head.

"Yes. I got the impression they weren't on good terms last week. Not sure what happened but it's all good now since they've apparently kissed and made up."

He nodded. "How long have they been together?"

"About six months now."

Flipper didn't say anything as he continued dressing. There hadn't been any mention of a boyfriend for Jamila Fairchild in the report he'd read. Another discrepancy. There were too many inconsistencies for his liking and he was determined to find out why. One thing was certain, he didn't like the idea of Swan being at her shop alone late at night.

He moved back to the bed, leaned down and brushed a kiss across her lips. "I'll see you in the morning."

"Looking forward to it."

He smiled down at her and then turned and left.

Later that night, Flipper, dressed all in black, moved in the shadows, careful to avoid streetlights and security cameras. He had scoped out the area and was familiar with where the cameras were lo-

cated. More than once, he'd had to dart behind a
shrub when people were out for a late-night stroll.

He reached the area where Swan's shop was located and when he heard voices, he darted behind a
building to hide in the shadows.

Two men stood not far away. One of them was
Rafe. Neither of the men saw Flipper. The other guy
was a little taller and appeared to be a foreigner.
Their conversation sounded like an argument and
was in a language Flipper wasn't familiar with and
he spoke four. Most SEALs spoke at least that many,
except for Coop, who had mastered seven.

When the men lapsed into English, they lowered
their voices and could barely be heard. Flipper did
make out the words *ink* and *roses*. Was someone getting a tattoo of roses painted on their body? If so,
did it mean anything?

Flipper was glad when the men finally moved
on. More than ever, he was determined to check out
the tattoo parlor. He waited a half hour to make sure
the men didn't return. When he was certain they had
gone, he went to work bypassing the security alarms
and cameras.

Using a sort of skeleton key, he opened the back
door and walked inside the tattoo parlor. Using night
goggles, he glanced around.

The place looked like a typical tattoo parlor.
He should know since he and his brothers had frequented a number of them. He was proud of the images on his body. Luckily, Swan hadn't asked him

about them. He was glad because the last thing he wanted to do was lie about why he was into dolphins.

Pulling off the camera attached to his utility belt, he replaced the night goggles with a high-tech camera, which was his own creation. This particular piece of equipment detected objects underground and under water. Looking through the lens, he scanned the room. It wasn't long before the camera light began blinking.

He moved toward the area and aimed the camera lower, toward the floor, and the blinking increased. Evidently something was buried beneath the wooden floor, a portion covered by a rug. The architectural report he'd been given of Swan's shop had not exposed any secret rooms or closets.

Putting the camera aside, he moved the rug and felt around to find a latch. He opened the trapdoor to find a small compartment beneath the floor. He saw more containers of ink. Why? There was a supply case full of ink on the opposite side of the room. Why was this ink hidden?

The first thing he noticed was the difference in the labeling. Was there something different about this particular ink? There was only one way to find out, he thought, taking one out of the cubby. He would overnight one of the containers to Nick instead of naval intelligence.

At this stage of the game, he wasn't taking any chances about who could be trusted.

Nine

Swan had just finished the last of her inventory when she heard the knock on her shop's door. Crossing the room, she peeped through the blinds to see who it was. A smile touched her lips as she unlocked the door. "David, I didn't think I'd see you until Friday."

He glanced around her empty shop before looking back at her. "I finished work early and remembered you saying you were working late tonight doing inventory. I wanted to make sure you got home okay."

That was really nice of him. "You didn't have to do that." But she was glad he had. They had spent Monday together celebrating Memorial Day. He had arrived at her place for breakfast and then they'd walked to where the start of the parade would take place.

After the parade, they'd gone to the island festival marketplace where various vendors had lined the streets with booths and a huge Ferris wheel. They had taken one of the boat rides around the islands and had ended up eating lunch on Key Largo.

She had thought about him a lot since Monday, remembering in explicit detail how he'd made love to her before leaving.

"I know you said Jamila would be off today," David said. "What about your tattoo guy? Is the parlor closed on Wednesdays as well?"

"Yes, but Rafe dropped by earlier. He was expecting a shipment of more ink to come in today but it didn't. He wasn't happy about that."

"He wasn't?"

"No. He said there was a particular shade of blue he was expecting."

Flipper nodded and checked his watch. "Ready to go?"

"Yes, I just need to grab my purse from my office." She was about to turn to get it when there was another knock at the door.

"Expecting anyone?" David asked her.

"No. I'll see who it is."

She walked to the door and David went with her. After glancing out of the blinds, she turned back to David and smiled. "It's Jamila and Horacio."

She unlocked the door. "Jamila, hi."

"Hey, Swan. Horacio and I were in the neighborhood and I remembered you would be here late. I thought we'd drop by to say hello."

Swan smiled at the man with Jamila. "Horacio, it's good seeing you again."

"Same here, Swan," he said in a heavy accent that Swan always loved hearing.

"And this is my friend David Holloway. David, you already know Jamila. This is her friend Horacio Jacinto," Swan said, making introductions.

The two men shook hands. Swan wondered if she'd imagined it but she thought David had tensed up when he'd seen Jamila and Horacio. "Nice meeting you, Horacio," David said. "I can't place your accent. Where are you from?"

"Portugal."

"Nice country," David said.

"Thanks."

"I hope you'll leave before it gets too late, Swan," Jamila was saying.

"I will. David came to make sure I got home okay." Usually whenever she worked late, either doing inventory or making her jewelry, she would catch a cab home even though she lived only a few blocks away. But since David was here, she would suggest they walk. It was a nice night and she would love to spend more time with him.

"We'll see you guys later," Jamila said. "We had dinner at Marty's Diner and now we're going to Summer Moon for drinks and live music."

"Okay. Enjoy. And I hope to see you again the next time the ship ports, Horacio," Swan said.

Horacio smiled. "I hope to see you as well."

After they left, Swan went to her office to get her purse. She returned and noticed David was standing in the same spot where she'd left him, staring at the door. "Are you all right?"

He turned to her. "Yes, it's just that Horacio looks familiar and I was trying to remember when I might've seen him. Maybe I've run into him before, here on the island."

She nodded. "That's possible. He's a chef on the Century Cruise Line that docks here once a week. Whenever it does, he comes ashore and meets up with Jamila. I think I mentioned that to you."

"You did, but I could have sworn I saw him a few nights ago. Sunday. After leaving your place."

Swan shook her head. "It wasn't him. The ship didn't arrive in our port until today. But you know what they say about everybody having a twin."

He chuckled. "You're probably right, but I'm sure you don't have one. I'm convinced there's not another woman anywhere who is as beautiful as you."

Swan knew better than to let such compliments go to her head, but she couldn't help the smile that spread across her lips. "You, David Holloway, can make a girl's head swell if she's inclined to believe whatever you say."

"I hope you do believe it because I spoke the truth." He took her hand in his as they headed for the door.

* * *

Flipper pulled out his phone the minute he walked into his hotel room later that night. He'd felt it vibrate in his pocket when he was walking Swan home but figured it would be a call he needed to take in private.

Swan had invited him inside but he'd declined, telling her he had a ton of paperwork waiting on him back at his hotel. That wasn't a lie. He'd begun rereading all those naval intelligence reports to see if he could determine why those investigators had failed to do their job and instead intentionally went after Swan as a scapegoat.

He checked his phone and saw Nick had called and Flipper quickly returned the call. "What do you have for me?"

"More than you counted on. All I can say is whoever handled that investigation did a botched-up job."

Or they did the job they'd been expected to do, Flipper thought. "I guess there's a reason you feel that way."

"Yes. That ink you sent to be analyzed isn't what it's supposed to be."

"It's not ink?"

"Yes, it's ink, but coded ink. When applied to the skin as a tattoo, it can be decoded by a special light. It's my guess that's how the classified information is leaving Swan Jamison's shop—with people's tattoos and not with any of her jewelry. Guess where the ink is being shipped from."

"Swan mentioned from some place in California."

"Yes, that's right and the distribution company is a few miles from the naval base in San Diego. That means someone on the base must be passing classified information that's being shipped in the ink."

Flipper frowned. "And because Rafe Duggers is conveniently including Swan's stones with each shipment, it makes sense for her to be suspect."

"Right," Nick agreed. "Someone is setting her up real good, Flipper. They are definitely making her the fall guy."

Flipper wondered who in naval intelligence had targeted Swan and why. "I have another piece of the puzzle I need you to check out."

"What?"

"The guy who was with Rafe Duggers two nights ago. The one I told you he was arguing with. I saw him today."

"You did?"

"Yes. He came into the shop when Swan was closing up. His name is Horacio Jacinto and he's Jamila Fairchild's boyfriend."

"That's interesting. I'll find out what I can about him," Nick said. "I wonder if Ms. Fairchild knows what's going on or if she's being used as a pawn."

"I don't know, but I'm going to make sure I keep an eye on all of them."

"Be careful, Flipper."

"I will."

A few hours later, after taking a shower, Flipper

was sitting at the desk in his hotel room suite when his cell phone went off. Recognizing the ringtone, he clicked on and said, "What's going on, Coop?"

"You tell us."

Us meant Bane, Viper and Mac were also on the phone. "I guess Nick called you guys."

"Yes, he called us earlier today," Bane said. "What's going on with Swan Jamison sounds pretty damn serious. Don't you think it's time to call the CO?"

Flipper ran a hand down his face. He glanced at the clock on the wall. It was close to three in the morning. "If Nick told you everything, then you know it's an inside job at the base. There's a traitor somewhere and until I know who I can trust, then—"

"You know as well as we do that you can trust our CO, Flipper," Viper said. "Once you tell Shields what you've found out, if he suspects Martin or Levart of any wrongdoing, he will know what to do."

"Yes, however, the three of them share a close friendship. What if the CO is blinded due to loyalty?"

"We're talking about our commanding officer, Flipper. Shields would turn his own mother in if he thought she was betraying our country. You know that."

Yes, he knew it. But still… "I don't know if Martin or Levart is really involved. Like Shields, they are Swan's godfathers and I would hate to think they are shady. I just know it's an inside job and right now I'm suspicious of just about everybody."

"We figured you would be, so open the damn door," Mac said.

Flipper frowned. "What?"

"We said open the door," Coop said, knocking.

Flipper heard the knock, clicked off his phone, quickly went to the door and snatched it open. There stood his four best friends.

"What are you guys doing here?"

"What does it look like?" Mac asked as the four moved passed Flipper to enter the hotel room.

"We figured ten pairs of eyes were better than two," Bane said, glancing around. "Besides, we need to keep you objective."

"But what about your families? Viper, your wife is having a baby!"

Viper chuckled. "And I plan to be there when she does. According to Layla's doctor, we still have a couple of months, so I'm good."

"And our families are good, too," Coop said. "They know we look out for each other and they agreed we should be here for you."

"Teri is glad I'm gone," Mac said, grumbling. "Maybe when I go back, she'll have a new attitude."

"Or maybe you'll have one," Bane said, frowning at Mac.

"Whatever," Mac said, picking up the hotel's restaurant menu book. "Is it too late for room service?"

Flipper closed the door and drew in a deep breath as he watched the men gather around the table, already rolling up their sleeves, ready to help him figure things out. They worked together as a team and he would admit that whenever they did so, good things happened.

"There's something all of you should know," he said, getting their attention.

They glanced over at him. "What? No room service at this hour?" Mac asked in a serious tone.

"That, too."

"What's the other thing we should know, Flipper?" Viper asked, sitting back in the chair he'd claimed as soon as he came in.

Flipper leaned against the closed door. "Investigating Swan Jamison is no longer just an assignment for me. It's become personal."

The men nodded. "And you think we don't know that, Flipper?" Coop asked in a steely tone. "That's why we're here. Someone is trying to frame your woman and we're going to help you find out who and why. But first things first. You know what you have to do, right?"

Flipper stared at the four men. Yes, he knew. Instead of answering Coop, he picked up his cell phone from the table and placed a call to his CO.

Ten

As far as Swan was concerned, Friday hadn't arrived fast enough. With every passing hour, she would glance at her shop's door expecting to see David walk in. One would think his surprise visit Wednesday would have sufficed. Unfortunately, it hadn't.

She'd had two days to think about how irrational her thoughts about David were becoming. He didn't come across as a forever sort of guy and she wasn't looking for a forever kind of relationship, so what was up with this urgency to see him?

The only reason she could give herself was that she'd been alone and without a man's attention for so long that now that she had it, she was in greedy mode, lapping it up like a desperate woman. And she had never done the desperate thing before.

The door chimed and she looked up to see that it was Rafe who walked in. Lately she'd noticed him using the front door a lot more, instead of the back door to his parlor. They had decided at the beginning of his lease that the entrance to her shop was off-limits so his customers wouldn't trounce back and forth through her shop on the days Rafe worked late.

"Did your box of ink finally arrive?"

He stopped and looked over at her. "Why would you be asking about my ink?"

Now that, she thought, was a silly question. Did the man have a short memory? "Because you came by Wednesday looking for the shipment and left in a tiff when it hadn't arrived."

"I wasn't in a tiff and yes, I did get my box of ink."

Yes, he had been in a tiff, but if he wouldn't ac-knowledge it, then she would leave it alone. "Good. I'm glad you got it."

She watched him walk off toward his parlor. He hadn't been in a good mood lately. But then, maybe she'd been in such an extremely good mood that she had a distorted view. In fact, come to think of it, it was pretty normal for him to be moody.

Moments later, while she worked with a customer, Swan watched as Rafe walked back through her shop and toward the front door. She decided if he did that again she would remind him of their agreement about which door he should use whenever he went in or out of his tattoo parlor.

After her customer left, she glanced at her watch. Her shop would be closing in a couple of minutes. David usually arrived early. It would be understandable if he'd gotten detained, but she hoped he hadn't been. She was so anxious to see him.

The thought of how much she was looking forward to being with him should bother her, but for some reason it didn't. Like she'd told Candy, Swan wasn't expecting anything from her relationship with David. There had been no promises made, so none would be broken. The only thing she was expecting was exactly what she was getting—a good time. He was excellent company and great in bed.

It had been almost three years since William, and during that time, although she'd dated, she hadn't allowed herself to get serious over a man. Instead she had concentrated on opening her shop and making it a success.

She had put her mind, heart and soul into Swan's. Especially her heart, deciding that if she put it into her business, she wouldn't run the risk of placing it elsewhere. Now it seemed there might be a risk after all and that risk had a name. David Holloway.

A part of her wanted to protect herself from another possible heartbreak by calling David and canceling any plans for tonight and then to stop sharing any time with him after that. He had given her his number so she could reach him. She could certainly come up with a plausible excuse. But did she really want to do that?

No, she didn't.

David would be her test. If she could handle a casual affair with him, then she would ace the test with flying colors.

The door chimed and she glanced up and there he was. She watched him lock her door and put the Closed sign in place before pulling down the blinds. Then he slowly sauntered toward her wearing a pair of khaki pants and an open white shirt and holding her within the scope of those laser-blue eyes. There was his too-sexy walk and a smile that made her heart beat rapidly.

Suddenly seeing him, when she'd been thinking of him all day, took complete control of her senses. Without much effort, the man had turned the sensuality up more than a notch. He had his own barometer of hotness.

Finally moving her feet, she strolled across the floor to meet him halfway and walked straight into his arms. The moment he pressed his body to hers, she reached up and looped her arms around his neck. He responded by wrapping his arms around her waist, drawing her even closer so she fit against him.

"I missed you, Swan."

She shouldn't let his words affect her, but they did—to the point where she was having difficulty replying.

"I missed you, too."

And she had, although they'd seen each other Wednesday. Even when she'd tried to convince herself that missing him to such a degree meant nothing. Now, as she stood wrapped in his arms, with her body pressed tight against his, hip to hip and thigh to thigh, she knew it meant everything.

"That's good to know, sweetheart," he said in a throaty voice.

Sweetheart? The endearment left her defenseless. She was trying to summon all her senses to regroup. And it wasn't helping matters that his arousal was cradled in the apex of her thighs. Good Lord, he felt so good there.

"Ready?" she found the voice to ask him.

His gaze studied her face as if he was seeing her for the first time. As if he was trying to record her features to memory. And then a mischievous smile touched his lips. "I'm ready for whatever you have in mind, Swan."

Shivers of desire skittered down her spine and Swan wished his words hadn't given her ideas, but they had. Ideas that were so bold, brazen and shameless she felt her cheeks staining just thinking about them. But at that moment, she didn't care. She could and would admit to wanting him.

She should wait until later to act on her desires. That would be the safe thing to do. But she knew she would be tortured during dinner whenever she looked at him. The way his mouth moved when he ate, or the way his hands—those hands that could turn her on just by looking at them—gripped his beer bottle. There were so many things about David Holloway that would do her in if she were to wait until later.

"You sure about that, David?"

"Positive. Do you want me to prove it?"

Did she? Yes, she did. "Where?"

"I will prove it anywhere you want. Right here in the middle of the floor if you like," he said. "But I suggest your office."

Flipper could tell by the way she was looking at him that she was giving his offer serious thought. He had no problems tilting the scale in his favor and he decided to do so. Lowering his head, he kissed her, trying to be gentle and finding gentleness hard to achieve. Especially when her taste made him greedy for more.

He knew she'd ceased thinking when she responded to his kiss by sinking her body farther into his embrace and tightening her arms around his neck.

Some things, he decided then and there, were just too mind-blowingly good, and kissing Swan was one of them. What they'd shared these last few days was a dimension of pleasure he hadn't felt in a long time—or maybe ever—while devouring a woman's mouth. And when his hands shifted from around her waist to cup her backside, he groaned at the feel of her body pressed tightly against his erection.

When he finally broke off the kiss, he buried his

face in the curve of her neck and drew in a deep breath. This woman was almost too much. She looked good, tasted good and as he drew in another deep breath, he concluded that she smelled good, too.

"You want to come with me, Mr. Holloway?" she asked, stepping out of his arms.

"Yes." The answer was quick off his lips.

She took his hand. "Then follow me."

He had no problem following her and the minute he crossed the threshold into her office, he recalled the last time he'd been in here. Namely, when they'd shared a kiss that had nearly brought him to his knees.

"It appears dinner will have to wait."

He glanced over at her. She had stepped out of her sandals. After locking the office door, he leaned against it and watched her undress. She was wearing a burnt-orange sundress with spaghetti straps. It looked good on her and the color of the dress seemed to highlight her hair and skin tone.

He had gotten little sleep since his friends had arrived in the Keys. But then they hadn't come here to rest. They had left their families to come here and help him solve a sinister plan of espionage against the country they loved.

And to protect the woman *he* loved.

He suddenly swallowed deep when that last thought passed through his mind. As he watched Swan remove her panties, he knew without a doubt that he had fallen in love with her. He wouldn't try to figure out how it happened but just accept that it had. Now more than ever he was determined to make sure whoever was trying to screw her over didn't succeed.

"Are you going to just stand there?" she asked, standing before him completely naked.

"No, that's not my intention at all," he said, moving away from the door to stand a few feet from her in what he considered his safe zone. If he got any closer, he would be tempted to take her with his clothes on. He removed his shirt and eased both his khakis and briefs down his legs at the same time. Quick and easy.

"I love your dolphins," she said. "I meant to ask you about them a number of other times, but always got sidetracked. So I'm asking you now. Any reason you chose dolphins?"

He decided to be as truthful with her as he could. One day he would have to explain to her why he'd lied about so many things. "Like the dolphins, I love being in the water. But this isn't just any dolphin."

"It's not?"

"No. This dolphin's name is Flipper. Surely you've heard of him."

"Not as much as I know Willy from *Free Willy*."

He chuckled as he moved toward her. "Willy was a whale. Flipper was a dolphin. That's what my friends call me. Flipper."

"Flipper?"

"Yes. Like I said, I love being in the water."

"You don't look like a Flipper."

He came to a stop in front of her. "Don't tell that to my family and friends. They wouldn't agree with you."

She reached out and touched the tattoo of the dolphin on his arm. Her fingers felt like fire as she traced along the design with her fingertips. "Beautiful. Not just your tattoos but all of you, David."

"Thanks." And in one smooth sweep, he picked her up and sat her on the desk, spreading her legs in the process.

"Did I tell you how much I missed you?" he asked, running his hands over her arms.

"Yes. Just a few moments ago when you arrived here and I told you I missed you, too. You also told me that you missed me when you walked me home Wednesday night and I invited you to stay."

Flipper heard the disappointment in her voice. If only she knew how much he'd wanted to stay. But once he'd found out Jamila would be out for a while with Horacio, he needed that time to check out her place. "I couldn't, but I intend to make it up to you when we have more time."

He was letting her know this little quickie didn't count. He had something planned for her when all this was over and he could sit her down and tell her everything.

"Not here and not now? What do you call this?" she asked when he reached up and cupped her breasts in his hands, marveling at just how beautiful they were.

"This is an I-can't-wait-until-later quickie."

"Interesting."

Shifting his gaze from her breasts to her eyes, he said, "Let me show you, Swan Jamison, just how interesting it can be." He leaned forward and kissed her while placing the head of his erection against her wet opening. The contact sent heat spiraling through him.

While his tongue mated greedily with hers, he entered her in one hard stroke. Pulling his mouth from hers, he let out a guttural moan when her muscles clamped down on his throbbing erection. That made him push harder and sink deeper.

And when she moaned his name, he knew she could feel the fire of passion spreading between them as much as he could.

Swan wrapped her legs completely around Flipper, loving the feel of him moving inside her. He was giving her body one heck of a workout on her desk. She could feel the heat in his eyes as he stared at her.

He used his hands to lift her hips off the desk's surface for a deeper penetration. When his erection hit a certain part of her, she gasped and arched her back.

"David…"

She whispered his name when she felt him going deeper and deeper. The intensity of their joining sent emotions skyrocketing through her.

She needed this. She wanted this. Like him, she needed it now, not later. This was more than interesting. This was a hot, frenzied, torrid mating. More than a quickie. David was thorough, meticulously so, and not to be rushed. It was as if he intended to savor every stroke.

Suddenly, she felt herself falling. Not off the desk but out of reality when an orgasm rammed through her at the same time as he shuddered with the force of his own release.

They stared at each other, realizing something at the same time. Wanting to make sure he didn't stop, she whispered, "Pill."

It seemed that single word triggered another orgasm and she felt him flooding her insides again while his deep, guttural groan filled the room. His release sparked another within her. His name was torn from her lips when her body shattered in earth-shaking and mind-blowing ecstasy.

As the daze from Swan's orgasmic state receded, she felt David slowly withdraw from inside her. That's when she forced her eyes open to stare at him and accepted the hand he extended to help her off the desk. Once on her feet, she wrapped her arms around his waist, feeling weak in the knees.

"It's okay, baby, I got you. I won't let you fall," he whispered close to her ear as he leaned down.

Too late, she thought. She'd already fallen. Head over heels in love with him. The very thought suddenly sent her mind spinning.

Hadn't she just given herself a good talking to moments before he'd arrived? Told herself he was someone she could enjoy, both in and out of bed and nothing more? That he was someone she knew better than to give her heart to because she hadn't wanted to take the risk?

What on earth had happened?

She knew the answer as she moved closer into the comfort of his warm naked body. David Holloway had happened. As much as she hadn't meant to fall in love with him, she had.

It didn't matter that she had known him less than three weeks. Somehow he had come into her world and turned it upside down, whether that had been his intent or not. When his work on the island was finished, he would move on and not look back. But still, knowing that he would leave hadn't stopped him from winning her heart.

"Ready?"

She lifted her head and look up at him. "You know, David, that lone question will get us in trouble."

He held her gaze for a long moment and then caressed the side of her face. "Or take us to places we really want to go and inspire us to do things that we really want to do."

Then he lowered his mouth to hers and kissed her.

Eleven

"Great work finding out about that ink, Lieutenant Holloway. I knew there was no way Swan would have betrayed her country."

"Yes, sir. Those are my thoughts as well," Flipper said. He had placed his CO on speakerphone so his SEAL teammates could listen to the call. "There's no doubt in my mind the persons naval intelligence should be concentrating on are Rafe Duggers and Horacio Jacinto."

"I agree. I met with Admiral Martin and Director Levart this morning and they concur there's a mole within the organization."

"By meeting with them, sir, does that mean you

feel certain they can be totally trusted as well?" Flipper felt he had to ask.

"Yes, Lieutenant Holloway. I do. I know that because of what you discovered and what went down with Lieutenant Westmoreland a few years ago involving those moles at Homeland Security, you're not sure who you can trust. I understand that. However, I assure you that you can trust the three of us to protect Swan with our lives if we have to. We knew she was innocent, which was why we sent you there to prove we were right. You have. Now it's up to us to find out who's behind this and bring them to justice."

"And in the meantime?"

"In the meantime, Lieutenant, you are free to consider this assignment completed. Go home to Texas and enjoy the remainder of your leave."

There was no way he could consider this assignment completed, although under normal circumstances it would be once the CO said so. "I think I'll hang around Key West for a while."

"Why?" Commanding Officer Shields asked. "Do you think Swan's life might be in immediate danger?"

"As long as Duggers and Jacinta don't know they're suspected of anything, then no. However…"

"However what, Lieutenant Holloway?"

Flipper had no problem being truthful to his CO. "However, Swan has come to mean a lot to me, sir."

"Oh, I see."

Flipper figured since his CO knew him so well,

he did see. "In that case, Lieutenant Holloway, how you choose to spend the rest of your leave is your decision. But keep in mind, since this is an ongoing investigation, you cannot tell Swan anything, including your reason for being in the Keys in the first place. That in itself will place you in what might be perceived by her as a dishonorable situation."

"I'm aware of that, sir, but I refuse to leave her until I have to. How long do you think it will take to wrap up the investigation?"

"Not sure. We will not only be investigating the original investigators but we'll have to restart the entire case, making Duggers and Jacinta the primary suspects. If you remain in the Keys and notice anything I need to know, don't hesitate to bring it to my attention."

In other words, Commanding Officer Shields was pretty much giving Flipper the green light to do his own thing, unofficially. "Yes, sir."

When Flipper clicked off the phone, he glanced up at his friends. "So what do you guys think?"

"Personally, I think you're doing the right thing not leaving here until you're certain Miss Jamison's life is not in any danger," Bane said.

"And since we don't plan to leave until you do, it's time we figure out just who is behind this," Coop added.

"I agree with all the above," Viper tacked on.

They all looked at Mac, who rubbed his chin as if contemplating something. Then he said, "Someone needs to play devil's advocate, so I guess it has to be me."

"No surprise there," Bane said.

Mac shot Bane a glare and then glanced back at Flipper. "Think about what the CO said. You can't tell Miss Jamison anything. Once she finds out the truth, that she was nothing more than an assignment to you, she's not going to like it, no matter how noble or honorable your intentions might have been."

Flipper drew in a deep breath. He knew Mac's words to be true. Although Swan had yet to tell him anything about her affair with William Connors, it had been in the report. The man had betrayed her and there was a chance she would probably see Flipper as doing the same. "So, Mr. Know-It-All, what do you suggest I do?" he asked.

"Start drawing a line in your relationship and don't cross it. In other words, stop seducing her," Mac said.

Too late for that, Flipper thought. All he had to do was remember what they'd done yesterday in Swan's office and again when he'd taken her home after dinner. Especially when he'd sat in one of her kitchen chairs and she'd straddled his body. The memories of what had started out in that chair and ended up in her bedroom made him feel hot. He hadn't left her place until dawn this morning. There was no way he could put a freeze on his relationship with Swan like Mac was suggesting.

"That's not an option, Mac. I'm going to do what I have to do now and worry about the consequences later."

* * *

"What's this about you having a boyfriend? I can't leave you alone for one minute."

Swan smiled when she glanced up at Rosie Mc-Call, one of her frequent customers. Rosie, an older woman in her midforties who'd been away for the past three months visiting her family in Nevada, had returned to the Keys just yesterday. "I see Jamila has been talking again."

"Doesn't matter. So tell me, who is he?"

Swan closed the jewelry case. "First of all, he's not my boyfriend. He's just someone I'm seeing while he's here on the island working, which won't be much longer."

"Um, short meaningless flings are the best kind. What's his name?"

"David. David Holloway."

"Where he is from?"

"Texas."

"You said he's here working. What does he do for a living?"

"Whoa, time-out," Swan said, using her hand for the signal. "You don't need to know all that. David's a nice guy and that's all you really need to know."

She knew how Rosie liked to play matchmaker. She'd been the one who'd introduced Jamila to Hora-cio. Rosie had met him at one of the nightclubs and thought he was cute, too young for her but just the right age for Swan or Jamila. Swan hadn't been interested in a blind date but Jamila had. Horacio and Jamila met, hit it off and had been an item ever since.

"You can't blame me for being curious, Swan. You seldom date."

"My choice, remember? Besides, you do it enough for the both of us." And that was the truth. After her second divorce, Rosie had made it known she would never marry again but intended to date any man who asked her out as long as they were the right age. Not too old and not too young.

Rosie smiled. "Yes, I do, don't I? But that doesn't mean you shouldn't go out and have fun every once in a while. There's more to life than this shop, Swan. I hope you're finally finding that out."

"Whatever." Swan had heard it before and all from Rosie. She liked the older woman and thought she was a fun person who had a zeal for life. There was never a dull moment around her.

At that moment, the shop's door chimed and Swan knew without looking in that direction that David had walked in. She also knew when he saw her with a customer that he would wait until she finished before approaching her.

Rosie leaned in. "Looks like you have a customer. Let's hope he buys something since he came in a minute before closing."

Swan inwardly smiled. "We can only hope, right?"

"But then he's such a cutie. Look at him."

Swan didn't have to look at David to know what a cutie he was, but she did so anyway. He was browsing around the store wearing a pair of shorts and a sleeve-less T-shirt with flip-flops on his feet. He looked laid-back and sexy as sin. "You're right, he is a cutie."

"I love those tattoos on his upper arms. Nice."

"Yes, they are." She knew Rosie was into tat-toos and was one of Rafe's frequent customers. The woman had them everywhere, visible and non-visible.

"You need to go wait on him. See what he wants. If he's not sure, offer him a few things."

Swan smiled. Little did Rosie know, but she in-tended to offer David a lot. "I will. Come on, I'll walk you to the door. I'm officially closed now," Swan said, coming from around the counter.

"You honestly want me to leave you here with him?" Rosie whispered. "For all you know he's not safe."

Swan chuckled and decided it was time for her to come clean. "He's safe, Rosie. That's David and he's here to walk me home. I'll introduce you on your way out the door."

"You mean that gorgeous hunk is your guy?"

Swan glanced over at David again. He was defi-nitely a gorgeous hunk but she couldn't claim him as her guy. "Yes, he's the guy I've been seeing a lot of lately."

"Smart girl."

David glanced up when they approached and gave her a huge smile. "Hi," he greeted.

"Hi, David. I'd like you to meet Rosie McCall. A

friend who has been away for the past few months and just returned back to the island. Rosie, this is David Holloway."

David extended his hand. "Nice meeting you, Rosie."

"Same here, David. I like your tattoos."

"Thanks and I like yours," he responded.

"Thanks. Well, I'll be going. I hope you guys enjoy yourselves."

"We will," Swan said, smiling up at David. "I'll be back after seeing Rosie out," she told him.

He nodded. "Nice meeting you, Rosie."

"Same here."

Swan returned to David a few moments later, after putting up the Closed sign, locking the door and pulling down the shades. She turned and studied him as he stood across the room, looking so amazingly sexy. She felt a lump in her throat. She loved everything about him, especially the muscles beneath his shirt, the masculine thighs and his tanned skin.

"Got more sun today, I see."

"Yes, I had to go out on the boat today."

"One day you're going to have to explain to me in detail just what your ocean duties entail."

"I will. But for now, come here. I missed you today."

She crossed the room to walk into his arms. "I missed you, too."

"That's good to know. Rosie seems like a nice person."

"She is."

"She has a lot of tattoos."

Swan chuckled. "Yes, she does. She's one of Rafe's best customers."

"Is that right?" David asked, still smiling. "He did an awesome job."

She checked her watch. "We can leave as soon as I grab my purse." They would be having dinner at Nathan Waterway and afterward would attend an art show. "I'll be back in a second."

Flipper watched Swan walk off toward her office while thinking of what she'd told him about Rosie McCall. He recalled what he'd overheard Rafe and Horacio arguing about that night behind this building. Ink and roses. Or had they said Rosie? Was she a part of the group? If she was, that meant she had an ulterior motive for befriending Swan.

Pulling his phone from his pocket he texted Nick. Check out Rosie McCall.

He received an immediate reply. Will do.

He then texted Bane. Excursion tonight.

The reply was quick. On it.

Most of today he and Viper had pretended to go fishing after Mac, who'd been tailing Rafe for the past two days, reported that Rafe had rented a boat and headed in the direction of another island close by. Today Flipper and Viper had also rented a boat, making sure they stayed a good distance behind Duggers.

The man had docked in Fleming Key. Bane and

Cooper, who'd arrived ahead of them, picked up the tail on Rafe. It seemed the man had gone into a sports shop where he'd stayed for three hours.

Pretending to be two guys enjoying their time out on their boat, Flipper and Viper had waited at the pier and knew when Rafe had left the island to return to Key West. Mac had been there to pick up the tail and reported that the man had been carrying a package when he went inside his tattoo shop. A package Rafe had gotten from the sports shop, according to Bane and Coop.

"I'm ready."

He looked up and when Swan met his gaze, she quickly clarified, "I'm ready *for dinner*."

He placed his phone back into his pocket and smiled. "That's all?"

The smile she returned made his insides quiver in anticipation. "For now, Mr. Holloway."

Twelve

It was getting harder and harder to leave Swan's bed, Flipper thought as he and his teammates docked at Fleming Key close to two in the morning. But at least he'd left her sleeping with the most peaceful smile on her face.

Without waking her, he had brushed a kiss across her lips and whispered that he loved her, knowing she would remember neither. But he decided to tell her how he felt when he saw her later today. He couldn't hold it inside any longer. She deserved to know. He wanted her to know. And when all this was over and she knew the truth, he would do whatever he needed to do to win her forgiveness and her love.

He jumped when fingers snapped in his face. He

glared at Mac, who glared back. "Stay focused. You can daydream later."

"I wasn't daydreaming," Flipper countered. He then realized he was the only one still in the boat. The others had already gotten out.

"Then night-dreaming. Call it what you want" was Mac's reply. "Just get out of the damn boat."

Flipper didn't have to wonder why Mac was in a rotten mood. Teri had texted him earlier in the day to say the new washer and dryer had been delivered. They were new appliances Mac hadn't known they were buying.

Moments later, dressed in all black military combat gear, the five of them circled around to the back of the sports shop Rafe had frequented lately. Being ever ready and not taking any chances, Glocks were strapped to their hips and high powered tasers to their thighs. Due to Viper's hypersensitive ears—known to pick up sound over long distances away—he would stay outside as the lookout. Flipper, Bane, Cooper and Mac bypassed security cameras to enter the building.

Once inside, they used Flipper's cameras and it didn't take long to find a hidden room. Making swift use of their time, they took pictures of everything. It was obvious this was the group's operation headquarters. More tattoo ink was stored here along with several specific tattoo designs. One design Flipper quickly recalled seeing on the side of Rosie's neck.

Flipper scanned the room with his camera and

then opened several drawers in the huge desk and took photos of the contents. When he came across a photo in one of the drawers, he suddenly froze. "Damn."

"What is it, Flipper?" Bane asked.

Instead of saying anything, he motioned his head to the photograph he'd found. Mac, Bane and Coop came around him to see it as well. They looked back at him and Mac said, "We've been royally screwed."

An uneasy feeling settled in the pit of Flipper's stomach. "I need to get back to Swan as soon as possible."

Swan was awakened by the knocking on her door. She glanced at the clock on her nightstand and wondered who on earth would be at her house at four in the morning. Was it David returning? She didn't recall when he'd left but knew it was the norm for him to leave her place around midnight to return to his hotel because of his work. Usually she would be awake when he left but tonight sexual exhaustion had gotten the best of her.

Pulling on her robe, she tied it around her waist as she headed for the door. Looking out the peephole, she saw it was Jamila and Horacio. What were they doing out so late and why were they at her place? She found it odd that Horacio was on the island when the cruise ship wasn't due back in port again until next week.

From the look on Jamila's face, it appeared she

wasn't happy about something. In fact, from her red-dened eyes, it appeared that she'd been crying. Swan wondered what on earth was wrong. Had something happened?

Suddenly filled with concern, she quickly opened the door. The minute she did so, Jamila was shoved inside, nearly knocking Swan down.

"Hey, wait a minute. What's going on?" Swan asked, fighting to regain her balance.

"Shut the hell up and don't ask questions," Hora-cio said, quickly coming inside and closing the door behind him.

Swan frowned. "Horacio? What do you mean, I can't ask any questions?"

"Just do what you're told," he barked.

Swan glanced over at Jamila and saw the bruise on the side of her face. "Did he do this to you?" Swan demanded, getting enraged. At Jamila's nod, Swan then turned to Horacio. How could he have done this when he adored Jamila? "I want you to leave now."

"If I don't, what are you going to do? Call the police? Or call that SEAL you're sleeping with?"

Swan frown deepened. "I don't know what you're talking about. Now leave or I *will* call the police."

"You won't be doing anything other than what I tell you to do. When I get the word, the two of you will be coming with me."

Swan placed her hands on her hips. "We're not going anywhere with you."

A cynical smile touched Horacio's lips as he

pulled out a gun from his back pocket. "This says you will."

Swan stared at the gun, not believing Horacio had it pointed at both her and Jamila. She was about to say something when Horacio added, "I'm giving you five minutes to go into your bedroom and put on clothes. Bring me your phone first. I don't want you to get any crazy ideas."

Swan had no idea what was going on, but from the pleading look in Jamila's eyes, she knew it was best to do as she was told. She went and got her cell phone and handed it to him, but not before she noticed several missed calls from David. Why had he been trying to call her? Her mind was filled with so many questions.

"You got five minutes to get dressed. If you're not back in five minutes or try some kind of funny business, your cousin here will pay for it."

Cousin? Why did he refer to Jamila as her cousin? At what was obviously a confused look on her face, he said, "That's right. Secrets. There are plenty more where those came from, Swan, and you'll be finding out about them later. Now go."

Swan got dressed in less than five minutes. If she hadn't thought Horacio was serious about hurting Jamila, she would have escaped through her bedroom window. That bruise along the side of her friend's face indicated the man was serious.

Swan was walking out of her bedroom fully

dressed when Horacio's phone rang. Instead of answering it, he said, "That's my signal that things are ready. We'll go out your back door to the beach. The boat is waiting."

"What boat?"

"Please don't ask him anything, Swan," Jamila pleaded, reaching out and grabbing her arm. "All of them are crazy."

Swan wondered just who were *all of them*. But she decided not to ask.

"Move!"

Following Horacio's orders, she and Jamila walked toward Swan's kitchen to go out the back door.

As soon as their boat docked, Flipper raced through the streets of Key West toward Swan's home with his teammates fast on his heels. He had tried reaching her on the phone but didn't get an answer. He immediately knew something was wrong because she kept her phone on the nightstand next to her bed and the ringing would have woken her up. He had tried several more times with no luck, which was why his heart was beating out of control and fear was gripping his insides, especially now that he knew who was involved.

They had contacted their CO and told him what they'd discovered. He was as shocked as they'd been and they knew Shields would be taking the necessary actions on his end. Flipper hadn't had to tell the man there would be hell to pay if anyone hurt one single hair on Swan's head.

When they reached her house, they found the door unlocked. Her cell phone had been tossed on a living room table and a quick search of her bedroom indicated she'd change clothes.

"Take a look at this, Flipper," Mac called out.

When he reached them in the kitchen, Mac pointed out the window. Flipper saw lights from a boat that was sitting idle in the ocean as if waiting to rendezvous with another vessel.

"I traced footprints in the sand that led to the water. A small watercraft probably took them out to that boat," Viper was saying. "There were three sets of shoe prints belonging to two women and a man. And they left around thirty minutes ago."

Flipper raced out Swan's back door and after putting on his night-vision eyewear, he stared out at the ocean.

"Intercept with our boat," he shouted over his shoulder to the others. Quickly dropping to the sand, he began removing his shoes, T-shirt and pants, leaving his body clad in a pair of swimming trunks.

"Don't try it, Flipper. The boat's too far out," Mac said. "It's too dangerous for anyone, even you."

Flipper glanced up at them while putting the waterproof military belt that contained combat gear around his waist. He then put a pair of specially designed water goggles over his eyes. "The woman I love is on that boat and I have no idea what they plan to do, so I have to try. Even if I die trying."

Without saying anything else, he raced toward the water and dived in.

Horacio had tied their hands before forcing them into a small boat, which carried them out into the ocean to a much bigger boat. Now they were sitting idle in the waves.

Swan wondered why. She glanced around and noticed that, other than the lights on the boat, there was only darkness. They were so far from land she couldn't see the lights from the homes where she lived anymore.

As if Horacio realized she was trying to figure out what was happening, he said, "I'm waiting for the rest of the gang, then we'll decide what we will do with the two of you."

What he said didn't make much sense. "Will someone please tell me what's going on?" Swan asked, getting angrier by the minute. None of this made any sense.

"I'll let your cousin go first since Jamila has a lot of explaining to do," Horacio said, grinning.

Swan turned to Jamila, who was sitting on a bench beside her. "What is he talking about? Why does he keep referring to you as my cousin?"

At first Jamila didn't say anything. In fact, it seemed she was refusing to meet Swan's gaze, but then she finally met Swan's eyes and said, "Because we are cousins, Swan. My mother is your grandfather's youngest sister."

"My grandfather?"

Jamila nodded. "Yes, Lawrence Jamison is my uncle. I knew for years that Uncle Lawrence disowned your father but I didn't know why until I was much older. Then I thought the reason was downright stupid and told the family what I thought. Everyone else in the family thought the same thing but were too afraid to stand up to Uncle Lawrence."

Swan didn't say anything. She was still trying to dissect the fact that she and Jamila were related. She'd known from her father that Lawrence had a sister and another brother. That was all she'd known.

"When I turned twenty-one and finished college, I decided to come find you. Uncle Lawrence didn't like it but I told him I didn't care. I'm one of the few who stands up to him. He said the family would disown me if I came here."

"Yet you came anyway," Swan said.

"Yes, I came anyway."

Swan glanced over at Horacio. He wasn't saying anything and didn't appear to be listening to what they were saying. Instead he stood at the bow of the ship looking through binoculars as if he was searching for someone. He'd said they were waiting for another boat with the gang and Swan couldn't help but wonder who the gang was.

She wanted to ask Jamila how much she knew and why they were being held hostage but figured that although Horacio was pretending not to listen to their conversation, he probably was.

Swan glanced over at Jamila. "Why didn't you tell me who you were when you first came into my shop that day? Why did you keep it a secret all this time?"

"Because I knew how my family had treated you and your mother. I figured the last thing you'd want was to meet a relative from that side of the family. I decided to let you accept me as a friend and then later I would tell you the truth that we were cousins."

"Now isn't that a touching story?" Horacio said, strolling back over to where they sat.

"Yes, it is touching," Swan said, defiantly lifting her chin. "Why are we here?"

He smiled. "You'll find out soon enough. And I hope you're not holding out any hope that your SEAL boyfriend will be coming to rescue you because he won't."

"Why do you keep saying David is a SEAL when he's not? He was in the military once but he was never a SEAL."

"Sounds like you've been conned by him just like your cousin here was conned by me," he said as if it was something to brag about. "Your lover boy *is* a SEAL and he was sent here to get the goods on you. Whether you know it or not, you've been his assignment."

Swan shook her head. "No, that's not true. I don't believe you."

"I don't care if you believe me or not but it's true. I only found out today what he's been doing and why he was sent here by naval intelligence."

Naval intelligence? Swan glanced over at Jamila, who said, "I don't know whether what he's saying is true or not, Swan, but he told me the same thing tonight."

"Why would naval intelligence suspect me of anything? It doesn't make sense." And more than that, she refused to believe David wasn't who and what he said he was.

At that moment, they heard the sound of a boat approaching. Horacio drew his gun and pointed the flashlight toward the oncoming boat. He put his gun back in place. "Hold on to that question, sweetheart. The person who will explain everything just arrived."

Swan kept her gaze trained on the boat that pulled up beside theirs and saw two people onboard. Both of them she knew. What in the world…?

She watched in shock as Rafe and Rosie came aboard. She was so focused on staring at them that she almost missed the third person who also came on board.

She gasped in shock when the person said, "Swan, you look well."

Suddenly losing her voice, Swan couldn't do anything but sit there and stare. There had to be some mistake. A very big mistake. There was no way the person standing before her was a part of this craziness.

No way.

She finally found her voice. "Georgianna? What are you doing here? What is this about?"

Thirteen

Flipper reached the boat and attached himself to the ladder on the side. Lucky for him, no one had thought to pull it up. Taking slow, deep breaths, he pulled air into his lungs while ignoring the pain in his arms and legs. He didn't want to think about just how far he'd swum, but like he'd told his friends, he'd had to try.

He quickly eased back into the water when he heard the sound of an approaching boat and was grateful the vessel pulled up on the other side from where he was hiding. He glanced at his watch. It was synchronized with the ones worn by his team-mates, and he knew they would do their best to get here soon. In the meantime, there was something he had to do.

Pulling a micro audio recorder off his belt, he moved back up the ladder to peek over the railing and into the boat.

Good. Everyone's attention was on the approaching vessel and no one saw him when he attached the audio recorder that was no bigger than a dime to the interior wall of the boat. He saw Swan and Jamila seated on a bench with their hands tied behind their backs and Horacio was standing not far away. Other than a man in the cockpit, there was no one else onboard. Flipper knew that was about to change when he heard voices.

Satisfied that the conversations would be recorded, he eased back down the ladder. When his watch began vibrating, he glanced down at the text message from Bane. On our way. Had 2 take care of a little problem 1st.

Flipper wondered what kind of problem his friends had to take care of. No matter. They were on their way and that's what counted. He listened to the conversation going on in the boat as he began pulling items from his belt. He intended to be ready to crash this little party when the time came.

He shook his head, knowing Admiral Martin would be heartbroken to discover his own daughter had sold out their country.

"I hate you," Georgianna said, glaring at Swan.

Swan was taken aback by the woman's words. "Why? What have I ever done to you? To any of you?" she asked, glancing around at the people she'd assumed were friends—Rafe, Horacio and Rosie. She hurt more at seeing Rosie than the others because she'd believed the woman had been a good friend.

"They work for me and did what they were told," Georgianna said.

"Work for you?" Swan was even more confused.

"Yes. I'm in charge of the entire operation. But I'll tell you all about that later. First, let me tell you why I despise you so much. I've waited a long time to get this out in the open. When your father died and your mother would send you to us for the summer, my parents thought you were golden. They put you on a pedestal, especially my father. Did you know he called you his little island princess?"

Yes, Swan knew but she also knew her godfather hadn't meant anything by it. It was just a nickname he'd given her when she was born. All three of her godfathers called her that sometimes. "It was just a nickname, Georgianna."

"For you, it might only have been a nickname, but for me, it was Dad shifting his attention from me to you."

"Godpop 1 loves you. He wasn't shifting his attention to me, he was just being nice."

"Too nice, and I despised you for it. He had a daughter, yet any time your mother would call, he and Mom would drop everything and take off. Just because your father saved Dad's life—that meant nothing. They were all SEALs and your dad was doing his job when he died. But it was as if Dad blamed himself and he needed to make it up by being nice to you, like you were somebody special. So, with the help of some friends, I decided to change everyone's opinion of you."

It was hard for Swan to believe what she was hearing. She'd never known that Georgianna harbored such feelings. Granted she hadn't always been overnice and had a tendency to be moody, but Swan hadn't detected animosity like this.

"What did you do?" Swan asked her.

Georgianna smiled like she was proud of what she was about to say. "I set up an espionage operation out of your shop with the help of Rafe and Horacio. Then, with Rosie's assistance, I made it appear that the secret information being sent to China was being done through your jewelry."

"What!" Swan couldn't believe it. Her head was spinning from all the shocks she'd received tonight.

"I have to admit I put together a perfect plan. This guy I was sleeping with at the time assisted me by tipping off naval intelligence with what you were supposedly doing. They did their own investigation and my team and I made sure everything pointed at you. It should have been an open and shut case and you were to be arrested and charged with espionage."

As if she was tired of standing, Georgianna moved to sit on one of the benches. She frowned over at Swan. "Everything was going according to plan until the final thread of the investigation reached Director Levart's desk."

"Godpop 3?"

"See what I mean? You have three godfathers and I don't have a one," Georgianna said in a loud voice, pointing a finger at her. "You don't deserve such love and loyalty, and I intended to tarnish their image of you."

Flipper's watch vibrated and he glanced down at the text message. Here. N place. Coop got layout of boat.

He texted them back. 1 N cockpit. 4 others. 2 hostages.

He quickly received a reply from Viper. Eliminating cockpit.

Got 4 in scope. That particular text came from Bane, a master sniper.

Flipper knew that although everyone was in place, timing was everything. Georgianna had no idea her words were being recorded so he wanted to let her talk before making his move. Then there would be no way she could deny anything.

From listening to what the woman was saying, it was obvious she had mental issues. That could be the only reason to have such a deep hatred of Swan that Georgianna would go to such extremes. Georgianna assumed she'd had the perfect plan for Swan's downfall and Flipper was glad things hadn't turned out the way Georgianna intended.

Before inching up the ladder to listen to what else she was confessing, he texted the message: Will give signal.

Swan shook her head. It was obvious Georgianna's jealousy had blinded her senses and fueled her hatred. Didn't the others see it? Why were they following her blindly? Swan glanced over at Jamila and could tell by the look in her cousin's eyes that she was wondering the same thing.

"When Director Levart saw the report, he refused to believe you could be guilty of anything, especially betraying your country."

Thank God for that, Swan thought.

"He requested a thirty-day delay before agreeing to take any actions against you. Even after we made sure the investigation clearly spelled out your role in everything. There was no reason for you not to be charged," Georgianna said.

She paused a moment before continuing. "Unknown to me and the others, Director Levart went to your other two godfathers and they put their heads together to see what they could do to prove your innocence. They decided to send one of their top SEALs to find out what he could and to prove your innocence."

Swan drew in a deep breath. *Oh no, please don't let what Horacio said tonight be true. Please don't let David turn out to be someone other than what he said he was.*

Georgianna's next words ripped into Swan's heart.

"The SEAL they sent was Lieutenant David Holloway. I guess you didn't know that all the time he spent with you was nothing more than an assignment. You meant nothing to him, Swan." Georgianna laughed as if she found the entire thing amusing while Swan's heart broke.

"Imagine how amused I was to find out just how taken you were with him, while not knowing the true purpose as to why he showed up here on the island. You were played, Swan," Georgianna was saying in between laughter. "But don't worry. I sent some other members of my group to take care of him for you. I think he's dead by now."

Suddenly a deep voice at the back of the boat said, "As you can see, I'm very much alive."

Swan gasped just as the others did. Standing with legs braced apart and wearing only a pair of swim trunks with a utility combat belt around his waist, David looked like a mad badass. It was obvious everyone was shocked to see him, especially Georgianna, who had assumed he was dead.

"Drop your gun," he ordered Horacio, who was still holding his weapon on Swan and Jamila.

"How the hell did you get here?" Horacio asked, enraged.

"I swam from Swan's home."

"That's impossible!"

"Not if you're a SEAL master swimmer," David said. "Now, do like I said and put your gun down."

"And if I don't? It will be a shame if I kill Swan or Jamila before you can get to anything on that belt you're wearing," Horacio sneered.

"Don't try it, Horacio. One of my team members who's a master sniper has all four of you within his scope. Before you could get off the first shot, you'd be dead."

"I don't believe you. There's no one else out here," Horacio said. When he lifted his gun to take aim at Swan, a shot rang out, hitting the man in the chest. The impact toppled him to the floor.

Jamila screamed and Swan understood. Jamila had fallen in love with a man who'd betrayed her and then gotten shot right before her eyes.

Suddenly, Rafe dived for the gun that had dropped from Horacio's hand. Before he could reach it, another shot rang out that hit him in the side. He fell to the floor as well.

"Either of you ladies want to join them?" Flipper asked Georgianna and Rosie.

Rosie looked like she was in shock and ready to pass out.

However, Georgianna looked furious. "You won't get away with this. No matter what you tell my father, he will never believe you over me," she said with absolute certainty. "I'll tell him that you decided to team up with Swan and she turned you against your country."

"I figured you would lie. That's why I've recorded your little confession to Swan detailing everything. I can't wait for your father to listen to it."

Suddenly the boat was surrounded by several naval vessels and sharp beams of light shined on them. A voice through a foghorn said, "Lieutenant Holloway, we are coming aboard."

A dozen men wearing SEAL gear rushed on board with their guns drawn, immediately taking Georgianna and Rosie into custody. Bane, Viper, Coop and Mac boarded the boat as well. Mac rushed over to check Horacio and Rafe. There really was no need since they were both dead.

Flipper rushed over to Swan and Jamila to untie their hands. More than anything, he wanted to pull Swan into his arms and tell her he loved her. He wanted her to put out of her mind what Georgianna had said about him until she'd heard his side of things. However, he knew when she pulled away from him to give her cousin a hug that she didn't want to give him a chance to explain.

He didn't intend to let her walk away.

"We need to talk, Swan," he said, looking down at her.

She glared up at him. "We have nothing to say to each other. Your assignment is over, Lieutenant Holloway. Now leave me alone."

Fourteen

Two weeks later

"How long are you planning to be mad at the world, Swan?"

Swan glanced over at Candy. Her best friend had returned to the Keys after hearing about what happened and she'd decided to stay. Swan was glad Candy had returned home but she was saddened by what had brought her back.

"I am not mad at the world," Swan said, taking a sip of her orange juice.

"But you are still mad at one particular man," Candy said, coming to sit beside Swan on the sofa.

Swan couldn't deny that was true so she didn't. "And what if I am?"

"He had a job to do, Swan. He was given orders. Surely you understand that."

Swan glared at Candy. "I'm sure none of my godfathers' orders included sleeping with me."

"I'm sure they didn't but David didn't force himself on you."

"No, but he deceived me."

"So did the others."

Did Candy have to remind her? "And I'm not talking to them either."

That wasn't totally true since Swan had reached out to Georgianna where she was being held at a federal prison in Orlando. The woman had refused to see her. Swan knew Georgianna was undergoing psychiatric evaluations to see if she was fit to stand trial.

Swan's godparents were heartbroken and she understood how they felt. Like her, they'd had no idea Georgianna harbored such hatred toward Swan, enough to do what she'd done. With both Rafe and Horacio dead, it was Rosie who was singing like a bird, telling everything she knew for a lessened sentence.

According to Rosie, Georgianna had manipulated a number of the men at naval intelligence into doing whatever she wanted them to do. When you were the admiral's daughter, you could wield that kind of power. She had even threatened a few with blackmail. She'd deliberately recorded several of the men having sex with her and then threatened to give the tape to her father and accuse them of rape.

Some of the men were not only married but a number were high-ranking military officers. Fearful of court-martial, the men had done whatever Georgianna asked, including falsifying records. So far, more than twelve men had been named in the scandal.

"I take it David hasn't called."

Swan drew in a deep breath. She had seen him last week when they'd had to show up at the naval station to give statements. "Yes, he's called. Several times. But I refuse to answer. Like I told him, we have nothing to say to each other. His assignment is over."

"And do you honestly think that's all you were to him, Swan?"

"Yes, but it doesn't matter."

"I think it does," Candy countered.

"And you think too much," Swan said, easing off the sofa.

The first week after the incident on the boat, she had closed her shop while naval investigators did a thorough search of Rafe's tattoo parlor. She had used that time to take care of Jamila, who was still broken up over Horacio. Jamila had loved him and in a single night had seen him become an abusive monster, a man she hadn't known. Then in the end, Jamila had watched him die before her eyes.

Swan knew Jamila was going through something that only time could heal. That's why when Swan had reopened the shop this week and Jamila had asked for extra work hours, Swan had given them to her.

"So what are you going to do?" Candy asked her.

Swan glanced over at her. "About life? Work?"

"No, about David."

Swan just couldn't understand why Candy couldn't accept that David was no longer in the equation. "I'm a survivor, Candy. Although it was hard, I made do after my parents' deaths and I will make do now." She glanced at her watch. "I'm getting dressed to go into the shop today. The cruise ship comes into port tomorrow, so business will pick up. I want to make sure most of my new pieces are on display."

Another thing they had found out was that Horacio had been fired from the cruise ship months ago but hadn't told Jamila. He had moved into Rosie's place while the woman had been gone. The duplicity of the people she'd thought she knew simply amazed Swan.

"And I need to be on my way," Candy said. "I promised my folks we would go out to dinner tonight. You can join us if you like."

"Thanks for the invite, but I'll pass. I just want to have a relaxing evening here tonight. I might go swimming on the beach later."

Swan had called Jamila and told her she would bring lunch from their favorite sandwich café. However, there were no clients in her shop when Swan got there, so she decided to do something she usually didn't do, which was close for lunch.

Normally, the shop remained open and she and Jamila would alternate lunch duties. But today she wanted to check on Jamila, talk to her to see how she was faring. Although Swan had been there for Jamila last week, they hadn't had a real honest-to-goodness talk since Jamila had admitted to being her cousin.

"What are you doing?" Jamila asked when Swan put up the Closed sign and pulled down the blinds.

Swan smiled over at her. "New store policy. From here on out, we will close at noon for lunch."

"What about the sales you'll lose?"

Swan shrugged. "Sales aren't everything. Besides, it's just for an hour. Come join me in my office."

"All right, let me grab some sodas out of the refrigerator."

A few minutes later, she and Jamila were enjoying their lunch when Swan gave Jamila a long look. "How are you doing?"

Jamila shrugged. "Okay, I guess. Trying to move on. I loved Horacio so much only to find out he wasn't the man I thought he was."

"I know the feeling."

"No, you don't."

Swan snatched her head up, frowning. "Excuse me?"

"I said you don't know the feeling, Swan. David Holloway was nothing like Horacio. David intended to save you and Horacio would have killed me if that woman had ordered him to do so. Big difference."

"But like you, I was betrayed."

"How?" Jamila countered. "Your godfathers sent David Holloway here to prove your innocence and he did."

Jamila put her soda can down and then added, "And another thing. What man takes a chance and swims across the ocean to save a woman? Do you know how far from land we were? Think about that."

Swan had news for her—she *had* thought about it. She could never forget how David had appeared seemingly out of nowhere on that boat, looking tough and ready to kick asses while wearing nothing more than an outlandishly tight pair of swim trunks with a military belt around his waist. Even when she'd been in what seemed like a dire situation, that hadn't stopped the woman in her from noticing how dangerously sexy he'd looked at that particular moment.

"When I mentioned what an astounding feat he'd accomplished to his friends," Jamila said, reclaiming Swan's attention, "they said that's why they call him Flipper. Did you know that's his code name as a SEAL?"

Swan wiped her mouth with a napkin. "Yes, I knew he was called Flipper. But no, I didn't know it had anything to do with him being a SEAL because I didn't know he was one. I assumed Flipper was his nickname."

Swan forced from her mind the day she'd asked him about those dolphin tattoos. He'd told her then they represented Flipper. That had been the day they'd made love in this office. Right here on this desk.

She wished she wasn't thinking so hard about that now.

She looked over at Jamila. "Why are we talking about me instead of you?"

"Because I think you should and because I think I should," Jamila continued. "Talking about your situation actually helps me believe that not all men are jerks and that there are some who still possess real honor, Swan. Whether you want to admit it or not, David Holloway is an honorable man. He couldn't help being attracted to you any more than you could help being attracted to him."

Swan stuffed the wrappings from her sandwich into the empty bag. "Now you sound like Candy."

"Maybe there's a reason why I do," Jamila said, stuffing her own wrappings into a bag. "It might be because Candy and I can see things that you refuse to see. I often think about what could have happened to us had David and his friends not shown up when they did. Do you ever think of that?"

Swan drew in a deep breath. "I try not to."

"I think you should," Jamila said, standing. "Thanks for bringing lunch. It will be my treat the next time." She then walked out of the office.

Swan stayed in her office after Jamila left, trying to put their conversation out of her mind. She was working on her computer, verifying inventory, when her office phone rang. "Thank you for calling Swan's. How may I help you?"

"Hello, island princess."

She smiled upon hearing her godfather's voice. "Godpop 2. How are you?"

"I'm fine. I just wanted to check on you. So much has happened and I wanted to make sure you're okay."

She had spoken to each of her godfathers and had thanked them for believing in her. They had taken a risk with their individual careers to do that. "I'm fine. How is Godpop 3?"

"He's fine but as the director of naval intelligence, he has his hands full with the investigation. It seems that more names are popping up in this scandal each day."

"And how are Godpop 1 and Barbara?"

"They are as well as can be expected under the circumstances. Learning about Georgianna was a shocker for all of us. We had no idea. When we decided to send Lt. Holloway to prove your innocence, the three of us weren't sure just what he would uncover. The only thing we knew for certain was that you weren't guilty of anything."

"Thanks for believing in me."

"You have Andrew's blood in your veins. You could no more be a traitor to your country than he could. Considering all that happened, I'm glad Holloway remained in Key West when he could have left."

Swan sat up straight. "Wasn't David on assignment?"

"Not the entire time. His assignment officially ended when he sent that ink in to be analyzed and we discovered it was tainted. I told him that he no longer had to stay in the Keys since by then we knew you weren't involved and we would take over the investigation from there."

"Then why did he stay?"

"To protect you."

"He told you that?" she asked.

"Yes. I remember the conversation like it was yesterday. I told him he could consider his job assignment complete and go home to Texas and enjoy the remainder of his leave. But he said he wanted to hang around Key West for a while."

Her godfather paused. "I asked him if the reason he wanted to stay was because he thought your life might be in danger. He said he felt that as long as Duggers and Jacinto didn't know they were suspects, then no, your life wasn't in any immediate danger. He informed me that the reason he wanted to stay was because you had come to mean a lot to him. I told him in that case how he spent the rest of his leave was his decision. And, Swan?"

She drew in a deep breath. "Yes?"

"As his commanding officer, I felt the need to remind him that although he was no longer on assignment, since the issue that had started with you was an ongoing investigation, he could not tell you anything."

When Swan didn't reply, her godfather asked, "You're still there, Swan?"

"Yes, Godpop 2, I'm still here."

"Did you not know how Holloway felt about you?"

"No. I thought I was just an assignment."

"You were at first and I'm glad you were. Otherwise you would be in jail wrongly accused of a crime you hadn't committed. But on the flip side, I'm also glad that when you stopped being an assignment, Holloway had the insight to stay and look out for you because he cared for you."

Long after her telephone conversation with her godfather ended, Swan remained seated at her desk, leaning back in her chair and sitting in silence while thinking about what Candy, Jamila and her godfather had said.

Some people never got betrayed, but she had been, a lot. William, Rafe, Horacio, Rosie, Georgianna and even Jamila. No one had been who she'd thought.

She remembered David and replayed in her mind all the time she'd spent with him since that day he'd first walked into her shop.

Was anything he'd told her true? Did he really come from a huge family? Was his mother even celebrating a birthday? Did he honestly have three sisters-in-law?

One thing was for certain, both Candy and Jamila

were right. David hadn't pushed her into sleeping with him. In fact, Swan was the one who'd invited him to dinner at her place with the full intent of having sex with him.

She got up from her desk and walked over to the window. She knew from Jamila that David had left the island with his friends after that first week, after he'd completed all the questioning by naval intelligence. Was he back home in Texas? Did his parents really own a medical supply company? What parts of what he'd told her were true and what parts were fabricated for his assignment?

And why did she still love him so much it hurt... even when she didn't want to love him? Even when she didn't know how he felt about her? He might have told her godfather he cared for her but David hadn't told her anything. Shouldn't he have? But then, had she given him a chance to do so?

The answer to that flashed in her mind quickly. No, she hadn't.

He had saved her life that night, swam across the ocean to do so, and then she'd told him she didn't want to talk to him. And he had honored her wishes...for that one night. Then he had called her almost every single day since, and yet she had refused to take his calls.

He hadn't called today.

Did that mean he'd given up and wouldn't try contacting her again? Was she ready to put her heart on the line and contact him?

She wasn't sure. But what she *was* certain of was that they needed to do what they hadn't done before. They needed to get to know each other. She needed to know which parts of what he'd told her about himself were true and which were false.

She wanted to get to know the real David Holloway.

Then what?

Hadn't she convinced herself she wanted no part of a man in the military? And what about her decision to never to get seriously involved in an interracial relationship like her parents had? Why did all of that no longer matter to her when she thought about her and David deciding to have a future together?

Maybe that's how love worked. It made you see the possible instead of the impossible. It made you want things you told yourself were not good for you because you were afraid to reach beyond your comfort zone.

Taking a deep a cleansing breath, she decided to call David tonight before going to bed. She had no idea what she would say to him but the words would come.

She doubted he would want to come back to the Keys anytime soon, so she would let him know she would come to him if he still wanted to talk. She would see what he said before asking Jamila if she could take care of the shop while Swan was gone. David might very well tell her that it was too late, that they had nothing to talk about. But there was a chance he would embrace her words. Embrace her.

Her mood suddenly lightened, knowing that was a possibility.

Flipper entered the hotel room and tossed his luggage on the bed. Different hotel but same city. He had given Swan two weeks and now he was back. They needed to talk and clear up some things. She hadn't accepted his calls, but now he was here and he wouldn't be ignored.

He shook his head when his cell phone rang. "Yes, Coop?"

"Have you seen her yet?"

"No, I just got here. In fact, I walked into my hotel room less than five minutes ago."

"Okay. And there's another reason I called. Bristol is pregnant."

"Wow, man. Congratulations. I didn't know you guys were trying."

Coop laughed. "We're always trying. But seriously, we figured it was time Laramie had a playmate."

"Sounds good to me."

"I hope things work out with you and Swan, Flipper."

"I hope so, too."

"And do me a favor."

"What?"

"For once, open up. Tell her how you feel. Don't

beat around the bush. You have a tendency to do that. Women love a man to get straight to the point and share their feelings. I hate to say it, bro, but you're not good at doing that."

Coop was right, he wasn't. "I never had to do that before. I've never truly loved a woman before Swan."

"I understand. But you do love her, so make sure she knows it. A woman has to believe she's loved."

Flipper chuckled.

"What's so funny?" Coop asked him.

"You're giving relationship advice. Do you know how much like Mac you sound?"

Coop chuckled as well. "You would have to point that out. I guess it comes with loving a woman."

"I guess so."

"No guess in it, remember it. Know it. Feel it. Take care and good luck."

After ending the call with Coop, it wasn't long before Flipper got calls from Bane, Viper and Mac as well, all letting him know they hoped things worked out for Flipper and Swan. All giving him advice. They were married men who had the women they loved and they wanted him to have the woman he loved as well.

He appreciated good friends who not only watched his back but who also cared about the condition of his heart. They knew about the pain he had lodged there and it got worse every day he and Swan were apart.

Flipper glanced at his watch. Swan's store would

be closing in less than an hour. He would give her time to get home and relax before paying her a visit. He refused to let her put things off any longer. They needed to talk.

He loved her and it was damn time she knew it.

Fifteen

Swan had just poured a glass of wine to enjoy while sitting on the patio when she heard the knock at her door.

She knew Candy had gone out to dinner with her family and Jamila had mentioned she would just stay in tonight and chill. Swan had invited Jamila to join her so maybe her cousin had changed her mind.

Her cousin.

That was taking a lot of getting used to but Swan knew her parents would want a family connection for them. Jamila was the only family Swan had and she appreciated their friendship more than ever.

She reached the door and glanced through the peephole. Her heart nearly stopped.

Was it really David? She blinked and looked again and saw it was really him. Back in Key West. And he was standing in front of her door looking like he always did, sexy as hell.

Drawing in a deep breath, she removed the security lock and opened the door. "David? I thought you'd left the island."

"I had but I returned today. May I come in?"

She nodded and stepped aside. The moment he passed her, she caught a whiff of his masculine scent, the same one she was convinced still lingered in her bedroom.

Swan closed the door and stood to face him. He was standing in the middle of her living room wearing a pair of shorts and a sleeveless shirt with a huge picture of a dolphin. *Flipper*. Her gaze moved beyond the shirt to his face to find his laser-blue eyes staring at her.

She cleared her throat. "I was about to sit out back and drink a glass of wine while enjoying the view. Would you like to have a beer and join me?"

She could tell he was surprised by her invitation. She hadn't bothered to ask why he was there.

"Yes, I'd like that."

Moments later, they were sitting side by side on a bench that overlooked the beach. They had been sipping their drinks for a few moments when he said, "I told you that night two weeks ago that we needed to talk, Swan. I think we still do."

Yes, they did. She would let him go first. "Okay, I'm listening."

"I want you to do more than just listen, Swan. I want you to engage by asking questions, giving me feedback, and I would like to be able to do the same with you."

"Okay, that seems fair because I do have some questions for you."

"Ask away."

She took another sip of her drink. "You didn't tell me you were a SEAL and I'd—"

"I couldn't tell you I was a SEAL, Swan," he interrupted to say. "That's why I lied and said I was no longer in the military."

"Yes, I know that now. I want to tell you, because of what happened to my father, I had made up my mind never to get serious about a military man... especially not a SEAL."

"Oh, I see."

She wouldn't tell him yet that she'd changed her mind about that. "Is your mother's birthday really next month and do you have four brothers?"

"Yes. Everything I told you about my family is true. I never lied to you about anything pertaining to them. I just omitted some details and couldn't elaborate on certain things."

She then put her wineglass down and turned toward him. "Why did you sleep with me, David, when I was just an assignment to you?"

* * *

Flipper knew this was the time of reckoning and what he told her would have an impact on their relationship for the rest of their days. He needed her to understand.

"You were supposed to be an assignment, Swan. But honestly, I don't think you ever were. From the moment I walked into your shop and saw you, a part of me knew I had to fight hard to be objective and do the job I'd been sent here to do."

He paused. "I tried to keep my attraction to you out of the picture but found it harder and harder to do. Each time I saw you while getting to know you, I fell deeper under your spell. It was hard pretending with you."

He decided to be totally honest with her. "Just so you know, that day you invited me to your place for dinner wasn't my first time there. I'd been to your home without you knowing anything about it. But at the time, it was just a house I was checking out as part of an investigation. The day you invited me to dinner, I saw it through another pair of eyes. Yours. And for me, it then became your home."

She drew in a deep breath. "You invaded my privacy by letting yourself into my home, but that's not why I'm upset. I accept that you had a job to do and I was your assignment but…"

"But what?"

"You still haven't fully answered my question, David. Why did you make love to me?"

David frowned, realizing that he *hadn't* answered her question. His teammates often teased him about beating around the bush, sometimes providing too much context instead of just sticking with the facts.

"The reason I made love to you, Swan, was because I desired you. Everything about you turned me on. Your looks, your scent, your walk…and then after our first kiss, it was your taste. Fighting my desire for you was no longer an option, although I tried being honorable enough not to seduce you."

"But then I seduced you," she said quietly.

He smiled. "No, I think that night we seduced each other. Everything we did was mutual."

"Yes, it was." She took another sip of her wine. "I spoke with Godpop 2 today and he told me your assignment ended but you decided to stay. Why?"

Okay, no beating around the bush this time, Flipper decided. "The reason is that by then I had fallen in love with you. In all honesty, in my heart you stopped being an assignment the first time I made love to you. I crossed the line of what was honorable, and I knew why. Because I felt you here, Swan," he said, pointing to his heart. "I felt you here in a way I've never felt before. No woman has ever been here, Swan. But during the one time you shouldn't have, you got there anyway."

"And now? How do you feel now?"

He placed his beer bottle aside and turned toward her. "Now you are still in my heart. Even more so. I love you so much I ache on the inside when I'm not with you. I love you so much I think of you even at times I shouldn't."

He reached out and took her hand in his. "Now I need to know, Swan, just how you feel about me."

Swan felt the gentle tug on her hand and, surprising even herself, she moved to sit in his lap.

When he wrapped his arms around her, she felt comfort flow through her. She turned in his lap to look down at him. He'd given her answers to all her questions, now she intended to give him answers to his.

"I love you, David. I fought it at first. I didn't know about you being present-day military, but I also had a problem…not with interracial dating… but with allowing anything to come of it. I saw how others saw my parents at times. Not as a beautiful couple in love but as an interracial couple in love. There should not have been a difference. I never wanted to deal with what they had to deal with in the name of love."

She paused. "But then I moved beyond thinking that way after I fell in love with you. Then I realized how my parents must have felt, believing nothing mattered but their love. Even if the world was against them, as long as they had each other, that's what truly counted."

"So you do love me?" he asked her as if for clarity.

Swan didn't have a problem clarifying anything for

him or anyone else. "Yes, I love you, David Flipper Holloway." And then she lowered her mouth to his.

Shivers of profound pleasure shot through every part of Swan's body when David slid his tongue into her mouth. Sensations bombarded her as she concentrated on his taste, his scent and the way he pulled her tongue into his mouth to mate with his. And when she felt his hands inch upward and slide beneath her top, his touch made her purr.

Both his taste and his touch were awakening parts of her, making her feel alive in a way she hadn't felt since the last time they'd been together. Here at her house. In her bed.

When his fingers touched her bare breasts, using his fingertips to draw circles around her nipples, she oozed deeper into the kiss, almost feeling like melted butter in his arms.

He slowly pulled his mouth from hers and looked at her. His blue eyes were sharp and filled with the same desire she felt. "Any reason why we can't take this inside?"

She wrapped her arms around his waist. "No, there's no reason."

"Good."

And then standing with her in his arms, he carried her into the house.

"Just so you know, David, I didn't ask you all my questions," Swan said when he placed her on the bed.

David glanced down at her. "You didn't?"

"No, but I can wait. None are more earth-shattering than this is going to be. And I need this."

He caressed the side of her face with his finger. "I need this, too. I know why I need it, tell me why you do."

She met his gaze and held it while she said, "I love the feel of you inside of me. I've never felt anything so right before. So pleasurable." She smiled. "Do you know I retired my sex toy?"

He chuckled. "That's good to know."

"Um, not too much information?"

"No. Nice to know what used to be my competition," he said as he began removing her clothes. Lucky for him, she wasn't wearing much. Just a top, shorts and a thong. Flipper had discovered outside earlier that she wasn't wearing a bra. He'd noticed more than once that she liked her breasts being free and so did he.

She reached out and tugged at his T-shirt and he assisted by removing his own shorts. Then he rejoined her on the bed. Reaching out, he lifted her by the waist.

"Wrap your legs around me, Swan. I'm about to join our bodies, to make us one."

As soon as her legs were settled around his waist, his shaft touched her core. She was wet and ready. Tilting her hips, he whispered the words, "I love you," before thrusting hard into her.

"David!"

Arching her back off the bed, she provided the

prefect position for his penetration to go deeper.
They were a perfect fit. They always would be. Not
just in lovemaking but in everything they did from
here on out. They had become a team.

He began moving, slowly at first and then harder
and deeper, over and over again. The only constant
sounds in the room were their breathing and flesh
slapping against flesh. The air surrounding them was
filled with the aroma of sex.

He felt on fire, like his entire body was burning
and the flames fueled his need, his desire and his
love. She was looking up at him, holding his gaze,
and he hoped Swan saw the depth of love in his eyes.

He clenched his jaw when he felt it, the stirring of
pleasure in his groin. The feeling was slowly spreading through his body and when Swan gripped his
shoulders and dug her fingers into his skin, he continued to thrust inside of her like his life depended
on it.

And when she screamed out his name, he knew
the same sensations that were taking him were taking her.

He drew in a sharp breath only moments before
calling out her name. Multiple sensations tore into
him, causing an explosion inside of him that had
him bucking his body in an all-consuming orgasm.
The sensations kept coming until he let go and his
release shot deep inside of her.

He knew right then that he wanted her to have his

baby. If not this time, another time. One day, he intended to make it happen.

Moments later, he slumped down beside her and wrapped his arms around her as he tried to get his breathing under control. After recovering from his explosive orgasm, when he was able to talk, he said, "I feel like I've been burned to a crisp."

"Hmm, speaking of burning, do you know what I thought was hot?" she asked, drawing in deep breaths of air into her lungs.

"No, what?"

"You on that boat wearing nothing but swim trunks and that military belt around your waist. Now, that was hot."

He grinned. "You liked that, huh?"

She smirked up at him when he straddled her body again. "I liked it." Then her features became serious. "I still can't believe you swam all that way to save me."

He leaned in and brushed a kiss across her lips. "Believe it."

He then pulled back and looked down at her. His expression was serious. "I'm a damn good swimmer. I'm known to be able to hold my breath underwater for long periods of time. Longer than what most would consider normal. But I wasn't sure I was going to make it to the boat, Swan. I told my friends I had to try even if I died trying because the woman I love was on that boat. That's what kept me going. That's what fueled every stroke I made into the ocean waters. And when my body felt tired, like I couldn't possibly swim another lap, I would think of a life without you and for me that was unacceptable."

He drew in a sharp breath. For a quick minute, he relived the feel of the cold water as he swam nonstop to the boat to save her, not knowing if he would make it in time. "I had to save you."

"And then I rebuffed you. I refused to have that talk you wanted."

"I understood. I had been listening to what Georgianna Martin was saying, the picture she painted. I told myself that once I talked to you and told you the truth that you would believe me. I was just giving you time to think about everything. I figured you would realize that I did care for you."

She reached up and caressed the side of his face. "You never told me you cared."

"I did. Our last night together, when you were asleep, I told you before I left that I loved you. I had planned to tell you the next day when we were together but that's when you were taken."

"And you came back," she said.

"That was always my plan, Swan. I never intended to let you go. I love you that much. And just so you know, my entire family is rooting for me. I told them about you and they can't wait to meet you. My brothers and I are giving Mom a party for her birthday next week. Will you go to Texas with me?"

When she hesitated, he added, "What I told you about them is true. My parents accept people for who they are and not how they look. Will you trust me about that?"

She met his gaze and nodded. "Yes, I will trust you and yes, I will go."

A huge smile spread across his face. "I can't wait to introduce you to everyone. And I've got the perfect thing for you to wear." He quickly eased off the bed.

She pulled herself up. "What's going on? You plan on dressing me that night?"

He glanced over his shoulder, chuckling as he pulled a small white box out of his shorts. "Something like that."

He returned to the bed and pulled her up to stand her on her feet beside the bed. Then he got down on one knee and looked up at her. "I love you, Swan. I know we have a lot of things we still need to overcome. But I believe we will do so together. Forever. Will you marry me?"

He saw tears form in her eyes when she nodded. "Yes, I will marry you."

He slid the ring on her finger and at that moment Flipper knew he was halfway to having his world complete.

He would get the other half the day she became his wife.

Sixteen

Swan glanced down at the ring David had put on her finger last week. Seeing it gave her strength and she definitely needed strength now, she thought as she entered a huge ballroom on his arm. It was his mother's sixtieth birthday party.

They had flown into Dallas last night so this would be the first time she met his family. Nervous jitters had tried taking over her stomach but a smile from David was keeping most of them at bay. He was convinced his family would love her and he had told her over and over that she was worrying for nothing. She was the woman he wanted and his family would love his choice.

"There's Mom and Dad," he said, with his arms

around her shoulders as she carried his mother's gift. The same gift he'd purchased that first day he'd come into her shop.

A man she knew had to be one of David's brothers whispered something to the older couple and they turned with huge smiles on their faces.

At that moment, Swan knew David had inherited his father's eyes and that the smiles on the couple's faces were genuine. She could actually feel their warmth. David's mom was beautiful and did not look like she was sixty or that she had five grown sons.

When they reached his parents, David made the introduction. "Mom. Dad. I want you to meet the woman who has agreed to be my wife, Swan Jamison."

"It's an honor to meet you," Swan said, extending her hand to his mother.

Instead of taking it, the older woman engulfed Swan in a huge hug. "It's wonderful meeting you as well, Swan, and welcome to the family."

"Thank you. Here's your gift. Happy birthday."

"Thank you."

She received a hug from David's father as well. Then suddenly she was surrounded and a laughing David made introductions. All his brothers had those same blue eyes and like David, they were very handsome men. She could see why when she looked at the older Holloways; they were a beautiful couple. And Swan could tell from the way Mr. Holloway looked at his wife and the way Mrs. Holloway would look back at him that the couple was still very much in love.

A few nights ago, David had shared the fact that because his mother had been married to a Navy SEAL for over forty years and had five sons who were SEALs, she counseled a number of SEAL wives who had difficulties with the frequency and longevity of their spouses' missions. Swan had been glad to hear that since she would become a SEAL's wife soon.

Because David would be leaving in less than four months on anther mission, they hoped to marry within a year. Surprisingly, David wanted a big wedding. She agreed as long as the wedding took place in the Keys.

The logistics of having a big wedding were enormous, given he had four brothers who were SEALs on different teams. Not to mention his closest four friends were SEALs as well. That meant Swan and David had to make sure everyone would be on leave in the States at the same time.

David also introduced Swan to her future sisters-in-law and they loved her engagement ring. The three were friendly and she liked them immediately. She was also introduced to other members of David's family—his grandparents, his niece, nephews, cousins, aunts, uncles—it was obvious the Holloway family was a huge one.

"Now I want to reintroduce you to four guys who are just as close to me as brothers. As you know, they came to the Keys to assist me in proving your innocence. And even when my assignment with you ended, they didn't leave. They stayed."

She had met his four friends that night after the incident on the boat, when they'd had to give statements. She had thanked them for their help but they hadn't been officially introduced.

"Did I tell you how beautiful you look tonight, sweetheart?"

She smiled up at him as they walked across the ballroom floor to the four men and their wives. "Yes, you told me. Thank you." She, Candy and Jamila had gone shopping in Miami. She'd known this was the perfect dress when she'd seen it on a store mannequin.

Within a few minutes, she had been introduced to Brisbane "Bane" Westmoreland and his wife, Crystal; Gavin "Viper" Blake and his very pregnant wife, Layla; Laramie "Coop" Cooper and his wife, Bristol; and Thurston "Mac" McRoy and his wife, Teri.

After spending time with the couples, Swan felt that just like her future sisters-in-law, the four women were genuinely friendly and Swan looked forward to getting to know them better. They loved her engagement ring as well and told David he'd done a great job in picking it out.

"So what do you think?" David leaned down to ask, taking her hand in his and leading her to where his parents, siblings and their spouses were getting ready to take a group picture.

She grinned up at him. "Um, for starters, I think I need to start calling you Flipper, since everyone else does. And then, *Flipper*, I think I am one of the luckiest women in the world right now. I love you."

He chuckled as he pulled her to the side of the room and wrapped his arms around her waist. "And I, Swan Jamison, think I'm the luckiest man in the world, and I love you."

"A very wise woman, my mother, once told me that when you meet a man who puts that sparkle in your eyes then you'd know he was a keeper. You, Flipper, are a keeper."

He smiled. "You, my beautiful Swan, are a keeper as well."

Flipper then lowered his mouth to hers.

Epilogue

A year later in June

Bane Westmoreland leaned close and whispered to Flipper, "Don't get nervous now. You wanted a big wedding and you got it."

Flipper couldn't say anything because Bane was right. He stood flanked by his father, who was his best man, and twelve groomsmen—namely his brothers, best friends and cousins.

Only his SEAL teammates knew Flipper had a tendency to tap his finger against his thigh when he was nervous. He stopped tapping but not because he noticed that Viper, Mac and Coop were grinning over at him. But then he figured both Viper and Coop had reasons to grin since they'd both become fathers this year. Viper was the proud father of a son, Gavin IV, and Coop had a beautiful daughter they'd named Paris, since that was where he'd first met his wife.

It was a beautiful day for a beach wedding and so far everything was perfect and going according to plan. Swan had hired one of the local wedding planners and the woman had done an awesome job. She had thought of everything, including the super yacht that could hold their five hundred guests that they'd be using for the wedding reception. It was anchored in the ocean near Swan's beachfront home. A fleet of passenger boats had been chartered to transport the wedding guests out to the yacht.

A ten-piece orchestra sat beneath towering balustrades draped from top to bottom in thin white netting. Chairs were set up on the beach, auditorium style, facing the decorative stage where Flipper and the men in the wedding party stood waiting.

Suddenly, the music began and all the ladies strolled down the beach and up the steps.

Swan had chosen her wedding colors of purple and yellow and Flipper had to admit the combination was striking. It took all twelve women long enough to do their stroll. His niece was a flower girl and Coop's son and one of Flipper's nephews were the ring bearers.

Flipper almost held his breath when what looked like a huge forty-foot golden swan was rolled onto the beach. When the orchestra changed their tune for the "Wedding March," the swan opened and his Swan appeared in a beautiful, dazzling white gown. She looked beautiful, stunning and breathtaking all rolled into one.

Flipper stared at the woman who would be his wife and felt so much love in his heart. He hadn't known until now just how much he could feel for one woman. They had spent the past year deepening their friendship and their love. He looked forward to returning from his covert operations, knowing she would be there waiting on him.

He watched as she slowly strolled toward him. All three of her godfathers participated in walking her up the aisle, passing her off to the other so many feet along the way. Then all three of them gave her away. When Swan reached his side and extended her hand to him, he accepted it while thinking she was *his* Swan.

His beautiful Swan.

The wedding ceremony began. What Flipper would remember most when he looked back was when the minister announced them husband and wife and told him he could kiss his bride.

Flipper pulled Swan into his arms and lowered his mouth to hers. She was his and he intended to keep her happy for the rest of his days. They would be flying to Dubai for a two-week honeymoon and then return to the Keys where they planned to make their permanent home.

When David released Swan's mouth, the minister said, "I present to everyone David and Swan Holloway."

Flipper knew they were supposed to exit by walking down the golden steps that led to the boat that would transport them to the yacht. But at that moment, he couldn't deny himself another kiss and lowered his mouth to his wife's again.

* * * * *

SEDUCED BY
SECOND CHANCES

REESE RYAN

For all of the amazing readers who read and recommend my books, thank you! Your support is invaluable.

For Building Relationships Around Books (BRAB), Round Table Readers Literary Book Club, Victorious Ladies Reading Book Club and Sistas' Thoughts from Coast to Coast (STCC Book Club), thank you for hosting me for lively book discussions. I cherish the time spent with you and appreciate all you do to promote authors.

One

Jessie Humphrey scrolled through her cell phone contacts and located the number she was searching for.

Her dream list of world-famous producers was a short one, but Chase Stratton reigned supreme. He'd worked with the top talent out there. Single-name artists at the pinnacle of their careers and critically acclaimed artists on the rise.

Jessie paced her tiny one-bedroom apartment in SoHo and chewed on her fingernails. Her entire future was riding on making this happen.

She sank onto the living room chair where she did much of her songwriting.

Her record label had offered her a new contract. To her agent's dismay, she'd rejected the offer. The studio wanted her to make cookie-cutter pop music rather than the soulful songs about love and loss that were her forte.

She'd been writing for some of the studio's biggest stars for years. As an artist, she had two albums under her belt and a growing base of die-hard fans. Including wealthy, powerful people like Matt Richmond, who'd paid her a generous fee to perform at his exclusive event in her hometown of Seattle, Washington.

With her current recording contract fulfilled, Jessie was at a stalemate with the label's top exec, Arnold Diesman.

She'd taken Matt Richmond's gig in Seattle because of the lucrative contract. Money she would invest in starting her own independent label where she would retain creative control.

Chase had a long line of artists with household names and the deep pockets of the record labels backing them. But Jessie needed to convince him to take a chance on working on her indie project.

She'd called in every favor she had to track down the phone number of Chase's personal assistant. Jessie dialed the number.

"This is Lita."

"Hi, Lita, this is Jessie Humphrey. I sent a couple of demos to Chase—"

"We received them. Thank you. But Chase's schedule is booked solid right now."

"I'm not surprised. He's the top producer out there right now." Jessie was undeterred by the woman's attempt to blow her off. "I know I'm not one of the single-name artists he usually works with and that I won't have the backing of a big studio for this project—"

"You realize you're making a case *against* me passing your demo on to Chase, right?" Lita laughed.

"Just acknowledging the obvious." Jessie paced the hardwood floors. "But he should consider my growing fan base. They don't care whether a big studio is behind the album. They only care that—"

"Look, honey, not everyone can drop an independent surprise album that'll shoot up the charts. And it's unheard of for an independently produced album to be Grammy-worthy. I know Beyoncé and Chance the Rapper made it look easy, but it isn't. And Chase only deals in top caliber projects. Now, if you have your studio rep contact us…"

"My contract is over and I'm not interested in signing another. I want complete creative control." Jessie continued when the woman didn't respond. "I've written huge radio hits for Top 40 acts. I know what sells."

"Look, Jessie… I'm a huge fan. But Chase has much bigger projects in his sights. And without studio backing…" The woman lowered her voice. "There's a reason Chase commands such an exorbitant payday. He selects his projects carefully. He always wins because he only plays the game when he's holding a royal flush. I listened to your demo. The songs are amazing and so is your voice. But Chase isn't willing to take on the risk of working with you without the backing of the studio."

"I see." Jessie stopped pacing. Tears stung her eyes.

"I'll hold on to your demo. When Chase needs a new songwriter, I'll recommend you. Maybe once he works with you in that capacity, he'll take a chance on your indie project."

"If I could just talk to him myself—"

"Sorry, Jessie. This is the best I can do for you right now. Chase is preparing to work on the West Coast for the next several weeks. But I'll keep you in mind when he needs a new songwriter. Promise."

"Lita, wait—"

The woman had already ended the call. Jessie sat at the piano that took up most of the space in her living room.

She'd have to find another way to get face time with Chase.

Jessie was determined to make authentic music. She wouldn't be strong-armed by the studio into cranking out forgettable songs.

It wasn't about the money or the fame. Playing the piano while singing songs she'd penned about the pain that had ripped her heart in two alleviated those feelings. It seemed just as cathartic for audience members who sang along with tears in their eyes. That connection with her listeners meant everything.

That was what she wanted to share with the world.

Chase Stratton had name recognition and a string of hits under his belt. He took an artist's raw material and spun it into gold while respecting their unique sound.

She had something different to offer the world, and she needed a team around her discerning enough to recognize that.

She'd find another way to get to Chase. And when she did, she'd be ready.

Jessie grabbed a pen from her little side table, and the pile of magazines on it shifted. She picked up the ones that had fallen to the floor.

The financial magazine bore the image of the incredibly handsome Gideon Johns.

After all these years, sadness still swept over her whenever she thought of Gideon. And she hadn't been able to stop thinking of him since her recent return to Seattle for Matt Richmond's event. She'd been equal parts hopeful and terrified that she'd encounter Gideon for the first time in well over a decade.

Gideon had been the reason she'd written her very first song. A song of heartbreak and unrequited love. It had been one of the songs on the demo that earned Jessie her first songwriting gig with a small record company. So rather than resenting Gideon's rejection, she should thank him for breaking her heart.

Nothing had really happened between them back then. And nothing would happen between them in the future. So why couldn't she let thoughts of Gideon go?

Jessie tossed the magazines back onto the pile and returned to the piano, pen in hand.

She hated that she was still so affected by a man to whom she clearly hadn't meant anything. But berating herself over it wasn't productive. Instead, she would allow those frustrations to fuel her creativity so she could write the next song.

Jessie scribbled a few notes that had been playing in her head all day on the blank staff paper. Then she played the corresponding notes on her piano and started to sing.

Gideon Johns sat on the front edge of his large cherrywood desk. He folded his arms as he sized up his assistant, Landon Farmer. He had something to say, and whatever it was, he was fully aware that Gideon wasn't going to like it.

"Look, Landon, whatever it is you're dancing around here…just say it. We're both busy people."

"Our top two investors just pulled out of the United Arab Emirates deal." The words rushed out of his mouth.

"What?" Gideon's voice boomed, filling the room. He hadn't intended to shout, and since the man looked like he wanted to flee the room, he felt bad for doing so. Still, it was a natural reaction to discovering that he'd lost half of the capital he was counting on for a two-billion-dollar building project.

"What the hell happened? The last time I spoke with them, they were champing at the bit to get in on this deal. In fact, I didn't solicit either of them. They came to me."

"Both cited the recent volatility in their own industries, Mr. Johns." The man reverted to addressing him formally whenever Gideon was displeased.

"Do they have any idea how much I have riding on

this deal? This is our first project in Dubai. If word gets out that the deal is collapsing—"

"Then we don't let it collapse." Landon sat a bit straighter.

"And where do you propose we get nearly a billion dollars in the next two months?" Gideon raised an eyebrow.

"The company has considerable assets, sir. You already know that—"

"No." It was a single, nonnegotiable sentence.

"But, sir—"

"Investing in the project isn't an option." Gideon returned to his seat. His chest felt tight and his head was beginning to throb.

"But you just said what a disaster it would be if the project fails—"

"It won't fail. I'll find the money." Gideon looked at him pointedly.

"I have no doubt that you will, Mr. Johns." Landon straightened his tie. "But what if you can't secure the funds? Wouldn't it be better for our company to invest in the project than to have to admit we couldn't raise the capital?"

"Making real estate deals using other people's money has been my policy for the past ten years. If investors discover that I needed to liquidate assets and sink that kind of cash into my own project, it'll wreck the brand I've spent a decade building."

"We could do it discreetly," Landon suggested.

"I believe in being transparent with my investors."

Gideon frowned. "Besides, liquidating that kind of cash will inevitably attract attention."

"All valid points." Landon stood and massaged the nape of his neck. "I'll scour our database of potential investors and see who might be right for the Dubai project."

"Go for the big fish. And focus on those who have liquid assets readily available. We need to stick to our original timeline or the remaining investors will start to worry." Gideon made a mental note of the effects this sudden change might have on the project.

"There is one potential investor who comes to mind right away."

"I know." Gideon tapped the table. "Matt Richmond."

Matt was a friend who'd mused about investing in one of Gideon's projects, but had yet to pull the trigger.

Gideon made it a point not to pressure investors to join his projects. He simply laid out the opportunity and return on investment to be had, and allowed his track record and reputation to do the rest. The timing wasn't great, but he'd need to prod Matt and see if he was serious about investing.

This project had the potential to make all of them a shitload of money. He'd never take the project on if he didn't wholeheartedly believe that. Nor would he ever try to rope his friend, or any investor, into a shaky deal. But he needed to be a bit more direct with his friend.

"I've got Matt. I'll try to meet with him within

the next week." Gideon woke his computer screen to send an email to his friend. Another email captured his interest.

It was the Google alert he'd set up on singer/songwriter Jessie Humphrey. She was beautiful, brilliant, talented—and the little sister of his ex, Geneva Humphrey. The woman he'd planned to marry a lifetime ago. Right up until the moment she'd broken his heart.

He'd gotten over the break with Geneva. Had even come to realize she'd been right to end things between them. But his relationship with Jessie was more complicated.

Two years after his breakup with Geneva, Jessie had shown up at his door wanting more than just friendship.

She was his ex's sister, so he'd promptly sent her packing. But he hadn't ever been able to forget that day. Or get thoughts of Jessie out of his head.

The first time he heard Jessie Humphrey's voice flowing from the speakers of his Aston Martin Vanquish Volante he'd been over the moon with happiness for her.

She'd walked around wearing headphones and singing her heart out for as long as he'd known her. And despite her parents' insistence that she pursue a "real" career, Jessie had always wanted to share her gift with the world.

Now she was and he couldn't be more proud of her.

Gideon had carefully followed her career ever since.

"Is that all, boss?" Landon furrowed his brow.

"Yes, thank you." Gideon waited for the man to leave, closing the door behind him.

Gideon clicked the link in the email. It took him to a video of Jessie performing at a small club, seated at a piano.

She was stunning. Who knew that she'd turn into such a beautiful, confident young woman and a rising artist?

Jessie had such a powerful voice and a unique sound, even back when he'd known her. Geneva had teased Jessie about her incessant singing and starry-eyed dreams, but Gideon had loved to hear her sing. He'd told her that one day she'd be famous. And he'd been right.

When the performance ended, he listened to it twice more. Despite following Jessie's career, he'd decided against reaching out to her. After the way they'd left things, he doubted Jessie would welcome seeing him again. And he didn't need the heartbreak of falling for another Humphrey sister.

It was safer to admire Jessie from a distance.

Which was a shame, because he'd love to see her again.

Two

Teresa St. Claire had spent most of the week hiding out in her office. Once she arrived in the morning, she'd only peeked her head out when it had been absolutely necessary.

Yes, she was the boss. But she felt like the screwup employee who'd put the entire company in jeopardy.

Every time she closed her eyes, she could see the ugly headline that had been running for the past week.

Mogul's Torrid Affair with Father's Mistress Ends after Her Surprise Inheritance Revealed.

She'd been pegged as a home-wrecking gold digger who'd had an affair with the late Linus Christopher and now had her sights set on his heir Liam. The ugly rumors, complete with uncomplimentary videos and photos, lit up the airwaves and seemed to follow her everywhere online.

Teresa had been hounded by gossip columnists and bloggers. Even a woman she'd always considered a reputable reporter had shown up at her home, inquiring about the nature of Teresa's relationship with both Christopher men.

The effect the rumors were having on her business was bad enough. But the additional tension it had created between her and Liam was unbearable. She could only imagine the embarrassment the rumors were causing him.

Teresa wiped away warm tears when she recalled the expression on Liam's face when he'd confronted her about the rumors. He'd even had the audacity to imply that she might've been behind them. Still, her brain was flooded with the warmth and passion that had been growing steadily between them, despite his constant mistrust of her.

She sighed. The outer office was uncharacteristically quiet. Other than calls from gossip reporters, the phones barely rang. Her employees spoke in hushed tones with their heads together rather than with the jovial, energetic nature she was accustomed to.

At this rate, the doors of Limitless Events would be shuttered for good in a few weeks, and it would be her fault.

A knock at the door startled her from her thoughts.

Teresa sat ramrod straight in the chair behind her desk. "Come in."

Corinne, her personal assistant, stepped inside.

The woman dragged a hand through her headful of red corkscrew curls with an exasperated frown.

"We've had another cancellation, haven't we?" Teresa practically held her breath. That made three this week already. Not to mention the three or four clients who'd gotten nervous about having her plan their parties. It had been all she could do to calm them down so they wouldn't jump ship. But she realized that any one of them might change their minds at any time.

Corinne nodded. "Maggie Ellington called to say that she's sorry, but she just can't take a chance that the scandal won't have died down by the time of her daughter's wedding."

"That's understandable." Teresa tried to sound unaffected by the latest news. "She wants to make sure her daughter and son-in-law are the center of attention, not me."

"You mean she wants to make sure that *she's* the center of attention, and she won't be upstaged by anyone. Not even the bride." Corinne folded her arms.

"True." Teresa laughed and gave her assistant a re-assuring smile. "But we'd both do the same if we were in her shoes. I can't blame her. In fact, I don't blame any of them for canceling."

"Well, I do." Corinne dropped into the chair in front of Teresa's desk. "They're all a bunch of hyp-ocrites. Most of them have done more scandalous things on an average Tuesday than you're being ac-cused of. Not to mention that the whole story is just a crock of—"

"I get it, Corinne." Teresa held up a hand to calm her assistant.

Corinne was fiercely loyal and feisty as hell. She knew how to get things done and she wasn't easily deterred. It made her an invaluable assistant. But it also meant that this situation wasn't sitting well with her.

"That may be true." Teresa shrugged. "But we can't force them to work with us."

"So what do we do in the meantime? The phones are barely ringing. If clients keep jumping ship…" Corinne's cheeks flushed.

"We won't let it get to that," Teresa said firmly. "I'm trying to drum up business with some new clients. The kind who don't run scared at the first hint of scandal."

"Reality stars?" Corinne asked, then rolled her eyes when Teresa confirmed with the nod of her head. "God, they're the worst." She heaved a sigh. "But hey, I get it. We have to do what we have to do. For now."

"The other key element of weathering this storm is that we hold on to as many current clients as we can. Keep reassuring them that this has all been a big misunderstanding and it'll blow over soon. Speaking of holding on to the clients we have now, have you heard from Matt Richmond?"

Limitless Events had planned an elaborate business retreat on behalf of Matt Richmond—the incredibly handsome and fabulously wealthy CEO of Richmond Industries—at The Opulence last week. The hotel was extravagant and luxurious, the food was going to be delectable, and the guest list was to include the rich and powerful. The event was the talk of the town, but for all the wrong reasons.

Torrential rains caused a mudslide that had knocked out the power and damaged the hotel before the retreat could take place. Matt Richmond's event should've been Limitless Event's pièce de résistance. Instead, it descended into a chaotic catastrophe for the dozen or so guests who'd arrived early. Though she obviously didn't control the weather, Teresa felt responsible for the calamitous party.

Thankfully, Matt Richmond hadn't blamed her for the disastrous nonevent. Undeterred by the incredible fail, he'd been determined to reschedule the retreat. Yet he hadn't called, as he'd promised, to initiate the planning.

Had he not returned her calls because of the scandal hitting the airwaves? Or had Liam, Matt's best friend, discouraged him from working with her?

"I haven't heard from him and whenever I've called, his assistant can't get a hold of him." Corinne shrugged apologetically. "Maybe we should call Nadia. After all, she does work for you."

"As an independent contractor," Teresa clarified. "And I don't like the idea of leveraging her marriage to Matt. That isn't why I asked her to work with me."

"Then maybe I should visit his office."

"No…don't." Teresa waved off the suggestion. She could imagine Corinne's friendly visit to Matt going wrong six ways to Sunday. "I'll try him again later. How is the search for a new venue going?"

Corinne's frown deepened and she blew a puff of air between her plump lips. "Not well. Not if Richmond is determined to schedule the retreat anytime soon. The venues with openings in the next couple of months don't meet our standards of elegance and luxury."

"I was afraid of that." Teresa heaved a sigh. "I know it's a tall order, but keep trying. Ask our top choices to call us first, in the event of a cancellation."

"Will do." Corinne popped up from her seat, her red curls bouncing. "Anything else, chief?"

"No." Teresa riffled through papers on her desk, knocking over a small four-by-six photo of her and her brother, Joshua, on a trip to Mexico together a few years ago. She picked up the photo. "Have you heard from my brother? He left me several messages when my phone went dead last week, but I haven't been able to contact him since then."

"I haven't taken any calls from him." Worry lined Corinne's forehead. "Should I try to raise him for you?"

"No, you have enough on your plate." Teresa set the photo back in place. "It's probably just Joshua being Joshua. I've left him several messages. He'll resurface when he's ready."

Corinne nodded, closing the door behind her.

Teresa relaxed in the comfy leather executive chair she'd splurged on when they'd opened the office. Now she only hoped she wouldn't be forced to shutter her doors and sell it along with everything else.

She was trying hard to keep it together, but it was a lot to ask when her entire world was imploding. The ill-fated weekend extravaganza, the false rumors, her brother's disappearance. But the thing that made her heart ache was Liam's rejection.

Amid the craziness of bad weather and a tree falling through the hotel that had nearly taken her out were moments that had taken her breath away. Her cheeks flushed and her entire body filled with heat whenever she thought of their steamy encounter in that spa room. And her heart stirred when she recalled the worry in his eyes when he'd rescued her from beneath that tree and tended to her ankle.

Without thought, Teresa rotated her ankle, still a little sore.

She'd been grateful he'd confided in her that night, explaining to her why he had such difficulty trusting people. But after all they'd been through and the moments they'd shared...how could he still not trust her?

Her desk phone rang and she picked it up. "Yes?"

"I tried Richmond's office again. His assistant was out and he answered," Corinne said triumphantly. "I have him on the line now."

Teresa smoothed a hand down her pant leg. "Thank you, Corinne. Please put him through."

"Hello, Matt, I know you're busy, so I'll only take a moment of your time," Teresa said cheerfully. "Last week, you indicated that you'd like to reschedule the retreat as soon as possible. I wanted to touch base so we can move forward with the plans."

There was a moment of uncomfortable silence. Teresa's pulse raced.

Oh no. He's going to cancel, too.

"When will The Opulence be available again?" he asked finally. "I know Shane Adams has people working around the clock, but..."

"Not anytime soon, I'm afraid. And once they do reopen, they're booked solid for several months. Would you like to wait until then?"

"No. It's for our fifth anniversary, so I'd like to keep the event as close to the anniversary date as possible. I realize not all of the people who were originally invited will be available if we reschedule with such a short timeline. So we'll need to expand the guest list based on how many from the original list will be able to attend."

"Just have your assistant pass those additional names on to Corinne and we'll take care of the rest."

"So then you have a venue in mind?" His tone was doubtful.

"Not yet," she admitted. "But my staff is working tirelessly to find a venue that's available on short notice and meets our standards and yours. I'll be in touch as soon as I have a few good options."

"And what about a headliner? Would Jessie Humphrey be willing to perform at the rescheduled event?"

Embroiled in a scandal and bleeding clients, Teresa hadn't considered whether Jessie would be willing to fly across the country again for the rescheduled event. Not to mention that she might have a conflict in her schedule.

"I'll do my very best to book her. Same deal?"

"Yes. I'll look forward to hearing from you once you've worked the details out."

Her phone pinged with a text message.

"I just sent you the two weekends that are most ideal for this event."

Teresa strained the panic from her voice. Both options were only a few weeks away. "I'll get right on it."

"Anything else?" he asked.

Teresa gripped the receiver tightly and nibbled her lower lip. She wanted desperately to ask Matt how his best friend was holding up under the glare of the rumors and innuendo about them. But this was business. Besides, she didn't want to drag Matt into this.

"No, but I wanted to say thank you for not giving up on my company or me despite everything that's happened. I can't tell you how much I appreciate it."

"You're welcome, Teresa," Matt said after a long pause. "Call me when you've got a venue and Jessie has confirmed."

Teresa hung up, grateful she still had Matt Richmond's confidence. She was more determined than ever to reward it.

"You can't just walk in there." She could hear Corinne's voice through the closed door.

Suddenly the door opened. Liam stood glaring at her.

"It's all right, Corinne." Teresa held up a hand. "I'll take it from here."

Corinne narrowed her eyes at him, then walked off in a huff.

"Have a seat." She gestured toward the chair when he closed the door behind him.

"I won't be staying long. I just came to remind you that, according to my father's will, your presence is required at Christopher Corporation's board meeting." He folded his arms.

His icy glare chilled her. He regarded her as if she were an untrustworthy stranger.

Had he forgotten that he'd shared his deepest vulnerabilities with her just a week ago? Brought her incredible pleasure on several occasions before that? Rescued her when she'd needed him desperately? They should be working together to clear their names, currently being dragged through the mud.

But the hardened look that distorted Liam's handsome face indicated that it would be a wasted argument. He was back to treating her as his enemy.

"In light of the rumors swirling about us, I didn't think you'd want me there." She raked her manicured fingernails through her shoulder-length blond hair.

"Pity my father's will didn't make allowances for bad press," he said dryly.

She folded her arms on the desk in front of her rather than raising the single digit that would best convey how she felt. "My assistant has access to my calendar. On your way out, stop by her desk and make an appointment."

Three

Liam's face and ears burned with heat in response to Teresa's brush-off. She'd summarily dismissed him and had returned her attention to the sheet of paper on her desk.

He clenched his jaw as he surveyed her. She was beautiful in a royal-blue silk blouse and white linen pantsuit. Teresa looked hurt and angry. She obviously just wanted him to be gone.

Liam couldn't blame her.

He'd blown into her office, behaving like an ass. But he was furious with her for putting his family and business in this position. *Again.* And he was furious with himself because he still wanted her...desperately. Despite everything that had happened. Despite the rumors swirling around about

them. Despite the fact that he wasn't sure he could
trust her.

Shit.

He must seriously be out of his mind because he
wanted to trust her. And he cared for her. But he
wouldn't allow anyone to make a fool of him. And
there was still a strong possibility that was Teresa's
endgame.

So why did he feel such a strong pull toward her?
And why did he want her more than he'd ever wanted
any woman?

Teresa insisted that her relationship with his late
father had been strictly that of a mentor and his men-
tee. But the man he'd known his entire life would
never have given a quarter of his company to anyone out of the mere goodness of his heart. Hell, he'd
often wondered if Linus Christopher had possessed
even an ounce of selflessness.

Was he really supposed to believe that the man
who couldn't be bothered to show his own son
warmth and compassion would've left this woman
25 percent of the company's shares unless there'd
been something more to their relationship than either
one of them had been willing to admit?

Teresa leaned back in her chair, narrowing her
blue eyes at him. "Are you going to stand there all
day brooding? This is my place of business. I have
work to do."

Liam sighed. "Look, I know I came off like a
complete ass just now. I'm sorry. But you need to
face the fact that if you want to liquidate that stock,

you'll need to comply with the stipulations of my father's will. That means we have to work together, and you need to be at the meeting this afternoon."

Teresa checked her calendar begrudgingly. "Fine. What time should I be there?"

"Actually, my car service is waiting. I thought we could ride over together so I could bring you up to speed on the meeting." Liam gestured toward the door.

"The sooner we leave, the sooner I can get back here." She pursed her lips in a sensual pout that made him want to take her in his arms and kiss her.

His hands balled into fists at his side.

She's the enemy. Why can't you remember that?

"It's best if we aren't seen leaving the building together," he mused aloud, more to himself than her.

"Then why are you here in my place of business? Or didn't you notice the stalkerazzi parked across the street?"

Liam straightened his tie. "I came in through the back entrance."

"Well, you can leave the same way you came in."

The hurt in her eyes and the pained tone of her voice made him feel as awful as his father. The last thing he wanted was to mimic Linus Christopher's cruelty. After his talk with Teresa, he'd thought a lot about his relationship with his father. And his relationship with her.

"If you need to bring me up to speed on the meeting, call me from your car. In fact, you could've done that in the first place rather than showing up

here and *demanding* that I drop everything and come
with you."

Liam squeezed the bridge of his nose. The situation was snowballing and he was the one to blame.
"I'd like to go over a few documents in the car. It'll
be much easier if we ride together in the limousine."

He shoved both his hands in his pockets and
leaned against a tall wooden filing cabinet. Hoping
she'd say yes. Because while every word he'd said
about them needing to work together was true, the
deeper truth was that he'd missed Teresa.

He missed the scent and feel of her skin, the way
her sparkling blue eyes danced when she laughed and
the sweet taste of her pouty lips. And he missed the
incomparable ecstasy of watching Teresa St. Claire
fall apart in his arms.

Teresa stood in the nude Stuart Weitzman block-
heel sandals she'd worn in deference to her still-sore
ankle. She retrieved her matching nude clutch from
her desk drawer and walked to the door, only slightly
favoring her injured leg.

"Your ankle…" He furrowed his brow. "Is it okay?"

"It's fine. Just a little sore." Teresa didn't want to
think of Liam as the man who'd rushed to her rescue that night. Nor did she want to forget that he'd
come charging into her office like an entitled ass who
thought the world revolved around him. Still, she
wouldn't behave like an ogre, even if he had. "Thank
you again for what you did that night."

"I'm just glad you weren't seriously hurt. When

I think of what could've happened…" He seemed
genuinely distressed by the near miss. "I'm just glad
it didn't."

Don't be swayed by a few kind words.

She walked out to Corinne's desk, not acknowledging the evil eye her assistant was giving Liam.

"We're a go for the retreat." Teresa forwarded
Matt's text to Corinne. "I just sent the dates Matt Richmond is interested in. Pull a couple of staff members
in to call the entire guest list. Find out if either date
is tenable. With such a short turnaround, we should
get a feel for whether either date will work before we
put too much time and effort into it."

"Got it." Corinne scribbled notes on a sheet of
paper.

"I need a list of viable venues as soon as you can
come up with them. I'll work on a few possibilities
from my end, too. There has to be something available
in Seattle that fits the bill for an event of this magnitude. Don't call Jessie Humphrey. I'll call her. A bit
of persuading might be required after the nightmare
we put her through last time."

Corinne nodded her agreement. She eyed Liam
again, then shifted her gaze to Teresa. "Will you be
returning to the office?"

Teresa cast a glance over her shoulder at Liam. He
was especially handsome in a navy suit that hugged
his strong frame and reminded her of all the reasons
she loved the feel of his toned body pressed to hers.

But he'd rejected her after their unbelievably hot
encounter at the spa. And again after the rumors

about her being a scheming gold digger surfaced, despite the poignant moments they'd shared the night before.

Teresa's spine tensed. She gripped the clutch under her arm and reminded herself to hold on to that anger. So she'd never end up in Liam's bed again.

"I have every intention of returning here as soon as I can." Teresa turned and made her way toward the door, aware that every pair of eyes in the office was focused on her and Liam Christopher.

They left the building by the back entrance, where Liam's driver was waiting. Her cheeks stung at the thought of being shuttled away under cover because he was embarrassed to be seen with her. She slid across the leather seat, putting as much space as possible between them.

Liam had the audacity to look hurt.

"I know you have things you'd like to go over, but I need to make a call first. If there's any chance Jessie Humphrey isn't already obligated on the dates I have available, I don't want to miss my window of opportunity."

"Of course." He picked up a black leather portfolio and shuffled through its contents.

Teresa pulled up Jessie Humphrey's number and hoped things would finally go her way.

Four

Jessie closed her eyes and settled into eagle pose, her left leg wound around her right and her right arm wrapped around her left. Unable to keep her mind still long enough to formally meditate, she enjoyed the moving meditation of yoga.

The ring of her cell phone disturbed her peaceful solitude.

She unraveled her arms and legs and peeked at the caller ID.

"Teresa St. Claire." She muttered the name under her breath, then considered ignoring it until she'd finished her yoga practice.

But Teresa had indicated that Matt Richmond wanted to reschedule his event. Despite the chaos of the heavy rains, power outage, and a tree falling into the hotel which nearly took Teresa out... Matt Richmond had generously paid her the full agreed-upon amount of her contract without quibbling.

If she was going to do this project independently, without the backing of her label or the blessing of her agent, she needed an infusion of cold, hard cash.

Jessie answered the call just before it went to voice mail. "Hello."

"Jessie, it's Teresa. I'm glad I caught you. Matt Richmond has decided to reschedule his retreat. The only bright spot to the entire ordeal at The Opulence was your impromptu concert in the lobby. I swear, it's probably the only thing that kept the guests from rioting." Teresa's words were rushed and her voice seemed tense. "So, of course, he'd like you to per-form at the rescheduled event."

Not wanting to sound too eager, Jessie hesitated before responding. "That's nice of you to say, Teresa. The situation got pretty intense, so I'm glad I was able to help. The event isn't going to be held there again, is it? It was a lovely hotel, but after the mud-slide I'm not in love with hotels situated on a cliff."

"Understood. It'll be a while before The Opulence is up and running again anyway. And Matt would really like to get this retreat done soon—"

"How soon?"

"He's considering two weekends this month." Teresa's tone was tentative. "I'm hoping you'll be available on one of them."

Jessie grimaced. She'd planned to spend the month writing songs for her next album and securing the producers and musicians she wanted to work with on her dream project. "Actually, I cleared my calendar to work on my next album."

"I can appreciate how busy you must be, Jessie, but if you have any flexibility at all, you know Matt Richmond will make it worth your while. We'd do the same generous deal as last time. In addition to your booking fee, we'll pay for your flight via private jet, and all of your room service expenses at the hotel."

Jessie chewed on her lower lip and paced the floor. "I don't know. This album is really important to me. I didn't tell you before, but I've decided not to re-sign with my current label. I plan to start my own, so I'll have the freedom to make songs like the ones I performed that day in the lobby."

"I applaud your decision, Jessie. I did the same when I broke away from MSM Events and started my own company. So I know how rewarding it can be, but I also know that you need money and connections when you're breaking out on your own. And at Richmond Industries' fifth anniversary gala, you'll have an opportunity to nab both."

"What do you mean?" Jessie sat on the edge of her sofa. "Who's going to be at the retreat?"

"Since not all of the invited guests will be able to attend on such short notice, Matt instructed me to expand the list. If there's a producer or music exec you're eyeing for your new project, I could try to have them added to the guest list. I can't promise you they'll attend, but I'll do my best to get them there. I'll even seat you at the same table."

Jessie sat on the piano bench. As much as she'd like to spend the next several weeks immersed in this project, if she was going to make it a reality, she needed the money she'd get from this gig. And if Teresa St. Claire could get her at a table with Chase Stratton or Dixon Benedict and allow her to showcase some of the new material she was working on for the album, all the better.

"And if you're looking for wealthy music lovers who might be willing to help bankroll your project, there'll be a few in attendance, I'm sure. Also, we might be able to increase your exposure by broadcasting your performance live this time. If that's something you want, I'll talk to Nicolette Ryan about it."

There were too many benefits to this deal to ignore. "You've got a deal. Send the contract over to my agent."

Sinking onto the mat, Jessie tried to resume her yoga practice.

She'd managed to avoid Gideon Johns the last time she'd returned to Seattle. Maybe she could again. The money and exposure were worth the risk.

If she did cross paths with him, things didn't need to be awkward. She couldn't stop thinking of him, but he probably hadn't given her another thought. So she'd hold her head high, greet him politely and move on with her life.

Jessie allowed her eyes to drift closed as she inhaled a deep breath. Everything would be fine. In fact, it might be good to see Gideon again. Perhaps it would prompt her to relinquish the silly fantasy she still held on to. Then she could finally let go of the past and any thoughts of what might've been.

"Good news." Landon knocked on the partially open door of Gideon's office. "You won't have to pin Matt Richmond down for a meeting after all."

"Why not?" Gideon looked up from his laptop where he'd been writing an email, trying to close the deal with a potential investor in the Dubai project. "Have we gotten all the capital we need?"

"Not yet." Landon frowned as he took a few steps inside Gideon's office. "But we're close. And I think we might've gotten even closer. I just confirmed that you'll be available to attend the rescheduled Richmond Industries anniversary retreat."

Gideon leaned back in his seat and rubbed his chin. "Matt is hosting the event, so it'll be hard to pin him down for a one-on-one presentation."

"I'll put together a quick video presentation with all of the basic facts. Something eye-catching that'll grab his attention." Landon slid into the chair in front of Gideon's desk. "You can hand him a copy of the prospectus as well as email it to him so he can review it at length."

"Good work, Landon."

"Thanks." He grinned, settling in the chair.

Gideon raised an eyebrow. "Guess that means you'd better get to work."

"Right." Landon hopped up quickly and headed for the door. "Oh, and I sent you over that list of prospective investors."

"I'm working on it now," Gideon confirmed. He peered through his thumb and forefinger. "I'm this close to securing another hundred million."

Landon's phone rang. But rather than a traditional ringer, it played a familiar song.

"That song..."

"Sorry, I usually turn my ringer off in the office, but I just came back from lunch and—"

"That's a Jessie Humphrey song, isn't it?" He'd recognize Jessie's soulful, heart-wrenching voice anywhere.

"Yeah, it's one of the more obscure songs on her recent album. It doesn't get any radio play, but if you ask me, it's one of the best songs on the album." Landon seemed impressed that he knew who Jessie Humphrey was. "My girlfriend loves the song, too. That's why I chose it as her ringtone."

"Well, you'd better call her back, huh?" Gideon went back to typing out his email.

"Right. But I'll send you the tentative dates for the retreat first. And I'll get to work on that presentation just as soon as I can."

Gideon hit Send on the email. Then he pulled out his phone and searched for Jessie's recent album. He'd purchased every album she'd made and the songs she wrote for other artists over the years.

Despite the debacle of the kiss, Jessie had been a

friend. Someone he truly cared for. He wanted only the best for her.

He stared at the album cover where Jessie sat in a leather chair wearing a short, flirty dress and a sexy smile. He often wondered if things would've turned out differently between them if more time had passed after his breakup with Geneva before Jessie had kissed him. Would he still have reacted negatively? Or would he have kissed her back?

Gideon shook the thought from his brain. They'd both gone on to fulfill their dreams. Wasn't that proof enough that things had happened just as they should?

He scrolled through the song list. Most of the songs on this album had an upbeat pop sound. But the song Landon had chosen as his girlfriend's ringtone was more like the soulful performance Jessie had given in that intimate little club. It was the kind of song that made her unique vocals shine.

Gideon shut the door to his office and played the song on repeat, losing himself in the mellow sound of Jessie's voice and her heartbreaking lyrics.

Five

Teresa ended the call with Jessie Humphrey, holding back a squeal of glee. In an otherwise crappy day, this was a victory worth celebrating.

She tapped out a quick email to Corinne confirming that Jessie Humphrey would perform. She asked her assistant to make sure the contract was ready to send the moment they selected a date and secured the venue.

Teresa checked the shared spreadsheet updating which guests were available on either of the possible weekends.

"Shit," Teresa mumbled under her breath.

"What's wrong?" Liam stopped scanning the documents in his folder. His smoldering blue eyes seemed to slice right through her. "You just secured your headliner. I'd think you'd be ecstatic."

"I'm thrilled that Jessie confirmed." Teresa ignored the fluttering in her belly and the electricity that danced along her spine when he stared at her that way. "But I'm not happy that most of the guests are selecting the earlier date. That gives us just two weeks to find a venue and get everything in motion. So far, every suitable venue in Seattle is booked. I'm going to have to venture outside the area."

"Have you considered Napa Valley?" Liam returned his attention to the documents.

"That's at least six hundred miles from Seattle."

"Seven, but who's counting?" Liam's eyes danced when they met hers and a sexy little smirk curved one corner of his mouth. It reminded her of the look he'd given her when he'd…

Teresa shut her eyes and tried to push thoughts of their amazing nights together from her brain.

"That would considerably increase the cost of the event."

"True. But it might also lure more people there. Especially those who are still unhappy about what happened at the previous event in Seattle. The beauty of the vineyards and an endless supply of wine will earn you a lot of forgiveness with this crowd. Besides, it's the company's fifth anniversary. Matt needs to make a big splash with this event so everyone will forget what happened at The Opulence."

"All good points, but I can't book a venue without seeing it for myself. I need to make sure there's adequate event space, suitable accommodations and trained, professional staff. I'd need to sample the

food and attest to the cleanliness of the rooms. I'd
want to talk to people who've used the venue before
to make sure their level of customer service is on par
with what my clients expect."

"So find a few possible venues and fly there and
check them out." Liam shrugged.

Teresa gritted her teeth. Was he being intentionally flippant about something that could make or
break her?

"I would, but my private plane is in the shop." She
dropped her phone in her clutch and snapped it shut.

Liam chuckled, his eyes twinkling. "Then by all
means, take mine."

"Now you're just being cruel." She folded her
arms and pursed her lips. "I know this doesn't mean
anything to you, but this event is important to me.
With everything that's going on right now, this might
be my only chance to keep my company from going
under."

"I wasn't being facetious." His tone and expression seemed genuinely apologetic. "I'm being sincere."

Teresa stared at him, blinking. "I don't get it. Not
an hour ago you could barely stand to be in the same
room with me. Now you're offering to let me use
your private plane to plan your friend's event?"

"That's just it," he said quickly. "Matt's my best
friend and this event is important to him. I want to
ensure his retreat succeeds. Besides, Matt and I will
be making the announcement about our joint venture,
the Sasha Project, so I'm invested in the success of

this event, too. That's why I'd like to accompany you on this scouting trip."

Teresa stared at him blankly, still waiting for him to pull the rug from beneath her. She sifted her fingers through her hair. "I'll have to check with Matt first. If he's good with relocating the event to Napa Valley, I'll gladly accept your offer. Thank you."

"Anything for a friend," Liam said calmly, though his heart danced in his chest. He could barely keep from smiling at the thought of spending time alone with Teresa in Napa Valley.

She's supposed to be the enemy.

Yet he wanted to haul her onto his lap and kiss her like it was the only kiss he'd ever need. The way he'd kissed her when last she'd been in his arms.

His eyes drifted to her momentarily, scanning the royal-blue silk blouse that was a welcome pop of color against her stark white linen pantsuit.

Teresa always managed to look so buttoned up and proper. It was a calm facade that gave no indication of the raging heat and unbridled passion that lay beneath her cool exterior.

Liam's face and chest flushed with heat and his heart thumped so hard in his chest he wondered if she could hear it, too.

Being in such close proximity to Teresa made it difficult to remain aloof and pretend he didn't want her as much now as he ever had. That he didn't think of her constantly.

It would be a painfully long twelve months.

According to his father's will, that was how long Teresa had to take a role in the company before she could divest herself of the shares he'd left her. That meant twelve months of working closely while rumors swirled around them and this palpable heat raged between them.

He honestly didn't know if he could take it.

Teresa had been tapping out a text message on her phone, presumably floating the idea of moving the event to Napa Valley past Matt.

"There." She put her phone on the seat between them. "We'll see what he says."

"Great. Now about this meeting." He handed a portfolio to her. "Here's the basic information you'll need to know this afternoon. We'll be meeting with the board to—"

Teresa's phone dinged and she picked it up. She grinned, turning the screen toward him. "Matt loves the idea. Now I just hope I can find a venue for our preferred date."

Liam flipped his wrist and looked at his watch. It was clear Teresa wouldn't be able to focus on anything else until she had some peace of mind about finding a venue.

Liam placed a call to his assistant.

"Duncan, please email Teresa St. Claire our list of preferred hotel venues in Napa Valley. Preferably those near a vineyard. And be sure to copy her assistant Corinne on it. Thanks."

Liam ended the call and put his phone away. "Let Corinne know she should call off the search for Seattle venues. Then maybe we can get to the business at hand."

Teresa stared at him. "Why would you—?"

"Same reason. I'm doing this for Matt and for myself. I need you to focus on Christopher Corporation right now, and until that was resolved, it was apparent you wouldn't be able to."

He opened his portfolio after she'd sent her text message. "Now let's get started."

Six

Gideon had been working in his office all morning with the door closed and Jessie's first album playing. She'd hit the music charts with one or two of the songs from her most recent album. But the songs on this older EP were far better. Her voice had a raw edge that reminded him of Alicia Keys's first album. And the songs all seemed so personal and heartrending.

He couldn't help thinking of her older sister Geneva and how heartsick he'd been when she'd broken it off with him. But he was also reminded of the day two years later when Jessie had shown up at his place.

Gideon couldn't help cringing at the memory.

He didn't regret rejecting Jessie's advances then.

It was the right thing to do. But he did regret *how* he'd handled the encounter. He would never forget the heartbreak and pain in those dark brown eyes. It haunted him still.

Gideon paused as he listened to the song.

"I was so young. Did you have to be so cruel? All I ever really wanted was you."

He rubbed his jaw.

Was the song about their encounter that day?

Maybe it made him arrogant to speculate whether the incident between him and Jessie had been the inspiration for the song. But it'd been fifteen years, and he hadn't been able to get that day out of his mind. Was it really so implausible that it'd had a lasting impact on her, too?

Gideon massaged the base of his skull, where tension always gathered.

The Humphrey sisters.

Painful memories of both Geneva and Jessie were inextricable parts of his past. As were the happy memories of them that he'd always treasure. So he could never regret the rainy Saturday afternoon he'd first encountered the pair at a local movie theater. Or the ways in which that encounter had shaped his life.

As painful as it'd been, the dissolution of his relationship with Geneva had been the best thing for both of them. He wouldn't be the man he was today if not for his drive to prove Geneva and her snobby, elitist parents wrong.

It had taken a while for him to get over the sting of

her rejection, but Gideon harbored no regrets about Geneva. But Jessie… He groaned.

Jessie was another matter altogether.

He'd considered contacting her, if for no other reason than to apologize for handling the situation so badly. But he'd decided against it.

He would welcome the chance to make peace with Jessie. But he wouldn't reopen an old wound just to absolve himself of guilt.

There was no point in revisiting old hurts. What was done was done.

So despite his desire to make it up to Jessie for hurting her, some relationships were better left in the past.

Seven

Liam lagged a bit behind Teresa and Evelyn Montague, the manager of The Goblet Hotel and Vineyards in Napa Valley, as the woman offered them a tour of the facility.

The vineyards and the grounds of the hotel were lovely. The hotel itself had loads of charm, something he knew both Matt and Teresa would appreciate. The art deco style hotel featured lots of chrome, silver, black and red. The furniture and wallpaper sported bold geometric shapes. The lighting, the mirrors, and much of the furniture and finishes exuded an iconic elegance of days past. Yet the hotel was tastefully modern and chic. The Goblet offered style and luxury without being pretentious.

It was the reason he'd fallen in love with the place when he'd visited it several years ago.

"I can't believe that you can accommodate our event on such short notice. A hotel this beautiful… I was sure you'd be booked." Teresa's eyes roamed the sumptuous space as they entered one of the ballrooms.

"Yes, well…" Evelyn glanced back at him, then cleared her throat. "We had some cancellations."

"I'm sorry to hear that." Teresa stared at the woman, following her gaze. She looked at Liam quizzically, the wheels turning in that pretty head of hers. She returned her gaze to Evelyn. "But it certainly worked out to my advantage, for which I'm appreciative."

Her thank-you seemed to be addressed to both him and Evelyn.

Teresa flipped her blond hair over her shoulder and straightened her suit jacket. "I've seen all I need to see. I'm prepared to sign the paperwork as soon as it's ready."

"Very good." Evelyn nodded. "I have a couple of items to handle first. So please, enjoy lunch and cocktails on the house. The covered patio overlooking the vineyard is quite lovely."

"That would be wonderful. Thank you." Teresa's blue eyes glinted in the sunlight spilling through the windows.

They followed the woman to the dining space, then she whispered something to their server before excusing herself.

There was an awkward lull of silence between them as they reviewed their menus. Finally, Teresa spoke.

"I honestly can't thank you enough, Liam."

"For?" He raised a brow, still surveying his menu. The offerings had changed since last he was there.

"For recommending Napa Valley and The Goblet." She put her menu down and leaned forward. "More importantly, thank you for whatever you did to convince them to make space for our event."

"Me?" He feigned ignorance.

"Please don't pretend you don't know what I'm talking about. I saw the look Evelyn exchanged with you. There was no cancellation, was there?"

Liam put his menu down and straightened his tie without response. He avoided her mesmerizing blue eyes, for fear his would reveal anything more.

He said instead, "What looks good to you?"

You.

Teresa bit back the automatic response perched on the edge of her tongue.

He was wearing a lightweight gray gabardine suit that fit him to perfection. His baby-blue shirt nicely complemented the icy blue eyes that calmly assessed her.

"You didn't answer my question." She sipped her water. "You must've gone to a lot of trouble to make this happen. As grateful as I am for what you've done, I'm completely perplexed. Why would you go to such lengths to help me?"

"Matt's my best friend, and I try to help my friends whenever I can. They'd do the same for me."

"You're a bit of a fixer yourself."

Liam chuckled. "Never thought of it that way before."

She hadn't heard the sound of his laugh in so long. It was nice to hear it again.

"Well, even if you did this for Matt, I want you to know how much I appreciate it. With everything that's been going on lately…" Her shoulders tensed as the weight of the rumors and lost business settled on her again. "Limitless Events won't survive if I don't pull this off. So thank you."

"You're welcome." He furrowed his brow. "And I'm sorry I accused you of leaking information about us to the media. Someone is obviously trying to damage your business and reputation."

"Do you have any idea who might've done it? Not many people knew about us. And I don't believe any of them would ever do something like this."

"Isn't it more likely it was one of the reporters you invited to your events?"

"Are you suggesting this is my fault because I invited the media?"

"No. But you can't blame me for being wary of them until we get to the bottom of this."

That she could understand.

What she couldn't understand was why Liam insisted on accompanying her on the trip and touring the hotel with her.

Did he really expect her to believe he'd done all

of that because he and Matt were best friends or because of their collaboration on the Sasha Project?

"Are you sure it's a good idea for us to stay overnight at the same hotel with all of the rumors already out there about us?" She glanced at the server, who seemed to be staring at them whenever she looked up.

"We're both part of Christopher Corporation for now. This is a working trip. Duncan is still trying to get me an early-morning meeting with the CEO of a local medical technology company I've been eyeing. It'd make an excellent acquisition for our portfolio, but the owner isn't very enthusiastic about the possibility."

"I didn't realize Christopher Corporation dabbled in the medical field."

"Our interests are quite diverse. Real estate, technology, entertainment...any solid investment that piques my interest and will provide a good return.

"If you'd read the company material I had sent over, you'd know this."

She ignored the jab. "So maybe this medical tech company just isn't interested in selling."

"I have it on good authority they are. I get the sense they just don't want to sell to me."

Liam thanked the sommelier when he brought out the bottle of four-year-old cabernet sauvignon Evelyn had recommended and decanted it. Then the server brought their appetizers. Artisanal cheeses with a charcuterie tray and crackers, both house-made.

"Why wouldn't they want to sell to you?" Teresa

sipped her cabernet. The savory, full-bodied liquid, bursting with the flavor of plums and berries, rolled over her tongue.

Liam's cheeks and forehead flushed as he studied her intently. He loosened his tie. "I'd say it has everything to do with the kind of person my father was."

"Linus shouldn't be an issue for them anymore." Teresa hoped she didn't sound insensitive.

"The culture and philosophy of a company often survive its founder. Especially when a family member takes over." Liam swirled the dark liquid in his glass, then took a sip. "They probably suspect I'll run the company the same way."

"Show them that isn't true." Teresa piled duck prosciutto and Fourme d'Ambert onto a cracker and took a bite. "Oh my God. That's good," she muttered, one hand shielding her full mouth.

Liam's eyes darkened and his Adam's apple bobbed as he swallowed hard. He spread duck rillettes and a savory goat cheese on a toasted baguette. "If they'd returned any of the calls Duncan made to them, I'd happily reassure them I'm nothing like my father."

She took another sip of wine and spread foie gras on a cracker. "Call the CEO yourself and request an informal meeting. Don't dance around the issue. Go at it head-on. Let him know that while you respected your father, you didn't always agree with his methods. You have a different vision for Christopher Corporation. One you'd like his company to have a starring role in."

Liam rubbed his chin, his head tilted thoughtfully. "My father might've been an asshole, but people respected him. I can't go into this deal with him thinking we're coming from a weakened position."

"Sometimes a softer touch makes a stronger impact. Besides, it'll give you a common enemy and a chance to bond because of it."

Liam put prosciutto on a cracker and popped it into his mouth.

"What I've been doing clearly isn't working," he conceded. "Maybe it's time to try something new."

"To new beginnings, then." She lifted her glass.

"To new beginnings." Liam clinked his glass against hers.

They both seemed to relax into an easy, comfortable conversation that reminded her of the nights they'd spent talking and making love. Before the will was revealed. Before those rumors had started flying, wrecking the fragile relationship they'd been building.

Teresa's mind whirred with unsettling thoughts. About her turbulent, off-and-on relationship with Liam. Her unpredictable brother, who still hadn't returned any of her calls. The rumors that were causing her to hemorrhage clients and whoever might be behind them.

"Teresa." Liam's large, warm hand covered hers. "Is everything all right?"

She glanced down at his hand and he quickly withdrew it, pressing it to the table.

"Yes, of course." She bit back the tears that burned her eyes. "I'm fine."

She most definitely was *not* fine.

Teresa was angry. With Liam for the distance he'd put between them when she was given shares of Christopher Corporation. With whoever leaked those ridiculous affair rumors to the press. But most of all, she was angry with herself. Because despite it all, she couldn't help still wanting him.

She longed for the heat that had raged between them during their past toe-curling encounters. But she also longed for the tenderness in his touch the night he'd rescued her from beneath that fallen tree. And the vulnerability he'd displayed later that night when he'd told her about the awful relationship he'd had with his parents.

Teresa drew in a deep breath. It was nice enjoying a delicious meal and incredible wine with Liam as they overlooked the vineyard, with no qualms about who might see them. But it was the exception, not the rule. So she shouldn't read anything into it or expect it again. She should just enjoy it.

She needed to get through the next year quietly, without any more incidents or negative press.

Liam's phone buzzed for the third time. He glanced at his watch. "I can't believe we've been here three hours." He'd forgotten how easy she was to talk to.

"No wonder the staff has been circling us." Her eyes gleamed.

Liam couldn't pull his gaze from her bright smile.

Teresa was beautiful, but there was something much deeper that appealed to him. She was smart and diligent, and she seemed so sincere.

He wanted to believe her interest in him wasn't a calculated ploy to grab a bigger piece of Christopher Corporation. That she genuinely enjoyed his company as much as he enjoyed hers.

"Is everything okay?" She regarded him with concern, her head tilted. "Do you need to take that call?"

"It's nothing pressing." Liam slid his phone into the pocket inside his suit jacket.

Teresa put her phone back in her purse and indicated to the server that they were finally ready to leave. She returned her attention to Liam. "Thank you again. You didn't have to do any of this, but I'm glad you did." She smiled. "Despite all of your posturing, you're a really good guy."

His heart swelled, but then it was seized by guilt over having accused her of running a scheme on his family.

"Let's make that our little secret. Don't want the competition thinking I've gone soft." He winked at her and then left some cash on the table for the server.

They'd spent three hours talking about the mundane. From Matt and Nadia's wedding to how Seattle's sports teams were doing this year. Over a second bottle of cabernet sauvignon, they discussed which Netflix shows were worth binge-watching.

All safe topics.

The server smiled broadly when he spied the additional tip Liam had left on the table. "Can I get you two anything else? A dessert perhaps? I can have it sent to your room."

"*Rooms*," Teresa clarified. "We're work associates."

The way the man's eyes danced made it clear he believed otherwise. "Shall I have something sent to your rooms?" He stressed the *s* at the end of the word. "On the house, too, of course."

"I couldn't eat another bite...until dinner." Teresa rubbed her belly. "But please give our compliments to the chef. The food was spectacular and your service was impeccable."

The man thanked them, then stepped aside, allowing them to exit the table.

When Teresa stood, she teetered slightly. Liam placed his hands on her waist to steady her. Their eyes met for a moment.

"That cabernet sneaks up on you." She pressed a hand to her forehead. "I'd better lie down before dinner."

"I'll walk you to your room." Liam guided her toward the exit, his hand resting on the small of her back. The server gave him a knowing grin.

Just great.

The server didn't believe they were simply business associates and Liam was to blame.

Accompanying Teresa on this trip was a bad idea. Suggesting they stay overnight was an even worse one.

They were in Napa Valley, rather than in Seattle where the rumors about them were swirling. He hoped they'd be safe here. He'd always been impressed by how discreet and respectful of his privacy the staff at The Goblet had been. He had no reason to suspect that this time would be different.

As they rode the elevator up to her room, his hand grazed hers. A rush of pleasure flooded his senses as he recalled the sensation of her soft, bare skin caressing his when last he'd held her in his arms.

He tried to block out the growing desire to back her against the elevator wall and claim her sweet mouth in a demanding kiss. Graze her nipples with his thumbs through the silky material.

Suddenly, the elevator chimed, indicating they'd arrived on her floor.

She exited the elevator. "Will I see you for dinner?"

"I'll walk you to your door." He stepped off, too. She'd seemed slightly tipsy, so he wouldn't rest unless he knew Teresa was safely in her room.

She seemed pleased by his offer.

"Dinner would be nice. I'll pick you up at your door around seven."

"Or I could meet you downstairs."

"It's like you said… I'm a nicer guy than I let on."

They stopped in front of her door and she opened it, stepping inside.

"Thank you again, Liam. The hotel is perfect for Matt's retreat. You have no idea how badly I needed this win." Her lips quirked in a soft, dreamy smile that lit her beautiful eyes. "This has been a really lovely day. After all of the crappy ones I've had this past week, I needed a day like this. So thank you." She looked at him expectantly.

Liam leaned against the doorway, his arms folded as he stood just over the threshold from Teresa. There was barely a foot of space between them. He wanted to lean in, erase the distance between them and take her in his arms. Kiss her until they were both breathless.

The eager look in her eyes and the soft pout of her kissable lips indicated it was what she wanted, too. But he'd promised himself he'd stay strong, so they wouldn't end up tumbling into bed.

There was too much unresolved baggage between them. So as wonderful as the good times they'd shared were, those moments where overshadowed by the pain, distrust and resentment that still bubbled just beneath the surface for both of them.

Liam heaved a long sigh as he pushed off the wall. "I'm going to give that CEO a call, like you suggested. Thank you for a lovely afternoon."

Liam strode toward the waiting elevator before he changed his mind.

Eight

Jessie put down her pen and huffed. She'd written two new songs for her album, but she was still struggling to write the title song. The one that would stand as a metaphor for her ability to rebound from both heartbreak and the disappointment in her mentor, Arnold Diesman, the record label's top exec, turning out to be a lecherous jerk.

She unrolled her yoga mat, sucked in a deep breath and went into her favorite sun salutation. It was the perfect way to alleviate the stress she was feeling, and it got her creative juices flowing.

Jessie bent over into a deep forward fold, her hands pressed to the mat and the blood rushing to her brain.

Her phone rang.

Figures.

Her phone had been silent all day, but the moment she'd gone into moving meditation, not wanting to be disturbed, it rang.

She checked the screen. *Teresa St. Claire.*

Jessie answered. "Hi, Teresa. What's up?"

"Hi, Jessie. Great news. We've nailed down the date and venue. The retreat happens in two weeks and you're going to adore the venue. It's a cute little art deco boutique hotel and vineyard in Napa Valley. I'm here now. The place is incredible. Very Old Hollywood glamour." The woman spoke excitedly.

"Didn't want to take another chance on Seattle rain and calamitous mudslides, huh?" Jessie wasn't sure if she was more relieved by not having to deal with the dreary weather or avoiding an encounter with Gideon.

She'd frittered away too much of the time she should've spent writing this album with imagining what it would be like to see Gideon again.

"With the short notice, we just couldn't find another venue in Seattle that was both available and luxurious enough for this event." Teresa's response brought Jessie out of her temporary, Gideon-induced haze. "Otherwise, I would've loved to keep the event in Seattle where most of the guests are based."

Lucky me.

"I've always wanted to go to Napa Valley, so I'm looking forward to it." Jessie sat on the piano bench with her back to the keys. "Send the updated contract with all of the particulars to my agent. We'll get it executed and return it as soon as possible."

"Corinne will send the contract first thing in the morning," Teresa said. "And more good news... Matt Richmond approved adding Chase Stratton and Dixon Benedict to the guest list. He was thrilled you suggested them. Both men were on his radar for future projects. He'll invite them both personally tomorrow. I can't confirm yet that either man will be there, but as promised, they'll both be invited."

"Keep me posted on whether they RSVP?"

"I will, and one more thing." Jessie could hear the grin in Teresa's voice. "I told you that wealthy music lovers who might invest in your indie project would be in attendance. Well, I'm reviewing the updated guest list and I just got confirmation that real estate billionaire Gideon Johns will be there as well as—"

"Gideon Johns RSVP'd?" Jessie began pacing the floor, her heart racing. She'd managed to avoid Gideon when the Seattle retreat was canceled. She obviously wouldn't have the same luck in Napa.

"Yes, and I'd be happy to introduce you."

"That won't be necessary," Jessie responded tersely. "We've met."

"I see." Teresa's voice registered worry. She was silent for a moment, then asked tentatively. "Gideon's presence won't be a problem for you, will it?"

Part of her was eager to show Gideon that the girl he'd dismissed was now an in-demand recording artist. But another part of her dreaded the encounter. A man as rich and powerful as Gideon probably barely remembered her, while she'd thought of him often over the years.

But she wouldn't allow the possibility to sidetrack her career. Nor did she need Gideon's help.

"No." Jessie forced herself to smile. "He's my older sister's ex-boyfriend, that's all. He probably doesn't even remember me. Thank you for the call. I'll look for the contract from my agent."

Jessie ended the call and continued to pace the floor.

Why should she care whether Gideon would be at the retreat? She should be over what happened between them fifteen years ago and over him. But her mind was buzzing with memories of the man who'd wanted to marry her sister.

The man she'd had a killer crush on from the first time she'd laid eyes on him when she and her older sister Geneva met him one Saturday afternoon at the movie theater.

Their parents hadn't been thrilled about Geneva getting serious with a poor kid from the wrong side of the tracks. But the more they objected, the more Geneva dug in.

Her sister had truly cared for Gideon, in the beginning. But at some point, it became more about defying their parents than genuine affection for him.

On her sister's birthday, Gideon had presented Geneva with an engagement ring. That's when her sister realized she'd let things go too far.

Geneva was about to embark on a year of traveling

in Europe and she wanted the freedom to see other people. So she'd kissed Gideon tenderly and ended it.

Gideon had been devastated, and so was Jessie. She'd adored him.

Jessie sat on her yoga mat, her legs folded in lotus position. Eyes squeezed shut, she inhaled a deep breath, trying to shut out the heartbreak she'd experienced the day she'd told Gideon how she really felt about him. But as a songwriter, she was in an unenviable position.

She needed to conjure up the raw emotions she'd felt that day. Feelings that compelled her to pen songs about unrequited love, living through the pain of a shattered heart and learning to rebuild it. How else could she convey that pain so palpably that the audience felt it, too?

But that meant that in moments like this, her wounded heart bled afresh. As if it had happened yesterday instead of a decade and a half ago.

She certainly hadn't spent her entire adult life pining away for Gideon. But in moments like this, it was clear she'd never really gotten over him.

"Gideon, we need to talk." Landon stood in the doorway of Gideon's office looking flustered.

The kid was brilliant, but Gideon wondered if he'd ever have the steely spine it took to deal with the ups and downs of real estate.

Financial and real estate journals had proclaimed that Gideon had the Midas touch. But he never fell for his own hype. He was good at the real estate game and had a gut sense of what deals and which investors were right for a project. But nothing was foolproof.

Gideon nodded toward the seat in front of his desk and leaned back in his executive chair. "What's happened now?"

"Some of the smaller investors in the Dubai deal are nervous because they've learned that our two largest investors pulled out of the deal. No one has jumped ship yet, but I get the sense they're considering it."

"You did the preliminary work on this deal. Are you confident in your research?"

"Yes, of course. I did solid background on everyone involved. I've run comps in the region. It's a hot area. Demand for and the price of hotel rooms continues to climb. New shops and restaurants are going up. Investors from around the world are clamoring to get in on deals in the area." Landon spoke animatedly. He seemed insulted by the insinuation that the preparatory work he'd done was lacking.

"*That* level of confidence…" Gideon pointed to the younger man. "That's what you need to convey to any investor who might be getting cold feet. They wanted to be part of this deal and they understood the inherent risks. So what they really want to hear is that *we're* still completely on board with the deal."

Landon nodded thoughtfully. "I can do that."

"Next time one of them calls, let them hear the fire and bass in your voice that I just heard."

"You can count on me." Landon was infinitely

more self-assured than he'd been when he entered the room. "One other thing…we have a limited window of time here. We'll all feel more confident about the deal once the remaining funding has been secured. I know you have meetings lined up with several potential investors, but Matt Richmond isn't among them."

Gideon had hoped to bring up the deal in casual conversation with his friend. But neither man's schedule had permitted for an impromptu lunch or meeting for drinks.

"We've both been busy." Gideon shuffled through a stack of papers on his desk without looking up at his assistant. "I'll give him a call."

"Preferably today."

Gideon narrowed his gaze at his assistant. "How about as soon as you leave my office?"

"You've got it." Landon saluted as he rose to his feet. "Keep me posted."

As soon as Landon was gone, Gideon pulled out his cell phone and dialed his friend.

"Gideon, what's up?" Matt answered, out of breath.

"I didn't catch you in the middle of—"

"No." Matt laughed. "I took a break to work out. I was on the treadmill."

"If this is a bad time—"

"It isn't. I could use the break."

"It's about that deal in Dubai I mentioned to you before. You've been griping about missing out on my last three projects."

"True. They had killer returns. I'm still kicking

myself for not getting in on that deal in New York. The price per square foot in that neighborhood is through the roof."

"Precisely," Gideon said. "That's why I'm trying to save you a spot on this Dubai deal. The ROI is going to be even bigger than on the New York project."

"I hear exciting things about the opportunities in Dubai. But I'm a little nervous about investing in real estate internationally outside of my part-time residences. Investing in the Middle East makes me particularly apprehensive."

"Have you ever been to Abu Dhabi or Dubai?" Gideon prodded.

"Can't say I have."

"Both cities are remarkable. In fact, if you and Nadia are still debating a honeymoon destination, Dubai would be a terrific spot. It's a luxurious oasis."

Matt had recently gotten married to his former assistant, Nadia Gonzalez, but with the anniversary retreat, they'd postponed their honeymoon.

"I was thinking somewhere tropical, like Tahiti." Matt chuckled. "But I get your point. Look, I don't want to be on the outside looking in on your next big deal, but I need to know a little more about what I'd be getting myself into on this one before I'm willing to invest the kind of money you're talking about here."

"Understandable." Gideon drummed his fingers on his desk. "We're working on a fairly tight window here. So why don't we discuss the details over lunch?"

"I'm in the midst of preparing for the retreat I've

rescheduled. So I'm pretty tied up," Matt hedged. "You'll be there, right?"

"I look forward to spending time in Napa Valley."

"Come in on Thursday instead of Friday. You and I can sit down over drinks and hash this out then."

Gideon's jaw tensed. The retreat was two weeks away, making the timeline even tighter. But if he squeezed Matt on a deal he was already squirrelly on, it'd scare his friend off.

"Sounds perfect," Gideon said.

"See you in Napa Valley two weeks from now."

Gideon hung up with his friend and sighed.

Nothing worthwhile ever came easy. His entire life had been a testament to that.

Gideon scrolled through his emails and came across the invite to the retreat again. A gorgeous photo of Jessie was plastered across the graphic. He was still a sucker for those big brown eyes and that generous smile. The one that still instantly made him smile, too.

He'd begged off the Seattle retreat at the last minute, deciding it would be better if he and Jessie didn't cross paths. In the end, it didn't matter since it was canceled, but the truth was he feared Jessie hadn't forgiven him. That she wouldn't welcome a reunion. But avoiding the rescheduled retreat in Napa Valley wasn't an option. So it was better that he went in with a plan.

He needed to approach Jessie first. Wipe the slate clean and let bygones be bygones. He only hoped Jessie was inclined to do the same.

Nine

Gideon Johns walked into the lobby of The Goblet Hotel on Thursday a little after one in the afternoon. He'd arrived even earlier than Matt suggested to ensure he got a chance to sit down and chat with his friend well ahead of the start of the festivities.

"Gideon." Teresa grinned as she approached him, a wide smile spread across her face. Her gorgeous blue eyes sparkled as she shook his hand in both of hers. "It's wonderful to see you again. Matt said you would be arriving today."

Gideon leaned in closer and lowered his voice. "I realize I'm here ahead of check-in, but I'm hoping my private cottage is ready."

"I anticipated that you'd arrive prior to check-in." Teresa grinned. "Your room was ready at 10:00 a.m."

"You're amazing." Gideon smiled.

Teresa walked to the front desk with him. "Melva, this is Mr. Gideon Johns. He's the guest I requested early check-in for. He's in one of the private cottages."

Gideon handed the clerk his credit card and identification. He turned toward Teresa, lowering his voice again.

"I'm glad you're in such a good mood." Gideon didn't want to wreck her upbeat disposition by going into the specifics of the ugly rumors circulating around Seattle about her and Liam. But he wanted to assure her he didn't believe them. "You're good people, Teresa."

Her smile deepened and her eyes were filled with gratitude. She placed a hand on the forearm he'd propped on the front desk. "Thank you. That means a lot."

He'd spent most of his adult life honing his ability to read people and decipher their intentions. Nothing about Teresa St. Claire made him believe she was the scheming vixen that the haters and gossipers in his circle would have him believe her to be. But in a business like hers, perception was everything.

It was a dilemma to which he could relate.

Gideon didn't believe for an instant that Teresa had nefarious motives when it came to Liam Christopher and his family's corporation. But as he spotted Liam sitting in a chair across the lobby watching them intently, it was clear that Liam's interest in Teresa wasn't just business.

The hunger in his eyes as his gaze slid over Teresa's body spoke more of the bedroom than the boardroom. The way the man's eyes narrowed and his nostrils flared when Gideon leaned in to speak to Teresa in a hushed tone indicated the slightest hint of possession.

Regardless of what might have gone on between them, Gideon refused to believe the woman he'd gotten to know was capable of the deceit and betrayal of which she'd been accused. But in his experience, many people born of wealth liked to believe that people who came from very humble beginnings, like him and Teresa, didn't belong, regardless of how hard they'd worked or how high they'd risen. They were a social experiment waiting to implode. And when they did, they'd shake their heads and wag their tongues as they mused about their moral defectiveness.

It was the reason he felt a kinship of sorts with Teresa.

"Your business partner over there is giving me the death stare." Gideon indicated Liam's general direction with a shift of his gaze.

Teresa's cheeks flamed and she cleared her throat. "I can't imagine why."

"Can't you?" Gideon gave her a good-natured smile as he returned his credit card and ID to his wallet while the desk clerk prepared his room key. "Relax, Teresa. I don't believe any of the bullshit I've heard. But it's obvious you two care for each other. I know it doesn't seem like it right now, but my gut tells me that everything will work out for the two of you."

"Who knew the great Gideon Johns was a hopeless romantic?"

"Maybe once upon a time, but that time has long…" Gideon turned toward a beautiful brown-skinned woman wearing expensive sunglasses, a chocolate-brown silk dress and a pair of rose gold high-heel sandals with a sexy crystal bow detail. The height of the heels and the thin, barely-there straps across the ankle and toe made the one leg exposed by her dress seem a mile long.

"Jessie Humphrey?" He whispered the name beneath his breath, but Teresa, who'd followed his gaze, clearly heard him.

"I hear you two don't require an introduction." Teresa beamed, clearly amused by how distracted he was by Jessie's arrival. She nodded toward the goddess with miles of creamy skin who approached the desk.

"Jessie, I'm glad you made it. I trust that your trip was less eventful this time around." Teresa stepped past Gideon and clasped Jessie's hands, as if the two of them were old friends.

"Yes, thank you, Teresa. And thank you for arranging everything. My flight was lovely."

"Well, I'm sure you're tired after your cross-country trip. I'll get your registration started so you can check into your room right away." Teresa stepped over to the desk.

"Hello, Gideon." Jessie finally acknowledged his presence, but she didn't remove her shades. "It's been a long time, hasn't it?"

"Fifteen years." He practically whispered the words as they exchanged an awkward hug.

He'd seen her PR photos on her cover and online. He'd even watched some of her performances on video. But nothing could prepare him for how stunning this woman was in person. Her creamy brown skin was flawless and her dark brown hair was pulled back into a sleek bun.

Jessie's high cheekbones and petite nose were reminiscent of her older sister's. Yet the similarities between the two ended there.

Gideon had always thought of Jessie as Geneva's little sister, which was why he'd reacted so poorly to Jessie's unexpected kiss that rainy afternoon nearly two years after Geneva had ended their relationship. He'd hurt her feelings, and they hadn't spoken since.

But that was then.

Gideon wouldn't dare reject a kiss from the woman standing before him now.

"How've you been?" He shoved a hand in his pocket.

"Well, thank you. And you've obviously done quite well for yourself." She gave him a cursory smile before handing her credentials over to another desk clerk.

"Sir…sir…" Melva gave him a knowing smile as she handed Gideon his room keys. The woman probably thought he was a shameless groupie way past his prime.

He nodded his thanks, then turned back to Jessie. "Your voice is amazing, Jess. But you know I've always thought so."

"Thank you, Gideon," she said quietly.

"How's your family?" He wasn't asking about Geneva because he was interested in her. He asked because inquiring about the health of her family without malice was the polite thing to do. Regardless of Geneva's heartbreaking rejection or her father's cruel remarks that he would never be worthy of his daughter.

"They're fine." Her shoulders tensed and she turned toward the desk clerk. "I hope yours are, too."

Even after Jessie had stepped out of Gideon's embrace, the heat from his body wrapped itself around her like a soft, warm blanket. His subtle, deliciously masculine scent tickled her nose.

However, when Gideon asked about her family, code for her sister Geneva, the warm, fuzzy feelings ceased instantly. Leaving her with the cold, dark memories of their last interaction and how broken it had left her.

Geneva had rejected him, but she was still apparently the only Humphrey sister he was really interested in. His inquiries about her were superficial niceties.

Maybe it made her petty to give him such a cryptic response. But if he wanted to hear all about his ex, he'd have to ask her directly.

"Last I heard, Geneva was living in Europe. Switzerland, maybe?"

Jessie drew in a tight breath, but fought to keep her expression neutral. She accepted her room key from the desk clerk.

"She was for a while, but she's lived in Amsterdam for the past seven or eight years with her husband, Edmond. She's Geneva Torian now." She gave him a manufactured smile designed to protect her suddenly fragile pride. "It was nice seeing you, Gideon."

Jessie turned on her four-and-a-half-inch-tall Aminah Abdul Jillil open-toe sandals and strutted toward the elevator. The bellman, who'd stacked all of her bags onto a luggage cart, moved with her.

"Jessie, wait." Gideon caught her elbow with a gentle grip. "We haven't seen each other in more than a decade. I have an important meeting today, but I'd really like to catch up."

You mean you want to hear more about Geneva.

Jessie bit back the caustic remark that burned her tongue and gnawed at her gut. Why give Gideon the satisfaction of knowing how much his rejection hurt?

She'd be cordial, but aloof.

"I hope to line up a couple of meetings of my own." Jessie tipped her chin so her gaze met his as she slipped her arm from his loose grip. "I'm performing tomorrow and I'm still tweaking some of the material. Maybe we can catch up after my final set on Saturday night."

"Of course." His voice reminded her of the pain she'd heard in it the day her sister ended things between them. "But if you're able to free up some time to grab lunch or perhaps drinks… I'd really like that."

Jessie nodded her acknowledgment, then resumed her trek toward the elevator with the bellman in tow.

They stepped onto the elevator and Gideon stood frozen, staring at her, as the elevator doors closed. As if he'd seen a ghost.

Jessie hated that she was still hurt and angry after all this time. She shouldn't be. If anything, she should be grateful to Gideon. She owed her career to him.

The heartbreak and subsequent longing she experienced drove her to pick up a pen and write poems and eventually songs. After writing songs for small local acts, Jessie had slowly climbed the songwriting ranks and written songs for chart-topping musicians.

She'd fought for the chance to sit center stage at her piano and sing her own songs. After a successful EP, she'd accepted a contract from a big studio, but she would only agree to a single album contract because the studio hadn't been willing to give her full creative control. She'd gambled on demonstrating that she was worthy of that level of oversight before she signed another contract. Hopefully for a multi-album deal. But Jessie hadn't anticipated the cost of that freedom. Nor had she been willing to sacrifice her soul for it.

Her experience with label exec Arnold Diesman taught her not to trust a wealthy, powerful man to do her bidding or have her back. In the end, that man's only real interest was his own selfish desires.

Jessie sucked in a deep breath as the elevator opened on the second floor. She followed the bellman to her luxury balcony suite. A bold silver wallpaper with a black geometric pattern welcomed her to the elegant art deco style space. She tipped the bellman once he'd unloaded her luggage, then locked the door behind him.

Jessie slipped off the flowing brown silk Cushnie designer dress with an asymmetrical hemline that skimmed her ankles in the back but rose thigh-high over her left leg. She kicked off her shoes and slipped into a pair of comfy gray sweat shorts and a white V-neck tee. Then she sank onto the sofa in the suite's well-appointed sitting area.

Seeing Gideon after all this time had been harder than she'd imagined. Which meant that the next few days would be difficult. It would be especially hard performing in front of the man who'd first inspired her to write songs of love and loss.

Chase Stratton and Dixon Benedict had both RSVP'd for the retreat. This was her best opportunity to get Chase and Dix on board with her project. So she wouldn't allow anything to throw her off course. Least of all handsome, uber-wealthy, aging-like-fine-wine Gideon Johns.

This project had the potential to change everything for her. So she wouldn't let a teenage crush distract her from her dream.

Later that evening, after making a few last-minute adjustments to her song, Jessie pulled out her cell phone in its pink rhinestone-studded case and tapped out a quick message.

You'll never guess who just asked about you. Gideon Johns.

Gideon watched as the elevator doors closed, his pride hurt by Jessie's chilly reception. He realized she wasn't happy about the way they'd left things. But he'd done the right thing. Was Jessie really still angry with him after all these years?

He'd be the first to admit that he'd handled the situation poorly. But what he rarely admitted was why he'd gotten so angry that day. Buried beneath all the practical reasons he'd rejected Jessie's proposition was the fact that he'd been startled by the way she'd made him feel. It was something he hadn't wanted to admit, even to himself.

He'd been attracted to her. Wanted her. Feelings he'd immediately rejected. She was his ex's sister.

The last thing in the world he'd wanted was to fall for another Humphrey sister. It was still the last thing he wanted. And yet, seeing her just now, he realized that he was as susceptible to it today as he'd been back then.

Gideon ordered a glass of wine at the bar.

Jessie had always been such a sweet and gentle soul. She was a ray of sunshine that he'd missed having in his life. But the woman he'd just encountered was unlike the girl he'd once known.

Was she still angry about how he'd rejected her back then? Or had fame and ambition changed Jessie?

Back when he'd known the Humphrey sisters, Jessie and Geneva had been like night and day. Geneva was confident, assured, ambitious and a bit entitled. Jessie was sweet, shy and thoughtful. Geneva always thought of herself first, while Jessie's primary concern was the people she cared about.

It had been Jessie's most endearing quality.

But maybe Jessie was more like her older sister than he remembered.

If Jessie preferred not to revisit their past, all the better.

Besides, rekindling a friendship with Jessie would sidetrack him from his primary goal this weekend. To seal the Dubai deal with Matt Richmond. Then he'd return to Seattle and forget about his encounter with the surprisingly aloof Jessie Humphrey.

Ten

Liam walked into the bar and sat down, leaving a space between him and Gideon Johns.

"Gideon." He nodded toward the man, who could barely hold back a smirk.

"Liam." Gideon took another sip of his wine. "If you've come to give me a back-off-my-woman speech, I can save us both time. My interest in Teresa is strictly professional."

"As is mine." *Now.* That critical detail he kept to himself.

Gideon's laugh made it clear that he wasn't buying it anyway. Not even for a moment.

"Do you make a habit of staring down the men who have close conversations with your business associates?" When Liam didn't answer, Gideon set his glass down. "Didn't think so."

"I thought you were too discriminating a man to believe the gossip mill, Gideon," Liam said after he'd ordered a Manhattan.

"If you mean the rumors disparaging Teresa… I don't believe a word of them." Gideon's expression grew serious. "But the part about your relationship with her being more than just business…you're the one who told me that."

"What do you mean?" Liam turned toward Gideon.

"You sat in that chair watching the woman's every move. Scowling at any man who dared smile at her." Gideon nodded toward Teresa as she walked past the bar with a male member of the hotel staff. "You can't keep your eyes off her even now. So, a word of advice, if that's the story you're going with, you might want to take it down a notch…or ten."

Liam groaned and raked his fingers through his hair. The man was right. Though it hadn't been intentional, he hadn't been able to keep his eyes off Teresa as she flitted about the hotel. Today she wore a fitted black pantsuit that perfectly complemented her figure. The sheer black blouse beneath it had a deep neckline that had his imagination and memory working overtime. Was it any wonder his eyes had a mind of their own?

"I'm sorry if I seemed—"

"Territorial?" Gideon offered, finishing his glass of wine.

"Something like that," Liam conceded. "It's a complicated situation."

"I'm no stranger to complicated situations." Gideon ordered another glass of wine. "So no judgment here. But if you're really going with the story that it's only business between you two, you might want to rethink your approach."

"Thank you for your honesty." Liam patted the man on the shoulder, then excused himself to go to his guest cottage and return an important call.

Pangs of guilt twisted Liam's gut as he picked up the telephone to return the call to Jeremy Dutton, the man he'd assigned to comb Teresa's background. The man was much more than just a private investigator. In fact, that barely scratched the surface of just what Jeremy Dutton was capable of.

While it was true that he'd come to the conclusion that it didn't make sense for Teresa to have gone to the press, there was still a lot he didn't know about the woman. Had she been honest about the nature of her relationship with his father? Was there a hidden agenda behind her interest in him? Did she have designs on acquiring a controlling interest in Christopher Corporation? Was Dutton able to dig up anything about her father, Nigel St. Claire, working for Christopher Corporation twenty years ago?

When it came to Teresa, there were too many questions and not enough answers. Answers that he needed since, thanks to the terms of his father's will, Teresa now owned 25 percent of the stock in his family's company. They were already dealing with all of the rumors and innuendo about her relationship with his father and now him. Liam needed to ensure that there were no additional skeletons that would come crashing out of this woman's closet to plunge his family and company name into further disrepute.

Anyone in his position would do the same, for the sake of their business. But he had an additional incentive to look into Teresa. He'd been given no choice about bringing her into the company. But the fact that he kept bringing her into his bed…well, that was all on him.

He genuinely liked Teresa St. Claire, but he had millions of reasons to distrust her. Most of which were sitting in local and international banks. Still, he was inexplicably drawn to her in a way he hadn't experienced with anyone else.

Common sense dictated that he leave Teresa alone. Deal with her only as he must. But the time he'd spent with Teresa at The Goblet made him remember just how much he liked her. And she seemed just as enamored with him.

Which made him feel particularly shitty about having her investigated. Despite the fact that any sensible businessman in his position would've done the same. Still, there was a question that kept running through his brain.

What if he chose to pursue a relationship with Teresa? How would she react once she learned of the investigation? Could she ever forgive him?

Despite his initial objections, in the few short

weeks since Teresa had been a part of Christopher Corporation, she'd demonstrated that she could be an asset to the organization. But he couldn't sustain any further liabilities where Teresa was concerned.

Liam dialed the private investigator. The man answered right away.

"What've you learned?" Liam asked after exchanging a cursory greeting.

"Straight to the point." The man chuckled. "My type of client."

Liam waited without reply for the man to give him the highlights of his report on Teresa.

It essentially amounted to nada. Zip. Zilch.

What the hell was he paying this guy for? He wasn't sure if he should be extremely pleased or incredibly suspicious about the lack of dirt his investigator was able to dig up after weeks of searching. Dutton was a thorough investigator on whom he frequently relied to vet potential businesses and potential business associates.

The only thing the man could confirm was that Teresa had spent a considerable amount of time with his father.

"Keep digging," Liam said. "Everyone has secrets. If there's something there, I need to know what it is."

"It's your dime, Christopher." Dutton chuckled. "I'll keep knocking on doors and kicking over rocks for as long as you're paying me to do it."

"Fine, but be subtle about it. Discretion is everything on this one."

Liam ended the call and slipped the phone into

his pocket. He was protecting his family's interest and his heart. Still, he couldn't help feeling like he was betraying Teresa by doing so behind her back.

Liam loosened his tie and opened the doors to the patio that overlooked the vineyard. He sat at the little café table, his thoughts immediately returning to the three-hour lunch he and Teresa had enjoyed together on the property just two weeks before. A memory to which his mind often drifted.

Liam could recall nearly everything about the hours they'd spent together. What she was wearing. How she'd worn her hair. Her delectable scent. The sound of her laugh. How much he'd wanted to kiss her. How his body had craved hers as he lay in bed alone that night.

Liam sighed. He was sure Teresa was hiding something. But then, he'd been holding something back, too. A secret he hadn't dared share with anyone.

He had reason to suspect he'd been adopted.

Eleven

Jessie checked her watch after she'd steamed the dress she chose for her performance the next night. It was nearly 10:00 p.m., almost 1:00 a.m. back in New York. She was already feeling the jet lag. If she went to bed now, she could get a decent night's sleep and still work out before breakfast. Her phone rang.

Geneva.

"Hey, big sis." Jessie yawned. A signal that their call wouldn't be long. "What are you doing up this early?"

It wasn't quite 7:00 a.m. in Amsterdam.

"Where did you run into Gideon? Did he recognize you right away?" Her sister completely ignored her question.

"I'm at The Goblet. It's a—"

"Luxury hotel in Napa Valley." Her sister sounded impressed.

"You know it?"

"Who doesn't?" Geneva scoffed. "What are you doing there?"

"That gig I got to perform for billionaire Matt Richmond and a bunch of his business associates—"

"The one that got canceled because of a mud-slide?" her sister said incredulously. "What about it?"

"They rescheduled the event and moved it to Napa. I'll be performing the next two nights."

"So Gideon is a friend of Matt Richmond of Richmond Industries?"

"It seems so," Jessie said through an exaggerated yawn. As if it were the least interesting piece of information she'd ever heard. "They both live in Seattle. You know the rich guys there run in the same circle."

"So what did he look like? Did he recognize you right away? After all, he hasn't seen you since I broke up with him."

Not true. But it wasn't a secret she wanted to share with her sister.

"He did recognize me right away. And he looks pretty much the same. Only more mature." *And infinitely more handsome.* A fact she didn't need to mention.

"Do you think he's as rich as the business magazines say he is?"

How the hell was she supposed to know? "I'm not a forensic accountant, Gen."

"I know, smart-ass. Tell me what he was wearing, and don't spare any of the details."

"It's not like I was cataloging his entire outfit."

A slim-cut charcoal-gray Tom Ford suit with subtle pinstripes, a crisp white shirt with a burgundy Tom Ford tie, and a pair of black leather Dolce & Gabbana shoes buffed to a high shine.

Not that she was paying attention.

"Well, what did he ask you about me? You do remember that, don't you?" Geneva said, impatiently.

"I do." How could she forget? For the first time it seemed Gideon saw her as an attractive woman. But then he'd burst any delusions she had about his interest in her by inquiring about her sister. The woman who broke his heart. "He asked how you were doing."

"And?"

Jessie sighed. "And if you were still living overseas."

That was the part that had irked her most. It meant Gideon had been keeping tabs on Geneva. Pining away for her, though her sister clearly hadn't wanted him.

"Why do you care so much, anyway? You're an old married woman, living the life abroad, remember?" Jessie teased.

Geneva suddenly got quiet. "There's something I haven't told you, Jess. Edmond and I...well, we're separated."

Jessie had moved into the bathroom and started unpacking her toiletries, but her sister's admission stopped her in her tracks. "Since when?"

Geneva was slow to respond. "The past three months."

"And you're just telling me?" She and Geneva weren't the kind of sisters who told each other everything. Still, Jess couldn't believe her sister would hold back something like that.

"We've spoken at least a dozen times over the past few months." Jessie returned to the main room of her suite and looked out the window at the surrounding vineyard, lit by strings of lights. Had she been that wrapped up in her own life that she hadn't noticed how unhappy her sister had been?

"Why didn't you say something?"

"I hoped it was only temporary. That I'd never need to worry you or Mom and Dad with this."

Jessie doubted Geneva's reasons for holding back the truth were as altruistic as she made them out to be. Like their mother, Gen had always cared about maintaining appearances.

"But you no longer believe you two will reconcile?" Jessie sank onto one of the comfy chairs in the room. "Or has the news that your old flame, billionaire Gideon Johns, inquired about you prompted that decision?"

"Don't be like that, sis," Geneva pleaded. "I know you think I'm the tough one, but this whole thing with Edmond has done a number on my ego."

"I'm sorry. I didn't mean to be…" Jessie raked her short, trim nails through her hair. "What happened? The last time I visited, you and Edmond seemed very happy."

"I thought we were happy, too. But that didn't stop Edmond from finding a younger, prettier model that made him happier."

"He cheated on you?" *It figured.*

"Don't gloat, Jess. Please. I couldn't take that right now."

"Well, for what it's worth, I'm sorry to hear it." Jessie returned to the bathroom. She needed to strip off her makeup and get ready for bed. "Will you be returning to the States?"

"I haven't given it much thought. I love my life here in Amsterdam, but I hadn't realized how inextricably it's tied to Edmond. Now that the people in our circle are being forced to take sides, it's clear that they're his friends, not mine."

"You should stay with me for a little while, as soon as I get back to New York. Or Mom and Dad would love to see you."

"Thanks. I'll think about it," Geneva said. "I have to get ready for work, and it sounds like you need to hit the sack. Love you."

"Love you, too." Jessie put her phone on the charger and got ready for bed.

Gideon's inquiry about her sister had prompted Jessie's envy, but it seemed to be just the thing her sister needed. She should be grateful to Gideon for that.

It was just as well because Gideon was only interested in Geneva.

Perhaps that was exactly how it should be.

Twelve

Gideon rose early and dressed in his workout gear, determined to get in a session before his meeting with Matt Richmond later that morning. They'd had to cancel their planned meeting over drinks the night before due to an emergency conference call Matt had to take.

Gideon walked over to the main building from his luxury cottage on the property and used his key card to access the workout facility. When he stepped inside, he was greeted by an angelic voice.

Jessie was running on a treadmill wearing a headset. Oblivious to his arrival, she was singing her heart out. Gideon couldn't help smiling. He'd always loved the unique, husky tone of her voice.

He was frozen where he stood as he surveyed her.

Jessie looked incredible in her tiny workout shorts and racerback tank.

Long, lean brown legs that seemed to go on for miles. A curvy derriere and generous breasts that bounced slightly with each movement. Her dark brown hair was piled atop her head in a high ponytail.

After Jessie's icy reception the previous afternoon, he'd planned to avoid any further interaction with her. But seeing her now, he just couldn't walk away. Jessie had once meant so much to him. He thought he'd been important to her, too. He needed to understand what had changed.

He stepped onto the treadmill beside Jessie's. She was startled, but grabbed the sides of the treadmill and recovered mid-stride.

"I'm so sorry, I didn't… Gideon. Good morning." Once she recognized him, her demeanor shifted from open and friendly to polite but shuttered. She yanked the key from her machine and it ground to a halt. "I'll leave you to your workout."

Jessie turned to leave, but he caught her elbow as he'd done the day before.

"I know you have to prepare for tonight, but if you could just give me a few minutes."

"Why?" She looked at him defiantly.

"Because I need to know why it is that I couldn't have been more thrilled to see you yesterday, but you obviously don't feel the same."

Jessie tugged her arm free, but her demeanor

softened, and he saw a glimpse of the sweet young woman he'd once adored.

A chill swept up his spine as her gaze met his.

Jessie was sexy and gorgeous. She had an incredible voice and a regal presence.

Any man would be attracted to her.

But what worried him most as he stared into those big, beautiful brown eyes was that the feelings he'd tried so hard to ignore came rushing back. Feelings he needed to shut down, for both of their sakes.

Jessie's gaze swept down Gideon's physique. He was obviously no stranger to workouts. The fitted sleeveless shirt highlighted his strong arms and broad, muscular chest. His athletic shorts showcased a firm ass, strong calves, muscular thighs and the outline of his...

She raised her eyes to his quickly, meeting his dark, penetrating gaze. The image of a young Gideon Johns was permanently burned into her brain. But fifteen years later he was more handsome than ever.

As she surveyed his fit body and handsome facial features what she felt was desire, pure and simple.

But then, her feelings for Gideon had never been as simple as her physical attraction to him.

"The last time we saw each other—" Jessie tipped her chin and folded her arms "—you made it exceedingly clear you wanted nothing to do with me."

She'd gone to Gideon's apartment. Kissed him. Admitted that she wanted him. And he'd flatly rejected her.

"I know I could've handled the situation better, but you surprised me and I overreacted. You were my ex's sister. I didn't want to cause friction between you two. And if I'm being honest, I wasn't willing to take the risk of getting involved with another Humphrey sister. Your father didn't believe I was good enough for one of his daughters. I wasn't interested in going through that again."

Jessie's central memory of that day was how harsh Gideon had been toward her. He'd yelled at her. Something he'd never done before. His eyes had been filled with what she'd perceived as anger. Now she wondered if it'd been fear. "You should've told me how you felt."

Gideon sat on a nearby weight bench. "I knew you well enough to know you would've tried to convince me otherwise. I didn't want to hurt you, Jess. But I didn't want to be hurt again either. It seemed best if we both walked away and didn't look back. I hope you can understand where my head was that day. I realize, in retrospect, that I was an ass about it. I'm sorry for that."

The sincerity in his voice and dark eyes made her chest ache.

"The resentment I've harbored since then wasn't fair to you. So I'm sorry, too, Gideon."

"I'm glad we finally had this conversation." His broad mouth quirked in a half smile. "It's something I've wanted to say to you for a long time."

"Thank you, Gideon. It really was good to see you again." Jessie turned to leave.

"Wait." He sprang to his feet, standing between her and the door. "You're still leaving? Why?"

"I was practically done with my workout anyway." She folded her arms, her gaze not meeting his.

Gideon had glanced at her machine. He folded his arms, too. "You had thirty minutes left."

She smoothed back her hair. "I'm on a tight schedule this morning. I have to grab breakfast and get some practice time in on the piano I'm performing on tonight. Then I hope to wrangle a meeting with a couple of music execs who'll be here this weekend."

"Chase Stratton and Dixon Benedict?"

"Yes. How'd you—"

"I overheard Teresa talking to her assistant about them. Neither of them has arrived. Stratton's studio session got extended another day and Benedict is coming in a day late."

"Oh." Jessie's heart sank. She didn't regret taking the gig. The payday was more than generous and she was grateful for the chance to have this conversation with Gideon.

But this retreat was her best chance of connecting with her two dream producers.

"Look, if meeting them means that much to you, I'll talk to Matt. I'm sure he can arrange some—"

"No." The word came out more harshly than she'd intended. After all, Gideon only wanted to help.

He frowned, confused by her objection.

"I mean…thank you, but no. I prefer to do this on my own."

"I admire your spirit and determination, Jessie. But if I can do this for you—"

"Then I'd owe you."

Jessie hadn't meant to say the words aloud, especially not so bitterly. Her face stung with heat, remembering the day Arnold Diesman had offered to give her complete creative control on her next album, if only she'd play the game.

She'd considered Arnold a friend and mentor until the moment he'd tried to convince her that quid pro quos were the way things were done in the industry. That it wasn't a big deal.

"When I reach the pinnacle in my career, it'll be because I earned it. Not because I knew the right exec or because I'm beholden to a billionaire."

Gideon's thick, neat brows came together. He stepped aside. "I'm sorry I offended you."

Guilt knotted Jessie's gut. Gideon was a good guy who wanted to do a wonderful thing for her. She appreciated that. But doing this on her own was important to her, and she needed to spell that out to Gideon in no uncertain terms.

"You didn't offend me. I just need you to understand my position on this." After a few moments of awkward silence between them, she jerked a thumb over her shoulder toward the door. "I'd better go."

"Wait, Jess." He stalked over to where she stood near the door. "If you want to do this on your own, I respect that. Hell, I even admire it. But that doesn't mean two old friends can't catch up over breakfast, does it?"

Jessie turned to Gideon.

God, he's handsome.

He seemed eager to absolve himself of any guilt where she was concerned.

"I could meet you at the restaurant in an hour."

He glanced at his watch and frowned. "I have a business meeting then. What about now?"

"I'm not going to the restaurant looking a hot, sweaty mess. I have my public persona to consider." She smoothed her hair back.

Gideon nodded thoughtfully and shoved his hands in his pockets. The move pulled the panel of fabric tight over his crotch and inadvertently drew her eye there. "Room service in my room?"

Oh. My. Gawd.

Her entire body flushed with heat and she resisted the urge to fan herself with her open hand. When Jessie raised her gaze to his, he'd caught her checking him out.

He was more than a little pleased with himself. The smirk on his face reminded her too much of the one on Arnold's face the day he'd invited her up to his suite to strategize the direction of her career.

It was like an icy shower had been turned on over her head.

She wouldn't make the same mistake again.

"I don't think that's a good idea. How about breakfast in the restaurant tomorrow at eight?"

"Sounds good." He pulled out his phone and added their breakfast date to his calendar. He assessed her tentatively. "We should exchange numbers.

In case there's a last-minute change of plans for either of us."

Jessie rattled off her cell phone number.

He sent her a text message. "That's me. Call me if there's a change in your plans or…anything." A broad, genuine smile spanned his handsome face.

Jessie's heart danced. She was as drawn to him now as she'd been then.

Thirteen

Gideon folded the burgundy pocket square and placed it in the front pocket of his suit. Tonight's festivities would officially be under way in just a few minutes. He removed a pair of platinum cuff links from their felt jewelry box and pushed one through the hole of his custom-tailored dress shirt. He'd just put the other cuff link in place when his cell phone rang.

He checked the screen.

Landon.

Gideon answered the phone and put it on speaker before returning it to the bathroom counter. "What's up, Land?"

"Mr. Johns…"

Oh shit. This wasn't going to be good.

"I'm sorry to bother you while you're at the retreat," he continued. "But I'm afraid I have a bit of bad news."

"Is another investor considering bailing on the project?"

"No. I think I've done a good job of addressing any concerns they may have had."

"Then what is it?"

"Some issues have come to light regarding the owner of the construction company whose bid we planned to go with. I know his bid was considerably less, but concerns are now being raised about the quality of his work. Complaints that weren't available when we did our preliminary groundwork. Even if it turns out that the information is false—"

"There'll still be the perception that the builder employs shoddy materials and workmanship." Gideon cursed under his breath. "We have no choice but to go with option two."

"Which is nearly ten percent higher than the initial bid. We'll also need a bigger contingency."

Gideon's head was starting to pound. "Of course."

"I don't mean to push, but have you had the opportunity to sit down with Matt Richmond?"

"There's been a lot going on." It was an excuse he'd call bullshit on if one of his employees had offered it. But his breakfast meeting with Matt had been interrupted when his friend's assistant alerted him to a problem at Richmond Industries' Miami office. "We still have a few days, so don't panic, Landon. Besides, we have a bigger issue."

"Even if Matt says yes, I doubt you anticipate getting the full remaining investment from him," Landon said. "And the total amount needed has just escalated." The man was silent for a few minutes. "Mr. Johns... I've been thinking. In light of everything that's been going on with this deal...maybe the timing just isn't right for it."

"It's the nature of the beast, Landon," Gideon said calmly. "It doesn't matter if it's a tiny residential rehab, a towering skyscraper or a commercial complex. Shit happens. Sometimes it's a little. Sometimes it's a lot. And the bigger the risk, the more shit is going to hit the fan. It's as simple as that."

"So you're not worried?"

"It's my job to worry. I do that whether we're behind the eight ball or way ahead of the game." Gideon checked his watch. He needed to get over to the main building for the welcome party. He didn't want to miss Jessie's performance. "Your only worry should be doing your job and doing it well. Everything else will be fine. Now, I've got this under control. Go out and enjoy your weekend. We'll hit the second-tier potential investor list hard on Monday morning."

Landon agreed, sounding more upbeat.

Gideon ended the call, straightened his tie and got ready to join the party.

Gideon stepped onto the patio of The Goblet. The tented space was elegantly decorated. The patio was overflowing with some of the most elite and powerful captains of industry in the fields of technology, information science, entertainment and more. A four-piece live band stood on the stage playing soft jazz.

"Good evening, Gideon." Teresa grinned as she approached him. "What do you think?"

The woman had traded her usual pantsuit for an elegant silver dress with a low-cut back and crystal detailing on the front. Her blond hair fell to her shoulders in soft, beachy waves. She stood beside him and admired her work. It was one of the few times in the past two days that he hadn't seen the woman moving so fast on her designer high heels that she was practically a blur.

"It's quite lovely, Teresa. I'm impressed, especially since you've done this on such short notice." Gideon accepted a glass of red wine from a passing server and took a sip. "And holding the event at a boutique hotel with a working vineyard. That was a stroke of genius."

"It was, but sadly, I can't take credit for the selection of the location. It was Liam Christopher who suggested it." She nodded toward Liam, who stood on the far side of the patio, eyeing them.

The man acknowledged them with a quick nod. Then he averted his gaze and moved to talk to another partygoer. A beautiful redhead wearing a long, flowing green gown.

The slightest frown furrowed Teresa's brow.

Neither of them is exactly subtle. No wonder rumors are flying about them.

"I'd like to keep this venue on the map for a real estate investor retreat I'm planning next year. I'm fo-

cused on another project right now, but give me a call
in a few weeks. I'd like to do some preliminary planning. You did such an amazing job at my last party.
You are the only event planner I ever want to use."

Teresa beamed. She tapped out a memo on her
cell phone. "I'll have Corinne give Landon a call
later next week."

She nodded toward her assistant, who spoke animatedly to a member of the hotel staff. The woman
wore a long, simple black gown. Her corkscrew red
curls were pulled into a low bun.

The mention of his assistant reminded him this
wasn't just a social call. He needed to nail down
Matt Richmond's investment and identify a handful
of smaller investors.

Teresa excused herself to go and speak with one
of her staff members.

Gideon finished his drink, then moved toward
Matt and Nadia, who stood together near the center
of the party. Now wasn't the time to pin Matt down.
But he could continue to sow seeds of interest and
perhaps reel in other potential investors.

He was embroiled in a lively conversation with
Matt, Nadia and two other guests when Jessie Humphrey swept into the space. She was stunning, steal-
ing his breath away in the midst of a conversation
about his most recent visit to Dubai and the building explosion there.

The flowing red floor-length gown had a simple
but lovely top with a deep vee that showed off the
buttery smooth skin of her toned brown shoulders.

The bottom portion of the dress boasted intricate beading over a sheer fabric that overlaid the satin skirt beneath it. The dress commanded attention and partygoers gave her a wide berth as she moved about. He'd venture that their reaction was as much because of the incredible beauty of this woman in her stunning ball gown as because of her celebrity status.

"Someone is certainly an admirer." Matt chuckled. "Pretty sure I've never seen you speechless before." He leaned in closer so only Gideon and Nadia could hear him. "I could introduce you."

"Not necessary." Gideon loosened his tie and cleared his throat. Suddenly the space seemed much hotter than it had been before Jessie arrived. "We're already acquainted. In fact, we have a breakfast date tomorrow morning."

Matt's and Nadia's eyes widened.

"There must be a story there." Nadia smiled. "Why don't I take these gentlemen to meet our guest of honor. That should give you a chance to tell it."

Matt gave his wife a quick kiss on the cheek before she ushered the other men toward Jessie.

"Nadia is working with Teresa now, isn't she?" Gideon inquired.

"As a contractor, not an employee. But not at this event. Teresa insisted that she should just enjoy the event with her husband. And I couldn't agree more. But don't change the subject," his friend teased. "You certainly didn't waste any time getting to know Jessie Humphrey."

"Actually, I've known Jessie for many years," he

clarified. "I dated her older sister, Geneva, when we were teenagers."

"Well, baby sis is all grown up now." Matt nodded toward her.

Amen to that.

Gideon sighed without response, his eyes trailing Jessie as she flitted about the room meeting party-goers.

She is so damn beautiful.

A partial updo allowed soft spirals to spill down one side of her lovely face. Her makeup was perfect. Naturally luminescent rather than overly done. Her eyes sparkled and her teeth gleamed as she flashed her brilliant smile or launched into the contagious laugh he remembered so fondly.

The woman was mesmerizing and she exuded confidence, which made her sexier still.

He was in serious danger of falling for her.

Jessie smiled and nodded as she mingled with a few of the guests before her performance. It was part of her contract.

Not that she wouldn't have mingled with the party-goers anyway. She'd just prefer to wait until after she'd performed, so that she could remain focused.

Despite being most comfortable onstage in front of an intimate audience, she still tended to get nervous before she performed. But the jitters she felt and the fluttering in her belly had more to do with the tall, dark, handsome man standing on the other side of the room staring at her.

Jessie hadn't met Gideon's gaze, but she'd angled her head so that she could study him. His tasteful black suit, complete with vest, fit his large, muscular frame well. A burgundy tie and pocket square were the perfect choice. And the shoes…gradient burgundy and black oxfords with an elegant style and shape that made her reasonably sure they were a pair of Corthays.

"Will you be performing songs from your current album tonight, Jessie?" a beautiful blonde woman in an elegant white dress asked eagerly.

"A few." Jessie kept a smile plastered on her face. It was a sore point. Of course people wanted to hear her perform the bubbly pop hits that they'd heard on the radio. But that wasn't what she wanted to play. "At an intimate event like this, I try to provide something you can't experience listening to a Top 40 pop station. So I'll also be performing new material."

The woman squealed, gripping the arm of the handsome man accompanying her. "I can't wait to tell all my friends I was one of the first people to hear Jessie Humphrey perform an original song. Would you mind taking a selfie with me?"

"Not at all." Jessie smiled graciously and stood beside the woman.

This part never got old. Sure, there were times when she just wanted to sit in peace and enjoy her dinner or get onto a plane in her sweats and baseball cap without being spotted. But in those inconvenient moments she always reminded herself to remain grateful. And she remembered how badly she'd wanted her name on that marquee, instead of solely in the songwriting credits.

After taking several photos together, the woman thanked her.

"You look absolutely stunning, Jessie."

Her spine stiffened at the sound of the smooth, honeyed voice that washed over her and made her pulse race and her spine tingle.

"Good evening, Gideon." She turned to face him.

The man was even more handsome up close, and he smelled absolutely divine. Jessie had the urge to lean forward, press a hand to his broad chest and inhale his delectable scent.

He bent toward her and whispered in her ear, "You're the most beautiful woman in this room, and you are incredibly talented. You're going to kill it tonight."

Jessie's face warmed as she inhaled his masculine scent and absorbed the heat radiating from his body. She smoothed down her skirt with trembling hands.

"Thank you, Gideon." Her words were soft, meant only for him. "You saying that…it means a lot to me."

"I'm only stating the obvious." Gideon seemed pleased by her admission. "Look, I know you have to mingle with the crowd, but I'd love to buy you a drink and chat later, if you have time."

"That would be wonderful." Jessie gave him a reserved smile, then watched as he disappeared into the crowd. Her body tingled with desire for this man. That certainly hadn't changed. But getting involved with Gideon was a bad idea.

* * *

The sun had just gone down when Jessie sat on the bench in front of the gleaming baby grand piano. Matt Richmond had introduced her and escorted her onto the small stage. She scanned the glamorous, well-dressed crowd of people eagerly anticipating her performance.

She hadn't seen Chase Stratton or Dixon Benedict in attendance at the event yet. It was disappointing, but it wouldn't change how she approached her performance. She would be authentic and give the audience her very best, leaving it all on the stage.

That was her policy for every performance, be it as the opening act on a stadium stage or in a small club that could barely accommodate a baby grand piano.

Jessie started to play the chorus of an older song of hers that she didn't intend to sing. She leaned into the microphone mounted over the piano.

"How are we doing tonight, beautiful people?" she asked in a soft, intimate rasp that prompted the crowd to shout variations of *good* or *fine*.

"That didn't sound very convincing, now did it?" she teased. The crowd laughed in response. "Why don't we try this one more time. I said, how are you incredibly beautiful people feeling on this amazing starry night?"

The crowd shouted back more enthusiastically.

"Now that's what I'm talking about." She nodded. "And are we having a good time tonight?"

The audience shouted back *yes,* many of them holding their drinks up as they did.

She started the set by playing snippets of a few of the songs she'd written for top acts. Something that always got the crowd going. Then she amped up the party by playing a couple of the songs from her recent album that had made it onto the pop charts.

Jessie played the bluesy intro from her first EP as a bridge to the emotional, deeply sentimental songs she'd play next.

"This next song is one of the first songs I ever wrote." Jessie continued to play the piano as she spoke. "I was a shy teenager and I'd had my heart broken for the first time." The audience *aw*-ed in unison. "I know, right? We've all been there. But it wasn't all bad. Because if it hadn't happened, I don't know if I'd be sitting here with you tonight."

Many people in the audience nodded as if they could relate.

"So I picked up my scented gel pen." The audience laughed. "Hey, I was still a teenager, y'all." She laughed, too. "But I picked up this pen and I decided to write some poetry. I wrote my little heart out and it was…trash." She laughed. "Utter and complete garbage. I filled two wastebaskets trying to get my thoughts on paper in a way that empowered me and healed my broken heart just the tiniest bit. Eventually, I wrote something that felt right, except it didn't quite feel complete."

She dramatically played the chords that made up the chorus of the song she was going to sing, and people cheered and clapped with recognition. Then she returned to playing the intro.

"It needed that little oomph. It needed music. The kind of music that touches people's souls. So I converted my sad little love poem into lyrics, and I wrote the bars of the chorus. The rest worked itself out from there. So if you've ever had your heart broken, if you've ever needed someone to remind you that no matter how bad it feels right now, it's not the end of the world, this song is for you." She scanned the crowd, pleased by their enthusiastic responses.

"The sun will shine again tomorrow. And when you wake up, in all of your fabulousness…" She waved one hand over the crowd. "You'll get the chance to eventually get it right. Whether it be with the same person—" her gaze involuntarily met Gideon's "—or with someone new."

Jessie launched into the opening bars of "Next Time I'll Get It Right," her voice strong and clear. She sang the song with every bit of her heart and soul. Just the way she'd written it. It gutted her every time she told the story of this song. Every time she performed it. But tonight it felt surreal, performing the song that had launched her songwriting and eventually her singing career. Knowing the man who'd inspired it was standing in the crowd, just a few feet away.

Fourteen

Jessie's pulse raced after the extended applause from the audience at the end of her performance. Regardless of how many people were in the crowd or how long she'd been doing this, an enthusiastic response was always exhilarating.

Matt Richmond returned to escort her off the stage. He and Nadia were gracious hosts.

She'd taken official photos with them before she'd gone onstage. Afterward, they both raved over how much they enjoyed her performance. Nadia even confessed that back when she was hopelessly in love with Matt, who also happened to be her boss, she'd taken solace in Jessie's songs.

Jessie returned to the party to mingle and take photos with many of Matt Richmond's business friends. After taking what felt like her hundredth selfie of the night, she was finally standing alone. Gideon, who'd been watching from his perch on a barstool all evening, approached her.

"I've been listening to your albums for the past few weeks, and I have to tell you, I didn't think you could possibly top the recordings. But that live performance was brilliant. It was intimate and gut-wrenching. Yet you left us on a positive note. It was truly outstanding."

"You've listened to my music?" Jessie had never given thought to whether Gideon was out there in the world listening to her music. He'd loved rock and hip-hop. What she sang was neither.

"Absolutely. I'm not stalking you on social media or anything, but I've followed your career enough to know you've written some pretty damn amazing songs for the biggest artists out there. You're unbelievably talented, Jessie. Guess those piano lessons your parents made you take paid off after all." He chuckled softly.

"Guess they did." Jessie couldn't help smiling, remembering how she'd whined and complained because Geneva didn't have to take lessons. "Of course, they're disappointed that I'm not making *real* music." She used air quotes.

Gideon's expression soured. His voice was suddenly tight. "How are Mr. and Mrs. Humphrey?"

He grabbed two glasses of champagne from a passing server and handed her one.

"As pretentious as ever." She accepted the champagne flute with a bitter laugh. "Though my mother isn't above musing to her friends about just how close she came to having a billionaire for a son-in-law."

Gideon frowned. "I doubt your father shares that viewpoint."

Jessie sipped the bubbly liquid. It tickled her nose.

"My father believes that had he not deemed you unsuitable for his daughter, you'd never have developed the drive to become a self-made billionaire." She hated repeating her father's words, but she wouldn't lie to Gideon. Besides, after his history with Milton Humphrey, she couldn't imagine that he'd have expected anything less of him.

"I've often contemplated that very thing." Gideon took a healthy sip of his champagne. He shrugged. "Maybe he's right."

"I don't believe that for a minute. Look at what you've accomplished over the last fifteen years. I refuse to give my father credit for all of that."

"I'm not saying I would be in the same situation I was born into. I know I would've made something of my life, if for no other reason than I loved your sister and would've done anything to give her the life to which she was accustomed. But this…" He took another sip. "I suppose I should thank your father for proclaiming me unworthy of his daughter."

They stood together quietly, drinking champagne and watching the crowd move around them.

Jessie set her empty champagne flute on a passing tray and rearranged the large flowing skirt of her beautiful designer dress. The ballroom gown took up so much space between them. But perhaps that was a good thing. It gave her room to breathe in a space where his close proximity and subtle masculine scent already seemed to overwhelm her.

The band had set back up and started to play again. Couples were filing onto the dance floor.

Gideon set his empty champagne flute on a nearby tray, then extended his large palm to her. "Care to dance?"

Jessie's gaze went from his offered hand to his incredibly handsome face and the dark, penetrating eyes that seemed to look right through her.

She couldn't speak. She nodded, placing her smaller hand in his, and followed him onto the crowded dance floor.

Gideon took Jessie in his arms and they swayed to the music in silence. He still found it hard to believe that the woman he was holding in his arms now was the same sweet, awkward girl with the big smile and beautiful spirit he'd once known.

It'd been one thing to see Jessie in a video or on an album cover. But standing with her now felt surreal.

It felt odd to be swaying with the beautiful woman she'd become and feeling such a deep attraction to her. And she was obviously still attracted to him.

His relationship with Geneva had ended long ago and she'd certainly moved on. He saw no reason he and Jessie couldn't explore their feelings.

"I guess I should thank you for not outing me as the lout who broke your heart back then." His lips grazed her ear as he leaned down and whispered the words in her ear.

"You're assuming you were the impetus for the song." Her back tensed beneath his fingertips. "I never said that."

"True." He nodded. "But I've been listening to the lyrics from that EP. It reminded me of conversations we've had."

"I write songs as a way to tell my story, not as a way to humiliate anyone else." She met his gaze. "I'm not a fan of revenge songs. Mostly because the people who've become famous for them tend to have a thin skin when the tables are turned."

"I agree," he said. "But I'm grateful just the same. I'd hate to become known as the cad that broke Jessie Humphrey's heart. Especially since it's the last thing I ever intended to do."

"I realize that now." Jessie dropped her gaze.

"What happened that day prompted you to become a songwriter. Just like your father's harsh dismissal set me on my path." He smiled faintly. "I guess there's some truth to those clichés."

"Like when one door closes, another opens," Jessie volunteered. "That was my grandmother's favorite."

"Mine, too." He smiled, thinking of the woman who'd meant so much to him. "We were destined to take separate paths, but I'm grateful they've crossed again."

"So am I." Jessie's eyes glistened with emotion as they danced beneath the stars.

He held her closer and she laid her head on his chest as they moved together.

She smelled like a field of flowers in spring and it felt good to hold her body against his. The attraction he'd felt for Jessie when he'd first seen her yesterday afternoon had only grown stronger.

He was glad they'd cleared the air. Perhaps they'd laid the foundation upon which they could rebuild their friendship. But as he held her in his arms, it was impossible to deny that he wanted more than just friendship with Jessie. If they could manage it without damaging this fragile thing they were rebuilding.

There was something about this beautiful young woman with an old soul who touched people's hearts. He wanted more than just a night or two with Jessie. But he had no reason to believe she wanted the same.

Jessie was thrilled Gideon was happy about their unplanned reunion.

She certainly hadn't felt that way initially. A feeling that was compounded by his inquiry about their family, in what she'd suspected was a sly bid for information about her sister.

But nothing about their conversations since made her believe Gideon was angling for a chance to renew his relationship with Geneva. So perhaps she'd been wrong. Especially since his reaction to her yesterday and tonight made it clear he was attracted to her.

She'd concentrated so much of her energy on her anger toward Gideon. But once that raw, jagged emotion dissipated, her heart was filled with the warmth and affection she'd once had for him.

Jessie had been thinking of him since their encounter in the gym that morning.

How would Gideon react if she kissed him tonight?

She was no longer a teenage girl crushing on her older sister's ex. She was a grown woman fully capable of entering into a consensual fling.

And that's all it would be.

Gideon had his life in Seattle. She had hers back in New York. But the desire to be with him burned strong. He was still the man she compared every other man to in the back of her head.

"You told me that Geneva is married, but you didn't tell me anything about yourself. Is there a special guy waiting for you back home?"

"No." Jessie's spine tingled, hope filling her chest. "What about you? Is there a Mrs. Gideon Johns?"

Gideon laughed, as if it were a ridiculous question. "No," he said finally. "Maybe that's because I've been so focused on chasing the next deal."

"With all the success you've had, I'm surprised you're not thinking of retiring to some tropical island. Maybe starting a family. And you've never been married."

Jessie wanted to take back those last words as soon as she'd uttered them.

"So you've been checking up on me?" Gideon grinned.

"Only after we talked in the gym this morning.

And I might have a financial magazine or two at home with your face on them."

"Somehow it makes me feel better that, even when you were angry with me, some part of you still cared enough to wonder what was going on in my life. I've always wondered about yours."

"And Geneva's," she said. It wasn't a question. He'd known her sister had lived in Switzerland. His information just hadn't been up to date.

"And Geneva," he repeated the words. "There was a time ten years ago, after I'd made my first million in real estate, that I wondered if there wasn't still a chance for us. I considered calling her up."

"Did you?" Jessie stared at him intensely.

"No. I flew to Zurich instead, planning to surprise her and sweep her off her feet."

A knot tightened in Jessie's stomach. "What happened?"

"I went to see her with a big bouquet of flowers in hand. But as I approached her flat I saw her with someone else. It was obvious he'd spent the night and she was seeing him off. I felt foolish for making the trip. For assuming that she'd want me."

"So you never really got over her. Is that why you never married? Because you were holding out hope that you and Geneva would eventually get back together?"

"No." The denial wasn't nearly as convincing as his earlier one. "We were never meant to be. I've made peace with that."

Jessie's gaze snapped to his. "What if Geneva weren't married?"

"She is."

"What if she weren't?" Jessie insisted.

"What I felt for Geneva...that was a long time ago. Truthfully, your sister was right. We wanted different things in life, even then."

Jessie gnawed on her lower lip in silence as she stared at the handsome man who held her in his arms.

What if she could finally trade her fantasies and what-ifs for a night in Gideon's arms? In his bed?

It was a thought that had consumed her all afternoon. But if Gideon still had a thing for Geneva, she'd be setting herself up for heartache, despite her intention to walk away at the end of their weekend.

Besides, she'd spent one evening with Gideon and she was already allowing his presence to distract her from her focus. She was here to convince Chase and Dixon to work on her project. But she'd spent the entire night drowning in Gideon's eyes and fawning over him.

"Thank you for the dance, Gideon. I should mingle with some of the other guests." She pulled out of his embrace. "And I need to check with Teresa to see if Chase or Dixon has arrived."

"Of course." He nodded, shoving a hand in his pocket. "I won't be able to make it for breakfast tomorrow morning due to an important business meeting. Maybe we could have a nightcap later?"

Jessie wanted to accept his offer. To whisper in his ear exactly what she'd imagined so many times.

But it would be a mistake. When he learned that Geneva would soon be free, he'd choose her instead.

"It's been a long day and I'm still jet-lagged. Another time maybe?"

"Sure." Gideon smiled, but his eyes revealed his disappointment. He kissed her cheek. "Good night, Jess."

She made her way to the other side of the covered patio, away from Gideon Johns.

Fifteen

Fifteen

Gideon watched Matt's reaction as the man surveyed the prospectus that Landon had put together for
him on the Dubai deal. After trying to meet with Matt
twice already this weekend, he'd arranged for them
to have room service breakfast at his private cottage.

It was the best way for Gideon to minimize the
interruptions as he tried to finalize Matt's partici-
pation in the deal.

"How much do you have on the line on this one?"
Matt asked calmly as he sipped his coffee.

"Everything." Even Gideon was taken aback by
his frank response.

He wasn't one to rely on a pitiful song and dance
in order to get investors on board. Not even when the
potential investor happened to be a friend.

"Not monetarily, of course," Gideon added when Matt regarded him skeptically. "But my reputation and the future of my company are riding on this deal. I won't lie to you, Matt. A couple of major investors pulled out recently. Not because of anything having to do with the deal itself. This deal is solid. We've done our homework on this and expect to see one of our greatest returns to date."

"Then why'd those two investors pull out of the deal?" Matt folded his arms, his brows knitted.

"Both men were spooked by volatilities in their industry. Teaches me a lesson going forward. Don't rely too heavily on investors from a single business sector. If market changes negatively impact that industry, the deal could go under."

"Makes sense." Matt nodded. "But I'm looking to invest ten million max in this deal. How do you plan to make up the shortfall?"

"Landon and I have been working the phones tirelessly for the past two weeks. We've secured most of the required funding for this deal. Once you're on board, I'll just need a few additional investments."

"And?" Matt looked up from cutting into his omelet.

"I've got phone meetings lined up for those this afternoon." Gideon took a bite of his crepe. He spoke calmly.

No pressure.

Despite the fact that he needed Matt's investment in order to complete this deal, his friend wouldn't be making this commitment as some favor to him.

It was an excellent opportunity for Richmond Industries to make an awful lot of money. That's what he'd focused on during his presentation to Matt. The solid return this deal offered with a relatively quick turnaround.

Matt picked up the prospectus and thumbed through it again in silence. Gideon didn't interrupt. He just kept eating his crepe and drinking his orange juice. As if all of this were no big deal.

"Okay." Matt put the folder down and looked squarely at Gideon. "I'm in. Send the paperwork to my office. Our attorneys will review it and then we'll cut you a check. Anything else I need to do?"

"No. We'll make this as convenient for you as we can," Gideon said nonchalantly. "The paper work will be waiting for you when you return to Seattle."

Matt shook his hand. "I look forward to finally doing business with you. It's been a long time coming."

"It has." Gideon kept his voice even, despite wanting to do a victory dance worthy of an end zone. "Welcome aboard."

"Speaking of something being a long time coming, it seems that your reunion with Jessie Humphrey was worth the wait." Matt took the final bite of his omelet.

"It's been great seeing her again. We were able to clear the air. Hopefully we'll rebuild our friendship."

"Friendship?" Matt's eyebrows drew together. "I saw how you were looking at her. Seemed like more than friendship to me. A couple of guys asked if you two were an item. They were hoping to ask her out."

"Who wanted to ask her out?" A knot formed in his gut and his hands clenched into fists.

"See, that face right there—" Matt laughed as he pointed to him "—that's definitely jealousy. You want to tell me again how she's just a friend?"

Gideon cut another piece of his crepe without responding. No need to add fuel to the fire. Matt was already enjoying this way too much.

"It's more serious than I thought." Matt finished his coffee. "You usually have a much better poker face. I should know. I've lost to you enough times because of it. Does Jessie know?"

"Does she know what?" Gideon tried not to be irritated with his friend. After all, the man had probably just saved his Dubai deal. "That I want to be friends again?"

"That you see her as more than a friend or a weekend hookup. I've seen you with both. Neither has ever produced anything nearly as intense as the vibe you're giving off right now or the aura surrounding you two on the dance floor last night."

"Vibes? Auras? Really, Matt?" Gideon teased his friend. "Next you'll be telling me the stars aligned to bring us together this weekend."

"Sounds more like something Nadia would say than me, but I can't disagree. Maybe this was the whole point of that disastrous mudslide at the original event. If that's the case, I've got a pretty hefty bill I'd like to send you." Matt climbed to his feet.

"Ha, ha, ha." Gideon stood, too. "You're a regular comedian."

"Nope. I'm just a guy in love who recognizes it when I see it in another guy. Especially one who still has no clue that he's already in over his head." Matt smiled broadly. "I have to prepare for my presentation with Liam later this morning. So I'd better go. Thanks for breakfast and for bringing me in on this deal. I'm excited about it."

"One more thing." Gideon drew in a deep breath, knowing he shouldn't ask but unable to stop himself. "The two music producers who are here—"

"Dixon Benedict and Chase Stratton. What about them?" Matt frowned. "Looking for more investors?"

"No, it's nothing like that. Do you think you'd be able to arrange a meeting with the two of them?"

Matt smirked knowingly. "You mean do I think I could secure a meeting for Jessie with the two of them?"

If he wanted to prove to Matt that he wasn't into Jessie he was doing a shit job of it. "Yeah."

"I'll see what I can do." Matt shook his hand again and left.

Gideon was as disturbed by Matt's observation about him and Jessie as he was excited to tell Landon they were close to finishing the deal.

Jessie was smart and beautiful and she made him laugh. Of course he was interested in her. He'd thought a lot about what would happen if she tried to kiss him again.

This time, he wouldn't stop her.

The image of Jess lying in his bed beneath him had kept him up, tossing and turning, all night.

Gideon grabbed his phone off the coffee table and dialed Landon. He would focus on the business at hand and let things with Jessie take their natural course.

Whatever that might be.

Jessie sat at the piano playing one of the songs she'd written for her new album. She was still tweaking the key in which she should sing it.

Teresa had confirmed that both Chase Stratton and Dixon Benedict had arrived at The Goblet the previous evening. She didn't think either of them had been there for Jessie's performance. But Teresa expected both men to be at the gala that evening and had promised to get them a table in front of the stage.

Jessie needed to deliver the performance of her life and impress both men. And she needed to stay laser-focused on her primary reason for taking this gig: securing the funding and ideal producers for her independent album.

She'd chosen to bet on herself, rather than accept a soul-sucking record deal. Or trade her integrity for the deal she wanted. *Everything* was riding on this project.

She wanted to create a collection of songs that would become part of the soundtrack of people's lives. If she succeeded, labels would be knocking down the door to offer her a deal. And she would establish her right to retain creative freedom on future projects.

The album needed to be brilliant enough to receive critical nods and outsell her last album, despite limited distribution. It was a skyscraper-tall order. But big-name producers like Chase and Dixon could help her get wider distribution than she could on her own, even with her past success.

She needed to remember what was at stake tonight for her career rather than obsessing over Gideon. What he meant to her then. The mistakes they'd both made fifteen years ago. How he'd react if she proposed a weekend tryst.

Jessie sucked in a deep breath, her head spinning as her hands moved across the keys. She hit the wrong note, then banged on the piano keys in frustration.

She couldn't lose focus, lost in thoughts of Gideon. It was a cruel catch-22, because the song she hoped to wow Chase and Dixon with was one that had been inspired by Gideon's rejection that day. Born of all the pain, hurt and anger she'd felt and the realization that it was time to let it all go and move on.

It was ironic that he'd waltz back into her life after she'd written that song. The universe had one hell of a sense of humor.

"Okay" was the most raw, emotional song she'd written to date. She needed to tap into the pain and loss she'd felt that day. And she had to transport the audience to that place where they could connect to their own experiences of love and loss.

It had been unnerving to perform with Gideon in the audience last night. Especially when she'd introduced the song that had clearly been about her feelings for him. But tonight, most of her planned set featured songs that would force her to relive those intense feelings. She'd be playing them all out in front of the man who'd inspired them.

She couldn't hold back any of those raw emotions. Her authentic sound and poignant delivery were what set her apart from her pop diva peers. So she would lean into whatever feelings arose and ride the wave of those emotions.

A piece of her hoped Gideon didn't show tonight. Then she could lay her heart out on the stage for everyone except him to see.

She doubted she would be that lucky.

The only thing that mattered was that Chase and Dixon would be there for the performance. They needed to understand what she was capable of. If she could manage that, she wouldn't need to convince them. They'd be clamoring to work with her.

"Jessie, is everything all right with the piano?" Teresa approached her with a platter containing a mug of tea and a saucer. "You're certainly deep in thought."

Jessie hadn't realized she'd stopped playing. She was sitting there as if the entire world weighed on her shoulders.

No wonder Teresa was worried.

"Everything is good. Thank you." Jessie took a sip of the warm chamomile tea the woman handed her. "In terms of attention to detail and anticipating the needs of the guests, you're one of the best event planners I've worked with. If you weren't on the West

Coast, I'd hire you to plan the album release party once I'm done."

"Thank you, Jessie." Teresa beamed. "And thank you for agreeing to do this event. After the disaster at The Opulence, I wouldn't have blamed you if you'd turned me down."

"Well, you did sweeten the deal." Jessie laughed. "I can't thank you enough for getting Chase and Dixon in the room for tonight's performance."

"I'm glad we could make it happen. If you give them even half of what you gave us last night, they'll both be *begging* to work with you." Teresa looked up when the banquet manager called her name. "I'd better go. Call me if you need anything. We want to build up the drama of your performance tonight, so don't mingle with the guests beforehand this time. Let's save it until after your set. If you could arrive in the staging area about an hour before go time, we'll make sure everything is ready."

Jessie thanked Teresa. Then when she had the space to herself again, she closed her eyes and let her fingers travel over the keys.

Sixteen

Teresa stood at the back of the auditorium late Saturday morning as Matt and Liam sat at the center of the stage concluding their talk on their new joint AI venture, the Sasha Project. The room was nearly filled to capacity. At the end of their presentation, they were greeted by thunderous applause.

The retreat was going better than either she or Matt had expected. More than half of the guests invited to the original retreat were able to attend, despite the short notice. They'd expanded the guest list to tastemakers and change agents in other industries. People like Chase Stratton and Dixon Benedict, both of whom had finally arrived and were seated in the auditorium.

After a quick update from Corinne and two other

members of her team, Teresa's next stop was the
kitchen. She consulted with the chef on the gala dinner menu. They also reviewed all of the special meal
requests of various guests. It seemed that nearly a
third of the attendees had dietary restrictions, but the
chef and his staff had everything well in hand.

Chef Riad offered to prepare her a lovely pasta
and chicken dish so she could have a quick, early
lunch. It would probably be her only chance to grab
a bite until later that evening.

Since it was such a gorgeous day, he suggested
that she enjoy her lunch on the patio beside the pool,
where he'd have it delivered.

It was the perfect suggestion. She could get a little sun, enjoy the gardens and inspect the pool to
ensure that everything was as it should be. As she
approached the large heated outdoor art deco pool,
Liam emerged from beneath the water.

She nearly dropped her cell phone at the sight
of him.

*The man is a ridiculously perfect physical speci-
men.*

He strode in her direction, his lips pressed into a
subtle smirk. The black Versace swim trunks he wore
were imprinted with a gold Barocco scroll print and
the iconic Greek key print at the waist. The length
of Liam's swim shorts showed off his strong thighs,
while the band at the waist highlighted his firm abs.

Liam ran his fingers through his dark hair, plastered to his head. His light blue eyes beamed in the
sunlight.

"Good morning," he said finally, obviously pleased by her reaction to his barely clad body.

A tingle of electricity ran down her spine and she involuntarily sank her teeth into her lower lip. Thoughts of when she'd last seen him wearing that little filled her brain, and her body ached for him.

Damn him.

"Good morning," she stammered. *Get a hold of yourself, girl.* "The Sasha Project announcement went well."

"It was great to finally make it public. But as soon as we were done I needed to clear my head. So I went for a swim." He accepted two towels from the pool attendant and thanked her.

Liam wrapped one towel around his waist and hung the other around his neck, drying his hair.

"You know Nicolette Ryan, don't you?" Liam nodded toward a beautiful woman stretched out on a lounger beside the pool with her bare legs crossed.

Liam collapsed on the chair beside her and she offered him one of the two drinks that a poolside server had just delivered.

The muscles in Teresa's back and neck tensed. Her free hand clenched in a fist at her side.

Nicolette Ryan. The reporter. What the hell was Liam doing cozying up with her?

Had Liam been the one who'd leaked the photos and information about Teresa to the press? Was he playing some sick game to drive her away before she could liquidate her shares in Christopher Corporation?

"Good morning, Teresa." Nicolette waved cheerily. The woman's brown eyes sparkled and her dark hair was smoothed back into a low bun. Her creamy, light brown skin shone. "Thank you so much for granting me a press pass for this event. The grounds are remarkable and Jessie Humphrey's show last night was one of the best live performances I've ever experienced."

Teresa forced a smile, despite her tense shoulders. "Glad you could make the retreat on such short notice."

Nicolette gave her a knowing smile. "I wouldn't have missed it."

She lay back, stretched out in the warmth of the sun and closed her eyes.

Teresa gritted her teeth. She looked for a patio table that would allow her to eat in peace without seeing or hearing Liam and his new friend.

She plopped down in one of the wrought iron chairs at a patio table beneath a large umbrella and sulked.

No, she and Liam weren't a couple. And she had no right to dictate what activities he engaged in and with whom. Still, she couldn't help the churning in her gut, thinking of Nicolette and Liam doing God knows what together.

She cast a sideways glance in their direction. Heads together, they were engaged in a private conversation. One to which they obviously didn't want her to be privy. She could barely hear them whispering in hushed tones. For a moment, she regretted selecting a table so far away.

"Here you are, ma'am. Chef Riad's special chicken Alfredo, just for you." The server set down her plate and laid out her silverware. He poured a bottle of sparkling mineral water in her glass.

Teresa wished he'd shift just a little to the right so she could see exactly what Liam and Nicolette were doing.

Spying on Liam wouldn't help her sanity with all that was already going on. What she needed was distance.

"I'm sorry, but would you mind if I moved to the cabana the hotel gave us access to for the weekend?"

The server politely gathered everything up on his tray again before heading over to the cabana.

Once he was gone, Teresa ate her meal in peace, trying hard not to wonder about Liam or his new-found interest in the beautiful reporter.

"I feel terrible about the photos that leaked after the blackout at The Opulence." Nicolette Ryan sipped her piña colada. "And those awful headlines. They weren't fair to you or Teresa." She nodded toward the woman who'd moved to the other end of the pool.

Without turning his head, Liam glanced in Teresa's direction in time to see her get out of her seat and follow the server to one of the more secluded cabanas.

"Liam." Nicolette called his name impatiently, as if it wasn't the first time she'd had to say it.

"Yes, I'm sorry. I was just…thinking." He took a gulp of his Manhattan. He turned to face her fully. "So you think someone has it out for me?"

"At this point, I'm not sure if their grudge is against you personally or against your father's company. It's even possible that Teresa is the real target of this cruel game someone is playing."

Liam frowned, glanced involuntarily over his shoulder at the cabana that Teresa occupied. If someone had it out for her…why? Had she done something questionable in her past that would make someone want revenge? If so, just how far would they go to make her pay?

"Teresa could be in danger."

"I don't know." Nicolette shrugged. "But I'd suggest that you both operate on the side of caution. Someone has definitely been asking around about the two of you and inquiring about her history with your father."

Nicolette adjusted her lounger, sitting upright. "People often discount me because of the topics I cover. Celebrities, fashion, Hollywood and society gossip," she said bitterly. "But I operate with integrity. *Always*. I don't want to see you or Teresa get hurt. Nor do I want to see either of your reputations ruined. Watch out for unscrupulous reporters and paparazzi. They're like sharks, circling in the water, sniffing out blood."

"Who has been asking about me and about my father? If you know that someone is asking, surely you know who it is."

"I don't have all of the details." She shifted her gaze from his and sipped her drink.

"There's something you know, but aren't telling me." Liam studied Nicolette's face.

Her brown eyes wouldn't meet his. "I have to protect my sources. I've already told you too much. In fact, I'd better go and get ready for lunch. Mr. Richmond doesn't want his guests hounded by the press this weekend, but a few have agreed to talk to me. I have some interviews lined up."

"Wait, Nicolette." Liam placed a hand on her arm. "Surely there is something else you can tell me."

Nicolette scanned the space before returning her gaze to his. "I'm not one hundred percent sure who is behind this, but it's quite possible that the source is much closer to you than you think. If I were you, I'd be careful about who I trust."

"I will." Liam ran a hand through his damp hair. "Thank you for sharing what you could."

Nicolette slid on her shades, gathered her things and headed inside the hotel.

A source close to him?

The number of people he could trust not to keep secrets from him steadily decreased, starting with his parents. His father had pulled the rug from underneath him by leaving Teresa 25 percent of Christopher Corporation stock. Then there was the even bigger secret…

When Linus Christopher lay dying in the hospital, Liam had caught a glimpse of his father's medical records. Linus's blood type was listed as AB. He hadn't given it much thought at the time. But later it occurred to him that his own blood type was O. If the information in his father's chart was accurate, there was no way Linus Christopher was his father.

Parents were often hesitant to reveal to their children that they were adopted. But he wasn't a child. He was a thirty-two-year-old man who needed to know his medical history. So if he was adopted, why hadn't his parents told him the truth?

After his father's funeral, Liam had asked his mother, Catherine, about the discrepancy. She insisted the hospital chart had been mistaken. And she assured him he was their biological son.

Still, he couldn't stop thinking about it.

Maybe his mother was right and the admitting staff had made an egregious error. But then there was the emotional distance he'd always felt between himself and his father. It had never made sense to Liam. But if the medical chart was to be believed, his father's resentment suddenly made sense.

Then his father had gone and left a quarter of the company's shares to Teresa—a virtual stranger. It only fueled his suspicion that he may not be a Christopher after all.

Seventeen

The Richmond Industries fifth anniversary event was going off without a hitch. The accommodations and food were fantastic. The guests were all well-behaved and seemed to really be enjoying the experience. And the hotel staff's customer service was unparalleled. Teresa couldn't have asked for anything more.

Liam had been a genius for suggesting this venue and a saint for using his pull to secure the hotel for her on such short notice.

Teresa closed her eyes against the memory of Liam and Nicolette whispering together beside the pool. Despite her growing affection for the man, he didn't trust her, and without that, they had no future.

She needed to get her head in the game and focus on her work at Limitless Events and the Christopher

Corporation. That should be enough to keep her busy so she didn't think about Liam or how incredible his body had looked dripping wet.

Her phone buzzed. She lifted it and checked the new text message.

Speak of the devil.

Urgent. Meet me in my cottage in ten minutes. Need to speak with you in private.

Teresa frowned. Why couldn't Liam have asked her to meet him at the bar or even beside the pool?

Because none of those areas offered true privacy. And from the sound of his urgent text, the issue was sensitive and meant only for her ears. Still, going to see Liam Christopher in his cottage was a profoundly bad idea.

Teresa dialed Liam's phone, but the call rang until it went to his voice mail. She called it twice more and got the same.

Teresa frowned and tucked her hair behind her ear as she made another sweep of the lobby to ensure everything was fine. She gave a few quick instructions to the staff setting up lunch in the banquet hall and followed up with Corinne and Evelyn Montague. Then she made her way across the property to Liam's cottage.

She knocked on the door, but there was no answer. Teresa knocked again, miffed that Liam had sent her such a cryptic text but now wasn't answering his phone or the door. She was just about to turn and leave when Liam answered.

"Sorry, I was in the shower. Got sidetracked by an unexpected call." He answered the door with a towel slung low on his waist. Droplets of water from the shower still covered his body. "Come in."

Liam stepped aside to allow her into the room, then he glanced around the courtyard.

"Liam, what's going on?" Teresa demanded, her arms folded. "Were you checking to see if I was being followed?"

"Yes." He took the towel draped around his neck and dried his hair.

"By whom?"

"That's what I'd like to know." He went into the kitchen and pulled out a bottle of water, offering her one.

"No, thank you." Teresa went to the window and peeked outside. She pulled the curtains closed once she was convinced no one was there.

The man was seriously making her paranoid.

"Then why would you think someone is following me? And what's up with the cryptic text? I have a million things going on right now. So spare me the drama and tell me what's happening."

Liam excused himself to go into the bathroom and change, leaving her to pace in the living space, which opened to the bedroom. She found herself staring at the bed. Thoughts of the nights they'd shared filled her brain. For one happy moment she had truly believed that they could have something more. Something real.

But there was so much baggage between them. Her history with his father. Liam's inability to trust

people, ingrained in him by his mother. The terms of
his father's will and the suspicion and animosity that
had created between them. The rumors that threatened both of their reputations and her livelihood.

"Is everything all right?" Liam placed a gentle
hand on her arm, startling her. She hadn't even realized that he'd emerged from the bathroom. "I called
you a couple of times but you were in a daze."

"I'm just running everything about tonight's gala
through my head. Trying to make sure I didn't forget
anything." There were enough secrets between them.
She hated adding an inconsequential lie to the mix.
"So you were going to explain the text."

"Right." He stepped away, creating space between
them. As if he needed it as much as she did. "You
might've noticed that I had a chance to chat with Nicolette Ryan, the lifestyle reporter for—"

"I know who Nicolette Ryan is, Liam." She folded
her arms, her jaw tight. "I issued her press pass."

"Yes, of course," he conceded with a little smirk.
He seemed to be getting a kick out of her spurned-
lover routine. "The reason Nicolette wanted to speak
to me so urgently was because she wanted to warn
me...*us*, really."

"About?" Teresa raised an eyebrow.

"Nicolette doesn't believe that the leaking of those
photos and videos of us was just some random act
by someone trying to make a buck." Liam sat on the
white sofa. "She thinks that someone has a calculated agenda to destroy one of us."

"Or perhaps both." Teresa sank onto the other end of the sofa and turned to him. "But who and why?"

"That's what we need to put our heads together and figure out," he said. "And soon. Preferably before they strike again and do more damage to our reputations and organizations. Christopher Corporation can easily ride out the current scandal, but if something else like this happens..."

"Limitless Events will be dead in the water." Teresa raised her eyes to his. "What do we do? I've invested everything I own in this company. I can't afford for it to fail. Too many people are counting on me. My staff, my family..."

"I know." Liam placed his large hand over hers, resting on the sofa between them. "And I'll do everything in my power to help keep that from happening. I hope you believe that."

Teresa nodded. "I do. You've already done so much. Getting Jessie Humphrey to The Opulence despite the weather. Getting this place for us on such short notice. You didn't have to do any of that."

Liam gave her a reluctant nod. He stood, pacing the floor. "We both need to be aware that there are unethical reporters out there who'd do anything to get a big story and some of them don't give a damn about the facts. They just want a juicy, salacious story, regardless of how fictitious it might be. I'm sure that people like that would think nothing of employing spies to get dirt on us or our companies. Perhaps even people we know and trust." He stared at her pointedly.

"You think there's a spy in my camp? Like one of my employees?" Teresa was incensed by Liam's suggestion. "I handpicked each and every member of my team. I'd vouch for any of them."

"I get it. They're good people. Seemingly trustworthy. But people aren't always who they seem."

"Like the fact that I'm not the home-wrecking gold digger you believed me to be?" She folded her arms, one brow raised. "Or that you're not the ogre I once thought you were?"

"Yes, people can surprise you for the better," Liam admitted. "But they can also stun you in truly terrible ways. We can't discount the probability of that."

Teresa stood, too. "Why do you automatically assume it's someone from my company? It could just as easily be someone from Christopher Corporation."

"True." He nodded sagely. "But aside from Duncan, I don't have a relationship with my employees that's quite as familiar as the one you have with yours. There's some truth to the saying that familiarity breeds contempt." He rubbed his jaw.

Teresa shook her head vehemently. "I still don't believe it. Besides, why would they do something that's jeopardizing their livelihood? I can see the fear in their eyes, Liam. They're all just as concerned as I am about the impact these rumors will have on the future of the company. I'm telling you, no one at Limitless Events would've done this. *No one*," she said again for emphasis.

Liam didn't try to hide his exasperation over her

unwillingness to believe one of her employees had sold her out for a quick payday.

"Maybe they are really honest, loyal, hardworking individuals." Liam focused his gaze on hers. "But if someone has an agenda against one of us, it's possible they'd stop at nothing to achieve their end. Even if it meant blackmailing someone close to us. Perhaps even threatening to harm a member of their family."

"Joshua..." Teresa pressed a hand to her forehead.

"You think your brother might've been compromised?" Liam asked. "Could that be why he went missing when you got that crank call about him?"

When she'd gotten a mysterious call implying that her brother may have been kidnapped, she'd confided that to Liam. He'd offered to have his investigator check into it and it turned out to be a hoax.

"Josh would never do anything to hurt me. Certainly nothing like this." Teresa didn't believe for a minute that her brother would be party to destroying her career. "Besides, he doesn't know about us. We haven't spoken in a while, and I certainly wouldn't tell my little brother that you and I..." Her eyes darted involuntarily to the bed in the other room. "It just couldn't be him, that's all."

Teresa paced the floor, her back to him. As soon as she left Liam's cottage, she needed to call her brother.

"Okay, if we can't figure out who, let's approach the other side of this."

"Which is?" Teresa turned back to Liam, studying his face.

He ran his hands through his dark hair and his expression offered an unspoken apology. "I need you to be completely honest with me, Teresa. Is there more to the story about what happened between you and my father? Are there any more stories that are likely to come out?"

It hurt that Liam felt the need to ask the question again. That he still didn't fully believe her though she'd told him the unvarnished truth. She was never romantically involved with his father. Linus Christopher had been nothing more than a friend and mentor to her.

"How many times and how many ways do I have to say it?" she seethed. "I did *not* have an affair with your father. I wouldn't. And I never saw him as anything other than a mentor. I hadn't seen Linus in years. I'm as shocked as you are that he'd leave me twenty-five percent of the company."

Liam grimaced when she mentioned the portion of the company she held. "I believe you about my father," he said quietly. He didn't want to ask about her father's connection to Christopher Corporation until Dutton gave him more to go on. "But is there anything else you might have to worry about? Anything that might cause a problem for your company or mine? Because, as you indicated, you now own a quarter of the company. So it's not just Limitless that's in jeopardy."

"I do have secrets." She shrugged. "Doesn't everyone?"

Liam stepped closer. "But is there anything that could be damaging to the reputation of Christopher Corporation?"

"I already told you about my brother and his problems. That he got in trouble with some dangerous people in Vegas and owed them a lot of money."

"The trouble that the Fixer helped you get him out of." Liam folded his arms and frowned. "It isn't ideal, of course. But we could probably find a way to spin the story. Everyone loves the story of a person who would go to bat for their family, at all costs."

"It isn't a story, Liam. It's the truth. Maybe this is all just about bad press to you, but this is my life." Her voice broke and tears burned her eyes. She swiped a finger beneath one eye, trying not to ruin her makeup. "Not that you'd understand."

"Teresa, wait…"

Before he could stop himself, Liam had caught her hand in his. She turned back to look at him. Hurt and disappointment filled the lovely blue eyes he'd found himself drowning in just a few short weeks ago.

"I realize how difficult this must all be for you. I didn't intend to come off as an insensitive, self-centered boor." He rubbed his thumb over the soft skin on the back of her hand. "I've been groomed my entire life to think of Christopher Corporation first and everything second…including the people in my life. I never much liked being on the receiving end of that treatment. That's something I need to remember going forward."

Teresa nodded, looking at him thoughtfully. The night the tree crashed on top of her, he'd told her about the rocky relationship he'd had with his parents. Had admitted how painful it was for him growing up. So he knew she understood what he meant. He appreciated the compassion in her eyes.

"There is one other thing I should tell you." She dropped her gaze from his momentarily. "The only reason I didn't reject your father's gift of shares in the company is because the man who made the threatening phone call about my brother implied that Joshua owed someone money. A lot of it."

"How much?"

"The caller said seven million dollars. I knew Joshua owed some money a long time ago, but I thought when the Fixer bailed Josh out, those debts were settled, too."

It was all starting to become clear to Liam. "So you'd like to have the money on hand, just in case."

"Yes." More tears rolled down her face and her cheeks turned crimson, as if she was embarrassed by showing emotion in front of him. She swiped at the tears angrily with her free hand.

"You didn't have to tell me that." Liam couldn't help staring at her firm, kissable lips. "Why did you?"

She looked at him squarely again. "Because I don't want there to be any secrets between us."

Liam cradled her cheek, wiping away her tears

with his thumb. He stepped closer to this beautiful woman who had an uncanny gift for making him feel an array of emotions. Anger, frustration, lust, jealousy, pain and a deep, growing affection that seemed to squeeze his chest whenever he thought of her.

He leaned in so slowly it felt as if he could hear the seconds ticking in his head. Teresa didn't object. Instead, she leaned closer, too. Her eyes drifted closed.

Liam pressed his mouth to hers and kissed her.

Teresa let go of his hand and relaxed into him, her hands pressed to his chest as she angled her head, giving him better access. He trailed kisses across her salty, tearstained cheeks. Then he pressed a soft kiss to her ear.

"Why is it that I can never resist kissing you?" he whispered.

"Maybe it's the same reason I can't help wanting you to kiss me." Her breathy reply did things to him. "Or stop thinking about the nights we spent together."

He kissed her again, and she parted her lips to him, inviting him to deepen the kiss. He obliged, his tongue gliding against hers. He reveled in the sweet, minty taste of her warm mouth.

The kiss that had started off slow and tentative escalated. The hunger in his kiss was matched by the eagerness in hers.

Her arms snaked around his waist, and her fingers pressed into his back, pulling their bodies closer. He wanted her. Hadn't been able to stop thinking about her. And he'd used nearly every excuse he could manufacture to spend time with her.

Everything he'd been taught from the time he was a boy told him he shouldn't trust her. That he should resent her intrusion into his life and the way she'd insinuated herself into his family's business.

But another part of him found Teresa to be a breath of fresh air in a world filled with self-important blowhards whose bank accounts were the most interesting thing about them.

She made him feel things he hadn't felt before. Things he wanted to feel again. So despite the promise he'd made to himself, he wanted to taste her skin. To experience the passion they'd shared as they brought each other mind-blowing pleasure.

Liam broke their kiss, his eyes searching hers for permission. Teresa sank her teeth into her bottom lip, her breathing ragged as she removed her suit jacket and tossed it over the chair. She turned her back to him, giving him access to the zipper of her bustier.

He leaned in and pressed a soft kiss to her neck and shoulder as he unzipped the fabric, threaded with a metallic silver. He tossed it on top of her suit jacket in the chair. His hands glided up her belly as he kissed her shoulders. He palmed her breasts.

Teresa whimpered. Her knees buckled slightly and her curvy bottom pressed against him. He slid the zipper down the side of her slim gray pants. She kicked off her heels, standing in her bare feet and a silvery gray lace thong.

He turned her around, pressing another kiss to her mouth as he lifted her. She wrapped her lean legs around him as he carried her to the bed.

Liam stripped off his clothing, thankful the boutique hotel provided a welcome kit that included a handful of little foil packets. He sheathed himself, then tugged off the little scrap of lace and dropped it to the floor.

He kissed her. Savored the sensation as her body welcomed his. Her fingers dug into his back as he drove deep inside her. Their bodies moved together. Their murmurs of pleasure growing more intense as they each hurtled closer to their edge.

Teresa froze, her fingernails scraping his skin as she called his name. The contraction of the muscles deep in her core sent ripples of pleasure up his spine that brought him over the edge.

He cursed, his body trembling as he collapsed on the bed beside her, struggling to catch his breath.

Neither of them spoke.

Finally, he rolled over and propped his fist beneath his head as he lay facing her. He trailed a hand down her stomach. "That was…" He blew out a breath, words escaping him.

A smile lit her eyes. "It was, wasn't it?"

"It always is between us."

Teresa's phone rang. She glanced at the clock on the wall, then cursed beneath her breath and climbed out of bed.

"I have to get back." She gathered her clothing.

"Of course, but do you have to go this instant?" He hoped for an encore as soon as he recovered.

"Yes." She rushed into the bathroom, but smiled over her shoulder at him. "But I'll take a rain check for later tonight."

He grinned, already counting the minutes.

Eighteen

Teresa smoothed the gorgeous blue floor-length Zac Posen fishtail gown she'd gotten for a steal down over her hips. She took one last look in the mirror as she carefully applied her matte red Dior lipstick. Then she dropped the tube in her clutch.

Today had been hectic. She'd handled several last-minute preparations, headed off potential problems and resolved a few unusual guest requests. But there were two events that had shaken her the most during the course of the day. Learning that someone may be acting on a calculated vendetta against her and…

Teresa's body tingled with electricity as it seemed to relive the trail that Liam's strong hand had taken as it moved across her skin. She'd allowed herself to be pulled under again by her attraction to him.

Not just because he was an incredibly sexy man. Though her eyes drifted closed briefly at the memory of Liam emerging from the pool in those swim shorts. She was attracted to him because, despite the distrust and bravado, at his core he was a sweet and thoughtful man. He'd come to her aid in countless ways in the past few months. Many of which he hadn't even wanted her to know about. He'd done it simply because she needed the help.

Still, were their physical attraction, similar interests and the fact that they enjoyed spending time together enough to overcome Liam's issues with trust and the nasty rumors out there about her?

Teresa pushed the disquieting thoughts from her mind. She had a gala to manage. And tonight would go off without a hitch.

She'd do whatever was necessary to ensure it.

"Teresa."

Matt approached with Nadia on his arm.

Teresa had brought Nadia on at Limitless Events as a contractor when it became evident that she wouldn't be able to keep her job as Matt's assistant once they became involved. She was smart, resourceful, hardworking and trustworthy. Which made her the perfect fit. But this was her husband's event, so Nadia was a client, too, serving as Matt's official cohost.

Nadia looked gorgeous in a strapless red gown with her blonde hair twisted in an elaborate updo. And despite his disdain for suits, the man wore an athletic-fit tuxedo that highlighted his muscular physique.

"This weekend has been fabulous. A wonderful way to celebrate Richmond Industries' fifth anniversary. It was a great call having the retreat here. Almost makes the disaster we endured last month worthwhile." He chuckled, his arm wrapped around Nadia's waist.

"It truly has been a wonderful weekend." Nadia's gaze met Matt's.

Her brown eyes glinted in the light and her cheeks flushed as her husband drank her in. As if he were seeing her for the very first time.

"You've honestly outdone yourself, Teresa." Nadia finally turned to meet her gaze. "Thank you for all of your hard work. With such short notice for the rescheduled event, I know it wasn't easy. Quite frankly, this was something of a miracle. Far more than we expected, given the timeline."

She nudged Matt, who was looking at Nadia dreamily once again.

"You've done outstanding work, Teresa. We'll be in touch to discuss the plans for our next retreat."

Matt excused himself and he and Nadia walked away to greet their guests.

Teresa was thrilled that Matt was so pleased. Just a few more hours and she could put this event in the books as a phenomenal success.

"Teresa St. Claire, I'm Brooks Abbingdon." A tall, handsome man with curly hair approached her. His wide smile gleamed. "We don't know each other, but—"

"Of course I know who you are, Mr. Abbingdon." Teresa smiled. "You're the CEO of Abbingdon Airlines, one of the fastest-growing private airline companies in the country." She shook the hand he'd extended.

"And you're the woman who put this incredible event together in just two weeks." Brooks grinned.

He was handsome with creamy, light brown skin. His dark hair had a natural curl and he towered over her at well over six feet in height. His liquid brown eyes and gleaming broad smile were simply mesmerizing. No wonder the man had a reputation as something of a playboy.

"I didn't do it alone, of course. I have an incredible staff." Teresa could barely contain her smile. After what she'd been through these past few months, it felt good to have everything going so smoothly and to receive such heartfelt acknowledgment from Matt Richmond and now Brooks Abbingdon, one of his high-powered guests.

"I'm sure you still have lots to do tonight, Ms. St. Claire, so I won't take up too much of your time." Brooks stepped closer and lowered his voice. "I'd like to discuss the possibility of engaging your services for an upcoming event."

"Call me Teresa." Her belly fluttered with excitement. A new, high-profile client like Brooks Abbingdon was *exactly* what Limitless Events needed right now. The success of the Richmond retreat and being tasked with planning an event for the popular bachelor could be just the thing to pull her company out of the sharp decline that began because of the recent scandal. "Thank you for considering Limitless Events. May I ask what kind of event you're planning?"

He grinned and his eyes, the color of dark, rich coffee, twinkled. "My wedding."

"Congratulations! I didn't realize you were engaged."

Teresa liked to keep up with the latest on the wealthy and powerful of Seattle. Especially when the news meant that they might need her services.

"I'd be honored to work with you to plan your wedding. If you give me the basics—your fiancée's name, the time of year you'd like to get married, the date, if you've set one, and any ideas you have about your ideal wedding—my assistant will work up some preliminary ideas to present to you when we get together."

Teresa pulled out her phone and started typing an email to Corinne.

"I appreciate your enthusiasm," Brooks said. "But I realize how busy your team must be. This is Matt's event, so I won't impose on his time, but I'll definitely be in touch."

Brooks flashed his megawatt smile and walked away before she could object. He was headed right for Nicolette Ryan, who had set up in a lovely area of the hotel lobby to interview some of the guests as background for her coverage of the retreat.

Not surprising.

The man could teach a master class on how to manipulate the press to one's advantage and have them love you for it.

Besides, he was right. She had a million things to keep watch over, beginning with making sure that Jessie had arrived in the staging area and would be ready to perform in less than an hour.

Liam stood by the bar and watched couples swaying on the dance floor to a big band song the musicians were playing. The retreat had been outstanding, and the announcement of the Sasha Project that morning had gone well, but the Saturday night gala was simply phenomenal.

The decor was modern glitz and glamour that played upon the Old Hollywood feel of the hotel's art deco style. And hiring a group to play big band songs and Rat Pack standards was a stroke of genius.

The food Chef Riad prepared had surpassed his expectations and The Goblet's private-label wine produced at the on-site vineyard was one of the best cabernets he'd ever had. It was so good that he'd forgone his usual Manhattan for the evening.

Liam caught a glimpse of Teresa as she darted through the crowd in search of the next fire to be put out. He wasn't sure how, but the woman seemed to get more gorgeous each time he laid eyes on her.

The stunning blue dress she wore complemented the color of her eyes and fit her body like a glove. It was sleeveless with a low neckline, so it showcased her strong arms and provided just enough cleavage to make his imagination go wild.

Only he didn't need imagination. He'd seen the full show and it was spectacular. Memories of that body haunted him in the middle of the night when he lay in bed alone, wishing she were there beside him.

Satisfaction washed over him when his gaze met Teresa's from across the room. Her eyes danced and a soft, sexy grin curved one corner of her mouth.

It took every bit of self-control he could manage to stay rooted in place when what he wanted more than anything was to pull her into his arms and kiss her. To remind her of what they'd shared earlier in the day when he'd made love to her in his cottage.

In fact, as wonderful as the event had been, he couldn't wait until it was over so he could take her back to his room and have her again.

"She looks amazing in that dress, doesn't she?" Nadia stood beside Liam. They both stared at Teresa as she dealt with one of the other guests.

"She does." Liam sipped from his wineglass and kept his response even. "As do you in yours." He nodded toward his friend's wife. "And nearly every other woman in this room, for that matter."

"Yes, but you are not staring at me or any other woman in this room." Nadia gave him a knowing grin. "You're staring at one woman in particular. And it seems that she is quite taken with you, too." Nadia cocked her head, watching Teresa for a moment. Suddenly the woman's eyes lit up. "Why don't you ask her to dance?"

"She's working and I—"

"The party is pretty much under control, and I know for a fact Matt wouldn't mind. So ask her." Nadia nudged him. "If you don't, I have the feeling you're going to regret it."

The woman sashayed off in her strapless red gown with her blond hair twisted up. Nadia was a beautiful woman and his best friend was a lucky man.

Perhaps she was onto something with her suggestion.

Liam finished the last of his wine and made his way to where Teresa stood near the back of the room monitoring the gala.

"You look stunning." He stood beside her, both of them watching the band on the stage. Liam placed a discreet hand low on her back and whispered in her ear. "But I happen to know for a fact that you'd look even better out of it."

Her cheeks flushed and she grinned. "You look pretty good yourself." She gave him a quick, sideways glance. Her grin deepened. "In or out of the tux."

Teresa surveyed the crowd, as if she was worried about who might be watching the two of them together.

Liam hated that it had come to this between them. They both needed to protect their business interests and their reputations. He realized that. But by allowing some shadowy figure to control their actions, they were giving the person power over them. Emboldening him to do who knew what next.

On the other hand, if they behaved as if the rumors had no effect on them, perhaps the culprit would realize he hadn't succeeded and just move on.

"I'd better go," Teresa said, pulling away from him.

He tightened his grip on her waist. "Don't. At least, not yet."

"Why not?" She turned to face him, a look of panic in her eyes.

The band played the opening chords of Frank Sinatra's "The Way You Look Tonight" and Liam smiled.

Perfect.

He removed his hand from her waist and extended it to her. "Dance with me."

"What?" She looked at him as if he'd lost his mind. "You want me to dance with you? Here? Where everyone can see us?"

"Yes to all of the above." He smiled. "This is my favorite song, and I can't think of anyone I'd rather dance to it with tonight."

"That's sweet, Liam." Her expression softened into a dreamy smile for a moment, but then she glanced over to the spot where Matt and Nadia stood. "But aside from all of the other reasons it isn't good for us to be seen dancing together, I'm working, remember?"

"Let me worry about Matt, okay?" He nodded toward the dance floor. "Come on. Just one dance. That's all I'm asking."

"One dance." She slipped her hand in his. "But

don't expect me to kiss you in the middle of the dance floor this time."

Liam burst into laughter, remembering when Teresa kissed him for the first time on the dance floor at Gideon John's party. It had been completely unexpected, but not unwelcome. He'd gladly kissed her back.

"Well, you never know. Maybe I'll kiss you this time."

They found a place on the dance floor not far from where they'd been standing. He took her in his arms and swayed to the music, singing along softly so only she could hear.

It felt right to hold her like this. To stop hiding and pretending that he didn't care for this woman as much as he did. It was obvious that they couldn't stay away from each other, no matter how hard either of them tried. So maybe they should stop fighting the growing feeling between them.

What was the worst that could happen if they just admitted that what they felt for each other was more than either of them had expected? That it was powerful and intense and worth exploring more fully, rumors be damned?

"This is one of my favorite songs, too." She tipped her chin to look up at him. There was a mixture of happiness and sorrow in her glistening eyes. "My mother listened to it when I was a kid. She and my dad danced to this song the first night they met. She plays it often, particularly when she's really missing my father."

"I'm sorry, sweetheart." He stopped singing and swaying to the music. "I didn't mean to make you sad."

"You didn't." She widened her smile and swiped the dampness from her eyes. "I hadn't heard the song in a long time. And I've never been serenaded with it before. It just struck me because…well, my mother always told the story of how my dad did the same thing the night they met. It just made me a little nostalgic."

"Happy memories, then?" Liam stared into her eyes, fighting the overwhelming desire to kiss her.

He wanted to articulate all of the feelings for her he'd been struggling with. But Teresa was here in a professional capacity, and he needed to respect that. Even if his body didn't.

"Happy-ish." She forced a smile.

"You haven't said much about your father," Liam noted, taking her in his arms again and slowly swaying.

"I guess I haven't. It's not something I talk about very—" Her phone rang and she gave him an apologetic frown. "I'm sorry, Liam, but I need to take this."

"Of course. You're working." He released her from his grip and shoved a hand in his pocket. "I understand."

She pulled the phone from her purse and read the screen. "It's Evelyn Montague. I'd better see what she wants. Besides, there are a few things I need to confirm about the farewell breakfast tomorrow morning. I have to go, but we're still on for later, right?"

"Nothing could possibly keep me away." Liam grinned. "I'll see you then."

Liam hated that Teresa had to go, but he thoroughly enjoyed the view as she sashayed across the room in that fitted blue gown, the fishtail hem swishing in her wake.

His body ached for this vibrant, brilliant, beautiful woman. In his head, they were already back in that cottage where his biggest problem would be finding the zipper so he could strip her out of that dress.

Liam went to the bar to order himself a Manhattan. As he sipped his cocktail, he silently assessed the crowd.

He felt secure in his decision not to allow the coward hiding in the shadows to dictate his life. But a small part of him hoped like hell he hadn't just thrown gasoline on the fire by pissing off whoever had an ax to grind with either him or Teresa.

Nineteen

Jessie paced the greenroom as she warmed up her voice and reviewed the final changes she'd made to both the lyrics and the musical arrangement of the song she'd be singing for the audience. Tonight's performance had to be absolutely perfect.

Teresa had confirmed that both Chase Stratton and Dixon Benedict were out in the crowd mingling. Dixon had even mentioned to Teresa that he was eager to hear Jessie perform live. In addition to the two dream producers for her project being in the audience, Teresa had informed her that entertainment reporter Nicolette Ryan would be broadcasting her performance live from her show's website and social media pages.

The live broadcast meant that tonight's performance had the potential to either be a viral sensation or a hot, flaming mess that could spawn a dozen memes and make her an industry joke.

Jessie preferred to believe it would be the former, not the latter. She just needed to showcase her songwriting and voice together in a way the syrupy pop album hadn't permitted her to.

Even if Chase and Dix passed on her project, maybe the live broadcast would capture the interest of another producer on her top ten list.

No. Don't think that way.

Jessie released a deep breath to drain the tension from her body. Tension in her jaw, chest and throat would make her voice tight and strained. In the bigger moments of the song, she'd sound like she was trying too hard instead of singing from deep down in the bottom of her soul. So she had to relax. Let go of all of her anxiety about the big moment ahead.

She smoothed her hands down the ethereal one-shoulder floor-length Laylahni Couture gown. Jessie had fallen in love with the dress the moment she'd laid eyes on it. She loved the contrast of the pale pink silk chiffon against her warm brown skin. And there was something so Old Hollywood about the twisted tulle overlay, embroidered skirt and bodice, and short but elegant train.

The gown made her feel beautiful, but also strong. She was a woman who was completely in control of her destiny. All she had to do was give an honest, raw performance. Leave it all out there on that stage for everyone to see.

Jessie continued her vocal exercises and warmed up her wrists and fingers.

With her entire future riding on this performance, Jessie tried not to think about Gideon being in the audience. Nearly impossible since her brain had been flooded with thoughts of Gideon all day. She couldn't help wondering how he felt about her and whether he was truly over her sister.

A mood which matched the raw, personal song she was unveiling tonight. "Okay" explored the pain of being in love with a person who loves someone else.

She wasn't a starry-eyed teen anymore and she now had a renewed understanding of their past. So why did this song still sum up exactly how she was feeling? And how would she react to singing those words with Gideon just a few yards away?

Lean into it. Use it as fuel.

Jessie drilled the words in her head again and again. She tried to release the apprehension rising in her stomach. To ignore the lingering feelings for the man who clearly still wasn't over her sister.

No matter how deeply she'd buried her feelings for Gideon over the years, they kept resurfacing. Maybe it was the same for Gideon where Geneva was concerned.

Even if he did have feelings for her, what did she expect to come of it? He had his life back in Seattle and she had hers in New York. She'd seen what happened to other female artists when they'd gotten serious about a rich and powerful man. It meant the death of their careers. And when the relationship was over, and it inevitably was, the woman was left to resurrect her career from the smoldering ashes.

That wasn't the fate Jessie wanted for herself.

Choosing Gideon meant *not* choosing her career. A career she'd worked for her entire adult life. One she wouldn't walk away from just because she'd reunited with her old crush.

Gideon had moved from his table near the stage and taken a seat at the bar at the back of the room. He didn't want to be a distraction to Jessie. He understood how much was at stake.

He sipped the whiskey he'd ordered neat. Gideon welcomed the heat building in his chest as the smooth liquor with a fiery bite washed down his throat. It'd been fifteen years since that incident with Jessie, and the shock of her kissing him felt as fresh now as it had then. But now he found himself in a completely new dilemma.

He felt something for Jessie. Something deeper than friendship or physical attraction. Something he wanted to explore. Yet the prospect of getting involved with his ex's sister gave him pause.

How would Geneva react to him and Jessie being together?

The last thing he wanted to do was cause animosity between the sisters. Nor did he want anyone to think this was some sick attempt to get back at his ex.

And what if things did work out between him and Jessie? He'd have to find a way to let go of his resentment of her parents.

Gideon took another swig of his whiskey. He should be celebrating right now, not agonizing over his feelings for Jessie.

Despite all of the drama, they'd secured the remaining funding for the project in Dubai and managed to pull the deal off. Construction would begin on time.

This was when he normally celebrated with a perfectly aged bottle of bourbon and the warmth and comfort of a beautiful stranger. But he hadn't looked at another woman since he'd laid eyes on Jessie.

It had driven him crazy to watch the men here fawning all over her last night. Most of them had no real interest in her other than the bragging rights of having slept with a celebrity.

He'd wanted to tell her last night that the tables had turned. That it was him who desperately wanted her. For a moment when they'd danced together, he believed she wanted the same thing. That she would be open to spending the evening with him, even if all they did was catch up on each other's lives.

But then Jessie had started asking questions about Geneva. Fishing to see if he had any lingering feelings for her sister. He'd answered her questions honestly. That included admitting he'd gone to Zurich ten years ago with hopes of rekindling what he'd thought they once had.

The evening had quickly gone off the rails from there.

After Jessie's performance, he would tell her the truth. Geneva had been his first love, so he'd held on to a romanticized view of their relationship. But they'd been too different from the start, and those differences had expanded over the course of their relationship. He'd tried to hold on to her by asking her to marry him.

It would've been a mistake.

One that would've left them both miserable and resentful. Altered the course of his life in ways he didn't want to imagine. He and Geneva were both exactly where they should be. And he was convinced that Jessie's reappearing at this point in his life was meant to be, too.

It would be a mistake to dismiss what he and Jessie were feeling just to spare Geneva's feelings when she was more than five thousand miles away.

Now if only he could convince Jessie of the same.

They announced Jessie's name and she emerged onstage to the sound of thunderous applause, aided by the fabulous acoustics in the room.

The sight of this woman, more beautiful than he could have ever imagined, stole his breath away.

Jessie wore an exquisite rose-colored gown worthy of anyone's red carpet. The goddess-style gown had a sheer overlay that covered one shoulder and added an elegant dimension to the dress. The fabric hugged her hips and dropped straight to the floor, but formed a short, graceful train behind her. And the dusty pink color popped nicely against Jessie's flawless brown skin.

She wore her dark brown natural hair in loose ringlets that dusted her shoulders. She'd captured the attention of everyone in the room and she hadn't even opened her mouth.

Jessie took a seat at the piano, adjusted the microphone and greeted the crowd. She went right into one of the songs from her recent pop album. But not one of the ones that got frequent airplay. It was a soulful tune about the highs and lows of being in love called "Nobody But You." As she sang about a love that, even in the tough times, was better than the best times with someone else, he couldn't help wondering who'd inspired that song.

Whomever it had been, Gideon couldn't help feeling a twinge of jealousy. For the first time in a very long time, he yearned for that kind of relationship. The kind that made you eager to return home at the end of a long, busy day because the person you loved was there waiting for you.

Jessie played the crescendo of the song, and the pounding of the keys brought him out of the daze he'd gone into. If he was looking for someone who'd be waiting for him at the end of a long, hard day, he'd set his sights on the wrong woman. He was in Seattle and she was in New York.

Gideon owned properties in New York, Miami and Los Angeles and on the beach in Costa Rica. Place wasn't the biggest challenge to exploring a relationship with Jessie. It was their careers.

He'd be making frequent trips to Dubai to oversee the deal and when the album was done, Jessie would undoubtedly spend several months out on tour.

How could they expect to make a life together when they wouldn't be on the same continent?

He was in a very different place in his life now. This weekend, he'd been quietly observing the joy and contentment of men like Matt Richmond. No longer moving from one conquest to the next, Matt seemed genuinely happy.

And for the first time in his life, as he watched the men around him on the hunt, he recognized the faint emptiness in their pursuits. Something he'd long felt deep down inside, though he'd always ignored it.

He'd focused on the high of the next big deal and the solitude at the bottom of a well-earned glass of whiskey. The temporary comfort and fleeting company offered by a pretty face.

He didn't want to live that way anymore.

Maybe it was because of Jessie. Or maybe it was a realization that had been a long time coming. Either way, he wouldn't let Jessie walk out of his life without telling her how he felt.

Gideon was mesmerized by her soulful performance. Her melodic voice had range. She was capable of going low with a voice that was gritty and raw. But she could also hit notes in her upper range that were simply angelic. Her lyrics touched him in a way no performance ever had.

He watched her onstage, completely rapt by her performance, like nearly every other person in that room, including the two producers she was so eager to meet with.

"Thank you so much." Jessie seemed genuinely

shocked by the enthusiastic applause that just wouldn't die down after her last song. "You all have been such a wonderful audience. So I'd like to show you my appreciation by sharing a new song with you that I haven't performed for anyone else. It's called 'Okay,' and I hope you like it."

Gideon finished the last of his whiskey and set the glass down on the bar as he turned back to the stage. For the first time that night, Jessie's eyes met his as she sang the opening lines of the song.

"You were the only one I ever wanted. Your heart was the only one that spoke to mine. But it was never me that you wanted. You loved the one I stood behind."

Her words and the pain in her voice and in her eyes as she said them felt like a punch to the throat. But he couldn't look away, no matter how deeply the words cut.

She turned her attention to Chase and Dixon, who seemed just as rapt by Jessie's performance.

Jessie's voice was raw and powerful. You could almost hear a pin drop in the space as she performed the song.

Her eyes met his again as she sang the chorus. "You deserve to be happy, for that I'll be glad in time. Right now my heart is still aching, but just know I'm gonna be fine. Because I'm okay, okay. Even though my heart is still breaking. I'll be okay, okay. So for that, love, one day I'll thank you. Because I made it to the other side…okay."

He'd wanted to stand up at the back of the room

and tell her right there in front of everyone how damn sorry he was things worked out the way they did between them. That he hated that it took fifteen years for them to find each other again. That the time was right for a second chance for them.

Instead, he placed his hand over his heart, then blew her a kiss.

Her eyes widened and she acknowledged his gesture with a quick smile, the emotion in her voice intensifying. When she was done, the entire room erupted with applause and Dixon Benedict jumped to his feet. The rest of his table and the rest of the room quickly followed.

Tears glistened in Jessie's eyes. "Thank you all so much. This has been such a tremendous night and I just want to say…"

Suddenly Jessie froze, her eyes filled with fear as a man babbling incoherently made his way to the front. He hopped on the stage, swiped the microphone from Jessie's hand and started to yell into it, his speech slurred.

Gideon sprinted toward the stage as quickly as his legs would carry him.

Twenty

It felt like everything was moving in slow motion. Liam had been lost in thought as he listened to Jessie Humphrey sing about loving someone you wanted to be with, but couldn't. He didn't see the man until he'd already climbed onto the stage.

Next, he saw Gideon Johns rushing toward the stage, leaping over a chair or two to do so. Liam was closer, so he jumped into action. He climbed onto the stage and tackled the man, who was still mumbling incoherently about rich liars and losers.

The man thrashed wildly. His elbow nearly caught Liam in the chin. Liam punched the man, knocking him out cold.

Liam shook his throbbing right hand and tried to catch his breath. "Jessie, are you all right?"

"I'm fine." She nodded. "How about you?"

"Jessie!" Gideon rushed onto the stage and gripped her arms. "He didn't hurt you, did he?"

"No, not physically." She turned to watch as the crowd was escorted from the room by members of the security team Matt had hired for the event.

"Where the hell were you guys *before* this drunk party-crasher leaped onto the stage?" Liam barked at the men, who lowered their eyes and continued to evacuate the room.

Gideon pulled Jessie against him as he stared at the man lying unconscious on the floor. It was as if he was waiting for him to climb to his feet so he could land his own punch.

Two members of the security team climbed onto the stage to assess the crazed man.

Another approached Jessie. "Miss Humphrey, I need to escort you to your room until we've assessed the threat."

Jessie turned away from the man and stared up at Gideon, her eyes wide. The poor woman looked traumatized.

"No." Gideon hugged her against him tightly. "She's staying with me. I'll see that she's okay."

Jessie gave him a grateful half-smile, then confirmed to the man that she was staying with Gideon.

The security man walked away reluctantly, then noticed Nicolette Ryan's cameraman with his camera still propped on his shoulder. "Are you still filming?"

Nicolette, who'd been staring at the stage in horror, was shaken from her daze. She rushed over to her cameraman and placed her hand over the lens. "Cut it. Now!"

He shut off the camera and the two made their way toward the exit. Nicolette turned back and mouthed "Sorry" to Jessie.

"Get me out of here, please." Jessie clutched Gideon's chest as she turned her head away from where other guests were filming the ruckus on stage as they filed out of the room. "Now," she pleaded.

"Have you got this under control?" Gideon asked Liam as he clutched Jessie, who'd buried her face in his chest.

"We're fine. Just take care of her." Liam wiggled his fingers, making sure none were broken.

"Thank you, Liam." Gideon shook his left hand, then escorted Jessie from the stage.

"I can't believe this." Teresa hurried toward the stage, going against the flow of the crowd. "I was in the kitchen speaking to Chef Riad when we heard screaming and people running. What on earth happened?"

"This dude crashed the party, climbed onto the stage and ripped the microphone out of Jessie's hand." Liam hopped down to the floor and pointed over his shoulder to the man still facedown on the stage. Liam shook his aching hand. "I had to sucker punch the guy before he hurt someone. He was behaving erratically, like he's on something major."

"Your hand is swelling." Teresa took his hand in hers gingerly and examined it. "We should get you to a doctor."

"I'll be fine." Liam shrugged. "I just need to submerge my hand in an ice bucket. Is there one around here somewhere?"

"At the bar, I'm sure. I'll take you back there and—" Teresa pressed a hand to her mouth and hurried onto the stage.

"Teresa, what's wrong?" Liam turned back to look at her.

She rushed toward the man the security guys had flipped onto his back. She dropped to her knees in her beautiful dress and hovered over him. Her hands were pressed to the floor on either side of the man's head.

"Josh, honey. It's me, Teresa. Are you okay?"

"Josh? As in your brother, Joshua St. Claire?" Liam stood in front of the stage.

"Yes." Teresa patted her brother's cheek, attempting to wake him. "I don't know what he's doing here or how he even knew where I'd be. We haven't spoken in weeks."

"Well, someone obviously told him where to find you." Matt Richmond approached them. He was clearly furious with Teresa. "How did this happen? You assured me that your personal issues wouldn't impact my event."

"It didn't, I mean I couldn't have known—" She stammered, her face red and her eyes brimming with tears. "I'm so sorry, Matt. I don't know how this happened, but I promise I'll find out."

"A lot of damn good that'll do me," he said bitterly.

"Take it easy, Matt." Liam held up his open palms. "I realize you're upset, but so is she." He gestured toward Teresa. "Your security team can sort out what happened later. I'll take care of this. Why don't you and Nadia go and try to calm the guests. Hopefully, everything will be back up and running soon."

"That's a good idea, Matt." Nadia squeezed his hand. "The guests need to see that you're calm and that this is just a minor inconvenience."

"Fine, but we will get to the bottom of this." Matt huffed, wrapping an arm around Nadia. "Your mother tried to warn me against using Limitless Events. I should've listened," he groused.

"My mother contacted you?" Liam turned to his friend.

Matt nodded. "Too bad I didn't listen."

Liam's mother still believed Teresa had had an affair with his father back when he mentored her as a college student. She hadn't been pleased that Liam no longer believed it. Still, he didn't think his mother would go out of her way to bash Teresa's business and hamper her ability to make a living.

"Will you be pressing charges against my brother?" Teresa asked quietly as she knelt beside Joshua. He was breathing normally, but still unconscious.

"I honestly don't know yet." Matt dragged a hand through his close-cropped hair in frustration. "Do you think Corinne and the rest of your staff can manage the remainder of the retreat without you?"

"Yes," Teresa stammered, her eyes wide.

"Good, because I want you and your brother out of here as soon as possible," Matt said.

Teresa nodded, tears streaming down her face.

Her career was over and her brother was in deep trouble. Even if Liam hadn't given him a serious concussion and Matt didn't press trespassing or assault charges against Josh, he had another problem. If anyone was looking for him, they might've seen him on the live internet broadcast. That meant they knew where he was.

She hadn't talked to him in weeks. Who knew what kind of trouble he might've gotten himself into this time?

Perhaps it was a good thing Matt wanted them to leave.

"Joshua," Teresa whispered, running her hands through her brother's dark hair to check for a bump. "What've you done now?"

"Teresa, I didn't realize this was your brother. Obviously, I wouldn't have hit the guy so hard if I'd known." Liam stood on the floor in front of the stage. A frown furrowed his brow.

She wasn't sure if it was because of the shitshow Joshua had just put on or because his hand was still throbbing.

"Your hand." Teresa scrambled to her feet with the help of one of the security guys who was watching Josh closely. "I completely forgot. Come on, we'll get you that ice."

Teresa walked to the back of the room and asked

the bartender to put some ice in an ice bucket for her. The man obliged.

They sat at a table at the back of the room, which was now empty, aside from the security team members and a bomb-sniffing dog they'd brought in.

She carefully set the vintage glass art deco style ice bucket on the table, shifted the ice around, then put his hand inside it.

He winced momentarily. "So about your brother... why do you think he showed up here severely impaired after dropping off the map?" Liam asked the question gingerly. "And since you two haven't talked, how did he know where you were?"

She was grateful for the kindness in Liam's tone. After her conversation with Matt, it was the lifeline she needed.

"Those are excellent questions, Liam. I only wish I had answers. And in Joshua's current condition, I don't expect we'll get coherent answers anytime soon."

"Does he drink a lot?"

"He did for a time in college, when he fell in with the wrong crowd. But what he's been up to of late, I'm ashamed to say I don't know." She shifted her gaze to where Joshua still lay on the stage. "I've been too consumed with my own issues. Trying to keep my business afloat and my name off the front page of the paper."

Teresa sighed, her hand resting on his wrist. "I haven't been a very good sister, have I?"

"Don't blame yourself for this. Josh is a grown

man, capable of making his own choices. You can't babysit him for the rest of his life."

"Maybe." Teresa sounded unconvinced. "In the meantime, I need to find transportation home for us."

"You and Josh can ride back to Seattle on my plane." Liam clamped a gentle hand on her arm before she could get up from the table.

"That's sweet of you, Liam. But what happened tonight makes it abundantly clear that I need to stay away from you. If I don't, I'll end up bringing Christopher Corporation down, too."

"Teresa—"

"I have to go before Matt changes his mind about pressing charges. He might even consider suing me. I wasn't to blame for the mudslide, but the same can't be said tonight."

"Don't worry about Matt. He's angry now, but he'll get over it."

"Like your mother has?" she asked, then shook her head. "I'm sorry. I shouldn't have said that."

"No, you shouldn't have. Given what my mother still believes about you, you can understand why she's holding a grudge." Liam hated what his mother had done and that she wasn't willing to reconsider her position. But he understood her resentment. In fact, he'd shared her righteous anger just a few weeks ago.

"That's all the more reason I need to stay away from you and from your company. I couldn't forgive myself if something happened to you or to your father's legacy because of his generosity to me." She stood.

"I can help you, Teresa. You said it yourself, I'm a fixer, of sorts. If we work together, I know we can—"

"Josh is my brother, and this is my problem, Liam. I won't bring you into this any more than I already have." Her chest ached at the thought of not being able to keep their planned date later that evening. "This is something Joshua and I need to figure out."

"So what are you going to do? You don't honestly expect to get a commercial flight back to Seattle tonight, do you?" Liam removed his hand from the bucket and dried it on a towel.

"Looking for a ride back to Seattle tonight?" Brooks Abbingdon approached their table and picked up his cell phone, which he'd apparently left behind when he was forced to exit the ballroom. "Since the festivities ended earlier than expected, I'm flying back tonight. Leaving in a little over an hour if you'd like to come along."

Liam tensed. If even half of the rumors about what a playboy Brooks Abbingdon was were true, he didn't want Teresa flying back to Seattle on the man's private jet.

"It isn't just me. My brother would be coming, too." Teresa pointed to Joshua, who was just starting to stir as the men stood watch over him.

"That's your brother?" Brooks gave a long, low whistle. "Is he gonna be a problem?"

"No, he won't. I promise," Teresa said. "But if

you don't feel comfortable having him on the plane, I can understand that."

"As long as you can keep him on a short leash, I'm fine with it. Truth is, we all have family like that, now don't we?" Brooks winked. "My car will be downstairs in a little over a half an hour. I'll see you then." He nodded at Liam and then walked away.

"Teresa, you don't need to go with him. You can go with me tomorrow morning. You can both stay in my cottage tonight, if you need to."

"No," she whispered, her eyes filled with tears. "I won't get you any more mixed up in this. But thank you for offering and for being a listening ear."

She leaned down to kiss his cheek, but he turned and pressed his lips to hers instead. A kiss that sent electricity down her spine and filled her body with heat as she remembered what had happened between them earlier. And that it would never happen again.

She slipped out of Liam's embrace and walked to the stage to collect her brother before Matt Richmond returned.

The security guy agreed to help her brother to the concierge's office, right by the hotel entrance, where they would wait out of sight for Brooks's car service to arrive. And he promised to stay with him until she and Josh left the property. It was less of a favor to her and more of an order from Matt Richmond, she was sure. But she appreciated it just the same.

She would need to coordinate with her remaining staff, go back to her room and pack all of her things and meet Brooks at the front door of the hotel in twenty minutes flat.

"Melva, I'll be checking out tonight." Teresa approached the front desk in a hurry. She apologized to the beautiful woman standing at the desk for interrupting.

"I'm so sorry, Teresa." Melva frowned. "Under the circumstances, I hate to ask, but this woman is—"

"You're Jessie Humphrey's sister. Jennifer?" Teresa had seen photos of the two women together on Jessie's Instagram account.

"Geneva." The woman smiled warmly as she slipped her hand in Teresa's. "It's a pleasure to meet you. I flew all the way in from Amsterdam to surprise my little sister, but both of my flights were delayed. It seems I missed both of her performances."

"You did, I'm sorry. They were both brilliant." Teresa nodded impatiently. She had no doubt Brooks would pull off with or without her. "What can I do for you, Geneva?"

"I wanted to surprise my sister, but she isn't in her room and she isn't answering her phone. Do you know where I can find her?"

"I don't." Teresa thought better of telling the woman that she'd last seen her sister leaving the ballroom with her ex, Gideon Johns.

"And I can't allow her to enter Ms. Humphrey's room without her express permission," Melva piped. "I'm not really sure what to do with her until her sister pops up."

"Right. Of course. And the hotel is completely

booked." Teresa thought for a minute. "I'll tell you what…my room is paid for through Monday. You'll just need to leave a card on file for incidentals and we can switch the room over to Mrs.…."

"*Ms*. Humphrey." A pained look dimmed the light in the woman's eyes momentarily before her easy smile slid back into place. "That would be wonderful. Thank you, Teresa."

"Give her my room number and a key," Teresa instructed Melva. "Just give me thirty minutes and I'll be gone. Perhaps you'll even run into Jessie in the bar while you wait."

Teresa said her goodbyes to both women and hurried to her room to pack as quickly as she could.

Twenty-One

Jessie collected her makeup and changed out of her Laylahni Couture ball gown in the greenroom while Gideon waited.

Her head was still spinning with all of the chaos that had ensued once the man made his way onto the stage.

She was in the midst of saying her thank-yous and had one encore song left to perform. Why couldn't the drunk party crasher have waited until then to jump onstage?

Jessie stared in the mirror. Her eyes were puffy and red from the tears that wouldn't seem to stop flowing once they'd started. She'd held them back until she'd entered the bathroom alone. But Gideon would know she'd been crying the moment he saw her eyes. Unless…

She dug into her leather Gregory Sylvia hobo bag
and pulled out her black Bôhten shades and slid them
on. She hated doing the obnoxious sunglasses-at-
night celebrity thing, but right now it was more
important to protect her pride.

Jessie put a satin-lined slouch hat on her head and
tucked her curls beneath it. Then she emerged from
the bathroom wearing a pair of GRLFRND high-
waist, ripped skinny jeans, a T-shirt and kitten heels.
She carried the beautiful Laylahni Couture gown
over one arm in a garment bag.

"You came out just in the nick of time." Gideon
smiled softly, taking all of her bags except her purse
from her. "I was just about to come in after you to make
sure you were okay."

"If that's a pun because of the song I sang tonight…it's too soon."

Jessie exited through the exterior door rather than
going through the lobby of the hotel. Party guests
still milled around and Nicolette Ryan and her cameraman were camped out there.

Nicolette had texted her and asked her for an
exclusive interview about the incident as she and
Gideon made their escape to the greenroom.

She declined.

Nicolette seemed understanding and sympa-
thetic. But Jessie had no desire to relive her performance going up in flames. All because some guy who
couldn't hold his liquor decided to be a complete ass
during the biggest moment of her career.

"I wasn't trying to be cute," Gideon said. "What

happened was no laughing matter. The guy turned out to be harmless this time. But what if he hadn't been?" Gideon seemed especially perturbed at the possibility that something could've happened to her. "And I know how important that performance was to you. But, Jessie, you nailed it. Your set last night was terrific. But what you did tonight…it was brilliant. You should be damned proud of yourself."

"Thanks." She came to a halt at the fork in the path and turned to face him. "And thank you for not being an ass about me writing these songs about you."

Gideon gave her a half grin. "Not everyone can say that they inspired someone to write a song. Let alone several. Especially one as good as 'Okay.'"

"Did you really like the song or are you just being unbelievably gracious about the whole thing?" She practically held her breath waiting for his response.

"Of course I really loved the song. Every damn person in that room loved it. Everything about it was perfect. The lyrics. The music. The way you sang the song…you poured your heart out on that stage."

"Until random drunk guy came and stomped on it." She took a deep breath and reminded herself there was no crying in record deals. This was a tough business. If she was going to break down in tears every time things didn't go her way, she needed to find another dream to chase.

"I know you're bummed about what happened, but let me tell you something, Jessie. Anyone who saw that performance tonight, anyone who experienced

it as deeply as I did…they will never, ever forget it.
I can assure you of that."

"Thanks." Jessie's mouth quirked involuntarily in
the slightest twinge of a smile. Her cheeks heated, and
her body tingled with electricity from his nearness.

"So, am I walking you back to your room?"
Gideon asked.

Neither of them had moved beyond the fork in
the path. Either they could take the route back to the
hotel where her room was located or they could take
the path that led to his cottage.

"Actually, if the invitation still stands, I could really use that nightcap you offered." Her heart raced
as she anticipated his response.

He studied her for a moment, as if he was debating the wisdom of taking her back to his cottage. "Of
course it still stands."

They turned up the path toward the private cottages.

"Chase and Dixon seemed blown away by your
performance," he noted. "I wouldn't be surprised if
both of them contact your agent, eager to work with
you. You knocked them off their feet."

"They seemed really into it when I was performing. Dixon was right there with me the whole time.
He even started a standing ovation."

"That was pretty incredible."

"It was." She couldn't help smiling. "Chase didn't
really seem to get on board until I performed 'Okay.'
But their table was among the first to be ushered out

of the room." The disappointment of not securing a meeting with either Chase or Dixon weighed on her.

Then there was the matter of Gideon.

She glanced over at him. He was handsome and tall with broad shoulders and such an incredible smile. He was still the smart, funny, determined guy she'd known back then. But he was also a successful businessman who employed members of his community and gave generously to important causes.

She'd always admired Gideon and expected great things of him, regardless of what her father and sister believed. But he'd exceeded her wildest expectations.

And she wanted to be with him more than ever. Not because of the schoolgirl crush she'd once harbored for him. But because he was exactly the kind of man she wanted in her life.

If she told Gideon that, he'd think she was still a silly, immature girl with a crush. After all, how could she know in just a few days that she wanted to be with him?

She just did.

That day when she'd shown up at Gideon's door, she told him that he was the only person who really understood her. That he got her in a way her parents, sister and even friends didn't. She was sure that Gideon was her soul mate. And it was her that he was meant to be with.

He'd probably thought she was a melodramatic teenager who didn't know what she was talking about. But here they were fifteen years later and the

more she got reacquainted with Gideon, the more
she believed she'd been right all along.

All of her fears about her career aside, what if they
really were meant to be together? Shouldn't she at
least be brave enough to give it a try?

"You're awfully quiet, Jess." Gideon set her bags
down on the doorstep of his cottage, but he didn't
open the door. "If you'd rather I walk you back to
your room, I understand. You've had an exhausting
day. You're probably ready to call it a night after everything that's—"

Jessie drew in a deep breath, clutched Gideon's
tuxedo shirt and lifted onto her toes, pressing her
mouth to his in a tentative kiss that built slowly.
Gideon slipped his arms around her waist and hauled
her body against his, the intensity of their kiss building.

Finally, she forced herself to pull away, her eyes
fluttering open as they met his. "Does that answer
your question?"

Gideon poured a glass of sauvignon blanc and
handed it to Jessie.

She took a sip and made a purring sound that sent
a shiver up his spine and made him want to cut the
formalities and tell her exactly what he'd been feeling these past few days.

That he hadn't stopped thinking about her since
she'd walked through the doors of that hotel. That
he wanted her in his bed.

There was something so compelling about Jessie.

Compelling enough that the idea of missing out on it was stronger than the fear of what he'd be letting go.

"You're right, this wine is fantastic." Her words jarred him from his thoughts.

Gideon filled her wineglass and then poured himself two fingers of whiskey. He sipped his whiskey slowly, then sank onto the opposite sofa.

He crossed one ankle over his knee and assessed the woman seated across from him as she sipped her wine.

"A lot has happened tonight. I know you're disappointed, but maybe it wasn't as bad as you think. We should look at the live stream from the event."

"No. Please." Her bravado faded momentarily. "I shut my phone off for the rest of the night. I don't want to see it. Not yet. Just let me live in my little fantasy realm where I killed it on stage tonight and everything is right with the world."

"It isn't a fantasy, Jess. You *did* kill it on stage tonight. And I'll bet that ninety-nine percent of the people who saw your performance would agree."

"And that one percent?" Jessie raised a brow.

"They have terrible taste in music, so they don't count." He grinned when she laughed. He'd always loved the joyous sound of her laugh. "Seriously, if the vast majority of listeners think you were amazing, why do you care about what an infinitesimal fraction of people think?"

"It's the nature of the creative beast. I can't help it." Jessie shrugged. "Besides, I learn more from my critical reviews than I do from the glowing ones that tell me exactly what I want to hear." She paced the floor. "Which is why I need to work with producers like Chase and Dixon. They have this uncanny ability to take a track that might seem good on the surface and turn it into something spectacular."

"About that…" Gideon set his glass down. "I know you asked me not to interfere on this, but what if I could pull some strings and get you a meeting with one or both of them?"

Jessie folded her arms and plopped down in her seat. "I want a meeting with them, of course. But I'd like to do this on my own. The same way you built your business on your own. You didn't rely on anyone else."

"Not true." He leaned forward. "I owe my success to a lot of men and women who were willing to give me opportunities and teach me what they'd learned." Gideon shrugged. "I pay their generosity and kindness forward by doing the same."

Jessie had kicked off her heels and padded over to the sideboard where the bottle of wine was chilling. She refilled her glass of wine, then sat on the sofa with her feet folded beneath her. "I've read business articles about you. They always call you a self-made billionaire." Jessie didn't seem convinced.

"Because it's the more compelling story." Gideon groaned. He gave credit to the people who had helped him every single chance he got. But the importance of those relationships was inevitably minimized in magazines and interviews.

"My assistant Landon...the guy is a work in progress, for sure." Gideon chuckled, thinking of some of their conversations. "But he's good at what he does, and he has a hell of a lot of potential. If I can help him get closer to his goals, even if that means leaving my company and striking out on his own, I'm going to support him any way I can. So let me do the same for you."

Jessie drank a gulp of her wine, her eyes not meeting his. "I don't like the idea of owing anyone anything. It gives people too much power over you."

"You think I'd want something in return?" He had to admit that one hurt. He thought she knew him better than that. Yes, it was fifteen years ago, but did she really think he'd changed that much? "Why would you ever think that?"

"It's happened before with someone I trusted."

Now he understood, and he wished he could give the fucker who'd made her feel that way a savage beatdown just to show him how it felt to be vulnerable.

"What happened?" Gideon sat on the edge of his seat, both of his feet firmly planted on the floor. "And whose ass do I need to beat?" There was a ticking in a vein in his forehead.

"Gideon, no." Jessie moved over to sit beside him. Her warmth enveloped him and her faint floral scent calmed the anger bubbling inside him over her revelation about her mentor. "I don't want to talk about that or the shitshow my performance turned into. Tonight, I want to talk about us."

She'd said it. Finally gotten it out into the open where they could discuss it like two rational adults. Though he found it difficult to have a reasonable discussion when she was sitting this close.

Jessie had already shed the sunglasses. Now she slipped off the hat and tossed it onto the sofa beside her, refluffing her headful of dark curls. Her short manicured nails were painted a deeper shade of pink and every other nail was affixed with a design.

"I'd like that." Gideon turned toward her and loosened his tie. "Spending these past few days with you has been special for me. I never stopped caring for you, Jess. The feelings I had for you then weren't romantic, but you were incredibly important to me. The loss of our friendship hurt as much as being dumped by Geneva."

Jessie frowned. Was it because he'd mentioned Geneva or because he'd admitted his feelings for her back then were platonic?

"One of my biggest regrets was how badly I'd bungled things between us. That my insensitivity that day hurt you." He traced the back of her hand with his thumb.

Jessie didn't respond to his confession, but her sensual lips spread in a slow smile. She leaned in, raised a hand to his cheek and kissed him again.

He wrapped his arms around her, his hand pressed to her back. Loving the feel of her in his arms and the taste of her warm mouth as he slid his tongue between her lips. He lost himself in her kiss. Lost all sense of time and place. Set aside his fears about what this meant for them.

He only knew he wanted more of this. More of her.

The longer he kissed her, the more sure he was that he would never get enough of her quiet murmurs. Or the way her soft, curvy body fit so neatly against the hard planes of his. That he would never tire of holding her in his arms.

Suddenly, Jessie pressed against his chest, creating space between them. She dragged her gaze to his, her chest heaving as she caught her breath. "There's one thing I need to know. It's about Geneva."

He already knew what she was going to ask, but she needed to say the words. "What do you want to know?"

She tucked strands of her hair behind one ear. "I need to know…if there was a chance for the two of you again, would you want it?"

"No." He kissed one corner of her mouth and then the other. "I loved your sister, but that was a long, long time ago. And we were never right for each other." He left a slow, lingering kiss on her mouth. Then pressed his lips to her ear. "It isn't Geneva I want, Jess. Or haven't you noticed?"

He lay her back on the sofa, his length pressed to her belly as he kissed her until they were both breathless.

He dropped kisses on her forehead and her eyelids. "Do you believe me?"

She nodded, her gaze meeting his. "I do," she whispered.

"Good." He kissed her again, savoring the taste of her sweet mouth and the feel of her body beneath his. "Because from the moment you strutted into that hotel lobby, I've only wanted you."

Twenty-Two

Teresa sat in the tan buttery leather seat on Brooks Abbingdon's private plane and fastened her seat belt. Then she double-checked to make sure her brother's seat belt was secure, since he was still fairly out of it.

One thing Teresa knew for sure, Joshua wasn't drunk. His clothing and skin were completely devoid of the scent of alcohol. Still, there was clearly something wrong with him.

Joshua had roused enough to walk onto the plane, but he was still babbling incoherently about rich liars and losers and the truth being exposed. When he wasn't ranting, he would doze off. So getting the truth from Joshua wasn't an option. In fact, as out of it as he seemed, she wondered if Josh would remember any of this, even once he became lucid.

He mumbled something that sounded vaguely like *sorry, love you, sis*. But then again, maybe that was just what Teresa wanted to hear. Something to make her feel the slightest bit better about the fact that her career was over. In fact, she was shocked that Brooks wanted anything to do with her once he learned that the party disrupter was her brother.

Joshua leaned his head on her shoulder, his dark brown hair tickling her nose. He muttered something again. This time she clearly heard *sorry* and *screwed up again.* Those words were followed by more incoherent babbling.

Joshua rubbed at his arm, complaining that it hurt like a bitch. *That* she heard quite clearly. He kept rubbing at his left arm, so she rolled up his sleeve and looked at it.

Teresa turned her head to one side and then the other, zeroing in on a small, nearly invisible mark on his forearm. She rummaged in her bag and took out her lighted pocket magnifier. Now she could see clearly what it was that Josh kept scratching at. It was a tiny, isolated puncture wound.

She breathed a sigh of relief that there was just the single mark. She checked his other arm and his ankle and saw no additional marks. If Joshua was an addict, he'd have several puncture wounds on his body, not just one. Which suggested that this was an isolated incident. But the more important question was, had her brother willingly injected himself with something?

"Your brother doesn't look very good." Brooks

switched to the seat across from her once they were able to freely move about the plane.

"He's been conscious more often, and I'm beginning to understand more of what he's saying." Teresa swept the hair from her brother's sweaty forehead.

"Should I request that the driver take him to a hospital once we land?" Brooks studied Josh with concern.

She could only imagine how inconvenient it would be to have someone die on one's private plane. Teresa banished the snarky comment from her head. After all, Brooks had offered to help when she was persona non grata to everyone but Liam.

"No, but thank you for the offer just the same." Teresa smiled warmly at Brooks.

"You're sure?" He didn't seem convinced that it was a good idea.

In any other circumstance, Teresa would've insisted that they rush Joshua to the hospital. There they could identify the substance he'd been given and flush it from his system.

But that could mean trouble for Joshua. She'd paid a hefty price to ensure that his earlier offenses hadn't ended up on his record. If she took him to the hospital, the staff would need to report the incident. Was this all Josh's doing or was someone willing to put Josh's life in danger to ruin hers?

Nicolette's warning to Liam that they should be careful whom they trusted suddenly came to mind.

"I'm sure. Thank you, Brooks."

Teresa heaved a small sigh of relief when Brooks

nodded and walked back to his seat. She glanced down at her still-shaking hands as she deliberated her next move.

Liam paced the floor of his cottage, still trying to figure out how everything had gone off the rails so quickly. The weekend started with so much promise and ended in a disaster, for which it would most likely be remembered. Particularly since the entire circus had been captured live on streaming video.

He was furious with Joshua for ruining his best friend's event and decimating what remained of the reputation of and goodwill toward Teresa and Limitless Events. He honestly couldn't imagine that her business could recover from what had just happened, especially in light of the fact that the person who'd crashed the party had been her brother.

Add to that his rant about rich people being liars and losers...well, the wealthy set could overlook a lot of things. Calling them out like that wasn't one of them.

Liam's phone rang. He dug it out of his inside jacket pocket, hoping it was Teresa saying she'd changed her mind and would accept his offered plane ride tomorrow.

Shit.

He heaved a long sigh and answered the telephone. "Hello, Mother. What can I do for you?"

"You can stop making a fool of yourself by your insistence on associating with that Teresa person," Catherine Christopher said without hesitation. "You know what she's done, who she was to your father, and how she destroyed our family. Emilia Cartwright one of my oldest and closest friends, sent me a video of you dancing with that woman as if neither of you had a care in the world. And, just as I predicted, the evening turned into a disaster. That woman destroys everything in her path. And that poor singer, assaulted! Just horrible!"

"You watched the live stream?" That didn't sound like something that would interest his mother at all. If she wasn't in the room holding court as the center of attention, she simply wasn't interested.

"Only because I received dozens of calls from people who saw you canoodling with that witch earlier and I wanted to see what else was going on."

"We were dancing together on a crowded dance floor. It's not as if I had her up against the wall in the back of the room."

"Don't be vulgar, Liam." His mother's voice was strained. "I did everything I possibly could to warn your friend Matt Richmond not to associate his brand with that woman, but he just wouldn't listen. Now that millions of people have seen the train wreck his party turned into, he's the laughingstock of the entire internet. And who would want to attend another of his parties? A life-threatening disaster is practically sure to ensue."

"You're being melodramatic, Mother. You weren't there, and it wasn't seen by millions. The situation wasn't that serious. Matt's security team just wanted to be extra cautious after the man was able to get onto the stage. It was an overreaction to their initial screwup."

"Where is that woman now?"

Liam hesitated before responding. "Gone. Matt asked her to leave."

"Good riddance. All of us will be better off with Teresa St. Claire out of the picture."

Liam ended the call with his mother and gulped his Manhattan. Maybe his mother's life would be better without Teresa St. Claire in the mix. But he'd felt a gnawing in his chest from the moment she'd walked out the door.

Twenty-Three

Jessie was in heaven. Gideon's kiss, his touch, had been every bit as wonderful as her mind had imagined. But as the intensity of their kiss escalated, she wanted more.

Gideon had rolled them over so Jessie lay on top of him. She shifted so that she straddled him on the sofa. Both of them murmured at the sensation when she placed her hands on his chest and rocked the apex of her thighs against his steely length. He cupped her bottom, bringing her closer as she ground her hips against him, the sensation between them building.

He still seemed tentative. Or maybe he wanted to let her set the pace. But she knew what she wanted.

She wanted his large, strong hands to caress her

bare skin. To glide her hands over his. And she wanted him inside her.

Jessie grasped the hem of her shirt and lifted it over her head, tossing it aside. Gideon quickly removed her sheer black bra and dropped it to the floor, too.

He pulled her toward him and laved one of her tight, beaded nipples. Jessie arched into him with an involuntary whimper as he licked and sucked the sensitive tip.

Gideon gently scraped his teeth over the tight bud and she cursed under her breath at the sensation his actions elicited in the warm space between her thighs. He shifted his focus to her other breast, lavishing it with the same attention.

"God, I want you, Jess," he whispered against her skin.

His beard scraped her flesh, adding to the mélange of sensations.

Gideon's gaze met hers as he unbuttoned her jeans, then slowly unzipped them.

Jessie sank her teeth into her lower lip and lifted her hips, eager to help him slide the garment off one leg and then the other. He stood suddenly, taking her by surprise as he lifted her. She wrapped her long legs around him and held on to his neck as he carried her to the bed and laid her beneath the covers.

She had wanted this for as long as she could remember. But now that she was here in Gideon's bed, her hands trembled and butterflies flitted in her belly.

Her anticipation grew as Gideon slowly removed his tie and then his jacket. As if he was putting on a show just for her. He took off his shirt to reveal his strong, muscular chest and chiseled abs. Then he slowly unzipped his tuxedo pants and allowed the fabric to pool around his ankles.

Dayum.

Jessie swallowed hard, her eyes tracing the pronounced outline of his thick erection beneath his charcoal-gray boxers. She couldn't tear her gaze away from the darkened circle over the tip.

She licked her lower lip, the space between her thighs throbbing as she was struck by the sudden desire to taste him there.

Gideon reached into the bedside drawer and removed one of the foil packets stocked by the hotel. He slipped out of his boxers and sheathed himself, crawling into bed with her.

She'd never seen anything sexier than this man, completely naked, crawling toward her. Like a panther in pursuit of his next conquest.

He dragged her sheer panties down her legs and settled between her thighs as he kissed her again, his tongue searching hers.

Jessie wrapped her legs around his waist and her arms around his back as he kissed her. His hips rocked against hers.

His kiss was hungry and demanding. Making her more desperate for him. The space between her thighs pulsed and her nipples prickled as they moved against the hair on his broad chest.

Gideon broke their kiss, leaving her breathless and wanting. He trailed kisses down her neck and shoulder as he shifted off of her. She immediately missed the weight and warmth of his strong, hard body.

He moved beside her and thrust his hand between her thighs, gliding his fingers through her wetness, over her sensitive nub. She whimpered, overwhelmed by the sensation as she writhed against his hand. He inserted two large fingers, then three. Sliding them in and out of her as his thumb teased her hardened clit.

Gideon brought her close to the edge, her legs shaking. Then he'd back off just enough to keep her from going over.

"Gideon, please." It wasn't like her to whimper or beg. But she was so close, her body trembling with need. "I want you."

"And I have never wanted anyone as much as I want you, Jess." He pulled his fingers from inside her, moving them over the needy bundle of nerves and all of the slick, sensitive flesh surrounding it.

The muscles of her belly tensed and she cried out his name, the dam inside her bursting. Overflowing with intense pleasure.

He kissed her neck and shoulders as her body shuddered. Finally, he pressed the head of his erection to her entrance, slowly pushing his width inside her.

Jessie dug her short fingernails into his back, her body tense as Gideon slowly entered her.

"Relax, Jess," he whispered. "Breathe. I would never hurt you."

Jessie hadn't realized that she was holding her breath and her muscles were clenched in anticipation. She breathed in and out slowly, her eyes pressed shut.

Gideon rewarded her with a slow, sweet, tender kiss.

"Open your eyes, Jess." His voice was low and deep. "I want to see those beautiful brown eyes while I'm inside you. And I want you to see exactly what you do to me. How badly I want you."

He moved inside her slowly, allowing her body to adjust to the sensation of being completely filled by him.

They moved together, their skin slick with sweat. Her belly tensed as her heels dug into the mattress. Another orgasm rocked her to her core. She called his name, her body quivering.

Gideon tensed, her name on his lips as he tumbled over the edge into pleasure. The pulsing of his cock pulled her in deeper, her walls contracting around him.

Jessie released a contented sigh, her head lolling back on the pillow. She smiled up at Gideon. His forehead was beaded with sweat and his chest still heaved. He traced her cheekbone with his thumb.

"That was amazing." He kissed her. "Is it bad that I already want you again?"

"No. Because I plan on taking every meal right here in this bed until Monday morning when I have to go back to…" Her words trailed as the reality of the situation dimmed the buzz she was feeling.

"Let's not think about Monday morning right now." He caressed her cheek.

"Good plan."

Gideon dropped a tender kiss on her lips, then lay on his back and gathered her in his arms, pulling the covers around them.

Jessie pressed her cheek to his chest, their intense encounter replaying in her head. She tried to do as Gideon asked and not think about Monday. But she couldn't escape the knowledge that in thirty-six hours they would go their separate ways.

Gideon cradled Jessie in his arms as she slept soundly with her hand and cheek pressed to his chest. Her quiet exhalations skittered across his skin.

He couldn't remember the last time he'd felt so content. Or the last time he'd been with someone who made him feel the things that Jessie did. He glided a hand up and down the smooth skin of her bare arm as she slept.

It was well after one in the morning, but it had been several hours since he'd last checked his email. Gideon reached for his phone on the nightstand and turned it back on.

He checked his email, directing the light from the phone away from Jessie so he wouldn't disturb her sleep. He replied to a few urgent messages, then noticed that he had several alerts for Jessie's name.

She hadn't wanted to see the video, and he got that. But at least one of them should see it. That way he could prepare her if it was as bad as she believed.

When he followed the link to view the video, there were already thousands of remarks. He sucked in a deep breath and started to read through them. He was pleasantly surprised.

"Jessie." He couldn't help waking her. She'd been so disappointed about how the performance ended. She needed to see this. "Sweetheart, you've got to see what people are saying about your performance last night."

She grumbled and buried her face in his chest before finally rolling over on her back and propping herself up on her elbows.

"All right, all right," she mumbled. "Let's get this over with."

He played the video and scrolled through some of the comments. The more she read them, the more excited she got.

"Oh my God. Did you see this? Dixon Benedict left an amazing comment. He said I'm one of the most talented singer/songwriters he's ever seen. He even says he'd love to work with me someday." Jessie sat up in bed, her back pressed against the headboard as she scrolled through the comments, most of which were rave reviews of her performance.

"This is incredible. Thank you, Gideon." She handed him back his phone and kissed him. "And I really do appreciate your offer to broker a meeting between me and Chase or Dixon. But I'd like to give it one more try on my own first. If I need your help, I'll ask. I promise."

"Whatever you want, beautiful." He cradled her

cheek. "I told you, you're a star, Jessie Humphrey. And you're going to do amazing things." He kissed her.

She gave him a sly smile as she reached into the drawer of the bedside table and climbed atop him. "There are a few amazing things I'd like to do right now."

"Oh yeah?" He rolled them over so that he hovered over her. "I'm all for that." He leaned down and kissed her. Then he made love to her again.

Jessie returned to her room on Sunday afternoon to gather some of her toiletries and fresh clothing. Gideon sat on the sofa watching the stock market news as he made calls to his assistant Landon.

There was a knock at her hotel room door.

"Gideon, would you get that, please?" Jessie called from the bathroom as she packed up her makeup and facial cleanser.

"Sure thing," he replied.

She'd expected him to call to her that it was the hotel staff or maybe Teresa or Matt looking for her. But there was silence in the other room.

"Gideon, who is it?" Jessie walked out into the main living space of the suite. She was stunned to see a face that resembled her own.

"Geneva, what are you doing here?" Jessie stammered. "I thought you were still in Amsterdam." Her voice faded and she wrapped her arms around herself.

"I was, but I thought I'd surprise my little sis. You said I should come to visit, so I thought I'd pop into Napa first and catch your performances. But my flights were delayed and I got in after your set ended last night." Geneva took a few steps closer to her sister. "But I saw the videos. Jessie, you were incredible. How is it that I didn't realize just how talented my sister is?"

Geneva opened her arms and Jessie stepped into them, hugging her sister tightly. Neither her parents nor Geneva had supported her decision to go into music. So it felt good to hear her sister's validation. It wasn't something she needed, but she hadn't realized until now how much she'd wanted it.

Her sister cupped her cheek and smiled, then turned to Gideon. She gave him what Jessie knew to be a forced smile.

"Gideon, it's good to see you." Geneva nodded toward him, awkwardness lingering between them.

"You, too, Geneva." He shoved his hands in his pockets, not moving toward her.

"So...you two, huh?" Geneva glanced from Jessie to Gideon, then back when neither of them responded. "Since when?"

"Since this weekend." Gideon pulled one hand out of his pocket and threaded his fingers through Jessie's. He squeezed her hand. "We hadn't seen each other in a really long time. We got a chance to get reacquainted during the retreat."

Jessie breathed a sigh of relief. She hadn't told Geneva or anyone else about the day she'd gone to Gideon's apartment. Maybe she'd tell her sister someday. But there was already enough tension between them. She wouldn't add to it.

Gideon wrapped an arm around Jessie's waist, as if he knew she needed his reassurance that he had no regrets about choosing her.

"I know you missed Jessie's show, Geneva, but there's lots to do here in Napa. Why don't I take you ladies to lunch later?"

"Great idea, Gideon." Jessie smiled at him gratefully. She turned to her sister. "What do you say, Gen? The food here is amazing and so is the wine."

"I'd like that." Geneva put on her biggest smile as she wiped dampness from beneath her eyes. "Can I meet you at the restaurant in say…an hour?"

"Geneva, I'm sorry if me being with Gideon feels uncomfortable right now. You're my sister and I love you. I'd never intentionally hurt you." Jessie took both of Geneva's hands in hers. "But… I love him. I think I always have." She glanced over her shoulder at Gideon. He grinned and mouthed the words, *I love you, too.* Jessie turned back to her sister. "And I did see him first."

"Yes, you did, Squirt." Geneva called Jessie by her childhood nickname through a teary-eyed laugh. "I guess technically I stole him first."

"You totally did." Jessie laughed, her eyes damp, too.

"Oh, Jessie." Geneva cradled her cheek. Her sister's smile seemed genuine, despite the tears that spilled down her face. "I'm so happy for you. For both of you." She turned to Gideon. "I've only ever wanted the best for both of you. I'm glad that the two